Also by Susan Shepherd:

A Vampire Story
Killing Esther
Killing Andy
The Grain God
Soul Of Rah

And coming soon: Returning Rah

City Of Rah

Book Three
of the
Saga Of The Rah

Susan Shepherd

ISBN:692434275
ISBN-13: 978-0692434277

"Before me floats an image, man or shade,
Shade more than man, more image than a shade;
For Hades' bobbin bound in mummy-cloth
May unwind the winding path;
A mouth that has no moisture and no breath
Breathless mouths may summon;
I hail the superhuman;
I call it death-in-life and life-in-death."

Byzantium, William Butler Yeats

The world was on fire, no one could save me but you

Strange what desire will make foolish lovers do

I never dreamed that I' d love somebody like you

And I never dreamed that I'd lose somebody like you

No, I don't wanna fall in love with you.

Chris Isaaks, "Wicked Game"

"Babylon, the jewel of kingdoms,
the glory of the Babylonians' pride,
will be overthrown..."

Isaiah 13

SUSAN SHEPHERD

CHAPTER 1

Rush is stabbing a piece of mutton. It's the sound of the blade sliding in and out of the carcass that he needs, the slicing, sucking noise that seems to him so obviously similar to the sound of the Hittite word for "darling".

I am mad, he thinks. I have defeated the Syrian army, enslaved the survivors, and returned my own men safely to Amega. Yet I can think of nothing but the Rah.

I am a joke. He has made me a joke. The great Antares, Master of Amega, Wolf of the Aegean. A lovesick joke. I will tear his entrails out and strangle him with them.

"You sent for me, Master?" The great oak door of the weapons room has opened and the boy from Punt, Akintunde, has entered and fallen to his knees. Rush looks up from his work. The cedar table is now covered in the blood of the ewe he is butchering for no particular reason. Akintunde bumps his fist against his heart, bows his head.

"Ah, nephew of my good servant, Ghedi," says Rush. "Did you know that your uncle was the best horseman in all of Hatti, Akintunde?" His voice is soft. But the soft voice of a beast is still a growl. He lowers his eyes to the carnage on the desk, sighs, and sits back into the iron chair behind it. "Best until the Rah...." his baritone growl drifts.

Akintunde swallows. This is his first meeting with the Master of Amega. He has been here only a week, has met the Master's sons, Quintus and Philip, also the charioteer, Keret,

1

who is the son of the great commander, Agrippa. He has met the stable master, Hagga, the archer, Pelet and the lance man, Lysias. All have advised him that the master loved his uncle, Ghedi, and that he has nothing to fear so long as he comports himself properly. But Akintunde's knees are weak and grateful today for the Hittite military bow.

"Akintunde," Rush muses. "A fleet name. Like the sound of water running over a stream bed. Can you run as fast as water, Akintunde?" The assassin has lifted the dagger as he speaks. He tilts his head, an innocent question. Looking keenly into the boy's eyes, he plunges the blade into the still warm flesh of the massacred beast on his table.

Akintunde swallows hard, fearing his throat too dry to allow speech.

"Master, I run as fast as you tell me," he responds.

"Hah, good answer, Akintunde. You are like your uncle. I like you already. And so here are your orders. You will take me a message to Babylon. You will carry my seal, and go straight to the palace, where you will insist that you must see the King immediately. You will say nothing to anyone until you are before his throne. Then you will tell Samsu-titana that he will return the Rah to me, or face my wrath. Tell him thus, 'King Samsu-titana, your darkest nightmare has yet to be dreamt. He will take a bone from your body for each day you keep the boy from him, beginning with today. Then he will take what you love first and second: first, your daughter Ephtheta, and second, Babylon. All of the armies of Syria will not protect you. Return him under guard with my servant to Amega, or face hell itself."

"I will tell him exactly thus," answers Akintunde, knowing that, whatever Samsu-titana's answer, he will be safe so long as he carries the assassin's seal. "Exactly thus."

"Good man," says Rush. Rising and lifting the bloody blade of his dagger from the carcass on his desk, he licks at it absently.

Akintunde remains motionless, waiting for permission to leave. But he feels the assassin's eyes burning through the top of his head, and he swallows a third time. What now? he thinks.

"Upon hearing his answer, Akintunde, you will leave the city on the west road, along the Euphrates. Five miles and you will find a fork in the river. At the fork, you will give the King's answer to my man. You will have no difficulty identifying him for he will wear the Mark of the Bull."

"Yes, Master," responds Akintunde.

"He will give you your next assignment." Rush holsters the now shining blade of his dagger in his weapons belt. Akintunde, still a boy, cannot help but sweep his gaze once over the carcass of the ewe. Its head lolls over the edge of the cedar table, its woolen hide almost entirely red now and matted with clots of blood.

"Give me your hand, boy," says Rush. As the boy obeys, he turns to hold his seal ring, still on his finger, over the flame of the lamp that stands beside the table. Akintunde's eyes follow the motion, not comprehending. Rush turns back to the boy and presses the heated ring into his right palm, holding it there as the flesh sizzles. The boy grunts in pain, but makes no effort to draw his hand away.

When the deed is done, Rush nods at the door, and the boy stumbles weakly to his feet and flees.

The litter sways gently in a southern breeze as the King's footmen carry Princes Ephtheta back toward the city gates, their crimson cloaks lifting and billowing in the arid air. Rah's wrists have been trussed and fastened to Ono's saddle horn. His mare is now being led by the captain of the King's litter guard, Petuk. Petuk rides a fine-boned gelding whose coat shimmers golden in the noonday sun like a mirage.

Rah cannot take his eyes from the horse's metallic hindquarters. He taps Ono's withers with his heels and draws her up to the shoulder of the burly captain. The man looks down at Rah, fury brewing in his black eyes.

"This Akhal!" says Rah in an excited mixture of Hittite and Greek. "This horse of king! Many story Rah is hear this horse. This horse he long travel. Thousand mile. Little food, little water. How you ride horse of king? In Babylon is all men ride Akhal?"

"What are you babbling about, you little fool," snarls

Petuk. But he is losing his anger in the depths of Rah's eyes, which seem to shimmer, as metallic-gold as his mounts rump, in the Syrian sun. And he is not a little impressed that the boy knows of the wonder of Babylon's Turkoman. He purses his lips, looks forward to the litter, remembering himself. He should not be speaking to this creature. The Princess has claimed him. Yet...

"These golden horses have been bred in Babylon for centuries," he answers gruffly, his pride tickled. "They are His Majesty's official horse of the City Guard. They do not leave the kingdom." He slides a glance back at Rah. "How is it that you, a puff of dance from gods know where, know of them?"

"I am best horseman in Gaul, Illyria, Hatti. All horseman know this Akhal! All know. But is, eh..." without the use of his hands, his pantomime is frustrated. He tosses his head and rolls his eyes to heaven. "Like dream."

"A myth. Hah," murmurs Petuk. "Well it is no myth, boy, as you see. And if you think Pala is fine, your head will spin when you see the palace stable." At this, again, he catches himself, lifts his beard and throws Rah a dangerous look. "Now get that common animal behind me and button your mouth."

In the litter, the princess Ephtheta sits with her wet nurse, Yesh, who has been with her since her birth. The woman, now in her thirtieth year, is nearly a head taller than Ephtheta, even sitting in the litter. She is built like a sapling, willowy, all trunk and long legs, and was imported as a child slave from Egypt, originating in the great kingdom of Kerma along the southern channels of the Nile. Her heritage was one of height, speed and beauty, and even now, after many years of service in a King's household, years of what amounted to little more than mothering a monarch's only surviving female offspring, she is lithe and fleet as a deer. Yesh remembers little of her capture, of the deaths of her mother and father, or of her days of slavery in Egypt, but she dreams often of her home along the canal that reached into the rich farmlands of Nubia, south of the Nile. Sometimes she awakes with a start, imagining herself on her grass mat in her father's house, the lowing of cattle in her ears, the scent of her mother's root mash, simmering on the fire, in her nose. Sometimes she hears her brother Mimba's voice, calling to the goats to come in to be grained, her brother's beautiful voice, not yet broken, and renowned in all the nearby towns for its height and range. Mimba, who saved her from the lioness with a walking sticks, and was killed and eaten by the beast a week later defending the family's sheep.

Sometimes she hears her mother calling her, "Wakeshtu! Wakeshtu! Wake now, you lazy girl. Eat your breakfast and help me milk the goats."

These voices only come to her in dreams, never in her waking life. Perhaps the dead can only speak at night, and in the dreams of the living. Perhaps, but why then could she remember nothing of her rape? Nothing of her pregnancy? After the slaughter of her people, she was taken into Egypt and sold with the other girls of puberty from her village to a merchant from Crete, taken across the great sea, and sold again to a rich man in Babylon. There she was impregnated by a ritualized rape, and when her son was born, he was immediately taken from her to be sacrificed to the Amorite god, Moloch, who demanded the burnt offering of living children.

They had ripped him from her body as she lay screaming in the blood of his issue. Yet she could remember none of this.

Yesh was given her master's twins to nurse the same day they took her son. Mad with grief, she nevertheless required the children, both in her body and in her Ba, her soul. Soon the sleep of denial took her memories of little Mimbabu, the son she was not allowed to hold before he was roasted in the arms of a golden statue. She forgot, but her body did not. Her breasts were full, as was her Ba, with enough nourishment for them both, and they thrived. A year later, when the Queen, who had lost three infants in as many years, demanded that the best wet nurse in the city be found for her fourth pregnancy, Yesh was sent to the palace to await the birth of the princess.

Ephtheta was born yellow, full of the withering sickness, just as her sisters had been. Yesh was assured that if the babe died, she would be buried alive with the child to care for her in the afterlife.

"This child will not die," responded Yesh calmly, for in

her heart she knew that she would never allow another child to be taken from her. "But I must have the leaf of the sweet potato plant to eat." This was a common and simple solution in her native land for the treatment of the withering sickness. The mother ate the boiled leaf of the sweet potato, which was as abundant as grass. But here, in this city of wealth and plenty, it was food for beasts. A Queen ate nothing green at all, but lived on delicacies, rich meats and sweets.

And in a fortnight's time, the little princess turned from yellow to cinnamon. In time, her eyes turned color too, from moss brown to amber gold, and the palace rejoiced that the first, and perhaps the only (for the Queen was no longer young) heir to the throne of Babylon had survived her infancy.

Yesh became a favorite servant in the palace, and any of her whims in the upbringing of the child were tolerated, indeed sought. As a result, the Princess Ephtheta did not become the spoilt and vain creature she might have been under the tutelage of the obsequious fools who typically cared for the offspring of a Babylonian king. She learned humility, humanity, and compassion from her nurse maid, a love for animals especially, and a certain obstinate courage that at times even frustrated the King himself. When in the year of her sixteenth summer her mother died of blood disorder, which caused such infernal itching that she could neither sleep nor eat, he ordered his only child to choose her future husband from all of the sons of the nobles in the kingdom.

"I will take no other woman to be my Queen," he said, looking down at his favorite's likeness. "You must produce for me an heir."

But Ephtheta stood before her father's throne with lowered eyes, and refused.

"I cannot, my King," she responded simply. "For there is no man amongst them who is half the man my father is." Then she looked up and added, "But I promise you with my own inheritance that when I find him, I will marry him, and give you a grandson."

That was last year, and though many suitors had since come and gone, her mind had not changed. There were the sons of generals, fine horsemen, brilliant young soldiers and even artists and scholars who sought her hand. Each time her father questioned her whether or not she found this one or that one handsome enough, smart enough, brave enough, she always responded the same.

"Enough for any woman in the land, my King. Any woman but the daughter of the great Samsu-titana, who has no choice but to compare her husband to her father for the rest of her life."

To this, the King had no answer.

But today, Princess Ephtheta has met a creature who might indeed turn her head. Certainly he was brave, having hailed the litter of the princess of Babylon like a nobleman hails a footman. And handsome? He was more dizzyingly handsome than the King's best Turkoman stallion. Behind a delicate, long-fingered hand, Ephtheta giggles, imagining herself bringing this golden sprite before the King and asking for his permission to marry him.

"What are you thinking, Theta?" whispers Yesh, who has bent to put the words in her ear so that the footman outside the litter cannot catch them before they reach it. "Are you up to mischief again? You will go too far one day."

"I will ask my father for his hand!" Ephtheta giggles, her tip-tilted eyes sparkling above the cage of her fingers.

"Hold your tongue, else they hear!" warns Yesh, but she has slapped her own slim hand over her mouth to keep the laughter in it.

"Nay, I shall never marry," says Ephtheta, chuckling still after a moment. "There is nothing to be gained by it. I have all I want, and what is it to me if there is an heir? Can I live past my own life? There is no freedom in marriage. Not even for a princess. It is a man's world."

"Tell that to the Queens of Egypt," responds Yesh.

"Few and far between," answers Ephtheta, peeking out of a small flap in the back of the litter to spy on the creature she intends to keep as her own personal pet.

"They will have to castrate him of course," she sighs. "Pity."

"You bring a golden lizard into the nest of a hen, he will still steal the eggs," murmurs Yesh, slapping the flap closed so that the princess turns to pout at her behind her silks.

"You say the funniest things, Yesh. That is no lizard. That is a cat, a pretty little ocelot for my collection."

But to this Yesh says nothing. Ocelots, she thinks. Has she lived in the delta? Has she lost a brother to a lion? She does not know a house cat from a hyena. Nothing with eyes like that one stays a pet for long.

Mochlos has had his first bath in a week. He has been forced to cling to the stinking animal, Ess, on horseback for the better part of the past three days, eating and sleeping with the man at night. As a result, the man's stench now clings to him. It is in his nose, the fine weave of his robe is sodden with it, even his fingernails carry the aroma.

Now he soaks in a rich man's bath on the outskirts of the great city of Babylon. The place is a maze of channels and ducts cut into the earth to feed the fields, all feeding off of the great river. The system sprawls north and south of the river as far as the eye can see, and this man, as his good fortune would have it, owns a great many acres of land, as well as hundreds of head of cattle, sheep and goats.

The bath water is chill, the fine perfumed oils of Crete he is accustomed to absent, but the luxury of a bar of goat fat soap, sweetened with eucalyptus, has made this morning almost tolerable. Mochlos and Ess were greeted and entertained civilly enough, though it was clear that the master of the house would not be joining them for meals, nor allow even the youngest of his seven daughters near them. They were put up in a separate quarters, behind those of the house slaves, and the Minoan priest's robes were washed while he slept. His only complaint is that these people seem to have an aversion to shaving their beards and, having been without a razor for days, his own pate has sprouted a ring of dark hair that sticks straight up from his head behind his ears. His beard, which he has not seen since he became a priest, is also sprouting, and is coming in with a white streak through the middle, making him look a bit like a badger, or worse a polecat.

"I look like a damned barbarian," he mutters, scrubbing at his nails with a brush made from a boar's bristles. "Surely there are barbers in Babylon? I cannot be seen in the city like this, nor in the company of that stinking animal. It is time to part company," he muses, smiling to himself. "Yes, I have had enough of that stench."

In the main house, Ess is hunting for treasure.

A soldier has rights, after all. It is the way of all soldiers to take from the land and the people around them. He is an Amorite soldier, returned from the battlefield, or at least from the campaign, and it is his right to take whatever he likes from the land and the people unfortunate enough to be along his route home. Today he is feeling randy. He has had a good bath, his first in months, and a few skins of good Babylonian wine from the house cellar, and he is looking about for a serving girl to take the edge off his temper, made worse by the last three days journey with that infernal Minoan priest.

"I'll take care of him next," mumbles Ess into his beard as he stomps about the main house, looking for a maid, a laundress, any female at all under the age of fifty. So far he has come across none but male servants, an old seamstress, and a cook as fat as a pregnant sow. He knows they're hiding from him, the young ones, knows the master's daughters are off limits too, but he's had enough of rules, having spent the last seven months on campaign. He's on his own now, and anyway, a girl's word against a soldiers amounts to little in Babylon. If he finds a daughter over ten summers old she's going to get an education.

As he wanders through the main house an old woman with a cloud in one eye, perhaps the master's mother-in-law, gives him a nasty scare, coming around a doorway like a ghost, her veil down, her wiry, corkscrew hair sticking out in all directions from her wizen old face. She looks up at him fearlessly, steadying herself against the door jam.

"Mot," she spits the word then touches the spittle on her mouth with one claw-like finger and reaches up to graze his face with a blackened nail. Her clouded eye, that whitened orb, cold as death, regards him. He smacks her hand away, shoves past her, too late. She has cursed him. She has called the god of death upon him.

He kisses his talisman then, to ward off the evil, though he doesn't have much faith in it. Even the great Ba'al fears Mot, god of death. Little good a talisman of weasel bone will do against him.

"Pah on you," he spits on the mud brick floor, pushing the curse from his mind. He is a superstitious man, all soldiers are, but he is also drunk and forgetting is easy now. He lumbers down to the end of the hall and is about to give up on this passage and go look for a shepherd girl in the fields when he spots a break in the stone wall above a cedar chest. "Hah," he pulls the chest away with a single motion, and finds a hole, half the height of a man, and a stairway leading down into the earth.

Even drunk, he is still a soldier. He waits, his ears perked for any sounds. They will have heard him pull the chest away. They will be cowering down there, the master's daughters, where their father has hidden them from the likes of Ess.

"No use hiding, pretties," he shouts down the hole, which is barely big enough for him to squeeze through. "Come up and entertain a hero of the realm now like good citizens. Else I'll be forced to come down and it'll go harder on ye."

There is a flutter of voices downstairs. One of them is weeping. He waits. Two. Two distinct voices. Ah, a good number. Didn't he hear one of the house slaves mention seven daughters? Where are the other five then? Perhaps visiting relatives in the city. Perhaps the elder of the seven are married off. These would be the youngest then.

"Are ye daughters of the master, or house slaves?" he calls. "Don't lie to me, I'll know soon enough by yer marks, or lack of 'm."

After a moment, a small, nervous voice answers him. "We are serving girls. Slaves."

"From where? How many, and how old?" shouts Ess.

"From Nubia," says the same small voice. "The Kingdom of Kush. There are three of us. I am the oldest. My sisters are not ten summers."

"And you?" Ess snorts.

There is another hesitation, then, "Fourteen."

"You come up and I'll leave the other two be then," he says. "Make me crawl down into this hole and it'll go hard with all of ye."

At their evening meal, taken in the guest house and still without the company of the master of the home, Mochlos is quite pleasant. He prattles on, without much input from his companion, about the well-known hospitality of the modern Babylonian home, the famed opulence of the palace, "Almost certainly influenced somewhere along the line by Minoan trade," he adds smugly. Mochlos has bribed a house man to shave his head, but he has decided to leave the beard, for now. "What do you think, Ess, am I more handsome with or without it?" he asks. "You'd look a mite better yourself, I must say, without all that ungodly hair. But the bath, and laundered clothing, has improved our chances of making a decent 'first impression' in court mightily."

"Neither," answers Ess, pulling apart a partridge with his hands and talking through a mouthful of the bird.

"Neither what?" Mochlos sets his cup down, regarding the man's brute table manners with stunned disbelief. "Do you eat from a trough in the Amorite army?"

"Neither with nor without," answers Ess. Ignoring this last, he smacks his lips and wipes his mouth on a bare forearm.

"There is a linen for that in your lap," frowns Mochlos.

"Handsome," continues Ess, picking up the cloth and throwing it at Mochlos' head, "Is not a word I'd describe you by. But *with* the beard, I'll admit you look more like a badger than a buzzard now. Hah!" He chokes on a bit of the hen.

Mochlos purses his lips haughtily. "I see. Well, perhaps I'll shave it after all, as soon as I can find a proper barber."

"That weren't no compliment, priestie. Yer between a rock and a hard place on that score. Maybe shave yer head off altogether, that'd be an improvement. Hah!" The big man convulses with laughter.

"What lovely dinner company," mutters Mochlos, his mood all but dampened. "Here now, let us drink a toast, shall we? This man has the most expansive wine cellar. Do you know I actually found an amphora of Minoan wine? Look here, pass me your cup and we shall drink to a future of riches beyond measure." He reaches for the henchman's cup as the man steadies himself, having nearly choked on a bone in his spasm of mirth.

I nearly had no need of you, thinks Mochlos, easily slipping a pearl of poison into the man's drink from a vial in his sleeve without the goon's notice.

"Here you are, sir. I drink to your health." Smiling, Mochlos hands Ess the cup, then pours a generous helping of the wine into his own and lifts it.

Ess has grabbed the cup and gulped it before Mochlos has had a chance to salute. The man is still coughing from his near asphyxiation on the hen bone, and has consumed the poisoned wine as if it were the solution to his distress. He bumps his enormous chest with his fist. "Hah, there's better."

Mochlos watches him coolly. The man returns to his meal, tearing another leg off his bird and sucking the meat off the bone with gusto. After a moment, Mochlos puts down his cup and squints at him. "Do I see something in your eye there?" He points a neatly groomed fingernail at Ess's right cheek. "Looks like you may need to have a doctor lance that."

"Wha? I got nothin' in my eye. Eye's fine," says Ess, losing interest in his partridge and wiping his greasy fingers on the linen in his lap. "Take a better look, don't want infection." He leans over, opening his lids with his thumb and forefinger so that the priest can examine the eye.

"That's damned strange," mutters Mochlos, peering at the man's face. "Not a damned thing!" Blinking, he sits back, remembering himself. "Must have been mistaken then. You're fine."

"'Preciate you lookin' after me, priestie," smirks Ess, returning to his plate.

"Well," comments Mochlos dully, "We can't have you go blind, can we. You're going to have to snatch the boy once we find him. I don't fancy having a physical confrontation with him."

"You afraid of that little mite? Hah, you're somethin' else, priest. Afraid you'll break a nail?" Ess chuckles, spitting grease.

"Hardly. That 'little mite' as you call him is not what you

think. He's a wildcat. You'd be surprised how strong-"

"Oh for crap sake, priest. Look at me. Do I care about a few scratches? I'll crush the little nipper, throw him in a bag and have done."

"No, no. We mustn't harm him, or mar him, in any way," answers Mochlos more seriously, and touching his lip with a long-fingered nail. "Not a hair of his head. Not a hair."

Ess shoots Mochlos a look, setting the hen bone he has been sucking down on his plate and pushing the whole mess away. He stares at the priest, waiting for an explanation, but Mochlos is silent. He picks up his cup of wine, looks into it, and takes a great gulp. Wine dribbles down his beard onto his newly laundered tunic. "You still worried about the assassin, priestie? Thought he couldn't catch us, that we'd be safe once we got to Babylon. Ain't that what you said?" He sets his cup down for Mochlos to refill. "The assassin..." he murmurs, belching. "The Wolf of the Hatti."

"It is over and done now, man," answers Mochlos, filling the henchman's cup a second time. "You could bring him back to Amega in a golden chariot with an olive wreath about his neck and the man would still lop off your head for your trouble."

Ess nods, then tosses back the entirety of the second cup of poisoned wine. "Why did you do it, priestie, eh? What were you thinking? You cannot outrun the beast. No one can."

"The boy thinks ..... the boy knows he needs me to survive. A slave-god cannot survive without his priest, without his House. I made him, he is mine. This was the law on Crete, where he was made. He will wither and die without me." Or with my replacement, he thinks, remembering that Rush had insisted he train the girl, Cara, before he left Amega. But there is no need for this towering monkey to know about Cara. It is bad enough that Rush holds that card yet.

Mochlos runs his index finger over the rim of his wine cup, nodding with certainty.

Suddenly his cup is flying from the table and his throat is in Ess' great paw.

"What of me, priestie? What's to keep me alive?" snarls the big man, his rank breath all but choking Mochlos.

"Did I force you into anything? Did I deceive you?" squeaks the priest though the man's fingers. As they loosen he continues, "Nay, if anything I have given you insurance against the death you had already secured for yourself! You were already on that monster's death list when you chose to kidnap the king! HIS king."

He pushes the man's greasy claw from his newly freshened robe, takes his own lap cloth and dips it in a bowl of water beside his plate, dabs his neck. "Besides," he puts down the cloth and picks up his wine cup, "can he walk right into the heart of his greatest foes' kingdom, slaughter us in our beds, and then expect to leave with the Rah on his shoulder?"

"That devil can do anything he likes and always has," spits Ess, rising to his feet. He wobbles a bit, catches his balance, then leans over Mochlos. "But I'll tell you this, priest." He pokes the man's chest. "If I smell that beast coming for me, if I get half a whiff of him, I'll make sure to secure you in your grave before he puts me in mine."

"Fair enough," answers Mochlos, leaning away from Ess' offensive breath. "I would expect no less from you, being a man of your profession." When Ess has left him he continues under his breath, "Though I doubt very much you will ever get the opportunity."

CHAPTER 2

"Rah is sleep here, with Ono," beams Rah as the man unties his wrists from the horn of his saddle and pulls him to the ground.

"Hardly," answers Petuk over his shoulder as he hops down from his own mount. Handing the reins to a stable boy he turns to take a better look at the prize the princess has caught for herself today. "Didn't need to go far to catch this pet for the princesses collection, did we? Barely got out the gates and there he stood, just waiting to be trussed and taken. Aamat, untie his wrists."

"You think the King will really allow this?" answers Aamat, who is Petuk's personal slave and valet, a youth from Egypt so newly sold to Babylon that he still hears the sacred ibis calling him like a trumpet from the rushes on the Nile in his sleep.

"What does he deny her?" says Petuk, taking Rah by the chin and musing into the blue-green ocean of his eyes. "Thought his eyes were gold," he mutters. "Play of light, I suppose-" he lets Rah's jaw loose and lifts his collar. "This is a good half pound of gold here. Where the hell did you come from?"

"Yes, he wears the gold of a temple slave-god, one of the holy ones." Aamat is at Petuk's side now. "In Egypt that emerald alone could buy you a fine house on the river."

"Rah come from north," says Rah to Petuk as Aamat

unties his wrists. "Far north. Priest make Rah in Knossos. Want to kill Rah, cut out heart," he braids his fingers around an invisible dagger and pantomimes Mochlos stabbing a victim laid out before him on a stone alter. "But wolf, he want Rah. Take Rah to Amega."

Petuk has turned into a statue, his lips paling. He stares at Rah, drops the collar, takes a step back.

"Put a triple guard on this creature," he barks at last to no one in particular. Several guards who have just dismounted from their horses step forward. "Yes, Sir!"

Petuk grabs the closest by his beard and wrenches him forward so that he is a hair's breadth from his face when he continues, "And make damned sure he is treated better than you would treat your own mother, understood? And that every man in this division knows that those were my exact words."

"Yes, Sir," answers the man.

"He may sleep wherever he likes. He may sleep with the King's mount if he likes." He looks at Rah. "Where would you like to sleep, boy? And what are you called?"

"Rah already say," frowns Rah, taking Ono by her bridle. "Rah sleep with Ono. This Ono. This," he taps his own breast, "Rah."

"Ra? The Egyptian sun god?" Aamat scoffs. "Egyptian gods do not come to earth to walk among mortal men. If you are Ra, where is your boat? Where is your crew? The sun shines today. Who carries it across the twelve provinces while you stand in the road to Babylon?"

"Rah is no sun god," says Rah to Aamat, as if talking to a child. "Rah is grain god." He makes a sweeping gesture toward the lush fields of barley outside the palace walls. "All kind grain. Barley. Rye. Hay. Where Rah is, plenty is. If no rain, rain come with Rah. If no crop, crop grow with Rah. But Rah must dance for king. Otherwise, no crop, no rain, no grain. Everything die. Maybe earthquake, too. Maybe flood. I don't know."

"Is this how it was on Crete then?" asks Aamat, looking from Rah to Petuk in alarm. "The Wolf of Amega took you, and so the island exploded?"

"Knossos gone," nods Rah solemnly, turning from Aamat

and stroking Ono's dun withers. "Wolf take Rah, sea take Knossos."

"Blessed Inanna," hisses Petuk, taking Rah by the arm, then remembering himself and releasing him as if the boy's golden skin had scorched his hand. "What are you saying, boy?"

Rah looks down at his arm where the man touched him, then back up at Petuk. "No touch Rah," he says, shaking his head solemnly. "Only Wolf he can touch Rah. Wolf, he is come. He is be mad now, you take Rah like slave. Tie up like chicken." He unties Ono's girth and pulls her saddle from her withers. He hands the saddle to Aamat, who is so stunned that he takes it, then hands it to a stableman. Rah continues, "He come now, come for Rah. He take this Bab-bee-lon city too."

"The Wolf of Amega," whispers Petuk. "Here, in our Babylon? No. Even he cannot breach these walls."

"He come. He take. Always he come, take." Rah shakes his head. His frown is a pout. After days without a razor the golden stubble on his cheek and jaw glimmers in the torchlight like the flank of the King's Turkoman. "Rah is tell priest, Rah must dance for king, save city from plague, save Ting Ya, save Hali," Rah continues casually. "Nobody listen. Rah dance for king, or city is destroy."

"Halki? Did he just speak the name of the god of fruitfulness?" Aamat looks at Petuk, as if he might know the answer.

"Do you know of another?" hisses Petuk bitterly, looking about at the guards who have collected around this exchange. "No one is to speak a word of this? Do you understand? Not a word or I will take your tongues!"

"But the King must be warned!" blurts the man who has taken Ono's saddle from Aamat.

"I for one do not intend to be staked for bringing the monarch bad news. Let the boy tell them himself," says Aamat.

"Rah tell," says Rah. "Rah is need priest. Need big-- many priest, many concubine. What is this?" He frowns at Aamat, makes a grand expression of awe at the invisible shrine he has suddenly discovered behind him, and Aamat nods and blurts to no one, "temple!" then looks sheepishly at his master, who narrows his eyes at him, his mouth a grim line.

"Ya, that," says Rah, continuing. "Need temple. Big. Must have concubine. Six. And dove too. Six. You have dance here? Must have, eh-" he gestures to the group of men that have gathered around him, "Like this, many. Many to dance. Men. Girl, too. Rah is teach. Must be take to princess so can tell. Take now!"

"*She* must summon *you*," says Petuk in alarm. "I cannot bring you to her otherwise! The King will have my head!"

"You no bring Rah now, Wolf he is have heart first, *then* head," Rah shrugs. "Can come any time. Maybe tonight. While sleep."

"Very well," swallows Petuk. He has removed his headdress to stroke his shaven head nervously. "I will speak to Mefali. If anyone can gain you access to the princess without losing his head, he can."

But Rah is staring up at the man's bald head. "You priest? Why you have head like this?" He reaches for Petuk's scalp but the man steps back.

"All Amorite men shave thus," Petuk blinks at Rah's innocence. "How is it you know so little of the world?"

"Rah know plenty," frowns Rah, walking around the man to make an exaggerated perusal of his scalp. "This for priest only in Knossos. Maybe here, everybody priest." He looks at Aamat. "Take off hat."

Aamat shoots Petuk a look, then, when his master nods, removes his own headdress, which is a cloth hood in red and gold, symbolizing his rank as a slave of a member of the royal palace. His head is shaved.

"Everybody no hair like priest," says Rah. "Stupid."

"He wants to see the princess," says Petuk to Mefali later that day. The older man is in his quarters off the military court in the palace. He is seated on a cushion of goose down, raised above the floor by a cedar platform. Beside him a fine-boned hound with a muzzle like a spear leans on him with obvious affection.

"You'd better get that animal off the King's silk mattress," adds Petuk, going for the dog's leather collar.

"Touch her and I will put a blade in your eye," answers Mefali, his arm sliding protectively around the bitches shoulder. The dog licks his cheek, as if in thanks.

But Petuk only frowns.

"Father, the boy is not what we think," says Petuk. He moves across the room to a bench, pulls it up to the bed and sits. He leans toward his father, his elbows on his knees.

"Oh? And what do we think?" answers Mefali, scratching the dog's back as she nuzzles his neck. Sitting beside him on the mattress, she is as tall as he.

"A performer from Larsa, lost from his troupe? A stray Mari palace slave? A tear from the golden eye of Shamash?" Petuk shakes his head. He closes his eyes and puts his face in his hands. "Father, he is the possession of the Wolf of Amega."

Mefali sits upright. He stares at his son, blinks. He takes a long breath. He shoves the bitch off the bed like so much laundry. She whimpers, and lies still at his feet.

"Inanna save us," he murmurs, then takes his son's arm and shakes it. "How do you know this?"

"There is more, father," says Petuk, looking up. "He says he must dance for the King, or else Babylon will suffer. He says the Queen will die. And he speaks of a plague. He says he must see the princess-"

"So the Wolf would destroy Babylon with a plague?" Mefali is stroking his pointed, grey beard, looking off beyond his son's shoulder to the doorway. "A plague. It is not his style, yet those coming back from the front have spoken of a plague animal being sent into Amega by one of our generals. Apparently the plot was undermined before any real damage could be done. But you know the legend of the man as well as I do. He has a genius for stealth, and a great fondness of symmetry. One would think he was an Amorite, so tenaciously does he hold to the laws of our Hammurabi. The fool who dared send a plague to Amega may well have brought down Babylon by doing so."

"You mean to say, an eye for an eye...."

"That is Hammurabi, my son. The Assassin, the Wolf, for

him, there is no eye for an eye. Pluck a lash from *that* eye, and he will take both your eyes... by removing your whole head, then leave you your eyeballs in your hands."

Later that evening, Mochlos hears his companion groaning in the room beside his own. The man seemed perfectly fine at dinner, and the telltale signs of the poison's effectiveness, broken blood vessels in the eyes, were not in evidence. Perhaps he is one of the few I have known who is immune to the weed, thinks the priest. No matter, there is breakfast, and a different concoction for the likes of him.

But then he hears the man's discomfort, the moaning, the pacing, on the other side of the wall they share. Ah, there it is. If you look in his face now his eyes will be bloodied. He is hemorrhaging. Soon he will be bleeding from both ends.

Sometime earlier a child had come to his door, begging him for help. That was the strange thing about being a priest. Even in a foreign country, they recognized him for what he was. Perhaps it was his bearing, perhaps his need for cleanliness, for order. Perhaps simply his soft-spoken, self-assured manner. They didn't seem to care that he worshiped a foreign god. He was a priest. They made the giant leap of faith that he had some power, some 'in' with the gods, and they ultimately came to him for help.

This child, a lovely Nubian girl in her early puberty, had fallen to her knees and clasped her hands together in supplication as soon as he had opened his door. Her face, when she lifted it to him, was the most enchantingly exotic ebony, punctuated by large, peach-colored lips, like an iris in bloom, and cheekbones to match those of a panther kitten. Her cheeks were glistening with tears now.

"Please, Sir," she said, "please take him away. Don't let him ruin my sisters, they are only babies, not even ten summers. Please," and then she stopped, choking on her own tears.

"My dear," said Mochlos in his most genuine voice, "What has he done? Has he hurt you in some-?"

But then he knew. Could all but smell the beast's stench on her. Yes, he had raped this exquisite child. The pig. The

Amorite pig.

Mochlos touched the girls shoulder. "Get off the floor, child. You have nothing more to fear."

She looked at him, her exquisite brow pinched. You, thought Mochlos then, would make a suitable concubine for the Rah. And given the proper silks, afforded the proper hairdresser, a suitable representation of the House of the Moon. Yes, I think I have found a delightful replacement for my current, miserable escort into Babylon.

"Come inside," and he stepped back, making an arc with his left arm to invite her in.

The look on her face told him his intentions had been mistaken, and to calm her fears he immediately stepped into the hall with her, lay his arm across her shoulders, and led her toward the door to the courtyard.

"Better still," he spoke softly into her hair, "let us sit alone in the fig garden where no one will overhear us. How long have you been a slave in this house?"

"Since I was a baby," said the girl. "I am fourteen summers now."

Passing Ess' door Mochlos hesitated, pressing his fingers lightly into the girl's shoulder to stop her. Within, Ess' moans rose. "Listen now. Do you hear him? He will be dead by morning, and you may thank me for it."

The girl looked up into the priest's face in awe. "But why would you poison him? You came together to my master's home," she whispered. "Is he not your friend?"

"Hardly," responded Mochlos, leading her on down the hall and out onto a stone colonnade toward the fig garden.

"Here now. Let us sit a while beneath this fig and speak plainly," said the priest, settling himself on a stone bench beneath the immature leaves of a young fruit tree.

"He found us in a cellar, and took me there. There," wept the child, "in front of my sisters. Oh, I am ruined..." she sobbed.

Mochlos sighed and nodded, "Yes, you are ruined....unless-"

"Oh, Sir. Can you make me a virgin again once I have been spoiled?" she cried, falling to her knees to lay her head in his lap and weep, "Oh, even a high priest cannot do this. What will become of me?"

"What is your name, child?" asked Mochlos, stroking her hair.

"I am Awiti," she answered, wiping her cheeks with her palms. "I was born in the Delta, in the Kingdom of Kesh. I was taken on the moon before my initiation-"

"Well, Awiti of Kesh, I am Mochlos, and I was High Priest of the House of the Moon in Knossos, in the land you Egyptians call Crete, where the Sea People live. I made a god-slave last spring, a sacrifice to Rah, Crete's god of abundance, and the god was pleased, and all of the valleys surrounding Knossos flourished. Then the Rah was stolen and the sea became angry. A great wave came, and wiped out the land of Crete, and many were lost. But I and my house were rescued by the Wolf of the Aegean, who desired the Rah and knew that without his maker the god-slave would die. He took us to his fortress in the land of the Hatti. But the Rah has fled the Wolf, into Babylon, and so I am here. For without me, he will surely wither."

The girl's tears dried as Mochlos told his story. She said nothing, only nodded, as if memorizing what she was being told, eager to hear more.

"This man, this unholy beast who has defiled you with his filth, is a bloodthirsty murderer, a mercenary. He, too, desired the Rah, and had me in his power until tonight. But I tell you, he is dying. No further harm will come to you, or your sisters, by his hands. Only now that I have told you all of this, you must swear your loyalty to me."

"It is yours, Sir. You have my word that I will never tell a soul. I am your servant," answered Awiti earnestly.

"Ah, in these times, a person's word means little, I am afraid. I will require more than that to keep my secret safe," said the priest.

"Anything, Sir. I owe you my life."

"And I will take it," said Mochlos, lifting his hand to quiet her when she jumped off the seat. "Hear me out. I will need temple concubines when I enter the city. Exotics, beauties fit for the house of the Rah."

"But I am nothing," said the girl, "Only a house slave for a rich man. How can I become a temple maiden?"

"Ah, all things are possible with magick," said the priest, smiling self-assuredly. "All things, save altering human will. A good magician knows that. Therefore I must know that you are willing, for without the subject's free will, magick can create disastrous results."

"No slave can ask for more in life than to belong to the house of a god," answered Awiti.

"Go and tell your master that the priest desires to purchase you. Tell him that if he is in agreement, in the morning he is to send you to me with his price on your lips. Tell him that I will add ten percent to that price if he will allow me to take you into Babylon, where I must sell certain property in order to repay him."

"Yes, Sir," the girl answered, then bowed to the ground. "Thank you, Sir, you will not regret your decision."

"No," thought Mochlos then, as she ran off toward the slaves' quarters to tell her sisters of her good fortune. "I think you will serve me very well."

Now, listening to Ess dying on the other side of the wall, Mochlos smiles quietly to himself. "Just like Siriona, she is. Not as tall, perhaps, but quite close enough to be a twin. And I dare say, even more beautiful."

Akintunde is running.

He has been running for seven hours, has crossed the plains of lower Anatolia, has found the mountain pass, and is making his way upward toward the setting sun, toward the Valley of the Gods, when he hears the kittens mewling.

Akintunde remembers.

He remembers his father, standing with his back to the setting sun in the doorway of his childhood home, with the kittens, three of them, in his arms. They were cheetahs, not yet weaned, their eyes crusted with puss, their ears filthy with mites and disease.

Akintunde was seven summers. He had hunted the lion with his father. He had seen a man return from his cattle with half his arm gone, taken by a leopard. And he did not

23

understand.

"They may die," said his father, putting a skin of goat's milk to the biggest kitten's mouth. "But we will try."

Akintunde watched. And for three days, his father nursed the cubs. One died the first night. The second, refusing the milk, died the next. But the third, the biggest one, took the gift of life from its enemy's hand greedily. It drank and drank. And when Akintunde's father brought it home a small hare, and showed it how to skin it with his teeth and gnaw at the meat, the kitten took the gift of the hare and ate its liver and its heart, then dragged it to a corner, though the corpse was bigger than she, and growled when Akintunde's father tried to take it from her.

"Ah," laughed Akintunde's father. "This one will live. This one we will call Themba, 'great in size'. This one will be yours."

And so the kitten grew, like Akintunde, into a lanky youth. It followed Akintunde into the pastures and lay by his side, watching the cattle lick the grass and low. It learned to leave the calves alone, to wait for food from its enemy's hand.

"You will always be enemies," said Akintunde's father. "But sometimes enemies can make the best of friends."

And one day, it happened that Akintunde was chosen to compete in a race with the five fastest youths in the village. He locked the cheetah in the grain hut and met the others at the appointed time on a hill on the outskirts of town. The boys would run for two days, out onto the veldt, where the village chieftain had sent ahead three elders to bear witness to who completed the race first.

The first day Akintunde ran fast. He overtook all of his competitors by the end of the day with several miles to spare. The second day he increased his lead. He did not know that two of his challengers were out of the race, one having unhappily made a decision to stop at a watering hole infested by crocodiles, another having shattered his patella in an unfortunate fall. On the third day, Akintunde had lost all sight of his competition. Cresting a low rise he made the fatal error of looking back over his shoulder to be sure, and took a misstep.

Akintunde fell into a rocky gully, made invisible to the eye by tall grasses, and landed in a bed of silt. Stunned and bruised, bleeding from a deep cut on his shin, he took a moment to catch his breath. Cursing at his own foolishness he pushed himself up on his hands, then raised his eyes to see how far he had fallen. It took him a moment to distinguish the tawny head of the jackal splitting the grasses. Alone, the animal might not have frightened him, but when a second dun head parted the vegetation beside the first, he realized he could lose more than a race today. The sun was fading, turning the sky above a dirty orange, and the pair began their siren call. Akintunde knew that this meant there were others. Though jackals rarely hunted in packs or challenged humans. This group was emboldened, and saw his fall as a sign of weakness that established him as prey.

Akintunde froze. It had been a dry season, no rain for many months, and the small animals these predators normally hunted had died off. These jackals were starving.

There was no solution. If he rose to his feet, attempted to climb back up onto the road, he would have to turn his back, another sign of weakness. They would attack him, first nipping at his wounded leg, sniffing the blood, tasting, then eating him alive. If he stayed where he was they would do the same.

And then she sprang.

At first Akintunde thought that a lioness had come to chase off the jackals and claim him for her own. In the fading light, in the shadow of the brachiaria that enclosed him, he saw only a flash of yellow and white, her belly, fly over his body and lunge for the boldest jackal. The others fled, but that one lost its battle to be free of her claws. The two disappeared in the rushes, and as the moments passed, Akintunde remained where he was at the bottom of the gully, hopeful that the lioness had forgotten him. Then, as suddenly as she had sprung, the cat was back, carrying the carcass of the jackal in her jaws.

"Themba! It is you! But I locked you in the grain hut-" Akintunde reached for his friend, and as he did so the great cat dropped the jackal and came to lie by his side.

"You have saved my life, Themba,' wept the boy that

night, lying against the mottled fur of his friend for warmth. "As my father once saved yours."

Now, hearing the cubs mewling in the brush along the mountain pass that would lead him to the Valley of the Gods, Akintunde thought of Themba, thought of the cub she had been, thought of his father walking in to their house with the three cheetah kittens in his arms, and recognized the same sounds of starvation and distress. And he thought of the debt he owed his friend, who might have been his enemy, and knew what he must do.

CHAPTER 3

Rush sleeps under the stars, a predator, exhausted after two days of travel, taking his rest only during the darkest hours of the night, not far off the soldier's road to Babylon. He has crossed the Table, dismounting his warhorse only when the safety of the animal's feet on the lava rocks would be compromised by his weight. He has taken with him the garb of Ameg The Merchant and enough gold and jewels to purchase anything needed to secure his ruse when he enters the city, but he travels under the guise of Samal-Etatani, an Amorite mercenary who will be well treated by any Babylonian he meets on his journey.

Samal-Etatani was, in fact, an Amorite warrior, and his exploits were well known by his countrymen. To his great misfortune, however, Samal was at the wrong place at the right time. He was among the men under Iamhad's command the night the Assassin burned their camp and took the general's heart and horse.

"Ah, it is Samal-Etatani," were the last words Samal heard in the land of the living before his throat was pierced by the infamous gold and silver dagger of the Wolf of Amega, thrust upward under the mandibles into the cranial cavity, to churn his brain like so much milk fat. "Forgive me, Samal," he did not hear as the Assassin stripped him of his leathers, his shield, his helmet and his boots. "But these things will serve me well, I think, if ever I should enter Babylon. You are a lucky fellow, that your life should be considered a worthy disguise for the Assassin. I will leave your head here with the rest of you, that you might find your way in the afterworld." Then he cut the man's ring finger off and pocketed it, for the ring was pressed with his seal, an identifier no one could argue with.

After all, the only way to own a warrior's ring was either to be that warrior, or the one who took it from him. And who could take the seal ring of the mighty Samal?

A dozen feet from where Rush makes his bed, Iamhad's warhorse stomps and blows. Before dawn the Assassin will dress the beast in Amorite battle tack, also stolen: a twisted iron bit, a deep, treeless saddle, and viciously spiked hind boots, fastened to the animal's fetlocks with leather wraps. Then he will continue his journey to Babylon, stopping only once for shelter and a warm meal at the house of the barley mogul, Attaru, and missing the departure of the High Priest of the Moon and his new temple maiden by mere hours. He will learn that the priest's companion, the man who was seen charging after Rah on horseback with Mochlos clinging to him, has met with death, incidentally, after having raped the very girl the priest has taken with him. And learning also of the manner of death which the Amorite dog suffered, Rush will deduce that the priest himself poisoned him, and conclude that whatever caused their merger is now in Mochlos' possession.

"Princess, a word," whispers Mefali into Ephtheta's ear as she leans together with her seamstresses, giggling over a sheave of rolled silks.

"What of this one, Mefali!" laughs Ephtheta, standing to unfurl a sheer sleeve of yellow. "I will make a dress to dance in and entertain my father's guests in it! Do you think it suits me?" She spins, winding the yellow gossamer about her naked neck and shoulders.

"It is quite invisible, Princess," says Mefali, biting his cheek to keep from screaming at his sovereigns daughter. She will drive me mad before I am another year older, he thinks. They will have to shackle me to a wall in the dungeon to keep me from strangling her with my bare hands.

"Invisible?" quips the princess, her copper brows pitched

upward in question. "But does it not suit my complexion? Do you not think it would make a lovely dress, just as it is? Just a simple shift, like so, tucked here and here. See? Can you imagine it?"

By now the seamstresses are falling off their stools, coughing on their laughter. But Mefali is not amused. No, you little minx, I will not imagine you in that, only that, for old as I am, my member will respond and then you and your allies will have a damned good laugh at my expense, and perhaps at the expense of my head!

"Come now, princess, you know as well as I that your father" (there, I need only mention him and all thoughts of you and that damned silk are gone) "would not allow it."

"Oh, where is your humor, Mefali. You are as sour as that stone faced son of yours, though I will admit he is a handsome stone, with his fierce eyes and his strong chin. What have you come to tell me? Can it not be said in front of my seamstresses?"

"Only that the … creature you … found today is … becoming a bit of a problem. He seems to be… well, it is possible that-"

"Oh, spit it out, Mefali!" Ephtheta has unwound herself from the yellow silk and handed it back to one of the girls. "Here, make me a new veil of this one. And," she gives Mefali a consoling smile, "a matching sheath in something a bit less… sheer. With this silk overlaying it, you see? To give the illusion of nakedness."

Mefali squeezes his eyes closed, clenches his teeth, and gives himself a moment to let that last dig go. In the dungeon, secured to a wall, he thinks. To keep me from strangling her myself. But to the princess, he says, "Would you like to see for yourself, Majesty?"

"See what?" asks Ephtheta, spinning around to give Mefali her full attention at last.

"The… the creature…"

"Oh, yes. The golden cat-boy! Have you discovered where he comes from? Is he an actor? Has he lost his troupe?"

"We… have an idea where he comes from, yes, Majesty,

but-"

"Oh for the sake of heaven, Mefali, bring him here to me. No, not here in my chamber. Bring him to the Queens visiting room. I will visit with him there. Then we will see what is what. After all, we cannot speak to my father about him before we know what he is, can we?"

An hour later Rah stands before the princess, Ephtheta, who sits on her mother's visiting couch in a room strewn with yellow and gold silks and brightly pungent with the scent of exotic flowering plants. Rah has been given a bath, his mass of curls brushed out, and his cloak and clothing taken and replaced with a simple white tunic and leather sandals. But unaccustomed to the tunic, Rah fidgets and pulls until, just outside the queen's appointment room, he stops and tears the cloth clear to his navel, much to Mefali's horror. There is little Mefali can do about it, save return to the guard's quarters to replace it, and it is a good half hour walk back.

"Ya," says Rah. That better, Wait, I do," he slaps Mefali's hands away and draws his arms out of the sleeves. Then he pulls the bodice of the garment over his Minoan belt, that circle of gold that cannot be removed except by a metal worker, and arranges it behind his back. He has made for himself an elaborate Minoan skirt. "This good."

Having not been present when the boy was stripped to be bathed, Mefali is taken back to see the rings of gold fastened to the boy's nipples.

"My gods, what are you?" he whispers, as to himself, but Rah only flashes him a dizzying smile and answers, "I tell you already."

"Bring him in behind me. And keep hold of him, he's unpredictable," says Mefali to the two palace guards who have been shadowing the boy since they left the military wing.

Mefali straightens himself, brushes some imaginary lint off his own sleeves, and lifts his chin. Then he walks deliberately into the queen's chamber.

"Your Highness," bows Mefali when he reaches the princess. Seated on a bench beside her is a willowy Nubian woman whose head is completely shaven, giving her extraordinary features, her plush mouth, her large dark eyes,

her broad nose, even more emphasis. Several sight hounds
lounge about the base of the dais, and lying on the couch
alongside the princess is a jet black cat with jade green eyes.
The princess wears her veil, her face obscure but for her tip
tilted eyes, now lined heavily in the fashion of the Egyptians.
Against the black lining, her amber eyes are startling. "I
present to you, Rah, god-slave of the House of the Moon of
Knossos."

But Rah has already taken Ephtheta's attention away from
the stately mannerisms of the elderly guard. As Mefali speaks,
Rah, held by two strong guards just behind him, has collapsed
gracefully to one knee, his mane of curls falling in a
honeycomb of ringlets to the floor.

"Step aside, Mefali, let me see him," says the princess.
"Stand up, little cat, and come closer. None of us bite, not the
hounds, nor I, not even Luter," she smiles, stroking the
miniature panther that lies against her side.

"Rah is come to dance for king," says Rah boldly, hopping
to his feet and stepping forward so swiftly that the two guards
move to tackle him.

"Oh leave him be, you silly men! Can't you see he is
harmless?" chides Ephtheta. "He is as graceful as any temple
dancer. Why if he leapt at me, what would he do? H-m? Sweep
me off my feet into a baladi? He is sweet. As sweet as my
Luter, though he looks like a young lion." She strokes her cat
reflectively. The animal's back rises to meet her fingers. It
pushes its head up against her cheek and pressing its flank
against her breast. "Now tell me Rah, where do you come
from?" continues the princess, dipping her head to rub her
veiled nose against the cats'. "And why do you insist that you
must dance for my father, the King?" She looks back at him, a
pout forming under the veil. "Has he sent for you?"

But Rah is pointing at the cat, and shaking his head with
distaste at the sovereign's daughter. "You tell him, 'I am
below'. Why you tell this cat princess below cat, eh? Princess
of Babylon?" He waves his arms, encompassing the mass of a
city he has yet to explore. "This bad. You princess. No kiss
cat. Cannot do everything you…" lost for the word he pounds
his heart with a fist.

31

"Feel," murmurs Yesh from the bench. She draws her hand from her mouth and stares at Rah. "Majesty, he is like a little lion," she breathes.

"Yes, Yesh, my sweet, he looks very much like a young lion," responds Ephtheta lifting her cat and placing him in a servant's hands. As she rises, Rah drops to the ground a second time in an elegant, formal bow.

Mefali is looking over Rah's head at the two other guards with huge eyes. He steps forward, in front of Rah. "Forgive me, Majesty," he blurts. "He cannot know what he is saying, nor whom he is saying it to."

But the princess only laughs and looks to the Nubian woman, who has risen as well.

"Do you hear it, Yesh? He has chastised me! For kissing my Luter!" She turns her attention back to Rah. "But why do you bow to me twice, Rah?"

"Servant is not great than master," says the roil of corn silk curls dusting the floor.

"It is the custom in Crete never to allow oneself to stand eye to eye to one's superior," offers Mefali.

"Up, up," says Ephtheta, motioning to Rah to stand.

"He is not Egyptian," counters the Nubian. "My people say there are yellow-haired men who live in the far north. They were dark once, like us, but loved the winter so dearly that they travelled further and further toward it, until they came to a land where the night never descended. They slept with the sun, and turned golden. This is one of these. A child of the gods."

"A young god?" muses the princess. "Come here, right here before me," she points to the floor at her feet, addressing Rah.

"His eyes!" gasps Yesh, bending to peer into Rah's upturned face. "Look at his eyes!"

Rah rises to his feet as the princess steps off the dais. He fidgets and keeps his eyes to the ground.

"Lift your chin," says Ephtheta, "come, come. Too formal!" She reaches to tap Rah's chin up, at which Mefali bristles.

"Majesty, you mustn't-"

"Oh, phoo. There now. Oh! Oh, look! They change

color before your eyes!"

Rah's eyes, jade green when he entered the queen's visiting chamber, have mellowed to a deep sapphire. The sun has begun to set and the only light remaining is the dancing lamplight. In it, the striated irises seem to spin.

"Like a god, Majesty. Look, look! Still they change."

"Are you a god, Rah?" asks the princess. "Now tell the truth or I will have you flogged!"

"Rah is god," answers Rah evenly, looking from one woman to the other. "Is no Rah in Babylon? No temple? Babylon must have temple for Rah. Must have priest. Concubine. Rah eat only milk from white goat, egg from white chicken. Fish, grain. Fruit. All is what come from Rah. Rah is god make grain. Make rain if no rain. Make baby if no baby. All good thing come from Rah. Rah come to dance for King. Need troupe. If no dance for king, plague come. Hali die."

"Halki? Can a god die?" whispers Ephtheta. "From plague?"

"If the god dies, the crops die," Yesh looks to Mefali.

"So he says, Majesty," Mefali answers, his eyes on Ephtheta. "And, Majesty," he begins, but suddenly Rah's eyelids flutter, and as the seizure takes him his body stiffens, then jerks, his eyes rolling back in his head. "Catch him!" cries Mefali to the guards, who break the boy's fall to the ground, then attempt to hold him down. "A pillow!" demands Mefali, but Yesh has already grabbed a silken cushion from the princess' couch and crouched to push it under Rah's head. "It is the rapture!" says one guard to the other. Both are using all of their strength now to keep the boy from bashing his skull on the tiles,

"Wait," Yesh has taken Rah's face in her hands. "Hold him like this, now. Quickly, else he bite the rest of his tongue off." She dips a slender hand into a fold of her costume and produces a bone flange, wide and flat on one end and sharp as a big cat's claw on the other. As one guard holds Rah's jaw, Yesh waits, the flange set against his cheek. Rah's mouth snaps open and shut and in the same instant she has inserted the bone, preventing him from closing his jaw completely.

"Excellent," murmurs Mefali, placing a gentle hand on Yesh's bare shoulder. "You are indeed a treasure, 'Kita."

"What is that device?" asks one of the guards. "It looks like a weapon."

But Yesh only smiles, her eyes drifting to the princess, then back to Rah, who has become still.

"You guards are not my last line of defense," answers the princess. "Though a tongue scraper, invented for cleansing a princess' mouth after a meal, is only a tongue scraper, if found in the folds of a governess' garment."

"That is, until some enemy makes an attempt on her life," nods Mefali. "Very wise, Ephtheta, to give a lioness a claw."

Yesh's smile widens. She stands and steps away from Rah, taking the flange with her. "The god rests within him," she says.

"This is more than I expected," Mefali gestures the two guards to pick Rah up. "And yet, it all begins to become clear. He is of immense value. If he were not, why would the assas-" he catches himself.

Ephtheta shoots him a curious look. "Put him there, on the couch," she says, motioning for the guards to do so. "Assa-? You begin a thought, Mefali, before a sovereign, and fail to complete it. Do you forget what happens to those who keep secrets from the royal family?" She turns and bends to brush Rah's mane back from his dampened forehead as he is laid out on the chaise.

"Certainly not, Majesty. However this is a matter best left to your father," says the old man, taking a cloth from his belt to mop his brow.

"M-m-m, yet I think this is not your plan," muses Ephtheta, still stroking Rah's hair. "He sleeps. I wonder, do gods dream?"

Mefali swallows, nodding harshly at the two guards to leave. They make a quick bow and turn in tandem toward the doorway.

"Majesty, I am in a terrible place. For if I tell you, his Majesty's beloved daughter, what the boy has disclosed, I will surely lose my tongue. But if I do not, I may lose my head."

"An easy choice then," says the princess, who has seated

herself on the couch beside Rah. She looks up at last at the old guard. "Better your tongue than your head."

"But Ephtheta you are but a child-" he begins.

"I am my father's daughter!" The princess is on her feet. "And he took the throne when he was younger than I! Do not underestimate me, Mefali."

That is enough to send the old guard to his knees. Head bowed, he answers softly, "Highness, we have reason to believe that the boy is the property of the Wolf of Amega."

The silence above his bowed head gives Mefali a moment to collect his thoughts. When the princess speaks again, he has already prepared himself for her words. I am thrust between them now, by this scrap of a boy, he thinks. This is the worst day of my life. Yes, the moment I set eyes on that creature was the worst moment. A moment cloaked in doom. For from whom shall I hold the truth and live? From my King, or his daughter?

Finally, unable to contain himself any longer, Mefali raises his head. The look in the princess's eyes does nothing to quench his fears.

"You will tell him nothing," says Ephtheta at last. "You are mistaken. You hear how he speaks. One can hardly understand a word regardless, even if one *can* understand his mishmash of Hittite, Illyrian, Greek and the gods know what else. He is an entertainer, that is all, a pretty dancer, no doubt a slave dancer who has run away from his master to seek his freedom. Owned by a rich man, I admit," she lifts the gold collar around Rah's neck, and as she does so, he stirs.

"Here, Majesty, he comes awake," offers Yesh. And just as she speaks the words, Rah's eyes flutter open.

"Gah," he says, sitting up and grabbing his head. "Head spin."

"From the weight of that emerald, no doubt," smiles Ephtheta. "Now, Rah, do not excite yourself. You will have all that you ask for. We have a splendid dance troupe here in the palace, easily the best in this part of the world. You may join them tomorrow. But it grows late and you need to eat and then to rest. We will put you in a room in the palace entertainers' wing tonight." She is absently playing with a curl of his hair as she speaks.

"Rah is sleep with horse," says Rah, ignoring her petting. "Sleep with Ono. You take Rah back to stable." He points to Mefali, then attempts to jump to his feet and wobbles.

"Oh!" Ephtheta attempts to catch him but Rah plops back down on the couch without her help.

"Highness, *pleeease*," sighs Mefali, at his wits end. "You must not become his servant!"

"Who is this Ono?" She raises her brow at him.

"His mare, Majesty. The animal he rode in on." And then, to Rah, "You will not be sleeping in the stable and smelling of manure so long as you live in the palace! Now come along and do as you are told." He grabs Rah's wrist, eliciting a snarl from the boy.

"Oh!" Says Ephtheta again, as Yesh puts two hands to her mouth in horror.

"No touch Rah," says Rah, pulling his wrist away and slipping onto his feet less than gracefully.

"He would bite you, Mefali!" says the princess. "He is strange indeed!"

"I fear we do not know the half of it, my lady," says Mefali, waving the boy to join him as he bows to leave.

"You snarl like an animal," spits Mefali to Rah as he leads the boy further west, toward the entertainer's quarters. The two guards, who had been waiting in the hall, jump to attention and follow smartly behind.

"No touch," says Rah absently, his head swinging from side to side like a child as his eyes attempt to follow the elaborately painted scenes on the walls. "This like in Cyrus too. Paint on wall. All kind place. Only is all-" he makes a sexual gesture with his hips and gives Mefali an innocent smile.

Mefali purses his lips. "You would do well to keep thoughts such as those far from the halls of the princess. These pictures tell the stories of the kingdom," he motions to the wall to his left, "Great battles, great victories."

"Is all kill, kill," says Rah. "To much kill, kill. Love better. This-" he moves his hips again, "better. Kill, kill. All dead. No live. Stupid. People go where people head go." He taps his temple with his finger, looking up at Mefali wisely.

Mefali gives him a long look. "M-m-m, maybe so," he says. "A rather philosophical construct, coming from a bit of dance like you. Maybe you are not so retarded as you would have us believe, eh?"

"Is easy. Dog can see," says Rah, shrugging. "Man, he make what he think in head, no?" Rah's stops to pantomime a man painting. Then, suddenly, he is a baker, kneading bread. Just as quickly he is on the ground sitting in a lotus playing a santur. The guards stand watching, too entertained to interfere.

Rah jumps to his feet. "Think all the time kill, kill," he taps his head again, "bring always dead, dead. More war, more cry, more bad. Stupid head."

Mefali strokes his beard, watching. Then he turns to continue toward his purpose. "And what is it that Rah keeps in Rah's head, hm?"

"Rah is always think dance. Make beautiful. Make people happy, people see what cannot see. People heart," he pounds his chest once, "is lift." He raises his hand and spreads his palms to the ceiling, upon which carvings of soldiers slay their enemies with swords and axe. "Lift people heart up, think beauty. No more think kill, kill. Then crop is good, rain come, plenty food, people happy, make baby."

They continue up a set of twisting stairs, down another hall, across the parapet that runs the length of a great theatre, where Rah stops in amazement.

"This where dance!" he cries, and he has leapt to balance on the polished stone balustrade to lift his arms, turning to bow with an actor's elaborate grandiosity to the four quadrants of the theatre.

"By the gods you will fall!" cries Mefali, grabbing the boy's arm at the same time one of the guards takes him by the waist and lifts him off the balcony and back onto the floor of the skywalk. But Rah only giggles his deep, man's giggle, clutching his stomach.

"Rah is no fall, Rah is never fall," he smiles at Mefali, then the guard who 'saved' him, and the two blink and stare, for Rah's smile has lit the theatre. Rah turns and, pantomiming caution with a devilish grin he approaches the wall again to look down at the place where he is destined to dance for a king.

"This good," says Rah, his deep voice soft with astonishment. "So good. Look," he points to the circle of concentric stone steps, made for his audience to sit upon to watch his show. "People see Rah from all place. Look!" he points up at a raised pavilion in the center of the mezzanine. Two enormous, polished stone seats face the stage below him. "King can sit there!" He looks back at Mefali and the guards, as if he has only just discovered the use of these structures for them.

"Yes, Rah, the King and Queen, or in our case, the King and Princess, sit there to watch our theatre. And if you are any good, you may well perform for them."

"I show you. Where dance master is? Show you now!" cries Rah.

"You will do no such thing," answers Mefali, nodding to the guards to move Rah along. "We are nearly there now. The palace theatre troupe, as well as the musicians, the acrobats, the animal trainers, magicians, singers, choreographers, they all reside down this hall, behind the theatre, you see?" He has reached a great swinging double door at the end of the skywalk. Pushing them open, he lifts his arm to motion to the enormous hall before them. The hall stretches as far as the eye can see, parallel to the north wall of the theatre and perpendicular to the stage. The place is bustling with people. Like the Knossos city market, the din is almost too much for Rah at first and he slaps his palms over his ears. People are walking in and out of doorways all down the hall, chattering, arguing, carrying props, costumes, even backdrops. A man with a tall silk hat that sits on his head like a cone approaches. He is tall and lean and wears a pointed beard. Under the cone hat his head is cleanly shaven.

"What have we here, Mefali? A gift? A dream come true for old Eliabus?" The man lifts his hands in a dramatic gesture of welcome. "A beauty! A superb delight from the far north! Step forward, lovely!"

Rah, released from the guard's grip, does as he is told. He stands, exquisitely still, before the man in the cone hat. As if by some heavenly magic the last of the sun's rays strike his crown through the clearstory windows above and turn his platinum mane into a silvery gold explosion.

"Eliabus, it is another of the princess' poor choices, I'm afraid. This one met us on the road into the city, standing there in the dust like a pauper with not but a cloak and a stolen war horse. Stood there, blocking the road until we were upon him, then–"

But Mefali need say no more, for Rah has taken his turn to tell the story. He throws back an invisible hood, extends his arms from his sides to open an imaginary cloak, and falls softly to his knee in the precise bow which stopped the princess' liter. There he remains.

After a moment, Eliabus lifts his eyes from Rah's golden head and looks at Mefali with stunned delight.

"What, you mean to tell me this beauty was found alone, on a horse, in the road?" he asks Mefali.

"Indeed I do." Mefali gives Rah's bottom a boot. "Get up, you clown. This is the Master of the Arts of the City of Babylon. This is Eliabus. You would do well not to mock."

"Is no muck!" says Rah, coming to his feet. But he has no more gained them than, lifting his eyes to Eliabus', drops again to his knee, his emerald crown clicking against the marbled floor.

Eliabus is laughing with delight. "Oh, oh quis letifico," he sighs. "Little golden one, you move like the rustle of leaves, like light on a quiet pond. I do believe this one can dance, Mefali."

But Mefali only purses his lips and pushes Rah toward Eliabus. By now a group of young men and women, many in costumes of brightly colored silks and plumes and some wearing head gear depicting animals and birds covering all but their peering eyes, have gathered in a half circle behind their master.

Mefali looks about at the outrageous group and snorts. He takes a step back, offers Eliabus a brisk military bow and says, "I do believe he will fit in here with you, Eliabus, and your circus of clowns, and I am glad to be rid of him. Good evening." He turns with his two companions and shoves open the great doors, grateful to be relieved of his charge.

"Rah is dance for you now," says Rah, making a shorter bow to Eliabus and the group, then making a show of shooshing them out of his way and giving them his back as he scans the retreating hall before him. Far from the din that greeted him only moments ago, the hall is now only a murmur. People stand along the walls and in doorways, watching, waiting.

"This good. I show you. Rah is good dance." And lifting himself onto the balls of his feet he takes in several long breaths, raising his hands over his head.

And launches himself down the hall in a series of cartwheels, handstands, back flips and spinning leaps that leave his audience dumb. At the end of the hall, Rah spins a petit, masked creature into his arms, bends her back and down onto his knee, his posture the very definition of desire, then releases her into the arms of a bystander and begins a casual, seductive saunter back up the hall. But he is still dancing, approaching a female every few strides, taking her in his arms, caressing her face, turning her in a spin, then abandoning her for another. He is a lothario, a jaded man of the world who has had too much of the fairer sex yet continues to seek what he has himself made tedious. When he is half way back to Eliabus the hall begins to echo with laughter and approval. Rah smiles, opens his arms to the applause, and offers a bow to each quarter.

"What a singular creature you are," breaths Eliabus. The man beside him, wearing the head of a jackal, turns his head to whisper into the Master's ear.

Eliabus chuckles, nodding. "I see it too, Iccubal. I see it too."

CHAPTER 4

In the guise of Samal-Etatani, Rush the Assassin enters the city of Babylon in the early hours of the following morning. He has circumvented the city along the outer wall in order to enter from the east, where he is less likely to be recognized as the imposter he is. Now, galloping the Black up to the Marduk Gate with the urgency of a messenger fresh from the battlefield, his Amorite shield and helmet glinting in the red dawn light, he has barely to extend his closed fist, offering the guard both the unquestionable authority of his benefactor's seal ring, and the palpable power in that flesh and bone weapon, to cause their captain to step back, signal the gatemen to open the great doors, and bow in homage.

You are here. He trots through the gateway, which is the length of his own house in Knossos, an arched tunnel through the walls of his enemy's heart, the Black's excellent hooves clattering on the paving stones. As he arrives at the interior end his predatory eyes adjust to the light quickly. He pulls the Black's rein harshly, the iron bit hitting its bars, and the animal rises on its hind legs, annoyed. He kicks it forward, back onto its feet, steadies it. He lifts his muzzle, as if to catch the boy's scent. I will find you. And then remembers. Cherry blossom, myrrh, and a knife of desire stabs him.

The streets are already bustling. A woman carrying a basket of figs looks up at him, pulls her hood over her head, hurries away. A wife. I will need a wife.

"The brothel," he barks at a beggar sitting cross-legged against the base of a fountain. The man holds up a braided basket, lifting his face to the sound of the assassin's voice. His eyes are gone, and sunken craters of skin, the lids sewed together, greet Rush.

Tossing a kakaru of silver into the man's basket, Rush bends toward the man's ear. "Let your fingers see what I have put in your basket," he says, lowering his voice. "Then tell me where to find a brothel best suited to a man who can pay for the life of a woman and do as he pleases with her."

The man stiffens. He reaches into his basket, feeling the weight of the silver pieces Rush has deposited there. He licks his lips.

"I have an ax here that can open your mouth. No one will take the great Samal-Etatani to task for it if I do."

"There is one such brothel," answers the man, "but I beg you sir, do not take your lust for blood out on a poor man's daughter there. Return to battle, where the fight is fair."

"I could take your head for that," snarls Rush. "Who are you to deny a soldier of the King his due? Where is this place? My patience is strained." He slides a short sword from its sheath, then whips it past the beggar's right ear. The man flinches at the sound of the blade slicing the air.

"Down this main street, past the palace, then south again, past the Temple of Adad. There is an alley running parallel to the wall. Follow it near to the end. You will find what you require there."

"Excellent," barks Rush, and without further hesitation he presses the Black forward down the main thoroughfare toward the palace.

Along the eastern wall of the palace fortification he finds a stable. He trots the Black up to the door, dismounts, unties his leather sack. A boy Rah's age runs to meet him and to take his animal. As he leads the steaming warhorse into the barn, a man in fine clothing approaches him and bows.

"Sir," he offers Rush a merchant's obsequious smile. "Will you be staying in the city long?"

"Indefinitely," responds Rush, tossing the man a sack of silver. "Take the best care of him. If I find so much as a chip in his hoof, if he loses so much as a pound of weight, if he is not gleaming when next I come to ride, you and I will have a moment of intimacy together that you will not soon forget."

The man's eyes grow large, his smile fades. He takes a step back, swallowing. "Yes, Sir. I will see to it," and he bows again, less gracefully.

"Now give me the name of a barber and another of a good inn."

"Just down here, Sir," motions the man, "toward Kumar, along the river, is an excellent inn, fit for a man of your... stature, Sir, and a barber next door. And may you have a pleasant stay, Sir. A prosperous and pleasant-"

But Rush has already dismissed him, and is sauntering down the bustling street toward the river.

The stable keeper waits. When he believes Rush is out of earshot he turns and shouts into the barn, "Put that animal in the west barn, do you hear? Give him twice the straw allotted and have someone walk him out 'til he is dry! I want him groomed morning and night so that you can see your face in his coat!" Shaking his head and stroking his shaved pate he mutters to himself, "I'll mix his grain myself."

"It is fortunate for you, Sin-Turami, that I am a generous man," says the whoremaster, skinning a pear with a small, hooked knife. He is seated on a bench in a back room, the room he calls his 'office', the room in which all of his darkest dealings are executed. He is a man of middle age, a man who likes to think of himself as handsome, although he is quite obese and has a sparse beard. To compensate for these faults he shaves his head like the nobles and wears expensively dyed garments. He also has a penchant for jewelry, and his ears are pierced and hung with gold bobbles, his fingers decked with jeweled rings. Gil-baal loves nothing more, in fact, than jewelry, unless it is the sound of a female pleading for mercy.

"She is not worth half of what I have given you, Gil-baal," answers Sin-Turami, spitting in the dirt at the whoremaster's feet. "She is a slave's child, and a stolen one at that. I could have you prosecuted." Sin-Turami tucks his money pouch back into his belt, disgusted at his own weakness. This lust will be my ruin, he thinks, scratching at his beard, which is running with lice.

"Perhaps so," smiles Gil-baal, pocketing the silver Sin-Turami has tossed on the table. "But then where would you go to satisfy your ... curiosity, eh? How would you manage to .... explore the delights only I am willing to provide you? Is there another like me, Sin-Turami, in all of the city? In all of Babylonia? It is easy enough to find a whorehouse, but one that specializes in delights such as this one? Nay, I lie my neck on the chopping block every day I live to bring ... adventurous ... men like yourself what you need. This is what drives up my prices, Sin-Turami. It is the risks I face. And so rather than bemoan the cost of your desires, give thanks to Mot that there is a man such as myself who is willing to face such hazards as I do to procure for you what you need, and then turn my back to what you might chose to do with it."

"Pah," spits Sin-Turami again. "Show me the girl."

"Ah, right this way," answers the whoremaster, struggling to gain his feet. When he does so, he waves Sin-Turami ahead of him. "Just down this hall," and he takes a torch from the wall, dips the wick in the fire at his hearth, and hands it to the man.

"What is it you said you did for a living?" Gil-baal asks as the two proceed down a stone stairs at the end of the hall. The smell of urine and fear are strong now, the air heavy with it.

"I am a tanner now, though I did my part for the King. Spent thirteen years in the army, living in shit and eating maggoty meat," mutters Sin-Turami. Ah, thinks Gil-baal, a tanner. How appropriate. Of course.

"And perhaps this... need.... spring from your work, yes? This... curiosity. Well, I am all for exploring ones... inner longings. I would not be in business if men like yourself were less ... adventurous."

"My knife?" Sin-Turami has reached a heavy wood door at the base of the stairs. He scans it with the torch, finds the bolt, lifts it. Gil-baal hands him his tanner's knife when he has thrown it.

"Be sure it is locked from the other side before you start, my friend," says Gil-baal, turning to begin the desultory task of hefting his bulk back up the stairs in the dark. "It would not due for her to escape, half way through your … process… and run out into the street."

"It will be bolted, I assure you," answers the tanner, opening the door to the sound of weeping and the stench of a week's worth of human defecation.

Across the great city, in the north east quadrant, now riding a mule he has procured with a bit of the gold he has been paid for the seal ring of Mursilis, the High Priest of the Moon of Knossos stops before an enormous structure with sheer, gleaming walls. The building, spanning several acres, consists of five tiers painted in a rainbow of colors and topped with a pyramid of gold. Flanking the sides of the structure are two staircases leading to the upper tier. Directly in front of Mochlos a paved ramp rises to the great golden doorways of the second.

It is the theatre of Ishtar, in the court of Kullab, the People's Theatre. Behind it, to the north, the Lower Fortress rises over the Kadingirra Road. There the city state's military is barracked, and their training facility, the Northern Fortress, is just on the other side of the Inner Wall, no doubt with passageways and tunnels leading though the wall. And beside it, rising gracefully above the Sacred Pools of the Ninmah Temple, is the new House of the Moon, though the owner does not yet know it.

"Quite like my Minoan estate," says the priest, nodding to the villa. Walking beside him, the First Concubine of Rah of Babylon stands open-mouthed in awe.

"It is the home of a high statesman," Awiti looks up at Mochlos. "You see the emblem on the doors? He will never sell his home to you."

"My dear," answers the priest, "He has no choice. It is the new home of the Rah. Once the King understands our relationship, and the needs of the little god, he will simply move the man out and give it to us. But for now, let us find a comfortable inn for the night. In the morning we will approach the palace, after we have done a little shopping."

And smiling with pleasure at his own wit, Mochlos turns

the mule around and kicks him on, past the Eridu Markets, and down the Uras Road which, he has been told, will lead him to a rich man's inn in the Suanna District on the other side of town.

"This is Horus, from the lower delta," says Eliabus, raising his open hand to usher Rah into a room on the upper floor of the theater wing. "He has been to Crete, that is, your Crete, part of the royal liaison last summer that accompanied the Nile king. He is a royal magician, and an animal trainer also. You may share this room with him."

"Horoos," says Rah, blinking at the young man, who lounges on a settee near a window. A long, painfully lean, spotted cat, the size of one of Rush's hell hounds, lies beside the settee, licking its paw. "Is big cat." Rah nods at the animal, somewhat awed.

The young man rises, daintily graceful. He wears a strange hat, shaped like a cone that leans back from his forehead and ends in a flat plate at the top. His face is painted, as if he has just left the stage, his eyes rimmed black, his lips darkened to crimson. He is dressed in a simple linen sheath but wears elaborate sandals with thick soles, making him half a foot taller than he is.

"Very pleased to make your acquaintance," bows the magician. "You are an acrobat then?" He allows his eyes to drift down the length of Rah's torso.

"He is a dancer," answers Eliabus for Rah, "and a profound acrobat. And the princess' newest pet. I'm sure you won't mind sharing your space with him, Horus. Take him about on your daily routine, show him the routine of palace life for an entertainer. Tomorrow we will see if we can find a place for him in our production."

Horus is smiling now from ear to ear. He has taken a few light steps on his strange shoes toward Rah. He puts his long-fingered and jewel-bedecked hands on his hips and, because of the height he has given himself in the sandals, bends to peer curiously into Rah's eyes.

"By the gods, his eyes!" breaths Horus. "They seem to be all colors at once!" He moves to touch Rah's cheek.

Rah lifts his lip in a soft g-r-r-r-r, one long incisor

exposed. Quickly, Horus snatches back his hand, and gasping, covers his mouth with it.

"What is he, Eliabus? This one is strange!" he looks at Eliabus with delight.

"Ah, perhaps this is why Mefali was so quick to be rid of you, little golden one? Bad manners? Raised with wolves, were you?" chuckles Eliabus. "No matter, no one will give you any reason to snap and snarl here. We are all strange here, one way or another," he gives Horus a good-natured once over.

"I should say so," responds Horus, returning Eliabus' look.

"Rah is no raise with Wolf," says Rah. "Rah is raise Rah." He gives Eliabus a pout, putting his own fists on his hips defiantly. "Wolf is kill cat," he adds, nodding to the cheetah that has raised itself onto its long legs and now sniffs his toes with considerable interest. "Like this. You train cat? How you train cat. Cat is no pet." He looks at Horus with veiled respect.

But Horus pays his question no attention. "Oh, do you hear him, Eliabus? They have cut his tongue. Oh, poor little sweetheart, no wonder-" he puts both hands to his mouth, tears gathering in the corners of his elaborately drawn eyes.

"Now, now, Horus, do not start this up. Whatever has made him what he is, he is here now, and whole. And come to think of it, you being so good with wild animals, I think this will do very nicely, the two of you together. You keep him out of trouble for me." And to Rah, "He will take good care of you, Rah. You just follow his lead."

When Eliabus is gone, Horus wipes the corner of one eye, smearing the kohl there. "Oh, dear," he sees that the black has come off on his finger and taps expertly on his strange shoes to a large polished mirror of bronze that leans against one wall. "Now we cannot go down to dinner like this, can we, Horus," he says to his reflection. "We will be a laughing stock, and embarrass our new friend."

Rah has come to stand behind Horus in the mirror, all the while exquisitely aware of the cheetah, who follows him, sniffing his leg, then his skirt.

"Mush likes you," says Horus, lifting his eyes to Rah's in

the mirror. He takes a stick of kohl off a small table beside the mirror and begins redrawing the eye liner he has smudged.

"Who this, Moosh?" says Rah, keeping one eye on the cat, another on Horus' pencil. "This too sad," he points to Horus' face in the mirror. "Make up, like…" and he has snatched the kohl liner from Horus' fingers with snakelike speed. "Now you watch Rah," he winks at Horus, then puts a line of black under his left eye, lifting the line up at the end. When he is finished, he looks at Horus in the mirror.

"Moosh is," but Horus has lost his words. "Moosh," he swallows. "Gods you are… exquisite." He takes the kohl from Rah's hand and moves to lift Rah's chin, stopping himself abruptly before he does so.

"May I?"

"Yah, you do," says Rah. "You try Rah, then you try Horoos." He closes his eyes, allowing Horus to lift his chin, then carefully draw a matching line under his right eye.

"Mush. Mushezibit. My cheetah here. She likes you," says Horus, and finishing his work he taps Rah's chin. "Go ahead, silly, open your eyes and see." He points to the mirror.

"Ah," says Rah, "Is good. Horoos good draw. Now you." He steps aside to give Horus the full surface of the mirror.

"Fix eye, same." Rah cocks his head at Horus, "Horoos, same like Rah."

But Horus has lost his train of thought again. "Sweetheart, nothing Horus could ever do to his face could match what the gods have given yours," he sighs.

The man standing in the doorway is a nightmare.

He is half a head taller than Gil-baal, who, being pure-bred Amorite himself, is quite tall. But he is also near as wide as the door in the shoulder, built like a man who spends life at his limits. His legs are long and muscular, his arms made for felling trees with an axe. Trees and men, thinks Gil-baal. And by his shield and his garments I can see that he is an Amorite captain. But his face is wrong. Pale, yes, but those eyes are pitch. And his head is unshaved, his beard trimmed neatly against his face, not pointed. There is something amiss here.

This man is not who he pretends to be.

Never mind, that is none of my business. My business is in this money sack, which by the feel of it, contains a good Kakaru of silver.

"What is your pleasure, sir?" asks the whoremaster, rising with some effort from his seat behind his money table. "Boy or girl, black or white, willing or ... not so willing?"

"Who is in use," growls the assassin. "That is the one I want."

"In u-" Gil-baal frowns. "I don't understand you."

"It is your job to understand," says Rush. "And so you do. I want the one in use. And the man who uses her."

"B-b-ut I cannot-" Gil-baal is already stepping back, back toward his table, which he will put between himself and this man before-

Too late. The table is turned over, nay, thrown across the room into a mud wall with so much force it has cracked clear in two. Gil-baal's throat is in the man's fist.

"You who promises he can do anything for any lust, can now serve his own lust for life. For his next breath."

Fingers like iron hooks press into Gil-baal's throat. For the first time in his life Gil-baal is made aware of the pipe that leads air into his chest. He is pulling it, thinks Gil-baal, he has found it and is separating it from its place. Gil-baal begins to thrash, his excessive weight taking him to the ground. This only makes things worse. The man is holding him up by the front half of his neck. Gil-baal can feel his eyes beginning to swell in their sockets.

"Hak-k-" he coughs through the man's fingers.

"You will be unconscious in less than a minute," says Rush. "Then I will do what I wish without paying you. And what good is that?"

Gil-baal, with no use of his throat, can only nod.

"Good. Lead me," says Rush, releasing the whoremaster's throat and dragging him to his feet by his garments, he shoves him through a bead curtain toward the back of the brothel.

"We will need a torch," wheezes Gil-baal, reaching toward one, but Rush only shoves him on.

"You know the way by heart, and I can see well enough in

the dark," comes the answer.

Indeed you can, devil, thinks Gil-baal, and when you are down there I shall throw the bolt, lock you in, and call my boys to take care of you! No one robs Gil-baal. And no one tells him how he will run his business!

"Open it," says Rush. They have descended a stair and have reached the place where the tanner entered moments earlier. Inside, a woman screams of terror, her voice muffled by the heavy door.

"I cannot. It is bolted from the inside."

"Have him open it, or I shall use you for a battering ram," comes the growl above Gil-baal's head.

"Sir!" cries the whoremaster into a small hole in the door just at his eye level, "You must come quickly! The authorities are at the door! Let me show you a passageway out the back, that you may escape safely!"

There is a shuffle behind the door, a wailing howl, then, "Please, please help me, please..." and then the bolt is thrust open from the other side. The tanner, however, does not have time to open the door. Rush has shoved the whoremaster out of his way with his left shoulder, using the man's bulk for purchase, then thrust the entirety of his weight and massive energy into the door, plastering the tanner effectively between it and the damp stone walls of the cellar.

"Uhh," says the tanner, the sound issuing forth from his abdomen like a backward fart. The bolt slides on the interior side of the door have broken three of his ribs, one of which has punctured his right lung. He lies in a heap, his bloodied knife, so eagerly slicing skin from living flesh only a moment ago, lies still in the fingers of his right hand.

The woman is bound and hangs from a hook embedded in the ceiling. Her sternum has been sliced open, and a cut runs deep under her right breast. Like a deer, thinks Rush, striding to the girl with such speed she has barely time to lift her eyes to see the monstrosity that has saved her whipping a glittering hand over her head to cut the rope with two slices. She falls, not onto the fouled dirt floor, but into his left arm, her entire body easily cradled against the massive bicep and forearm. Just as quickly, her legs are lifted from beneath her. Pain and fear evaporate. She looks up into the face of her savior, who, for a brief instant, drops his eyes to hers. Black pools of strength, fringed with thick, soft lashes greet her. She faints, unutterably content.

Rush turns to the whoremaster, who himself has sustained a dislocated rib. The man is panting, holding his bulk up by supporting himself with his opposite hand against the doorway. He watches Rush, defeated, a dog waiting for a command.

"Take her to the surgeon. If she dies, you die," says Rush, handing the limp body to the man. "The death that you chose for her."

The whoremaster lifts his arms, his left side throbbing in agony. How can I carry this woman up the stair, across the street, to my brother's house, he thinks, to fetch a surgeon? And yet I shall. Or die trying. He accepts the girl's body, which is, fortunate for him, quite slim, and turns to make his way up the stair.

"She is mine now," says Rush from the dark behind him. "I will collect her in a week's time."

My gods, if she dies I must find him her twin, thinks the whoremaster, lumbering with greater speed than he knew he possessed up the stair and out into the street.

Rush turns to the man on the floor.

"An expert cut," he says, "You are a tanner then."

"You..." breathes the tanner weakly from the floor, "you... are not...."

"No," Rush is testing the hook in the ceiling as he speaks. "Not from the palace. Not even from this kingdom. But a king in another. I like your skin, tanner."

He turns back to the man moaning on the dirt floor, bends to crouch over his head, and takes his beard.

"You have two faces, tanner," says Rush. "One for the world, one for your victims." He pulls the man up with him by his beard, drags him easily over to the hook.

The tanner, who is beginning to understand, whimpers. "No, no, no, sir, do not..."

"Only a small man would need a rope," muses Rush, picking the tanner up by the torso, causing him to scream in agony as his broken rib tears further into his lung. He thrusts the man onto the hook like a slab of meat. The iron prong is driven into his back, catches his ribcage, holds him firm.

"You are a small man," continues Rush, and slipping his gold and silver dagger from his weapons belt, he lifts the man's chin once more, "with too many faces."

Across the street, at his brother's home, the whoremaster, Gil-baal, is pacing and wringing his hands.

"Tell him I have money enough to feed his family for a year, Il-Bethyr," moans Gil-baal to his sister-in-law. He is clutching an ill-smelling poppet to his side. "It will draw out the pain," she had said. "And send it back to your enemy." Then she had taken the naked woman from his arms and set her near the hearth on a rug, sending his nephew up the street to fetch the surgeon. "The surgeon will need hot water, to boil his things," she had explained, when he chided her for putting on a pot, thinking she meant to make him a meal as she always did when he visited his brother and twin, Bil-baal.

An hour later the surgeon is finished stitched the girl's wounds with a boiled string of goat gut and a bone needle. "Keep this on for twenty-four hours," he advises, applying a poultice to the injury. "Then change it, using this mixture here," and he points to the bluish paste he has mixed, "and fresh, boiled linens. Give her a bit of this," and he hands Gil-baal's brother's wife a packet, "each day, to fight infection. When you see the wounds healing, you may wean her off it." He mops his brow with the sleeve of his garment, looking at Gil-baal and shaking his head. "I cannot promise you she will not die of infection, that is in Mot's hands, not mine," he continues, rising to his feet to dip his hands in the bowl of warm water that Il-Bethyr extends to him, "and if she lives, she will have a terrible scar of course, I should say no man worth a mina will have the stomach for it. Too bad, such a pretty girl." He shakes his head again, sighing.

"She needn't be a beauty," says Gil-baal, who is sweating so profusely that his bald head shines. "Only alive."

"What is your name, girl?" asks Il-Bethyr, who is kneeling by the woman's head, mopping moisture from her face.

But the woman is silent. She looks up at Gil-baal's brother's wife with pain-dimmed eyes, struggling to lift her head, then moans and drops it back onto the rug.

"The sedative has taken her tongue. I doubt she will do more than sleep for the next twelve hours or so. All the better. The worst of the pain will be over by then."

But the whoremaster is paying no attention. He has begun to pace again, back and forth before the hearth. "He said he would be back to collect her in a week. A week, dear gods. A week."

Rush has found an inn in the Suanna section of town, just above the Uras Gate. He likes the location, for despite its proximity to both the Ishara and the Ninurta Temples, making it an upscale neighborhood for Ameg the Merchant to reside in while he looks for a villa to purchase, it is just across the river from Tuba and Kumar, seedier neighborhoods where Rush can harvest whatever he might need from the criminal element that infests those locals. Better still, there are several routes out of the city from here, the Uras Gate, the river itself, and across the river in Tuba, the Samas Gate. It is the weakest quarter of the city, though there is still the Outer Wall to breach, should a fighting force be inclined at some point to do so. They put their weakest flank to the south, thinks Rush, as if I cannot turn a corner. As if I cannot cross a desert.

Rush changes into the garb of Ameg the Merchant in an alley behind the inn. Then he finds a barber. Ameg is not new to Babylon, and his reputation as a premier silk and Egyptian cotton merchant is established in the market. He need not change his Minoan style, and will keep his beard trimmed, distinguishing himself from the Amorite, who wears his pointed. Only a fool would grow a long beard, let alone enter a fight with one, thinks Rush, and this place is full of fools.

Rush takes a suite of rooms at the top of the inn. It is a moderate vantage point, high enough to overlook the river to the west, dwarfed by the towering palace wall rising from behind the Marduk temple to the north. Ameg is displaced from his home in Knossos and will need a story. I was out to sea, trading in Mycenae, when the volcano erupted. I fled south to Egypt, then east, to Phoenicia. My family in Knossos are dead. I am estranged from my daughters in Greece. I must build a new life, and for a merchant, there is no better place, now that Knossos is gone, than Babylon.

Rush waits until nightfall, taking a few hours of rest in his plush new quarters. Then he dresses again, this time in a simple wool robe. He uses a bit of charcoal from the fire to create dark circles under his eyes, wrinkles on his forehead, and hollow cheeks. He pulls a loose cowl over his head, hiding his profile. Then he makes his way out of his suite via an east window that is tucked behind a chimney and invisible from the road below. He scales the wall, easily dropping to his feet silently in the soft loam of a garden, and makes his way toward the palace district to learn what he can learn from the streets.

CHAPTER 5

"He instructed me thus, Great King," says the runner Akintunde, as he stands before the throne of Samsu-titana glistening with sweat. "You will say nothing to anyone until you are before his throne. Then you will tell Samsu-titana that he will return the Rah to me, or face my wrath. Tell him thus, 'King Samsu-titana, your darkest nightmare has yet to be dreamt. The Wolf will take a bone from your body for each day you keep the boy from him, beginning with today. Then he will take what you love first and second: first, your bride, that is, Babylon, then your daughter Ephtheta. All of the armies of Syria will not protect you. Return him to me, or face hell itself.'"

Akintunde has been running for four days and three nights. His only sustenance, a quick drink from a stream and the dried fruits and meats he carried with him. He has allowed himself four hours of sleep every night but the first, which he ran straight through. Every time he wanted to rest except for these, he simply opened his palm and looked at the burn there, the brand of the Assassin. I am forever yours now, he thought then, as he ran. And this was not a harsh thought, nor did it depress him. He was the property of the Wolf. No one would dare touch him, nor remove so much as a fingernail clipping from his person, lest the Assassin relieve them of their whole hand. But he also knew that if he failed in his mission in any way he would not live to see the following sunrise. It was a precarious precipice upon which he stood, but wasn't this what he had trained for all of his life? Could he ever have imagined that his fleetness of foot would be put to such a purpose? His first assignment a message to the king of Babylon from the Wolf of the Aegean?

And how had he come by this assignment? By a trick of fate, wherein his uncle, sold at quite another time and place, was purchased by the Wolf, came under his favor, then lost his life to a plague sent by the Assassin's enemies.

Akintunde ran. He ran until he reached the east gate of Babylon, gave his urgent message to the guard there, then ran to the palace front gate where he explained his purpose a second time. No one intervened, even when, after obtaining directions through the huge complex of halls and theatres, he took off at a run toward the throne room. Not once they saw the still-scabbing brand on his hand. To a man they stepped back, waved him on, then touched their talismans and murmured prayers to their gods.

"Who is this boy, this 'Rah'?" King Samsu-titana is looking to his advisors, his mouth set in a grim line. His fists, clenched in anger a moment ago, for the messenger had interrupted his afternoon liaison with one of his favorite harem girls, are now clenching instead the ends of the arms of his throne. His three advisors stand together beside his perch, their heads together like so many hens, murmuring among themselves. "Why have I no knowledge of such a creature?" shouts King Samsu-titana, gesticulating to the runner.

A mewling from the folds of Akintunde's cloak brings all three to attention. Instantly, an enormous guard, tall as Akintunde and twice his girth, steps forward, slicing a lance through the air between the King and the messenger.

"What on earth did you bring into the King's visiting room with you?" cries one of the three advisors.

Akintunde is on his knees, head bowed. He swiftly takes the cub from a hammock tied to his belt and offers it to the King.

"It is a gift, Lord, a leopard cub, for your personal collection of exotics."

"From whom?" says the King, confused. "From *him*?" He looks at his advisors with a shocked expression.

"From his country, yes, Highness," answers Akintunde carefully.

"He threatens me and gives me a gift, all at the same time?" cries the King, standing up. "Damnable beast! He will not threaten me as I sit on my own throne, in my own palace, in my own kingdom! Who is this boy? Someone find him and bring him to me or I will have you all quartered! And you, messenger, you will not move from this palace until I have an answer for you. Take him to the Wing of Commerce, and put him up there, with a guard on him. He is not to leave the palace, you understand?"

"Yes, your Highness, bows the guard, and he pokes Akintunde with the lance. "Come with me."

The three advisors are still huddled together, whispering amongst themselves. One pops up a head, sees that the guard has taken the messenger, and approaches the throne.

"My Lord, it seems that the princess has the boy," he says nervously.

"What are you saying, my daughter? Ephtheta? How in the name of Abad-"

"She came back with him from her outing," answers the spokesman. "He is housed now in the entertainer's skene, under the tutelage of our Master of the Arts, Eliabus. He is said to be a profound acrobat."

"Bah, the Wolf of the Hatti does not threaten the King of Babylon with open war for an acrobat. Bring him here to me. Bring him here this instant!"

"Yes, my King," answers the spokesman, waving at a guard by the door to do just that.

In the palace theatre, Rah watches a man wearing only a loincloth juggle three small torches as he stands on the croup of a spritely white mare. The mare is trotting briskly in a circle while a second man lunges her. At either side of the circle two more men stand holding hoops, also lit, so that the juggler must jump through their flames as the horse trots beneath them.

Rah yawns, leaning back on the bench he occupies to look up at the sky overhead. The portion of the theatre above the stage, the choir and the lower benches have no roof, and great billowing white clouds stand above him like angels hovering in the still spring air.

"Are we boring you, dancer?" asks a girl with a plume of ostrich feathers for a tail. She carries a mask with a long hooked beak encrusted with glitter.

"What this," Rah frowns, "bo-o-r-ig?" He sits up, cocks his head and scans her, paying special attention to her bare legs and feet.

"Boring, Boor-Ring," she smiles, plopping onto the bench next to him. "It means to be unamused. Unimpressed," she nods at the juggler's routine. "Uninspired."

"Pretty girl," says Rah, lifting a finger to touch her cheek. "You dance bird? What kind bird is pretty girl be?"

The girl squints at Rah's mouth, quizzically. "Ah," she says, then pops the mask onto her head to speak through it. "I am a falcon! Trained to bring you whatever you wish!" She stands, raises her wings, which are made of painted papyrus feathers attached in rows to her sleeves.

"Watch!" and she spins, causing the feathers to fly out from her arms and lift. "You see him? The falcon?"

"Ta-hah! Rah is see now! Dance is make bird fly!" Rah hops to his feet.

"Rah is be white dove in Knossos. Dance for King! Make all," he waves one arm up and behind him, turning in a circle to show her the Great Hall of Knossos, filled with his adoring fans, "people of Knossos love Rah, cry for Rah when Wolf he come to take Rah."

"You danced for the King of Knossos?" the girl pulls her falcon head off, her eyes wide with wonder. "Oh how wonderful that must have been! Was Egypt there?"

"Yah, Rah is dance for Egypt King, Queen too. All there. But," now he lowers his hand, his shoulders slumping, he bows his head. He is sorrow itself.

"But Knossos is no more," says the girl, lifting a hand to set gently on Rah's golden shoulder.

"Knossos no more. Only Rah. Rah Priest. House of Moon," he looks up, his eyes, dizzily pretty with sadness, snap suddenly with anger. "And Wolf!"

"Oh," says the girl, moving closer, "Poor, poor, Rah!" though she understands only that he is a sweetness filled with grief and history. "Well," she brightens. "Babylon will never fall, Rah! Babylon is the greatest city in all the world! With the best soldiers, the best horses, the best chariots, the best land, here between the Great Rivers! Only," she purses her lips, looks up into the still sky above the theatre. "We have had no rain in some time. And they say the farming has turned the soil to salt. The crops were poor last spring."

"This good," nods Rah. "Good Rah is here now. Rah is make rain. Make crop come. But need to dance for King. What is name this king?"

"Samsu-titana," answers the girl. "But how can Rah make the rain? How can Rah fix the soil?" She tilts her head at him.

"Samsam," Rah mulls over the word. "King Samsam. Is good name. Strong."

"Samsu-titana," repeats the girl, watching Rah's apricot lips as he mouths the word carefully. The dance master's clapping for attention brings her back to her senses.

"I must go now. Watch our little play, Rah. I think we are very good." She turns, lifting the falcon head, then looks back at him. "I am Rhinna," she smiles, before fixing the mask back onto her head with a strap under the beak and flitting off toward the stage.

"Reen," repeats Rah, as the girl moves off. "Good leg," he watches the girl's strong, well-trained calves as she darts into line. She is one of many falcons, standing in a row behind a tall dancer with a great headdress. He is a king, it seems, and the falcons are his retinue. "He maybe Egypt, maybe," says Rah to himself, remembering the costume of the Egyptian King the night he danced for Knossos. He is studying the dance, hunched forward on his seat, elbows on knees and head in hand when two guards storm into the theatre from the King's entrance on the upper balcony.

"Hold there!" one cries, and all of the movement on stage winds to a soft halt. Eliabus appears from behind a curtain stage left. He walks primly toward the chorus pit, his hands clasped together. Without hesitation he begins down a short set of steps toward the soldiers.

"Where is the boy, the one called Rah?" shouts the taller of the two guards. "Give him over to us, for the King has sent us to collect him!"

"There is one named Rah here," answers Eliabus. He lifts his hand to gesture to Rah, sitting in the first row of bleachers. "But he is only acrobat. A foreign dancer, that is all."

"I care not if he is a cow, who came into Babylon by means of a row boat," says the guard, whose companion is already flying down the ramp that leads to the mezzanine. "The King has summoned him."

Rah rises to his feet. "King, ya," says Rah, nodding to Eliabus, who shoots him a confused look. "I tell you, Rah must dance for King. Meet King now." He makes a quick bow to the master, turns to make another toward the stage, then strolls up the center aisle to meet the guard. The man moves to take his arm as they meet, but Rah is too fast for him.

"No touch Rah," he says, lowering his brow. "Only Wolf is touch Rah," he points to the glittering emerald on his forehead. "Wolf is give Rah, you see? No touch."

The guard steps back, withdrawing his hand as if he had been reaching for the wrong end of a lit torch. He looks up at his superior, who is leaning over the wall of the upper balcony.

"Is okay, Rah come," beams Rah to the man above. "But you no touch. Or Wolf he come when you sleep. No good," he shakes his head sadly. Then, looking at the man beside him, who swallows hard, "No good," Rah shrugs. "Wolf he always come when you sleep. Take eye. Take tongue. Take head, maybe," Rah smiles again. "You no touch, maybe you be okay. We go, now! Rah is meet King!"

"Your father has sent for the boy, My Lady," says Mefali to the princess. She is standing in her garden, an open courtyard in the northwest corner of the palace. About her, an assortment of parrots, flightless birds, monkeys and tree climbing animals, chatter and call. On the couch behind her a serval licks it's paws, and a black sight hound with a fine coat and long, pointed snout follows her about as she tosses bits of food into a large stone pool.

"The boy? Whatever for? And how has he come to know

of his existence, Mefali?" she answers coolly, leaning over the wall of the pond to feed an enormous calico carp.

"Not from my tongue, I assure you, Princess," answers Mefali. "A messenger has come from Amega."

Now Ephtheta turns to give Mefali her full attention. "From Amega?"

"Yes, Majesty. From the Wolf himself. And he has threatened, nay, promised, your father that if he does not return the boy to him at once he will … he will take Babylon, and then-"

"And then? Is there something worse?" Ephtheta looks at Mefali with sloe eyes. Her calm is chilling. And still you do not shudder? thinks Mefali. What are you made of, woman? You are either an imbecile, which I know you are not, or braver even than your father.

"You, princess. He will take you."

"M-m, well, someone must," says Ephtheta her strange composure unwavering. "What can my father do? Will he start a war over a god? For he *is* a god, isn't he, Mefali? What other reason would there be for the Assassin to make such a threat? The man who needs nothing, who takes everything, the man of shadows, suddenly communicating with my father. Has no one discussed with the King the meaning of these things? If the Wolf of Amega would threaten Babylon for this boy, then this boy must, by reason, be worth all of Babylon. Even more."

"I am in no position to suggest these things to your father, My Lady," answers Mefali.

"No, but he has advisors for that very purpose," she responds. "And far be it from me, a mere woman, to suggest you carry this thought to their ears." Ephtheta smiles, turning back to her carp, whose whiskers ruffle the water's surface as it mouths for more bits of barley bread.

When Mefali is gone, Ephtheta drops the last of the crust of bread into the pool and grasps the wall. She sinks to her knees, gasping for breath. From beneath a fig tree, Yesh runs to her side, helping her to a bench.

"You bring the sickness on yourself, Princess," Yesh chides, holding the girl's head against her chest and willing air into her lungs. "You know you cannot involve yourself in such intrigues. Leave the boy's fate to your father. He will know what to do."

Ephtheta closes her eyes. She stills her heart. She counts her breaths. One, in. Two, out. Three, in, Four, out. I will not succumb to this. Release me, Mot, I will not go to you just yet. I am like the carp. I need no air. See, I disappear beneath the water, fading, fading to the bottom like a stone.

"What do you think, girl. A nice enough inn for the Priest of the Rah?" Mochlos waves his fingers, gesturing to the grand view through the open air windows. From here, the glimmering painted walls of the Marduk Temple split the blue sky, ending in a point that seems to touch the very heavens. Behind it the palace sits like a sleeping dragon, stretching from the banks of the river to the Ishtar Road. The room he occupies is strewn with finery. Woven silk rugs hang from the walls, telling the stories of the Babylonian gods. There is Shamash, riding across the sky in golden raiment. There is Enki, with his horned crown, dressed in the skin of a carp and standing with his staff, the double helix snake, outstretched over the valley of the Euphrates, and there, his mother, Nammu, giving birth to the oceans.

"It is fitting for the High Priest of the Rah, Sir," answers Awiti. "But perhaps his first concubine should occupy a lesser room, a common woman's quarter in a servant's inn," she adds carefully. Awiti sits on a small stool beside Mochlos while a barber shaves her head, revealing a perfectly balanced skull.

Another barber is shaving Mochlos' from head to foot, and the priest lies on a bench in nothing but a loincloth. He seems completely oblivious to Awiti's discomfort at seeing his nakedness through the sheer curtain the barbers have hung between them.

The barbers were summoned by the innkeeper shortly after Mochlos arrived. The top floor, the entire floor, of the inn, was occupied by a wealthy foreign merchant, and despite his newfound wealth, Mochlos was unable to have him routed and relocated to a lesser room.

"Well, that is a fine thing," he whispered to Awiti as the mistress of the inn led them to their quarters on the second floor. "Does my silver shine less brightly than his?"

"Perhaps he has some influence other than silver, Sir," responded Awiti softly. And this made Mochlos take a second look at her, narrowing his tigerish eyes.

"Yes, yes," he answered, nodding. "Clever girl," he said, a wicked smile pulling at his lips. "Well then we shall have to introduce ourselves, won't we?"

Now the First Babylonian Concubine of the Rah lifts long fingers to touch her smooth scalp as her barber rubs a flowery scented oil into her skin. With her head shaved, her large eyes dominate her exquisite face.

"I have never had my head shaved, Sir," she says, turning her face in a hand mirror the barber has given her.

"This is a city of shaven heads," chuckles Mochlos from behind the curtain. "And you, my dear, must be more stunning than any other temple concubine in a city that boasts of thousands of them. Therefore," he smiles at his own image in the mirror his barber has handed him, "you must be unique, a thing of magick, a mystical creature, created by the hand of a master priest for the mystical Rah! And so you, my dear, have just become…" he sits up on his couch as his barber rubs an exotic oil onto his shaven chest, "Babylon's first and only hermaphrodite!"

In the dark of a moonless night, one week after he has entered the city, Rush the Assassin returns to the house of Gilbaal for his new wife.

He slips out of the open air window of his bedroom suite, crawling with a panther's ease past the window behind which Mochlos sleeps, dreaming sweet dreams of priestly glory in a city made of gold, and drops, in Iamhad's boots, on silent feet to the garden below. He moves up the street, slipping between houses like a black wraith, toward the palace. In the muted city darkness, which is eclipsed only by the rows of torches along the wall of the palace, he stops to watch the guards make their rounds along the parapets. There you sleep, my angel, my mystery, my darling, my passion. The image of Rah's beautiful eyes flashing opened, his mouth curling in a puppyish snarl as a silver and gold dagger rips open his fine breast to find his heart, causes him to lose his orientation momentarily. Damned you. I shall have you. I shall have you in chains. I shall make you cry out for me one day. Look now. Fool that I have become. To lose my senses, even for an instant, in a foreign city, in the bowels of my enemy. You will pay for this you little devil.

Rush turns west, slips beneath the noses of the guards along the flank of the palace, cutting two down for no particular reason, other than the heat that the image of Rah has caused to rise in his blood. He crosses the river bridge, then turns south again, past the Temple of Adad. He finds the alley running parallel to the temple's north wall, follows it to the end, finds the brothel of Gil-baal lurking, feeding in the stink of the south west corner of the city like a dung beetle.

Inside, Gil-baal snores noisily in a room separated from his business office by a curtain of painted wooden beads. Against him and trapped beneath one fleshy arm, a boy half Rah's age, the son of a man who could not pay his debt, lies awake, listening to the clicking of the beaded curtain as a soft breath of air lifts it, as if a door had opened, and pulls the foul atmosphere in the room, created by Gil-baal's digestion, away, replacing it with a fresh desert breeze.

"Come to me," says a voice so deep, so dark, that the boy at first believes he has imagined it. But the silhouette standing now inside the room, in front of the curtain, blocking out the torch light and making the curtain man-shaped and solid, is no dream. The boy lifts his head from the mattress.

"Papa?" he whispers, though he knows this thing is not his father. Gil-baal stirs. He rolls off the boy, snorts, farts, comes to rest on his back. The boy slips off the mattress and stands.

"Come now," says the thing in the doorway, and in the sliver of light from behind it's masked head the boy sees a hand is outstretched toward him. The fingers are long and elegant, the palm broad and meaty. "You are safe."

The boy looks back at the enormous lump of flesh in the bed. Gil-baad continues to snore, oblivious.

The boy looks back at the shadow in the doorway. He can hear it breathing through the gauze mask. It is a predator, all strength and size, inhumanly large, yet he is not afraid.

The nails of a mouse, scurrying through the office behind it, causes it to tilt its head momentarily toward the sound, and the long lashes of one exposed eye blink in profile. It gives the thing a personhood, a softness. It is all the boy needs to decide. He runs to the blackness, hits a wall of bone and muscle, wraps his arms around its trim waist.

His head is palmed by a warm, heavy hand and pushed through the curtain into the office. "Stay," says the voice. And the boy obeys, listening for some action behind him. Even when he hears Gil-baal scream, he stays, facing just as he was left by that hand, his back to the beaded curtain and the end of Gil-baal's reign.

Behind the curtain, roused by the crushing weight on his chest, Gil-baal wakes.

"Foul stench," says a voice as deep as Hades above him, "where is my bride?" But before Gil-baal can answer, fingers like the talons of an enormous bird of prey encircle his throat. Long, sharpened nails pinch the flesh at the back of his neck, crossing each other like scissors.

"U-g-g-h-h-" Gil-baal makes his best effort to force a word through his gullet but succeeds only in vomiting a bit of his last meal onto Rush's hand. The pressure is off his chest immediately. Glorious air, a mixture of sweet night wind and his own farts, rushes into his lungs.

"Filth!" He hears the word growled from a corner of the room, the corner where he keeps a wash basin. There is the tinkling of water. The monster is washing his hand!

"She is in my brother's house," coughs Gil-baal, rising onto his elbows. "Directly across the alley. She is there now, alive and well, I swear on my life! Go and take her, take her for the love of Marduk! I have done all you ask, let me live!"

"How is it you gorge yourself thus," the voice is by the window now. Gil-baal turns, gasps. The thing is beside his bed again, leaning its masked head out the window. In the torch light from the alley he can see a strip of black cloth flutter at its mouth as it sucks in the fresh night air. "How is it you can give up your very freedom to move about with ease, simply for the-" the head turns to regard him and Gil-baal starts, involuntarily, "the pleasures of the single organ, the tongue?"

Gil-baal lies, like a slab of mutton, on his bed. He has barely the courage to continue to pull air into his hungry lungs. Do I speak? Do I answer him? What is there to say, what-?

"Better to cut off the offending part." The monster is musing, one elbow resting on the window ledge. An exposed eye glitters in the flickering torch light. "Better for the whole person. You must learn to respect the whole body."

"I," pants Gil-baal, "I do, I do, Sir. I tell you, if my habits offend you, I will change them. Yes! I will! Only let me show you! Give me time to-"

"How much time have you had already?" wonders the voice.

"Sir?" peeps Gil-baal.

"How much time? How old are you, whoremaster? How many years did you waste, gorging yourself, defiling yourself and everyone around you, with your monstrous appetites, before I came for you?"

Gil-baal swallows another burp of bile. Oh, dear Ishtar, only get him out, get him out of my house, and I will give your temple every piece of silver I have ever made!

"I am almost forty summers, Sir," he hears himself squeak.

"Have you not had enough time?"

But the voice is no longer at the window. It is in his right eye. A cool breath, sweetened with cinnamon, puffs against his eyeball, as iron fingers pinch open his jaw.

"Your tongue." A silver crescent glitters against Gil-baal's cheek. "Do not make me use this blade to find it."

"Oh, dear gods no!" cries Gil-baal. "I can give you anything you desire! Please! I am a man who fulfills the most secret wishes!"

"That is your tongue. Give it hence, and I will split it for you, and you will become lean and slither about on your belly as you should. No more talk. Extend it, you adder, or I remove your jaw."

The blade above Gil-baal's head is swift and accurate. It slices down the instant the man pokes his tongue past his lips, accurately splitting the end of the muscle into two smaller tongues. The pain is instant, then gone, and then replaced by a throbbing agony. Gil-baal's mouth fills with blood as he pulls the wounded organ back into his head to nestle behind his teeth. He draws his hands up to his face, moaning.

"You cannot give me what I desire." The monster's bottomless voice is sad. "But I will have my bride." And he is off the bed, the light tinkling of the beaded curtain the only evidence of his departure.

I must go to my brother's wife, thinks Gil-baal. She will stop the blood. But I must be sure that he is gone from there before I do.

Across the alley, Rush kicks open Bil-baal's door, leaving a hairline crack in the poplar that will ultimately compromise the wood. The sound is an explosion that blows Bil-baal and his wife, Il-Bethyr, out of their beds and onto their feet.

In the dark, Bil-baal attempts to catch his breath. "He is here, wife," he says, reaching for an oil lamp. "Get the girl, that we might be rid of him."

In the front room, Rush sets the boy, whom he has carried out of the brothel on his shoulder, onto his feet. "Stay beside me," he says, then moves off into the darkness. Presently a light glows in the hall, and in the glow the boy sees the broad back of the assassin bend to accommodate for his height under the low ceiling. A woman's sharp intake of breath emanates from behind his shape.

"She has healed well, sir," says Il-Bethyr, "I have taken great pains to reduce the scarring to a minimum, but of course, she is maimed."

"Her face?"

"No, her face is quite pleasant enough. But her breast, well..."

"I saw. It is nothing to me," answers the black wraith. "Bring her."

Il-Bethyr vanishes down the hall as Bil-baal appears behind her with a lamp.

"Extinguish that," says the mummy. Bil-baal hesitates only a moment, not wishing to be in the dark with the thing that has entered his house. When Il-Bethyr returns, the girl is with her, dressed in a dun sheath.

"Put an outer garment over her," says the wraith from the darkness.

"Sir, she is still healing of course," says Il-Bethyr. "She will need to take with her this preparation, and this salve to put on the wound." She extends her hands toward the voice, each holding a small earthenware jar. Small, child hands take the jars from her.

"Oh!" gasps Il-Bethyr.

Bil-baal has returned from an inner room with a cloak to throw over the assassin's new bride. He pushes her forward as he does so. "Here she is."

"Speak, girl," says the darkness.

"I am Tiamat," says the girl toward the voice. A small hand takes hers in the dark and pulls her away from Bil-baal. She sighs a soft "oh".

"Tiamat, it is I, Mukkan," whispers the boy into Tiamat's ear. "He is taking me, too."

"Speak a word of my visit to another soul and I return," says the darkness, still thickening the shadows in the center of the room. "And tell your brother the same, else I will finish carving him into the viper he is." Then the thickness softens, and Bil-baal hears the door shut softly.

"He is gone, praise the gods," he says.

"I have cursed him," answers Il-Bethyr. "He will suffer for what he has done to your brother."

"Curses will not harm the devil, wife," answers Bil-baal, turning to lead her back to their bedroom in the dark.

CHAPTER 6

"The boy, Rah, Highness," says the burly guard who had shoved Rah before the King.

Rah instantly floats to the ground in his most elegant bow.

The King's throne room, which is packed with a glittering array of state sycophants and royal slaves, is silent. Rah remains in position, a golden thing, a sheaf of finest wheat, tossed in homage before a monarch. Though he has been ordered to rearrange his tunic properly, it nevertheless is rent, and slips lazily over one shoulder. The scents of cherry blossom and myrrh lift as he falls into the bow and caress the King's nostrils.

"Get up, boy," says the guard behind him finally.

Rah slips to his feet, head bowed.

"Let me see you," says the King. "Show your face."

Rah lifts his chin, eyes alighting on the King's own.

"What is he," whispers King Samsu-titana after a moment.

"We believe he is a god-slave, made on Crete, Majesty," says one of the King's advisors, who has been thrust forward by his two fellows.

"A god-slave? What is this?" asks the King. "Is he a god, or a slave?"

"On Crete, my King," answers the man, coming forward less timidly, "The Minoans are known to do such things. There are such tales coming forth from that…now desolate…land. It is said that the priests of Knossos could create such creatures in ceremonies. Ceremonies in which a chosen slave was executed in some manner conforming to the particular god being honored, then brought to life again, by the priest, who has the power to summon the god himself into the body of the slave."

"And he is one of these, then?" asks the King, leaning forward on his throne to peer into Rah's face.

"We believe so, Highness," says the King's advisor, looking back to his companions for support.

"Died, and was returned to life by a priest, you say?" muses Samsu-titana, stroking his beard. "This is witnessed? This is sworn to?"

"If he is one of these, yes, Highness, absolutely," answers the second of the King's advisors, now coming forward, a bit more emboldened. "And given the - the Amegan monster's threat, we," and here he turns to his fellows for support, "we all agree that it must indeed be so. For why else would ... well, for what other reason would the Assassin make such a threat? The man who needs nothing, who takes everything, the man of shadows, suddenly communicating with Babylon?" Now the man looks at the taller of his two companions, nods, steps back. That man comes forward to complete his argument. "Highness," he says, "If the Wolf of Amega would threaten Babylon for this boy, then this boy must, by reason, be worth all of Babylon... Even more!"

"Bring me the messenger," barks the King then, standing up and causing everybody in the throne room to drop to the floor on one knee. All but Rah, who simply lowers his eyes.

King Samsu-titana peers at the boy's coppery head in disbelief. He takes a step forward, then makes a sudden, rash flight down the three stairs from his throne to the floor of the chamber. The hall murmurs with shock. Rah is still. The King is tall, taller even than an average Amorite male. His crown sits on a shaved skull that gleams with rare oils. His beard is long and grey and pointed, the tip reaching nearly to his belt. He is decked in gold and jewels and his gown is stained a brilliant crimson.

The King reaches out to touch Rah's cheek.

"Lift your face to me, god-slave," he says, and the hall

hushes.

Rah does as he is told. Sunlight through a high casement catches the emerald on his forehead and it explodes with color. But even the emerald cannot distract the King from Rah's prismatic eyes.

Rah smiles.

And Samsu-titana himself steps back, blinking.

"Rah is dance for King," says Rah, dimples popping. "King see now, all this city be happy now. Good crop. Good year for Babylon. Rah is come. People be happy, dance in street. You see. Hali is no die now. Rah must dance for king, save from plague, save everybody," Rah continues casually. "Rah dance for king, and city is no destroy."

"Halki? Did you hear him? He speaks of Halki!" The King turns to his advisors. "So the Wolf of the Hatti knows of our...situation?"

But the throne room has begun to buzz so loudly around him that his advisors can barely hear his words. The word 'plague' hops from here to there all about the King, the noise rising to a near panic.

"Silence!" cries the guard who brought Rah in. He thumps a staff against the stone floor so hard that the wood splits.

"This is a powerful spirit!" someone cries. "We must do as he says" says another. "Did you hear him? He must dance, or a plague will destroy Babylon!" shouts a third.

"Silence!" It is the King's booming voice this time, and this time the room quiets, though a soft buzz of whispers still persists.

"He knows of our... situation..." Samsu-titana looks at his advisors with fury brewing in his grey eyes.

"He has been told nothing, Highness, I assure you!" responds the taller advisor. "He has been housed with the entertainers until now."

The King's eyes shoot back to Rah. "How is it you know of our problem? Did the Wolf of Amega tell you this? Is that why you have come? Have you fled him, fled him to come to the aid of Babylon?"

"Wolf, he come for Rah," says Rah. "He come, take Rah.

Must dance for King before Wolf is come."

"It could be a trap, Highness!" pipes the third advisor, who has been silent until now. He is the oldest of the three, and limps forward slowly on a staff.

"He sends the creature here to us, knowing our situation, then accuses us of keeping him here for our benefit and mounts an attack!" cries the second.

"An excuse, Highness, that is what this is! An ill-conceived excuse to invade our city!" says the first, pointing a long finger of accusation at Rah's golden head.

"M-m-m," nods the King, and, stroking his beard, he turns and climbs back up the three stairs to his throne. The three advisors give each other sidelong glances.

"Well, there is one way to know," he says. "We must see his magic for Ourselves. He says he must dance for Us. So be it. I order henceforth a dance be performed. Therefore inform Our Master of the Arts of the City of Babylon, Our Eliabus, that this dance is to be performed for Us on the night of the next full moon, in the Palace Theatre. This creature will dance for Us. Then, if he is not what he says he is," and here he looks down at Rah, his grey eyes growing cold as the north wind in the mountains, "we will send him back to the Wolf of Amega in a box."

Akintunde lies on a pallet in the far corner of the clerks' quarters in the Wing Of Commerce. In his lap is the leopard cub, suckling a skin filled with goat's milk. The cub has growing stronger daily, despite its ordeal. When it has finished its meal it claws and nuzzles Akintunde's chest, mewling for more.

"You are ready for meat, little one," murmurs Akintunde. "This is the last of it." He pulls a strip of dried quail from his running sack and puts it on his chest in front of the kitten's nose. The animal pounces with both claws, causing Akintunde to wince. Then it licks the string of meat up with a gritty tongue. When it has ingested the meat it sniffs Akintunde's ribs, nuzzles his nipples. Akintunde lets out a burst of reflexive giggles.

"What kind of messenger comes into Babylon with a beast

such as this in his sleeve?"

She is a girl of less than fifteen summers, dark-skinned, like himself, her head shaved. She has entered the clerks' quarters, which is otherwise empty, without his notice, and now moves from pallet to pallet straightening linen and gathering soiled clothing. She looks up from her work and smiles, and Akintunde is, for an instant, home.

"A messenger from the greatest warrior in all the Mediterranean world," responds Akintunde, rising to his elbows and setting the cub onto the floor. "A messenger from Amega."

"But the messenger did not bring the beast from Amega," smiles the girl, returning to her work on the opposite side of the room. "The messenger found the beast, starving and motherless, on his way to Babylon. And the messenger's heart was touched by the sight, for the beast reminded him of the land of his birth. Perhaps he had a pet such as this. Perhaps his father brought him a cub in his youth, and the boy and the cub became one."

"How can you know all this?" asks Akintunde, rising to his feet.

"Do not approach me, messenger," says the girl, glancing over her shoulder at the door. "They will cut your hands off if they think you meant to touch a palace slave."

"I mean to touch no one," answers Akintunde. "Only you are like a sister, who looks the same as me, and knows my childhood as if you shared it."

"I am from the Ta-Antyu tribe of Punt," responds the girl. "I lived in a small village at the rise of the Nile."

"I too am from the Ta-Antyu tribe!" cries Akintunde. "I was famous in the land for my speed. And so, when I was taken by Egypt, I was sold to an Amorite general for a messenger. But the Wolf of Amega crushed him, and took me for his own."

"Many were taken from the Ta-Antyu," says the girl, glancing now at the cub, who is digging his claws into Akintunde's bare feet. "Your friend needs meat. I will get you something from the kitchen."

"Yes, thank you, he is always hungry now. I found him

without a mother, trying to suckle the bodies of his dead brothers. I had a cheetah once, in the land of Punt. She saved my life..." his voice trails off.

"You told the King this one was from the Assassin. A gift. But this is a lie. You meant only to honor your friend, your cheetah, by saving this cub. But a cheetah and a leopard, especially an Anatolian leopard, are two different things, messenger. This is a dangerous animal to make a pet," the girl says, moving toward the door to check the hall. "I will go now, and come back with something for it." She disappears.

Akintunde lifts the cub off his foot to look into its face. Now, he thinks, you are a sweet little ball of fur. But in six months, you will be a terror. I will have to release you, before you understand that my people and your people have always been enemies.

Ephtheta is lying on her royal couch in her visiting room when Mefali returns.

"You are unwell, highness?" he asks softly.

"I have been better, uncle," says Ephtheta, lifting herself onto her elbow.

"Your father has seen the boy, and has ordered that he dance for the palace. On the night of the next full moon."

"That is only two weeks away," answers Ephtheta. "How can an entertainer perform for the palace with only two weeks' time to prepare?"

"We suspect that the Assassin is using him as a ruse to excuse an invasion. We believe he may have knowledge of our situation and that this boy, whether a hoax, or slave truly possessed by a god of prosperity, is here to cost us a war with the Hittites, whom we could not defend against in our current condition. Nevertheless, your father intends to discover if he can, by his magic, somehow replenish our failing soil."

"My father would judge a god," sighs the princess. "And what if the golden cat-boy is, in fact, a Minoan god-slave? What if the crops flourish? What then, uncle?"

"Well then," responds Mefali, walking to a western window to look out over the Great River, "we will hope he can restore us fast enough to feed our troops, and we will defend ourselves."

He will take the city, thinks Ephtheta, and he will take me. The only man capable of either. So be it. I have always, secretly, adored the legend of the Great Wolf of the Hatti. He is smart, and he is dangerous. Perhaps he is as handsome as he is lethal. Perhaps I will have babies fit to rule Babylon after all.

In a suite of rooms on the top floor of the finest inn in the Suanna section of Babylon, Tiamat and Mukkan are curled together on a pallet, sleeping soundly under a duck down quilt. After giving the girl a copy of Ameg's seal ring the assassin left them in the alley opposite the front door and told them to show the innkeeper the ring. "Touch nothing of mine," he said, then disappeared into the night.

Tiamat took Mukkan's hand and did as she was told, showing the seal ring to the inn keeper with bowed head. But he will ask questions, she thought. Who am I to say I am? And what will I do if he does not allow me, a woman in such simple garments, into the inn at all? Will we sleep here in the street? But she quickly discovered that there was no need to explain anything once the man saw the ring lying in the palm of her extended hand. He stepped back, bowed deeply, and waved her in. Then he led her and the boy to the merchant's rooms himself, and, half an hour later, interrupted their sleep with a tray of meats and delicacies fit for a visiting celebrity.

"I would offer you my best wine, Madam," he babbled, for the innkeeper had a problem with pressure of speech when he was nervous, "but alas my cellar is locked. My wife holds the key, you see, and I dare not wake her at this hour. She has quite a temper." Then he bowed low and backed out of the door, murmuring, "And a good evening to you both. Anything I can do to improve your stay, anything and all, you need only ring that bell there, in the hall across from your door, you see? Ring it hard, and I will come myself, or else have one of my servants answer it. Good evening then," and he was gone.

After stuffing themselves the two curled up on a good sized bed at the back of the suite, leaving the larger room to their rescuer.

Now a cool spring breeze through the open air windows,

lifting an edge of the down blanket against Tiamat's nose, awakens her. She bats at it, sees that the boy is still sleeping, and crawls off the mattress carefully. She is just backing away from the bed, as quietly as she can, when she hits a wall of sinew and heat and cries out.

"Good sleep, my wife?" The black menace behind her pulls its head off, revealing an extraordinarily handsome face, glacial eyes, and a trimmed beard.

Tiamat is instantly on her hands and knees, though her breast throbs where the tanner has mutilated her. She lowers her forehead to the floor, and whisper, "Master."

"Not in this town," he answers, a strange mingling of amusement and authority in his voice. "Here you are to be my wife. The new wife of Ameg The Merchant. Richest man in Babylon, save, perhaps, the King himself."

"Your wife, My Lord?" answers the girl, determined to keep her head pressed to the cool tile floor, though her left bicep, the one furthest from her injury, is now encircled by a firm hand, which is gently ushering her to her feet.

"Do not be afraid," the voice responds softly, and in its placidness she can barely recognize the monster who saved her. "No one will hurt you now. You are safe now."

At this, Tiamat is drawn to her feet. Her eyes filling with tears, look up into the face of her savior. "Master," she says again, although it is barely a breath.

"Your breast," says the man, releasing her arm. "Let me see your wound."

Tiamat blinks away her tears. She hears Mukkan stir behind her and instinctively looks over her shoulder at him. He is sitting up in the bed, staring with enormous eyes at the man who calls himself Ameg The Merchant. Her hand moves to the front of her garment, which is a simple night slip, loaned to her by the wife of Bil-baal. But the man is not looking at her breast. His black eyes are pinned on the boy. She can feel them above her head, glittering like polished onyx in the afternoon light. Mukkan slips off the bed and out the door, turning his face to the wall as he goes. The man returns his gaze to her. Tiamat swallows, closes her eyes hard against her tears, and opens the bodice of the slip. She holds the edges open, eyes slammed shut, lips trembling. She feels the coolness of a single finger trace the wound. Still she cannot open her eyes. She bites back a sob, determined to give her submission completely to this man. To her savior. She feels the power of his shadow bend closer, and then the finger taps her chin, asking her to lift her face to him. He is a full head taller than her, but he had bent so that his lips are at her ear.

"There is no shame in this, girl. You are a warrior now," he whispers. Whispers with such gentleness that she feels her knees attempt to fold and she must order them to stop! You cannot simply fall into this man's arms! This is your master!

She looks up into his face to see the most peculiar combination of kindness and dominance she has ever seen.

"What shall I do, Sir?" she whispers back. "Am I not ruined? Am I not maimed? I have but one breast."

"Who shall know? You are the wife of Ameg now, and if another man's eyes behold you," and at this he cups her right breast in his hand, caresses it gently, and then releases her and closes the bodice over her wound, "Ameg shall give them to you as a keepsake. Two eyes for one breast, that is the price to look upon my wife." He smiles, a devilish smile revealing long, clean, wolfish teeth, and she instinctively steps away from him.

"Y-yes, Sir." She curtseys.

"Now you have had a good sleep, you and the boy. What is his name?"

"Makkan, Sir."

"You and Makkan will take this," and he has tossed a money sack into her hands, "and go shopping. You will find the best seamstress in the city and order a wardrobe fit for a princess. Do the same for the boy. Have them dress him properly. He is your son now."

"But Sir," responds Tiamat, "My...condition will be obvious to all. I will bring shame on you," she lowers her eyes, her lip quivering.

"That is a job for the dressmakers," answers the black animal that now begins to undress, revealing an oddly pale, but beautifully carved chest, decorated with a black star of hair just there, between the striated pectorals. He turns from her to address the curtained door in a booming baritone. "Makkan!"

"I don't understand, Sir," says Tiamat, as Makkan dashes into the room, fast as a squirrel, to drop at his new master's feet.

Rush is pulling off his leggings. "Fetch water and soap, and wash these in the cistern. Do not allow that simpering idiot innkeeper to take them from you to give to the laundress. They are not to leave your possession, you understand?"

"Yes, Sir!" says Makkan jumping to his feet to reach for the assassin's muslin tunic and leggings with eager and reverent hands.

"If he tries, you tell him precisely what I told you," Rush takes the boy's chin and gives it a stern shake. "Repeat it."

"DO NOT ALLOW THAT SIMPERING IDIOT INNKEEPER TO TAKE THEM-" says Makkan, careful to pronounce each word boldly, and making every attempt to reach Rush's baritone.

"Excellent," Rush fluffs the boy's hair. Then he takes his arm, spins him, pats his bottom, and shoves him through the curtain. "Now go."

When the boy is gone, and he turns back to the girl, she is staring at his nakedness. He narrows his eyes at her, and she quickly lowers her head.

"Did I give you an order, woman?"

"Yes, Sir," says Tiamat, who curtsey's quickly and moves to tear past him and out the door. But he is too fast for her. He seizes her left arm, again careful not to cause any stress to her still fresh wounds. Tiamat stops in her tracks. She makes no attempt to lift her eyes to him.

"Disguise is nothing. All people wear disguises of one kind or another. A good dressmaker will form you a simple lambskin pad to disguise your injury. To fill out the bodice." He gives her bicep a little squeeze and she winces. "Be sure not to give my money for poor work, or he will suffer for it."

"Yes, Sir," says Tiamat, waiting for the grip to loosen. When it does, she curtsey's again, then flies out the curtained door.

"Makkan, wait! We are to go shopping!" Rush hears her trill excitedly as she dashes after him.

CHAPTER 7

"A thief sleeps in a city of thieves."

The words are a Hittite hiss in the priest's left ear. He has been dreaming of cream cakes, fruit-sweetened yogurt, fried dough dipped in honey and custard in flaky pastry. Now a man beside him at table is looking over his left shoulder with an expression of amusement on his face. The man wears fine purple silks and is decked in jewels. He lifts his hand, points to Mochlos' ear. The Hatti king's seal ring is on his finger.

It is the man he sold the ring to.

Mochlos becomes confused. Why am I at table with this man? And what does he point at? Is there something behind me?

Low, like the growl of a bear, the voice returns. "Wake, Priest," it says, and this time, Mochlos recognizes it. His heart gives one good kick against the bars of its rib prison, and he stirs. He turns on his side, away from the voice. I dream, he thinks, fading back into the blackness of slumber.

And he is on the floor.

And a man, the size of a bear, straddles him.

"Gods be merciful!" he hears the stupidity of the words before he realizes he has uttered them. The assassin has slapped a paw over his nose and mouth. Making noise has cost him his air.

"Hello, little priest," purrs Rush, his masked face inches from Mochlos'. One eye surveys his scalp, his face, his beard.

The head cocks, amused. "Gone Amorite, have we?" he runs a hot palm over the priest's cranium. "Can I remove my hand, priest? Or will you wake the girl, and make me silence her, h-m? She is a pretty one. Quite fit for our Rah. Pretty enough to eat."

Mochlos glares up at the monstrosity on his chest, waiting. There is no point struggling with this madman, he thinks. It only makes it worse. Yet he fails to realize that his angry eyes constitute a struggle in the assassin's world.

"That is no way to look upon your master, villain," growls the hood.

Instantly Mochlos shuts his eyes, having no other course of action available to him with which to display his submission. But his mind boils with rage none the less. After what seems an eternity, the broad palm that blocks his wind lifts. Mochlos sucks in air, greedily.

"You found me," he gasps, making a weak attempt to put his hand up to ward off further suffocation.

"When have I ever not?" says the assassin, a lilt of mirth in his growl.

"I would have found you," says Mochlos, swallowing. "Could you perhaps allow me to rise? I have no intention of speaking above a whisper and having an eyeball ripped out and shoved down my throat."

Rush lifts himself off the priest and pulls him to his feet. "Sit then. Tell me a story, priest." He shoves him onto the bed in a sitting position.

Mochlos adjusts his nightgown, which has twisted around his torso like a tourniquet. "Very well. I have followed the Rah into Babylon."

"This you say to impress me?" The mirth is still in the assassin's voice. Mochlos swallows, bathing his throat in spit in order to continue.

"Someone had to. That scum, Ess, and his band of thieves, well I convinced them he was the greater treasure, thus negotiating the release of the king."

"Go on, priest. Your tongue is an excellent shovel. It digs your grave deeper by the minute," says the assassin.

"He is your king, is he not? The one you were fighting

for? Did I do wrong?"

"And you thought I would trade the Rah for him? I could have done that myself, priest."

"Not exactly. Only a third party could have convinced the Amorites that the Rah was worth more to you than the King of Hatti, your king."

"Go on. You amuse me," says Rush. He has drawn his crescent blades. Mochlos can see them flashing above his head in a sliver of moonlight. It is the only thing visible in the otherwise pitch dark.

"I also had to convince him to take me with him. That without his priest, his creator, the god-slave would wither. This is how I came to be in his company when he rode off in pursuit of the boy toward Babylon."

"Ah," muses the assassin above his head.

"You will be pleased to know that Ess has died at my hand," says Mochlos rather cockily.

"You will be pleased to know that the other two have died at mine," answers Rush, "Far more unpleasantly, I expect."

"Yes, well, poison is no fun either," snips Mochlos. "He was bleeding from both ends when last I saw him."

"Mm," says Rush, and for an instant, Mochlos imagines that he has impressed the murdering ape. "That leaves you to enter Babylon, sell Mursilis' seal ring, and set up your house. But how did you plan to lure the Rah back into it?"

"I have not been asleep!" spits Mochos. "I plan to purchase a fine house near the People's Theatre, where he will surely be drawn. There I will establish the first Temple of Rah."

"Mm," says Rush again, turning to the blackness of the open window through which he entered Mochlos' suite. "And with the girl," he waves his hand in the direction of Awiti's bed, "who looks to be a twin of his Seriona, you thought you would bait him. But did you know he is in the palace, priest? That the Babylonian King believes I sent him here deliberately, a god-slave, made by a master magician on Crete? A god-slave who can thwart Babylon's impending famine?"

"Famine? I-"

"The streets talk," says the assassin, "and the dark

listens." Now the dark hulk moves from the window, vanishing left, and suddenly Mochlos is pinned to his bed by the gullet and one pitch eye is glaring at him, an inch from his own.

"Augh-eh," chokes the priest miserably.

"You have brought death to Babylon, priest," says the assassin, anger and sadness mixing into a strangely soft base in the depths of his throat. And just as suddenly, he is gone. A thickened darkness blots out the slim light peeking through the open window, and vanishes.

"Famine," whispers Mochlos to himself, rubbing his windpipe. "Well, well, well. What better magick is there than the Rah, for famine? Did Knossos not flourish by his creation? Did Cyrus not thrive? True, after the thriving came the... well, that is another thing entirely. An act of nature, entirely separate. A terrible misfortune, yes. But what could it have possibly to do with the slave-god? Yes, this is better than I thought! All I need do now is install myself here as the High Priest of the Rah, and Babylon will be at my feet!"

In the morning, the King receives a visitor.

It is not Samsu-titana's custom to allow a foreigner into the palace, but this visitor is from Crete, from the very city that the god-slave, Rah, originated. Eager to learn more about the boy and his true worth, the King admits the man to his throne room. He is surprised to see that he is accompanied by a smaller figure, completely cloaked in yellow silks.

"Why did you not inform me there were two?" he snaps at his advisors as the two forms traverse the enormous length of the room toward his throne.

"Majesty, he claims to be a priest. He must be attended at all times. She is apparently a personage of considerable holiness."

"Your Immensity," says the man when he reaches the foot of the King's dais. And making an elegant full bow, he remains with forehead to the cool tile floor until one of the King's advisors sighs, "Rise."

"What is your purpose in Babylon?" the King barks, leaning forward to peer at the man's peculiar dress. "Turn around, that I may see this robe you wear. What are you, then? A priest from Knossos? You have heard of this boy, Rah?"

"Highness, I have more than heard of him," says Mochlos, now unable to contain a tigerish smile. "I made him."

In the entertainer's dining hall that evening, Rah sits beside Horus, a bowl of raw vegetables before him. In a cup beside the bowl is a mixture of watery yogurt meant to be poured over the dish.

Rah is unaware that the hall is quieter than usual this evening, that the whispering he hears about him is a result of his presence, and that what might occupy his corn silk head is the discussion of everyone but his companion, who nibbles a radish as he watches Rah stare at his own dish with dismay.

"This what dancer eat? How can dance? Rah need fish, need bread, too. How can be strong now? Rah can no jump eat root!" and he flings a carrot from his bowl. The vegetable lands on the next table, narrowly missing the naked shoulder of a man dressed only in a skirt made of horse tail hair. The man turns to fasten his wide eyes on Rah. Horus shrugs at him dramatically, and the man looks to his companions, then turns back to his meal.

"Rah, you mustn't throw your food about! We are dressed, some of us, as animals, nevertheless, not permitted to act like them in the dining hall!" Horus hisses in Rah's ear. But Rah is on his feet before he can finish. He has hopped onto the table and is now making his way down the long line of diners, looking from plate to plate for something palatable to eat.

"Where is egg? Fish? Bread? How you dance eat like this?" He bends in half to swipe a bowl of salad from under a pheasant-girl's nose. "Eat like cow. Move like cow," he shakes his head with terrible sadness, holding up a fist full of chard. "Dancer want to move like cat!" he makes a sudden turn on the balls of his feet, and he is a blonde panther, snarling at the tiger-man whose bowl of greens he has just overturned with a toe. The man starts, then smiles and claps, as his companions nod and smile and follow suit.

"Rah fix." Suddenly, Rah is in the air. He has sprung onto his hands, cart-wheeled to the opposite end of the table, and jackknifed into an impossibly high pike. He turns his body twice in the air before landing soundlessly on the ground in a crouch.

He stalks on silent feet toward the kitchen, and Horus, sensing danger, hops off his bench and rushes after him on his platform sandals.

The kitchen help are cleaning up their stations when Rah pushes open the swinging doors and enters the room. A tall man with a white scarf tied around his head looks up from his cutting board, which he has been wiping down with a wet linen. The man is clean-shaven, his face doughy.

"What is *he* doing in here?" he snips, throwing the linen down and wiping his hands on his aproned belly. Rah ignores him and begins a thorough search of the bins, baskets and barrels of grain and vegetables for something to his liking.

Horus follows after, tapping along on his outlandish shoes in double-time, his long-fingered hands fussing at the scarf at his throat.

"He's looking for something else to eat," Horus explains, giving the head cook a tortured look. "He's a bit wild, you know, not quite, well, civilized I suppose is the word. But if you get to know him he really is quite charming. Quite charming," he makes a grab at a Rah's wrist as the boy plunges his hand into an open barrel of barley. But Rah is too quick, he holds the fist of grain away and over his head, puts the flat of his opposite hand against Horus' chest. Horus looks down at that hand, up into Rah's narrowed eyes, and desists.

"Take him out of here! I will not have him mucking about in my kitchen!" shouts the head cook, pointing the sharp end of his knife at the door.

"He will bite," says Horus, flicking a look at the cook. "Anyone who touches him without his consent." Rah smiles suddenly at Horus, looks over his shoulder at the cook, then discharges the fist of barley into the air over his head and carries on his search.

"Rah is need fish! Is need grain, cake, make Rah strong so can jump high," he is headed right for the head cook, right into the point of the vegetable knife. Horus clops after, slipping on pearls of barley, hands waving.

"Entertainers must be light, Rah! We must be very careful how we eat! How we eat is how we look!" Horus stops short behind Rah just as he reaches the head cook.

"You cut Rah, when Wolf he is come, he cut you. He cut you in half," Rah pokes the cook's belly. "You make good fish for Rah. Grain cake. Maybe you make sweet cake too, like Ting Ya. Wolf he is like Rah be strong, jump high, run fast. Rah be weak," Rah shakes his head sadly at the cook, using one finger to press the handle of the knife down and away from himself, "Wolf he come, maybe skin be good, eh..." he looks at Horus for the word. He is pantomiming a man stepping into leggings. "Suit," says Horus dully, his carefully lined eyes moving from Rah's to the cooks. "He speaks of the Wolf of the Hatti," he adds, swallowing.

"Yah, is wolf of hat. You know him? He eat meat. No cook. Rabbit, deer, any meat. When he come, you cook for him too. But now, you cook for Rah. Only white meat, fish, egg from white chicken, milk from white goat. And everything," he swings his arm up and over himself, "what come from Rah."

All this time the head cook has been staring into Rah's face. Having seen him only from a distance, from the kitchen pass way, he is now doubly stunned both by the boy's appearance and his speech. He has heard very little of what he has said, being a man who concentrates entirely on one subject at a time. Now he raises his eyes to Horus', shakes his head, shrugs.

"What the devil is he saying? He's got a cleft tongue, and speaks three languages at once," he lifts the knife again, for it is his habit to use it as a pointer, at Rah's mouth.

"You get used to it," says Horus, attempting a smile of condolence. "But you had better put down the knife, Chef, for he is quick, and impulsive, and he may well cut himself on it."

"And what is it to me if he does?" snaps the chef, nevertheless withdrawing his knife to plant his fists on his doughy hips.

"You stupid?" Rah's brows have furrowed. "Why he is so

stupid, Horoos? This why dancer eat like cow! Need better cook! Need Crispo! We get Crispo here, he cook right for Rah!" and for emphasis, Rah smashes a fist down on the chef's cutting board.

"No, ... how I say it Horoos, like-" Rah is on his toes, punching the air, puffing and feinting.

"Energy," answers Horus, looking back at the Chef and shrugging.

"Yah, this. No energy in cow food. Everybody dance like sleep. I tell Wolf he get here. I tell him Rah is need Crispo. This cook, maybe can make-" he is chopping the air with the edge of one hand, "vegetable."

The chef's teeth are grit, his face a pomegranate. "I understood THAT!" he shouts as the pair retreat from the kitchen, Rah snatching a handful of rolled oats to munch on his way out. "You'll eat greens like all the rest, you little fool!" the chef continues, wiping his forehead with his apron and turning back to his cutting board to continue his toweling.

"Rah, you mustn't insult Chef like that," hisses Horus as Rah flings the doors to the dining hall open. "He is a very influential man. Eliabus and he go way back, you know."

But Rah is already lifting his fists over his head to the applause of the entertainers still seated at table.

"Dancer eat like cat now!" he shouts. "No more eat like cow, move like cow!"

"Dear heaven," murmurs Horus, lifting an index finger to his lips to chew a cuticle.

In the kitchen, the staff stiffens at the applause, and turn to watch the head cook throw his towel down on his cutting board and stomp out the back of the kitchen in a fury.

In the palace stable, Aamat is enjoying his favorite time of day. The horses have finished their morning grain and he has pulled his master's Turkoman from its stall and clipped its halter to the cross ties in the aisle. He has picked out the animal's feet, wiped down his legs with a damp cloth, trimmed the feathers of hair about his pasterns and scraped any manure the beast lay in during the night off with a bronze comb. Now he is currying the animal's shimmering golden coat with a boar hair brush. When he is finished, when the entire coat has been curried with overlapping circular strokes, then he will use the fine brush to stroke the gelding's coat toward the tail, so that his neck, his shoulders, his basket and loin all glimmer like the light coming through the open barn door, that morning sun that turns the air to golden smoke this time of day, making everything, even a pile of straw left outside a mare's brooding stall, translucent and magical.

Another groom has entered the stable from the open doorway leading a yearling. The colt whinnies, happy to see his stable mate. Petuk's gelding dances on the cross ties and snorts. The two animals are becoming too accustomed to one another and they will have to be separated. But for now, Aamat simply nudges the big animal aside, unclipping one of the ties to allow the groom room to lead the colt through to his stall.

Petuk's Turkoman dances sideways, nearly stepping on Aamat's boot. "Hah! Where are your manners, Petuk!" chides Aamat, taking the beast's halter and giving it a shake. The horse an Amorite warrior takes into battle inherits the man's name as a gift, an honor given it for surviving its first battle. But the Turkoman's namesake is just entering the stable, and, hearing his own name reproached by his servant's tongue, he clears his throat, crosses his arms over his chest, and waits for an apology.

A disturbance at the doorway on the opposite end of the aisle interrupts him. The early risers who have begun to fill the stable with their morning chatter turn to see a slim figure dressed in a simple white tunic strolling into the barn, leading King Samsu-titana's stallion with nothing more than a lunge rope. At first, Aamat is confused. It seems the sun is rising at both ends of the stable. There is an ethereal glow surrounding the figure and the horse. Aamat blinks, even brings the thumb and forefinger of his free hand up to his face to pinch his eyes. Dreamily, he reaches for Petuk's right cross tie to reattach it to the gelding's halter. He has forgotten that his master stands in the north doorway, ready to berate him for using his name in a reproachful tone. His mind is soft, like the soft morning light that glows now in the southern doorway.

A man has come storming out from the passage to the inner riding arena. He is dressed in full military riding gear. Behind him a handler grabs at the reins of the horse he has clearly just dismounted. It is the Master of the Royal Stables, whose habit it is to rise an hour before dawn to begin training the green two year olds who have been selected from the royal breeding program to become war horses. The man wears a leather helmet and leather leggings trimmed in red. He is exceptionally tall. He carries a short reed whip, which he has raised.

"What is this? Who has given you permission to handle the King's personal animal?" He strides toward Rah, the whip raised in his right hand, his left arm extended to expertly swipe the lead rope from Rah's hand and separate him from the horse before he cracks the whip down on Rah's golden head.

"Ayyy-Eeeee!" Rah cries, releasing the lead and dropping to his knees, his arms over his head to protect him from the blows that are now raining down upon it. And the light, that strange, ethereal glow, has vanished. Aamat is shoved into Petuk's flank as his namesake rushes past the pair and down the aisle toward the scene.

"Do not harm him! Put down your whip, Stable Master!" Petuk cries, and when he reaches the man he grabs his whip hand, pitting strength against strength to prevent the next blow.

"How dare you, Petuk?" spits the furious Stable Master. "How dare you lay a hand on me?"

"No, Hatu-Hadu! I save you from yourself! This boy is here by decree of the King! This is no slave, Sir! This is a royal entertainer!" cries Petuk, putting himself between the Stable Master's whip and Rah's snarling whimper.

"I do not care if he is a royal consort, Captain," responds Hatu-Hadu, who, though taller even than Petuk, cannot match his strength. Careful not to lose face in front of his staff, he snatches his whip from Petuk's grasp and snaps it sharply against his own leather legging. The King's Turkoman starts, tripping backward and snorting at the sound. Petuk takes his eyes off Hatu-Hadu long enough to look down at Rah. Blood is dripping from the boy's left ear into his curls. His golden coronet has been dislodged, ripping hair from his scalp in the process. Rah is warbling like a stricken dog. He turns fierce green eyes onto the Stable Master, and lifts a hand to search for something on his earlobe. But the lobe has been sliced in two.

Rah's fingers are running with blood.

"Take him to the surgeon, quickly, Aamat! Have him clean that wound and stitch it!" Petuk has lost interest in the Stable Master. Is this creature truly the property of the Amegan Wolf? he is thinking, his head spinning. Have I just witnessed the first blow in Babylon's last war?

Aamat has rushed to his master's side. He lifts Rah onto his feet. "Cold water!" he shouts to a young groom. "A clean linen, man, quickly!" he adds, for among the soldier's valets he is king, being the Captain's own. The boy dashes out the back doors, returning in seconds with a pail from the stable well and a fresh linen he has filched from Hatu-Hadu's own grooming box.

Aamat plunges the linen into the icy water, then presses it to Rah's ear. "Hold it there now, tightly, Rah," he says, rushing the dancer toward the stairs that lead up into the Royal Guard's quarters, where the surgeon is making his morning rounds.

"He will not die from a split ear," spits Hatu-Hadu, turning to lead the King's Turkoman back to its stall on the opposite end of the training arena. "What did he think he was going to do with the King's finest breeding stallion, hm? Ride it? Use it in a play, perhaps? He would have been killed. And you can thank me for saving him from it."

"Perhaps," responds Petuk, taking a deep, worried breath. "But I doubt very much if the Hatti Wolf will see it that way."

But Hatu-Hadu is already out of earshot.

The royal surgeon is lancing a boil on a young guard's rump in the palace barracks when Aamat calls for him at the top of the stair. The surgeon looks up at his assistant, his lips pulled down in a frown.

"What a morning, Kalak. Is it not enough I must be reduced to such ailments as this?" he points to the oozing slice he has made in the man's buttock, "and now no doubt some groom has got his toe smashed by a stud?" Rising from the side of his patient's mattress, he hands the clean end of the lancing instrument to his man. "Oh, how I long for war wounds. Finish up here, will you? Make sure to boil the needle and thread as I showed you before you stitch." He turns to see that the Captain's personal slave is bringing him an androgynous creature with a mop of creamy curls. "What the devil?"

"Surgeon, he bleeds profusely! He cannot be marred! He is a god-slave from Crete, sent to the King by the Wolf of Amega!" Aamat is out of breath with excitement. He settles Rah on a cot and gently takes the blood soaked linen from his ear. The surgeon bends to examine the wound, which is already beginning to cake.

"It is nothing," he remarks. "A few stitches. You see, it already begins to dry." He looks up at Aamat quizzically. "A god-slave from Crete? Sent to Babylon by the Hatti Wolf? This is strange by any stretch, Aamat. Why on earth-"

"It is said that the Wolf has threatened Babylon with war, should this boy be harmed in any way. He demands that he be returned immediately to Amega, or he will take Babylon!"

"Well why the devil did he send him to us in the first place?" frowns the surgeon, who is a man with little patience for rumor. "This is a fat lot of nonsense. An entertainer with a head full of stories to tell, I'll wager, that is all he is. He's no more come from Amega that I have come from Lelwani." He turns to snatch the now sterilized needle and thread from his assistant.

"It is said that he is a slave-god made by a great priest, who took on the spirit of their Rah, a grain god alike to our Halki. His priest arrived only yesterday, the one who made him. He tells of the crops and seas overflowing with abundance in Knossos, so pleased was Rah with his dance."

"It is a clean tear," observes the surgeon as he sets to stitching the wound. But he has only to press the needle to Rah's ear to cause the boy to flinch and snarl, brows furrowed, teeth bared.

"He has the spirit of the cat, Sir, and he takes fits," Aamat nods at the surgeon as he looks up for an explanation. "Truly, he is indeed a god slave, one of great value."

"Not much pain tolerance, has he?" mocks the surgeon, who is used to working on brave men. "Very well. Kalak, bring me the dreaming tea. We shall have to send him to Upelluri to close this."

When Kalak returns with the tea in a small earthenware cup, the surgeon takes it and offers it to Rah.

"Drink this, now," he says mildly, "and you will sleep while I stitch up your ear, which has been rent in two."

"Rah sleep? No die?" says Rah, looking into the surgeon's eyes for some comfort. Finding none, he looks to Aamat.

"Yes, Rah, you will fall into a gentle sleep, and dream of good things, good places, people you have loved and lost," says the valet.

"Take off crown," says Rah, raising his hands to tear at the emerald and mail circlet that has been woven into his hair since he left Amega. "Is hurt."

"Let me, Rah, you will damage yourself further," says Aamat, untwisting the braided curls that have held it fast until now. Rah grimaces, but tolerates Aamat's fingers, which at times become trapped in the knotted strands and must be pulled free, yanking several hairs from his head at once.

"Such an abundance," mutters the surgeon, watching. "A head full of fluff, in and out."

"There now," offers Aamat, releasing the coronet from the golden nest at last. Several locks of corn silk hang from the band. "Ah, look here, surgeon! His scalp is cut as well!" Aamat separates a patch of curls above Rah's left ear. A fissure, about the length of a man's thumb, runs with blood. Aamat hands the coronet to Rah.

"It can be stitched as well, but not while this creature is awake and in possession of his teeth," answers the surgeon.

"You keep for Rah," says Rah, handing his tiara back to Aamat. "I go, maybe see Ileah," and taking the cup from the surgeon he drinks the tea down in one gulp.

"Is bad," he spits, wiping his mouth with his forearm. "How is bad tea make good dream, Aamat?" he looks up at Aamat with trusting eyes. When the slave offers no answer, Rah looks to the surgeon. "You fix Rah," he says, "Or Wolf is come. Be mad. Be mad Babylon make Rah," he moves to touch his torn ear …. "Ugly now." He is beginning to feel the effects of the drug and lies back on the cot. "Rah is sleep. Maybe go to see Ileah," he murmurs, drifting off.

"We must be quick now," says the surgeon. "The heated knife, Kalak." And he makes the first of two clean cuts that will sever a wedge of Rah's ear away so that he might restore the symmetry of the lobe.

CHAPTER 8

In the Kullab section of the city, in the north eastern quadrant, the High Priest of Rah, for so he introduced himself to the King, and his consort, the hermaphrodite, Awiti, arrive at the doors of their new home. The pair have travelled by royal litter, and house servants quickly dash out of the house to greet them. Yesterday, a messenger from the King himself came to warn the nobleman who occupies the house that he would be moving to a more modest accommodation closer to the palace, and that the High Priest of the new Babylonian god, from Crete, a unique god of fertility and plenty, will be taking up residence at the villa. The man balked only momentarily, for the house was owned by the palace, as were most of the more stunning homes in the Kullab. He understood that his cooperation was not requested, but demanded, and that anything less than complete submission would be considered treasonous and met with a harsh response, perhaps a capital one.

The man inquired how long he had to move his household and was told that two days should be sufficient. At any rate, the Priest would be moving in immediately, and he was to make him completely welcome.

Now Mochlos and Awiti descend from the litter to look up in awe at the painted façade of the house. The building sits upon itself in smaller and smaller squares, like a wedding cake, each layer painted either a solid color, or a story-telling collage.

The first floor is twice the footprint of the House of The Moon in Knossos, and all around the dwelling is a maze of tropical greenery, through which red brick paving stones weave a winding path. Birds of marvelous and kaleidoscopic color flit through the trees and tiny blonde monkeys cry in alarm at the duo as they enter through an iron gate twice the height of the priest.

"Your luggage will be brought in and unpacked, Sir, by the King's staff. Only give them some direction as to which rooms you will be occupying," says the palace secretary, who has accompanied Mochlos to the home to insure that the current occupants are appropriately gracious. "If I may, I would suggest that you, yourself, take the third floor. This is where the King stays when he visits the People's Theatre. There is a lovely view of the Temple of Ninmah from the master chamber there. And you will want to house the god-slave in the tower," he points to the top layer of the cake-house. "All of the Temples house their holiest relics in their towers, as a perpetual offering to the heavenly ones for whom they were built." He smiles, a man proud of the wisdom of his city.

"There are no other slave-gods here in Babylon?" asks Mochlos, not a little shocked, but thoroughly delighted by the thought.

"No, Sir. It is a dangerous business, is it not? Few priests are willing to take the chance of disappointing a King these days. But your god-slave, he is proven, yes? Certainly you must be utterly certain of his powers, else you would not have come forward as his maker."

Careful not to change the pleasant cast of his expression, Mochlos nods, "Of course," and quickly turns to put an arm around Awiti's shoulder. "Come. Let us find these rooms then. I have yet to offer prayer and sacrifice and the light is fading. Tomorrow, the Rah arrives."

He turns away from the secretary and gives Awiti wide eyes, then calmly guides her through the gates, which have been opened for them by two house slaves. There is a wide, stone paved walk leading to the front door of the house.

Inside Mochlos stops on an enormous expanse of polished stone flooring. A row of pillars line either side of the room, which is itself larger than his own courtyard at the House of The Moon on Crete. Behind the pillars the walls are carved stone depicting battlefields, migrations, births and deaths. Above, light filters through open air windows cut into the exterior walls of the house. The greeting room, for that is where Mochlos and Awiti are told to await their host, is furnished with upholstered couches, seating pillows and vases as tall and as broad as a man, all carefully arranged on a magnificent green and white stone parquet flooring.

A house slave in a gold trimmed green gown rushes down a long, shallow set of stairs at the opposite end of the greeting room. He is very tall, very slender, and wears an elaborately woven beard down to his waist. His head and brows are shaved.

"Welcome to the House of Seven Cisterns," the slave draws himself down into an elegant bow, offering Mochlos the crown of his shining, well-oiled head. "We are honored by the presence of the great High Priest of Knossos, maker of the Rah."

Word travels fast in this city, thinks Mochlos, bowing in kind as the man rises. But aloud he only returns the expected response. "And I, Mochlos, High Priest of the Rah, am equally honored to be greeted by the hospitality of the House of Seven Cisterns."

"I am Nipu, senior house slave. I have been assigned the honor of familiarizing you with your new home." And the slave bows again, less dramatically, and raises his arm to wave Mochlos and Awiti forward, toward the staircase from which he has just descended.

The stairs, in fact, run the length of the back of the greeting room, then turn and make a second shallow run along the eastern wall. The entire ziggurat will continue in this manner, so that the house is in fact surrounded by a single revolving staircase cut into the exterior walls. The second floor is a series of rooms and suites extending inward from the stair. The third floor opens onto a single enormous room which at first appears to match the greeting room below. The room is decorated with bright red and gold tapestries and a wool rug, also red and gold, covers two thirds of the floor. Settees, seating pillows and low tables furnish the room, and a buffet table along the west wall overflows with vases filled with white lilies, fresh fruits, steaming dishes of lamb and pheasant. Mochlos' eyes are fixed immediately on a tower of yellow at the far end of the table. The creation is a replica of this very house, right down to the red brick path leading to the front door.

"Is that…edible?" he begins, forgetting himself.

"The King's favorite, lemon cake, with a honey glaze and a cream filling. Quite delightful."

Mochlos takes Awiti's arm, as if it is she he must hold back from attacking the buffet. "Yes, quite," he murmurs.

"If you would, Sir?" Nipu folds his hands together over his breast and begins across the parquet floor. When he passes under the archway at the far north side of the room, he turns. "The King's apartment," he motions for Mochlos to enter an opening to the right. "And the Queen's," he motions Awiti toward a second opening, across the hall. "Of course, we have not had a Queen now for some years. The room remains decorated as she desired, however. Her favorite color was yellow, like your gown." He lifts his hand to wave Awiti into the Queen's apartment. The room is crowned with gilded woodwork. The walls are a white and yellow fresco, a Queen's wedding party traveling across a fertile valley toward a grand palace, were a King awaits in a golden chariot lead by five golden stallions.

Mochlos has entered the King's apartment. There is more gold in this one room than I have seen in my entire life, he thinks, and I have been to the Palace of Knossos. Yet here I will sleep! Here I will be High Priest of the Temple of Rah! Unless I am proven a fraud. Which of course I am. Are not all high priests frauds of some sort or another? Is not all magick fraud, to a degree? A confidence game? We believe our own lies, and convince others to believe them. My life, now, rests in the hands of an imbecile. A demented boy who can barely speak, who thinks like a wild animal. They expect him to replenish their valley, which is simply over-farmed and barren. There is no act of nature that can accomplish this, much less can a wizard and his idiot.

"Sir, there is the tower yet to show you, and it grows late. I would not want to be the cause of your missing your evening oblations." Nipu stands in the doorway, waiting for Mochlos to follow him out of the King's suite. "There are two entrances to the tower. The exterior stairs, and this." They have reached the end of the hall, where a stairwell rounds to the left, spiraling up to the fourth level of the building and the tower.

The stairwell enters onto the center of a clean white space. The area is empty of furnishings, and a slave is repainting a mural on the circular wall of the room. On the far wall the sky god, Enlil, stands on a mountain and blows his golden breath down onto a lush plain of waving barley. In the next segment of the mural, the eastern wall, Enlil opens the crust of the earth with a great hoe, and men spring forth from the opening. Mochos turns to follow the mural to the south wall, where the god impales his consort, Ninlil, with an enormous phallus, and to the west, where Enlil falls toward the underworld, banished from heaven for the rape.

"The previous occupant kept his valuables here but as you see, the space is perfect for the worship of a god of agriculture," says Nipu. Mochlos nods, turning about one more time to take in the circular story.

"How interesting. The walls here curve, yet the exterior of the tower is rectangular."

"In Babylon, it is believed that it is best to give ones gods a circular area in which to live. The curved walls are meant to mirror their heavenly home, which is, of course, infinite."

Well, thinks Mochlos. Clearly the Moon has little to do with abundance here in Babylon. Have they no knowledge of her influence on earthly things? Have they, being inland as they are, not noticed that she rules the tides? This is a backward, ill-informed people. Astounding that they have come so far, culturally, as they have. "This god, what is his name?" he asks aloud.

"This is Enlil, god of agriculture," responds Nipu.

"This god, Enlil, does he not have a temple of his own in Babylon?" Mochlos has crossed the room to peer behind a blue and gold embroidered drape that hides an aperture in the north wall. A smaller room, barely large enough to lie down in, hides behind the drape. Perfect for the tools of my trade, thinks the priest.

"He does, however," Nipu pauses, "I fear that his High Priest has not found favor with his god. As you have by now heard, our soil is depleted, and crops are poor. Some believe that Enlil has salted the land with his tears, so tiresome does he find the priest's worship and sacrifice." Nipu shakes his head. "I do not think the King will tolerate this priest much longer if things do not change soon."

"This will be rectified," says Mochlos confidently, though his stomach clenches at the thought of his fate, should his own magic fail to solve the King's problems. "And now you must leave me to my prayers, Nipu. Have our things brought up to the rooms you showed us, and have a slave bring me up the trunk I carried on my lap in the litter. I will need what is in it for my evening oblations."

When Nipu has gone, Mochlos turns to Awiti. "Well, child, it is either the most stunning luck, or the worst, that we have come to this city with our Rah at a time like this."

"We must be like the fishes, Sir," Awiti smiles weakly. "We must swim, and swim well, or we will sink, and feed the hungry beneath us."

Akintunde is under guard in the Wing of Commerce on the night he is to return to the fork of the river to make a report to the assassin's messenger. The girl slave from Punt has brought him meat and milk for the leopard cub, which he has named Themba, in honor of his friend, the cheetah. The cub is growing strong, and is already twice the size it was when he rescued it. Tonight, the girl has brought him something else, something from the land of his birth, something to give him strength and to keep him safe. In a basket of clean linens, she has wrapped the tooth of a lion. It is a precious gift, but Akintunde has no way of thanking her. She can only leave the basket at his door, at the feet of the guard who watches him. When she is gone, the guard allows Akintunde to come out to take the basket of linen.

No one has made any decision about the cub. Indeed, no

one has broached the subject. The stigma, that it is a 'gift' from the Wolf of Amega, follows it wherever Akintunde takes it. He is allowed to give it full access to a small garden courtyard behind the Wing of Commerce, which is conveniently adjacent to the room he is held in. Although no one has made provisions for its care, Akintunde is given a robust helping of meat with his evening meal and he suspects he is expected to share it with the cub, if he chooses. Even so, the girl from Punt has been diligent in providing Akintunde with fresh, raw poultry for the kitten, as well as goat's milk, tucked inside the linen basket.

That the house slave should come so frequently with fresh linen has not occurred to the guard, as they work in shifts, and thus far she has been careful to come at different times of day, avoiding suspicion.

But one day, playing on the floor with the cub, Akintunde hears a commotion down the hall.

"You have a visitor," says the guard at the door. "Get to your feet and present yourself properly to the Princess of Babylon."

Akintunde is barely on his feet when a miasma of gold and green silk glides through his chamber door. The girl is young, perhaps not even his age, and delicate. Her face is veiled but for her eyes, which are extraordinary: large, tip-tilted, the color of honey.

Akintunde is back on his wrists and knees again in a full bow almost instantly.

"You are the messenger from Amega," she says, and before he can catch it the cub has romped over to her and she is kneeling to stroke its mottled coat.

"Careful, Madam, the cub is wild," blurts Akintunde, making a lurch across the floor from his knees to grab the kitten. But a guard has planted the blade of his lance in the wood floor. The gleaming edge is an inch from the boy's nose.

And the girl in the silk cloud has picked the beast up to pet its head and cuddle it. "Not so wild, I think," she smiles, stroking the cub's head. The animal has begun to purr, not the soft throb of a housecat, but the deep, earthy burble of a leopard.

"I was told by a trusted advisor that this cub was a gift to Babylon from the Assassin," she says into the cub's fur. "Surely such a clever man must know that my father detests cats, while I, his favored daughter, adore them."

"Surely," answers Akintunde, sure only that he is in the presence of a princess and that he would be wise to agree.

"I am Ephtheta, Princess of Babylon," the girl sets the cub down at her feet, where it pounces an imaginary mole under the hem of her diaphanous skirt. "It must be difficult for you, unable to return to your master with your message as you are, a creature who loves nothing so much as to run, trapped in a room with no company but the kitten you must now wish you had not saved."

Akintunde looks up at the princess with wide eyes. Then, defeated, he sits back on his haunches and drops his chin.

"Yes, Madam, it is difficult for me. It was my first mission, and so great a mission! To bring a message to the King of Babylon from the greatest-" but he stops himself before he insults his hostess.

"Do not be afraid to speak the truth to me, messenger," answers Ephtheta. "Everyone knows what he is, even my father. There is no greater warrior, not even here in Babylon, whether we care to hear it or not. Now tell me, how have you managed to keep this cub alive under these circumstances? No, I see that you would betray someone to answer. But would you not prefer to hand her over to a very stubborn and demanding princess? Who would make very sure that she was cared for properly, given live food to hunt in an open enclosure, until she is ready to be released near the place of her birth?"

"How wise you are, Madam!" answers Akintunde, looking up at the princess with open lips.

"I have made it a hobby to study animals all of my life," answers Ephtheta, bending to pick up the cub. "What is your answer?"

"I would be greatly relieved, Majesty," answers Akintunde. At least in this I will not have failed, he thinks to himself.

Ephtheta turns, the cub in her arms, to face the doorway.

"And as to your mission, messenger," she says softly, "Consider it accomplished. For the man who sent you to Babylon knows my father well enough to know that your failure to return…is his answer."

In the evening of the same day, Rush visits the palace. Tonight, he intends to lay his eyes upon his treasure, his Rah, come what may. Already from the streets he has learned that a laundry maid who works in the Palace Hall of Commerce has been sneaking food to a certain messenger, a boy from Punt, who claims to have brought the Royal House a gift from the Wolf of the Hatti himself. What the gift might be is uncertain, but it eats raw meat. Rush is more than a bit perturbed that this is almost certainly an Anatolian leopard, a great cat exclusive to the Anatolian peninsula, and therefore a creature to be owned solely by the Hatti royals. He has also learned that today the "gift" has been confiscated by the Babylonian princess, Ephtheta, for her own collection.

Not as long as I draw breath, thinks the assassin as he spirits up the palace walls with nothing more than an iron hook and a rope. The House of Samsu-titana will not own a beast who represents the identity of the Hatti kingdom! I will dispose of it tonight, and the princess may wear its hide in the morning.

The boy must have come across a cub in distress and taken pity on it, thinks Rush, entering the palace through a laundry window on the southwestern corner. Then, in Babylon, he found he had no means of explaining the creature, and he found himself embellishing on his master's message, and offering the whelp as a gift!

Bed sheets dry on ropes traversing the low ceiling of the laundry, and Rush moves between them silently. A sleeping guard is muffled with a pillowcase and neatly garroted as Rush makes his way toward the door.

But did I not say, 'tell him exactly this, no more, no less?' Pah, what must a Punt boy think of an Anatolian leopard? He was raised among lions. Two more guards are felled in the hall. Rush removes their daggers, drives them to their hilts into the men's bellies, and moves on. The distinct smell of hay takes him through a second doorway, down a long, dark hall which opens onto a dirt floor. In the dark, Rush can make out only the lamps that remain lit on the far side of the indoor arena.

What is far more disconcerting to him than the story of the leopard is the news that the little grain god from Crete was struck by the Palace Stable Master this morning and taken to the surgeon with a bloodied ear. No one has seen him since, and as he is usually quite evident in the palace, his absence is disturbing.

But it started here, thinks Rush, and so here is where I begin.

Hatu-Hadu is sound asleep in his room off the indoor arena when the sound of his own bone breaking wakes him before the pain finds his brain.

A hand the size of a plate is slapped over his mouth and nose before he can scream. His whip hand is hanging useless, an appendage at the end of a limb that has been snapped over the knee of a huge black monstrosity wrapped in muslin like a mummy and breathing heavy like an enraged bear. But even more terrifying is the sense that he cannot take a breath. His starving lungs quickly begin to burn.

"One sound, and I crush your gullet," breathes the horror through the muslin strips that cover its mouth.

Hatu-Hadu manages to nod 'yes' under the enormous paw and his face is released.

"You will never raise a whip again, Stable Master, for this elbow is shattered, and you are not fool enough, though you are a fool, to see what happens to the other if you so much as look at as whip again so long as you live. And you *will* live. You will live to see me take Babylon, and everything of value within it, before I spit it out again like the poisonous pit of a ripe peach."

Rush is holding Hatu-Hadu's face firmly in place with the hand that had been cutting off his air. With the other he begins carving his unique signature under the man's left eye. Hatu-Hadu, his shattered elbow a throbbing agony, clenches his teeth against the moan that is forcing its way out of his throat. The Wolf, he thinks through the thick blanket of pain that is making him faint. It is the Wolf of the Hatti. No one lives...and yet he says I will...

"You will live," continues Rush, his one exposed eye narrowed as he contemplates his work, "And you will pray to every Babylonian god you can think of that my little cat bears no scar from your work. And while you are praying, day and night, night and day, you will be my puppet. And when Babylon needs horsemen, Babylon will have none. My little puppet will see to it." Rush, finished with his incision, flicks the pea sized bit of flesh he has carved from the man's face off his dagger and holsters the weapon. He gives the man's chin a shake. "Yes?"

"Y-y-ess," whispers Hatu-Hadu. "As you say," he swallows, desperate to remain conscious though the pain in his arm threatens to black him out. "I...am your ...s...servant," he manages, and he is gone.

Rush heaves himself off the man's body. The broken limb falls off the side of the mattress at a gruesome angle. "Better have that looked at," Rush growls, turning to find his way to the door.

Rush moves through the palace with the stealth of a wolf, felling guards strategically. It is his wish to leave his alarming signature, for it to be known that the Great Wolf of the Hatti has been padding through the very bowels of his enemy's kingdom. In the morning he will revisit the place as Ameg, the Merchant of Knossos, and watch the palace shiver and gape in confusion and horror at his night's work.

He has no difficulty finding the entertainer's hall, for the palace's open air theater is in the north eastern quadrant, and it takes little effort to extrapolate that the skene must be the long flank of the building extending from the far end of the stage. Rush moves toward his mark, taking the path Rah took less than a fortnight ago to meet his new troupe. He crosses the stage on the skywalk above, stops a moment to look down and memorize the lay out, the whereabouts of the King's seat, then continues through the double doors at the far end of the catwalk and slips through.

There are no guards in the entertainer's wing. Down the hall the snores of the performers, most of whom have been pushed to their limits these last weeks by a certain newcomer, are the only sounds. Rush slips past door after door, listening. He is nearly at the end of the hall when he hears what he has been keening for: the soft, kittenish purr of the sleeping Rah.

Horus awakens to the sensation of asphyxiation. His kohl rimmed eyes fly open, and when his eyes adjust to the darkness, he sees one sad black orb, heavily lashed, looking down into his with all of the compassion of a shark. Two polar emotions crash together like cymbals in his breast as the thing speaks.

"One sound, and I open your throat." The burly voice is muffled behind the muslin strips of the monster's headdress and his thick Hittite vowels, but Horus understands the command. He nods his head furiously, and the great, warm palm is removed. Just as suddenly, the glitter of a silver bladed dagger replaces it.

"You are too silly to kill," says the beast, and the onyx eye flits downward over Horus' prone body. He is wearing a sheer, salmon pink bed dress tonight and his orangey hair springs in corkscrews from his head in every direction. For an instant he feels the twinge of embarrassment. I should have worn the pale blue chemise, he thinks, and a sleeping cap to hide these awful, kinky curls.

"Where is the surgeon?" Growls Rush, tightening his fist on the clothing at Horus' breast. His hand is heavy and hot, and Horus' looks down at the dark hair rising along the powerful wrist. He swallows a bolt of craving to touch it, tears his eyes away and looks up into the eye of the assassin.

"He has taken a bed in the next room, Sir, to be nearby should the Rah awaken," Horus whispers conspiratorially, and nods toward Rah's bed on the far side of the room.

The shark eye peers at him.

"The ear is nicely stitched," responds the black brute warily. "What need has he to remain with the boy?"

"Sir," answers Horus carefully, "The Rah has not awakened since the surgeon treated him." When the beast makes no effort to interrupt him he continues, looking over at the boy's mattress. "He is quite self-possessed, you know, quite a handful. Not at all as pretty in manner as he is in body. Quite cat like, all spit and snarl. Well, I myself am good with cats, big and small, and though I am only a magician, I suppose this is why he was given to me to keep an eye on. All the same, he has created quite a stir-'

"Get to the point, fop," rumbles Rush.

"Yes, Sir! Well he simply would not allow the man to stitch him up, you know, and so the surgeon gave him a sedative. The dreaming tea-"

"Dreaming tea?"

"Yes, Sir, and hasn't awakened from it. They say the god he entertains has left him, lost in the land of dreams, in the kingdom of Upelluri."

Horus stops himself from saying more. The monster's head has dropped.

"No."

Silence. The crow of a cock across the river. Horus can hear his own blood beating in his ears.

"No, I will not lose you to this," says Rush, lifting his head to see that the dawn is rising in the east window over Rah's head. In its dim glow he can make out the boy's form under the crisp white linens. He would never sleep under a linen, thinks Rush, and never on his back like that, his head on a pillow. What is wrong with me that I did not see it myself? It was the ear. I was too fascinated by it. That bit of flesh, laced like a doeskin boot.

And the missing pearl.

Rush turns his attention back to the magician. "Who am I?" he says suddenly, in Greek.

Horus blinks. He works the muscles in his throat, wets his lips, but makes no answer.

"Wolf got your tongue, cat man?" even behind the mask the smile is evident.

"You... are....the W-wolf...." Says Horus warily. "The Amegan."

"One and the same," sneers Rush, rising to his feet. "And you are still a fop, and so I will not mar your painted face with the Tear of the Bull, for you are not man enough to wear it, even in death. Therefore live, and watch over my little cat until

I return."

"Watch? Oh, but I have, Master, I watch over him like a hen-"

"Yes, you are like his Aros, aren't you? But would you take my blade for him, like his Aros would have? What strange packages bravery can mask itself in." Rush touches the magician's lip with his thumb, brushes it roughly. "You rouge your lips? Why do you want to look like a woman, magician? Are you not made like a man?"

"I am, yes," answers Horus, suppressing the urge to lick that electric thumb. What is wrong with me? he thinks. This is the Terror! But to Rush he only mutters, "How I wish that I were not. For I have a woman's heart."

"Well, Man-who-is-a-woman, I will tell you this. A woman's heart is fiercer. And so watch that cub for me, like he was your own. Let him come to no further harm, and do not leave his side, and you will be rewarded." Rush is at the window before Horus finds the strength to rise onto his elbows in his bed.

"Master, what should I say? Shall I keep your visit secret?" he whispers.

Rush looks back at him. In the warming dawn glow, the exposed eye is a dagger. Horus starts. My gods, he thinks, that monster was just upon me!

A chorus of screams in the hall answers his question. He looks to the door, and when he returns his eyes to the window, the assassin is gone.

"Fourteen guards, two slaves." The King is pacing across his elaborately tiled balcony. Today his hip aches from an old axe wound, a wound he took in his first battle, and he walks haltingly, leaning on his scepter every few strides. "And a cat."

"Not a cat, Your Glory, but the very animal he is said to have given Babylon as a gift!" responds Mefali, whose unfortunate duty it was this morning to advise the King of the carnage that has taken place in the palace while he slept.

"Well," grumbles Samsu-titana, "Had he not garroted them, I would have staked them myself. For letting him in." He turns to his valet. "Bring me wine!"

"A palace guard, no matter how heroic, cannot be expected to stop the Amegan, Your Greatness," responds Mefali.

"Perhaps not," answers the King wearily, "But they'd have been staked all the same. And the cat is dead also?" he turns to swipe an enormous goblet of wine from his valet's serving plate.

"The cat is gone, my Lord. Whether it escaped from its enclosure, as the princess believes, or was slain, we do not know."

"No," sighs the King, limping to his couch to sit down heavily. "Bring my daughter here to me at once."

The pounding of the old man's fist on her outer door awakens Princess Ephtheta.

"Your father summons you, Princess!" she hears her hand maid hiss from her visiting room.

"Very well, Yesh," answers Ephtheta dreamily, rubbing her eyes with her fists. "Tell Mefali I will be down just as soon as I am decent." She lifts herself on her elbows, and for a moment, reaches down to the foot of her bed, where the cub was curled, and sleeping, before her visitor changed her world forever.

"Oh, he is a dream, Luter," she smiles, cradling the cat who has leapt up to greet her with his morning sniff. The cat struggles from her grasp, unaccustomed to her passionate embrace, and trots to the foot of the mattress to lick its paw.

"A man to make all others look like imitations." Giggling to herself, she remembers the encounter, now so firmly imbedded in her psyche. She had been sitting up in bed, wheezing, and contemplating waking Yesh, for the sickness was upon her, when a darkness eclipsed the predawn window. She knew instantly who it was. Could there be doubt? Just as the legend described him, wrapped in strips of black muslin like a dead Egyptian king gone mad, with shoulders wide as an elm, a long, nipped torso, the legs of a messenger, and that one pitch diamond of an eye. She startled him in her wakefulness, in her breathlessness. Her fist was clenched to her chest as she fought to drag air into her narrowing lungs, and as she looked up at the man, she saw that eye widen, then soften.

He was instantly on her. Pressing her shoulders back down onto her mattress, he quickly pulled the mask from his disguise and whispered in a delicious Hittite baritone that she would never, ever forget, "Be still now, and do not fight, but take my breath." And then his mouth was on hers, lips that tasted faintly of cinnamon, strong, soft, moist, delicious lips, and air, air as sweet as life itself, was being forced down into her stubborn lungs, opening them, filling them.

And she melted, every muscle, every sinew, became unstrung like an untuned lute, and there was no struggle, he was doing it all for her, breathing for her, filling her with air, filling her with life. And as he drew back she raised herself and slipped her arms around his neck, stretching up to taste again the mouth that saved her. And he let her. His black brows forming a quizzical peek over those sad, softened eyes, he let her. She nuzzled his mouth, pushed her tongue past his lips, hungry. He released his jaw, cautious, and she slipped the tip of her tongue into his mouth to tickle his own.

"M-m-m…ore," she heard herself whimper before he pushed her down again, his arms outstretched so that the dawn light shone in her eyes.

His face, an extraordinary face, a handsome face but stern, fierce, determined, fatherly, closed in a frown. The brows dropped, the jaw clenched.

"Daughter of my enemy," he whispered through his teeth. "An asthmatic," and he was on his feet, and the cub was scooped up in one hand and tucked under his arm.

"No!" she cried, but whether it was for the loss of the cub or the wolf, she would never truly know.

An hour later the Princess stands before her father in his visiting room. This is a more informal setting than the throne room, and she sits to his right, on a couch, her handmaid, Yesh standing quietly behind her, while he paces in front of his own couch, back and forth, the length of the windows overlooking the People's Court.

He limps today, thinks Ephtheta. Poor father, no longer the warrior he was, he looks like his enemies' advertisement.

He should not limp so in front of his servants, his staff. People will think him weak. I wonder what he would think if he knew that the man he credits with that wound, the man he hates so violently, forced breath into his daughter's lungs last night, and then withdrew with her leopard, and her heart, tucked under his arm?

But to her father she says, "My sovereign, he is already here, as you say. He has marked each of his victims with the Tear of the Bull. Yet you live. I live. Even the Stable Master lives. It would seem even to me, a mere child, a simple-minded girl at that, that the Wolf if the Hatti has no intention to slaughter either one of us."

King Samsu-titana leans on his scepter. His hip is an agony today. Your teeth are in my hide, he thinks to himself. But to his daughter he says, "My child, my seed. You are no simple-minded girl. God help him if he takes you. You will bend his brain like a baker's knot."

"You flatter me, Father," smile Ephtheta, though she cannot wait to try it. He was already quite confused, I think, she muses, unconsciously bringing her hand up to cover her smile, though she wears her veil. Even her father is denied the sight of her lips, but the Wolf took them, like they were already his.

"You are peculiar today, daughter. Here is a terror, loosed upon our Palace, coming and going as he wishes, slaying and marking my guards, stealing his own 'gift' back but leaving his god-slave untouched, and yet you have a tickle of mirth in your eye I have not seen since you sat upon your mother's knee, hand feeding that little monkey I found for you in my visit to Heliopolis."

"I am grateful you are unharmed, My King," responds Ephtheta, tempering her expression, and making every effort to dull the gleam in her eyes. When she realizes this is impossible this morning, she lowers them. "And myself."

"Do you think that beast could have walked right into my bed chamber and taken my head? I, the King of Babylon the Great?" Samsu-titana slams down his scepter, his quick temper lost. "Is that what my own daughter thinks?" His raised voice brings three guards into the room, with looks of amazement on their faces. They have never heard the King speak to his favorite above a near whisper.

Ephtheta raises her eyes slowly. When she looks into her father's face she is for a moment speechless. There is something there that she has never seen before. King Samsu-titana is more frightened than angry.

"Of course not, My King," she answers gently. "You are the most powerful man in all of Asia."

But in that instant, both understand that this is no longer a certainty.

"He does not wake, Majesty," says the surgeon carefully. He kneels before King Samsu-titana, his fist at his breast, his head bowed. On his face is a poultice, the cake of blue mud cracking with the movement of his lips. Beneath the poultice, the Tear of the Bull stings like a wasp.

"Who is responsible for this?" demands the King, springing to his feet from his couch for the third time that day.

"He was given the dreaming tea," answers the surgeon. "He would not allow me to stitch his ear and there was no other choice but to send him to Upelluri while I sutured it." He looks up, warily. "I have never known a patient to fail to wake, Lord," he adds.

"Indeed, you have never sent a god-slave to Upelluri!" booms the King. "Do you know what you have done, surgeon?"

"My Lord, how could I know-" begins the surgeon.

"Were you not informed that the boy is the property of the Wolf of the Hatti? A god slave, made by a high priest on the lost island nation of the Minoans? And did it not occur to you, surgeon, that the spirit of a god, trapped by a master priest in a human form, would not willingly return to that body if released to Upelluri?"

"He was injured, Lord, and I was told he must not be marred-"

"Do you know what you have done? That the Wolf of the Hatti has vowed to take Babylon, to take my *daughter*, if a hair on that boy's lip is plucked?" shouts the King at the top of his lungs. "Guards, put this man in the pit! And send a messenger immediately to the priest, Mochlos! Perhaps he will know how to seduce the spirit of a god back into the world of men. Send for him at once!" The King slams the butt of his scepter down on the tile floor at his feet.

"Your Greatness, the Merchant, Ameg, his new bride, Tiamat and son, Makkan."

"Majesty," Rush makes the pretense of a formal bow, hindered by the mass of his own belly, which has grown since his days on Crete. In fact, there is an entire duck down featherbed beneath his brilliant blue-green silk today. Even so, the assassin might easily execute a bow, were his feelings for this King so inclined. But it is his hatred that keeps his back straight, and it is all he can do to keep from breaking the man's fingers, twisting his arm behind him and cutting his throat with his ankle weapon when he offers his seal ring to be kissed.

The 'merchant' clumsily clicks his teeth on the ring. He will not hand me that thing again, thinks Rush, without losing it.

The merchant looks about the King's visiting room, rudely indicating that he would sit. I'll not stand here like a donkey while he lounges on his couch, thinks the assassin. King or no, though today I am his guest. I am a dog on a chain, and want nothing more than to leap, and bring my jaws down on the throat that hides behind that idiotic Amorite beard.

The King waves a hand at a slave, his face belying measured patience. Instantly, two elaborate ottomans are carried into the room and placed before the merchant and his wife.

Rush seats himself with a 'huff'. He is breathing loudly, a glutton with a permanent wheeze resulting from the effort of simple movement. He nods at Tiamat, who curtseys to the king, takes Makkan's hand, and sits him down beside her on her ottoman.

"I understand you lost your home on 'Crete, and, regrettably, your wife and sons," says the King as two servants carry in a low table covered with a plethora of gastronomic dainties for the guests.

"Yes, Lord," responds Rush, his eyes opening wide at the

elaborate setting of treats. Without hesitation he palms a handful of stuffed dates and shoves them into his mouth. Talking through the treats, he continues. "Crete... that is, the island you here in Babylon call Crete... is no more. Rather, what is left is uninhabitable. My home was destroyed, my dear wife and my two sons, twins they were, gone. I myself was out to sea, and escaped the disaster. I am estranged from my Greek wife and daughters many years now, and so I have determined to make Babylon my home."

"Yes, and quickly took a new wife I see," muses the King. "But how is it you have a son of eight years here in Syria?" His eyes narrow at the merchant.

"Ah hah!" spits Rush through a mouthful of sugared hazelnuts. "You catch me out, Lord! Yes, as I am a frequent trader in Syria, I have long ago adopted the customs of your people. The liberal approach to marriage is best for a man like me, one of," he opens his arms to expose his girth more readily, "large appetites! Haha! My son is a product of such.... enthusiasm for your broadminded ways!"

"So you are not the mother?" the King regards Tiamat.

"I am, Lord," Tiamat squeaks, her head swimming with the notion that not a moon ago she was hanging by her wrists in a brothel, about to be carved up by a butcher, and today sits before the King of Babylon beside the man who saved her.

"I see," says the King. "An early start," he adds, unruffled. "And your purpose here at the palace?" he returns his attention to Rush.

"Highness, I am surprised you have not heard of me before now. I have done considerable business in Babylon. I am in silks and fabrics, mostly, as well as precious gems. My merchandise is quite celebrated in other parts of the world and my name is a household word all along the Mediterranean coastline."

"I see," the King begins, still unsure of the merchant's reason for visiting the palace. Does he mean to sell his silks to the royal dress maker? This is a matter for the Secretary of Commerce, and well he should know it. Irritated, Samsu-titana looks over Rush's capped head at his Royal Guard Captain, and sees that the man has drawn his lips back in a firm line.

His cheeks bulging with the honeyed fig and nut roll he has just stuffed into his mouth, Rush continues. "However, be your ignorance of my business acumen as it may, I did not come to the Palace on this particular day to discuss the needs of your house hold wardrobe, though of course I could not help but notice that your guards' are a bit frayed about the edges, not to mention your palace slaves," he looks behind him at the guard by the door, the man who led him in, and gives him a menacing once-over. The guard's eyes grow wide. Then he collects himself, huffs, and straightening his shoulders, disregards the fat merchant's insolence and pins his gaze to the tapestry behind the King's settee.

"I am here because you have something that is mine," smiles Rush jovially, enjoying the disbelief and exasperation that has blackened the King's face.

This is more than Petuk can bear. The Captain of the Guard steps forward, the point of his spear suddenly at the merchant's throat.

Rush looks up at the man calmly, and placing one manicured finger on the hilt of the weapon, moves it with a dandy's touch off his jugular. What the King sees is an effeminate movement, and the jewel encrusted crown of the merchant's cap. What Petuk sees is the black death lurking in a frustrated assassin's eye. Petuk blinks and steps back, disconcerted.

Now Rush turns to the King, having had sufficient pause to rearrange his face into a doughy pooch by digging his chin into his chest and lifting his shoulders just so. He has played Ameg a thousand times, he reminds himself, and except for his hatred of this King, he can do it once more.

"Sir, you offend your sovereign," pipes the tallest of the three royal advisors who stand to the right of their ruler's couch in a cluster, like a batch of addled hens.

Beneath the featherbed the assassin takes a long, even breath. *My* sovereign, he thinks, would be on his way here in a sack, the victim of the honorless dogs you call an army, were it for you. But to the advisor Rush only lifts a hand and then places it politely on his breast and nods. A seated bow, hardly an appropriate apology, but an apology none the less.

"Forgive me, Lord. I am wise only in the ways of trade. As a man, I am a bit of a fool, I admit, and have never properly learned the manners of the great ones I serve. What I mean to say is that your new acquisition, the god slave from Crete, is in fact, my property."

The King sits up on his couch. He waves Petuk back to his post at the door, looks to his advisors with fury brewing in his grey eyes, and waits.

The taller advisor turns to his associates, and seeing that he is on his own, steps forward to confront the merchant himself.

"We were told that the boy was the property of the Amegan Wolf," he says through his teeth.

"Ah," nods Rush, then casually reaches for a plate of cinnamon-rolled cheese puffs. He palms two, offers the plate to his wife and son who blink at the balls of spiced dough like spooked rabbits before taking them from his hand and making a brave attempt to nibble on them without choking.

"The monster has threatened to take the City if we do not return him, and yet what slave could escape him? We believe he has sent him here as a ruse to excuse an attack when we are at our weakest."

Almost as soon as the man utters the word he steps back in horror of his own tongue. The King smashes the royal scepter down on the tile floor and stands.

"Enough!"

"Forgive me Majesty," sputters the advisor, though he knows full well the unlikeliness of this.

"Will you tell the world of our disadvantage by way of a merchant?" the King bellows. "I will have your tongue for that!"

No, thinks Rush. I need that tongue right where it is.

"Majesty," he raises a hand in protest. "I am in a loathsome position here, I see. For by some bizarre set of circumstances I seem to know more about your enemies than your own spies do. Your 'situation' here in Babylon is quite common knowledge elsewhere in the world. Why, I was told of it myself by the very man you accuse of sending you my slave!"

The King, who was in the process of reseating himself when the merchant began his speech, rises to his feet a second time.

"What are you saying man? You have been in communication with the Wolf of the Hatti?" He brings his hands up to his face, then remembers himself and clenches his fists at his side.

"He is a very good customer, indeed, Sir," responds the assassin, "and a man of fine tastes I might add. He buys gems for his wife, who is quite a talented jeweler. Yes, in fact that marvelous pearl earring you have no doubt noticed on the boy-god, that is her work. I found that pearl in the Orient. Priceless," he adds, turning about to give the Captain of the Guard a strange, cold glance. Without knowing why, Petuk shivers, straightens his back, and fixes his gaze on the wall behind the King's head once more.

"You have dealings with the assassin?" whispers the King, seating himself once again. "And how is it he then claims the boy-god to be his? When you say in fact the creature is yours?"

"Well, he has not completed payment, has he? This is a priceless thing, a god slave from the extinguished land of the Minoan kingdom. The very last, and best of them. I was there, King Samsu-titana, I saw what occurred on that island paradise not seven moons ago. This boy, once he was made from a northern slave off the boats of the slave trader, Kephas, he brought great prosperity to Knossos, yes, it is true, but did you not know that he was made a target of the assassin by the Southern King, Cyrus, who envied the North King's fortune? Cyrus was in grave drought that year, hard to believe it was only last summer. Cyrus purchased the assassin's skills to kill the boy, but the assassin could not accomplish the task. Imagine, the Great Wolf, the scourge of the Aegean, unable to take a blade to a mere boy, such was the magic of the child."

Rush purses his lips, licks them, takes a deep, even breath under his feather belly, steadies himself. I will not lose my identity now, he thinks, I will not allow myself to think of that day. I am Ameg, a fat flatulent fancy, telling a story. I do not tell my own story. I do not tell of my own failure. I feel no fury. My blood is cool.

Nevertheless, the eyes of the merchant, Ameg, seem to the King to grow hot, like black marbles, as he continues.

"I knew nothing of this," murmurs the King, who leans now at the edge of his settee waiting for more.

"Indeed, it is all over the Great Sea. How is it your informants have not reported it to you? There can hardly be a more urgent message, Your Greatness, than the story of the boy god, the Rah."

"You say the assassin, the Wolf, he himself could not kill the boy on assignment from the Minoan King, Cyrus?"

"He could not," sighs Rush, turning his attention once again to the table of confections and palming a handful of honeyed hazelnuts. Popping several in his mouth, he continues. "The assassin, being what he is, chose instead to steal the boy. But what he stole, he stole from me! Can you imagine! For I had only recently purchased him in half from the High Priest, Mochlos-"

"He is here! In the city!" cries the tall advisor, who quickly stops himself from saying more when the King turns to give him a dark look.

"He, this priest, came here to the palace only yesterday, claiming he made the god slave on Crete last spring," says King Samsu-titana to Rush.

"He is a slippery fellow," chuckles Ameg, "but in this he told you the truth. I'll warrant he did not tell you that the boy is half mine, however."

"He did not. He mentioned nothing about a sale," responds the King.

"Being a man of the sea, Highness, I was aware of the coming eruption on Thera. As many men of business did, I had been using the island as a gathering place for my commodities. I had barely time to remove the better part of my merchandise before the gods' rage tore the island to bits. I informed the priest to move himself as well from the coast of Crete, and made a bargain that I would take him with me, he and his entire household, for a half share of the boy-god. He agreed."

"And how is it that you did not have the foresight then to

remove your wife and sons from the Minoan Kingdom before the catastrophe?" asks the King, his eyes narrowing.

"Alas, they were not in Knossos at the time. They were in Gornia, staying with relatives. There was simply no time to collect them."

The merchant's demeanor is callous, and King Samsu-titana is suddenly struck with the idea that Ameg may well have left his former life on Crete behind on purpose. He glances over at Tiamat, then Makkan. A pretty girl, an exceptionally beautiful little Amorite boy. Yes, I see what he has done. This is a heartless man. No wonder he does business with the devil.

But to Ameg he says, "Ah, how unfortunate. And yet how fortunate that you had a life here in Babylon waiting for you." The merchant's smile is corrupted by a glint of humor left lingering in his eye. The King continues, "Now, what do you mean, coming to the palace to claim the boy-god as your property. Do you expect us to hand him over to you, when the Wolf has demanded his return to his fortress in Amega? What difference does it make to us whether a merchant and a priest own equal shares in the creature, when the enemy of Babylon demands him for himself? Do we not all know that what the Wolf of Amega takes, by whatever means, is his?"

'Ah, but Lord," responds the merchant, stopping to suck honey from his thumb, "I can be of service to you now that I am here. You see, as long as the assassin understands that the boy is here in my care, and in the care of his priest of course, for he cannot survive without his priest, he will stay his hand. I can assure him that his property is simply on loan, to a beleaguered city, and that, with the proper payment of course, transacted through me, his trusted broker, no harm need come to Babylon. Then, when Babylon is restored by means of the boy's magic, he will be returned, again by me, to the Amegan!" Rush pats his profuse belly and chuckles. "These are truly delicious," he takes another cheese ball and pops it in his mouth.

"You think that our gravest enemy would be willing to loan us a god slave who is capable of restoring our strength? Are you completely daft, man?" blurts one of the two royal advisors who have, as yet, said nothing during this entire exchange.

"Indeed I do, Sir," nods Rush, wiping honey from his lips daintily with a red and gold embroidered linen off the table. "For I know the man. And he will take Babylon when Babylon is fattened, like a calf, and ready for slaughter."

CHAPTER 9

Rah dreams, and in his dream he dances.

Behind the wolf-skin tent of the barbarian soothsayer, he and his twin dance for bread. The old woman stands in the flap doorway, clapping to their rhythm. Around them, the men and women of the tribe have gathered. They laugh and point at the pair, and now and then, someone throws a turnip, a fish, a round of bread at their feet. They will not go hungry today and they are happy. Their happiness lifts them, and they are leaping higher and higher, so high that Ileah's feet no longer touch the ground. She laughs and beckons her brother to join her in a tree, far above the barbarians below. And Rah's spirit follows. It leaves the crowd beneath, leaps into the tree with Ileah, who takes his hand and draws him further and further up into the branches to the clear sky above.

"Stay with me, Alahai," she says, "High above."

"I must return," says the spirit inside him. He speaks clearly, in the language of his parents. His tongue is whole. "I must dance for the King of Babylon. I must save the city from plague."

"You will," she smiles. "But for now, you must remain with me, while the Wolf eats Babylon."

"You say he was given a 'dreaming tea'?" asks Mochlos, stroking his new, salt and pepper beard. It gives me an air of dignity, he thinks to himself, gazing into the small bronze mirror in his hand.

"Yes Holiness," responds the King's messenger, accustomed to calling the many clerics in the city by this title. "A tea to send him to Upelluri, the dream world. None have ever failed to return," he adds, nervously.

Turning to look over the parapet of his third floor apartment, Mochlos sighs at the man's ignorance. I must not despair. I must use this turn of events to my advantage, he thinks. I will not consider that if I cannot awaken the boy my limbs will be hacked off by the carnivorous madman who thinks he owns him, and roasted over a slow fire while I watch. I *will* wake him, and when I do, my supremacy as a priest in this city will be established.

"Yes, well then I do believe your surgeon has never given it to a god slave," he says wearily. "Did he not realize that the spirit I worked miracles to trap in that body is the spirit of a god, the god of abundance, the Minoan Rah? Your surgeon has released him, you see? You have all but undone my work." He raises his hands to his face, cups his cheeks, shakes his head with abject disgust. You are a pack of imbeciles, his body says to the messenger, but I keep my tongue. "I will need the boy here, in the House of Seven Cisterns," he says finally. "This is his temple. Tell the King that the god, Rah, will only return to the land of men with gifts, supplication, prayers, and fasting. The whole of the city must participate. You understand? He must see that he is honored in this city. And," he turns to the messenger with a crafty glint in his eye, "I will need to know the ingredients of that 'dreaming tea' he was give, of course. I cannot be expected to work in the dark."

"But the King has asked you to return to the palace with me," responds the messenger, growing more anxious. "You can then explain this to him yourself."

Mochlos looks the messenger over with annoyance. "I must prepare, fool. Do you think we have time for that? The longer the god is lost in the land of dreams, the less chance we have of seducing him back to the land of men. Now get out of my sight, and bring the boy and the surgeon whose mistake has caused this calamity back here within the hour."

When the messenger is gone, Mochos folds his arms over his chest and leans against the parapet, his back to the Lower Fortress, which hunches against Babylon's north wall like a huge animal, overlooking the Kadingirra Road. To the east the Sacred Pools of the Ninmah Temple glitter in the noon day sun. It is nearly summer, thinks the priest, and I am expected to bring this dying, overworked soil back to life with a boy and a dance. There is no work of man nor nature that can accomplish this.

Rah sleeps, and in his dream he visits the fortress of the Wolf.

He stands on a parapet. It is night, and sheets of rain drive angry clouds across a moon soaked sky. His curls cling to his neck and shoulders. Rivulets of rain run down the fine line of his backbone, soaking his loincloth. I am really hear, this is no dream. I have perspective. I stand here, facing north, and if I turn around the Great Sea will be behind me. I can hear the waves crash against the cliffs. Yet I cannot turn around. I am compelled to move forward, though I do not know my way, off the wall, toward a stone stair, down into the bowels of the beast's lair.

Rah moves, as if on wings, down and down, two levels. He passes a guard making his rounds on the second stair. The guard turns, but ignores him. The he is gliding, ghostlike down a hall, this is Ting Ya's hall! Ting Ya! Why have I come? Where is my mother?

Rah passes through a guarded door. Again, the sentinel ignores him. The door is thick maple wood, and he feels the soul of the old, elegant tree as his being traverses its depth. He cannot see what is ahead, but a warning greets him inside the wood core of the door.

"Be brave, Jin yu!" It is the voice of his mother.

No! No, Ting Ya, do not leave me! Rah's spirit explodes from the lulling core of the maple door. Ting Ya's room is a garden of yellow lilies. The flowers are strewed over the cold tile floor. They sit in vases on every surface. They cover the bed, but for the face of the little Keeper of the Dead. Ting Ya sleeps, and her face is beautiful, even in death. Her long hair is a braid, woven with yellow wild flowers, and lies alongside her diminutive body, reaching the foot of the bed.

"Bad day, Jin yu. Remember what I say."

"Ting Ya!" he hears his own soul scream the name, helpless.

"No look for living in dead body, Jin yu. I be with you always now. Many lives. Always friends."

But he is no longer in the death chamber of the little priestess. He is above the city of Babylon, in a tower that rises high over the surrounding houses. Sheets of rain pound against the roof and damp air fills his lungs. I am here. This is the house of my priest.

"Jin yu," she says again, her voice soft with love, "remember what I say."

Rush returns to his suite at the inn as Ameg, to gather his things. He sends his 'wife' and 'son's' recently purchased wardrobes back to the palace with a servant, but he must find a solution to the problem of the leopard cub before he can join them there. Tiamat and Makkan remain at the palace and are even now being installed in a private guest wing, reserved for royals visiting from other lands, across the palace courtyard, which is immense, but on the same floor as the King's suite of private rooms. The suite suits Rush, for it offers a good view of all three of the southern gates into the city, as well as a view of the river, which bisects the city just west of the palace. The river feeds Babylon, but to Rush it is the whore's greatest weakness, for it forms an ideal point of penetration, both north and south, for an army of expert boatmen.

Ameg has been invited to remain at the palace for as long as the god slave is 'on loan' to Babylon, with the understanding that he will communicate personally with the Amegan Wolf, and, hopefully, delay him from carrying out his threats before the god-slave can be awakened and returned to him.

Alone in his suite of rooms at the inn, Rush releases the cub from his sack and sets a bowl of milk down for it to lap while he removes the gilded robes of his alter ego, unties the featherbed from his waist, and lies down for a nap. He has slept only an hour or two in as many days, and he nods off easily, the cub cuddled against his ribs. He has fixed the door with a trap, a simple rock and leather sling tacked to the jam above which insures that if anyone attempts to open it they will wake him. The door has a sturdy bolt, but he has no intention of using it, no more than he would throw stones in a pond before he settled down to fish.

The afternoon is softening to dusk when a commotion on the floor beneath his own draws him out of his dream of grouse hunting on Crete. Muffled voices rise through the still air as one set of heavy footsteps approaches the window beneath his own.

"Might have left something of value. Rich priest like that."

Thieving maids, thinks Rush, not particularly aroused. But information comes from the most unlikely sources and it is not his habit to miss an opportunity to eavesdrop on the least of it. Pushing the cub aside gently he rolls over to press his ear to the floor. A second voice, this one male.

"Not the door, fool! Up through here...say he's the richest man in all of Syria, spare maybe the King!"

Idiots, thinks Rush. And then, ahh! Idiots! Perfect.

Rush pulls his upper body back onto the mattress and rolls his back to the window. He pulls the sleeping cub against his bare loins, and waits.

He does not have to wait long. The pair of fools clamor up into his window so noisily that he cannot continue to pretend to be sleeping, else his own ruse is realized. He makes a start, rolling over to face the noise, in time to see two ragged ruffians, daggers drawn, standing over him. One shoves the point of his blade up under Rush's throat and is instantly flying over the assassin's broad chest to land on his own head, his arm snapping at the wrist as Rush gives it a twist and a yank before releasing it. The other man has raised his own weapon, intent on plunging it into Rush's breast before the rich merchant cries out for help. Rush back fists the tough's throat, careful not to crush the windpipe, and takes the knife as the man wobbles backward, clutching his gullet.

"Piece of pig shit, this," he spits, tossing it out his open window. "Couldn't open a linen bag with it, let alone a man."

Rush sits up in the bed, strokes the waking kitten off-handedly, lifts himself to his feet to find his dressing gown. He rifles through his assassin's bag, which rests on a low stool beside the moaning man with the splintered wrist. The man's dagger is lying in the dying light, inches from his face. Rush watches the man lift himself off the floor with his good arm and grab for the knife. He makes a heroic effort, palming it and drawing back to slice the assassin's Achilles, before Rush stomps his face.

"My dose!" The man moans, drawing his good hand to his smashed and bloodied proboscis.

Rush slips the yellow dressing gown over his broad shoulders, looks about for his featherbed belly. The other man is scrabbling to his feet. He makes a rush for the open window, takes the sill in both palms, intent on flinging his body out and down two stories onto the shrubbery below. He is caught by the back of his tunic and tossed over the bed and onto his miserable companion, who curses when his flying weight smashes his face, nose first, onto the floor.

"Toss me that pig shit blade," mumbles Rush, tying his feather belly on under his gown. He is slipping his feet into a pair of expensive, silk and pearl-beaded slippers as the man with the injured larynx rises to his feet and begins backing toward the door.

"What did I say?" asks Rush, adjusting his sash over his newly acquired belly.

The man is silent.

"Did I say, sneak out my door?"

The man blinks, looks down at his friend, who is crawling to his feet.

"Did I say, look at your friend?"

The man looks across the room at Rush, shakes his head.

"You want to see if you can make it out that door before I put the pig shit blade I asked you for in your back?"

The man swallows, looks down at the dagger at his feet, looks up at Rush.

"I have yet to meet a man I have had to give an order to twice, who still owns both his ears," says Rush, as he expertly twists his braid into a bun with one hand and extracts his merchant's cap from the paws of the cub, with the other.

"You ...*want* me to pick up the knife?" the man squeaks, finally.

"You have just lost one ear," answers Rush, giving the kitten a scratch on the head as he moves across the room. The thief drops to his knees, grabs the dagger by the blade, tosses it lightly, handle up, into Rush's waiting hand. "Good, just the one then," says Rush, and before the man has risen to his feet, the better part of his left ear has been sliced off.

Waves of blood gush forth from the stub of the ear. The man screams, cupping his hand over the wound as Rush tosses the Amorite dagger out the window. "Pig shit Amorite weapon. Made by mules. Couldn't cut a roast." The man with the shattered wrist is looking up from the floor in horror, still moaning with his good hand cupped over his bloodied nose. Rush kicks him in the forehead and he somersaults into a heap against the wall.

"You are less than useless to me. A mouth to tell the whole of Babylon who Ameg is. But you," Rush picks up his bag, nods to the man with half an ear, "Will be my mule."

"As you say, Sir!" sobs the man, making yet another attempt to rise.

"Did I say, rise?" asks Rush, taking his attention off the cub, which he has scooped up in his free hand.

The earless man is back on his face in an instant. "No, Sir," he says loudly into the floor.

"Well then, rise," says Rush, and as the man rises gingerly to his knees, he hands him the squirming kitten. "Take this to the priest, Mochlos, at the House of Seven Cisterns. You know it?"

"I do, Sir!" answers the man.

"Tell him only this: 'The biggest rat in Babylon has caught a cat, and he desires that this cat, which is the property of the sovereignty of Hattusha be kept safely, and away from prying eyes, until he comes for it.' You have it?"

"I have it, Sir. The biggest rat-"

"Never mind. Do as I say and you will find the surgeon's assistant to stitch your ear at the priest's house. You'll be a bit lop-sided from now on, but a better listener, I'll warrant."

Rush slips a golden-handled dagger from an ankle holster under his robe and throws it, with exquisite precision, into the eye of the second thief. The man writhes, clawing at the hilt with one hand, then faints. The earless thief draws himself up to his feet, cub pressed against his heaving breast.

"From now on, you are my mule. Need I explain what will happen to you if you fail me, Mule?" asks Rush.

"No, Sir, I will not fail, Sir," says the man, clutching the kitten.

"Your accomplice, downstairs, the maid, she is a sister?"

"My wife, Sir."

"She will wrap that body in a rug-"

"He's not dead, Sir-"

"Irrelevant. In a rug, and have him carted off and tossed in the communal dump."

"Yes, Sir. He-"

"He what?"

"He is my brother, Sir."

"Then do it yourself." Rush takes a step toward the man. "Go." The man flees, taking the window as an exit, and leaving Rush to extract his dagger from his brother's eye, rinse it in a jug of water on the dresser, and return it to the holster at his ankle.

At the House of Seven Cisterns Mochlos the priest is preparing the waking concoction in the tower room. It is a dangerous mixture, meant to thrust the heart of the patient into such a panic as to force the mind to wake, and take control, or die of fright. But there is no other solution to the problem at hand. The 'dreaming tea', as it turns out, was the very worst thing the palace surgeon could have given Rah's epileptic brain, and it has sent the boy into a coma. Brewed from the highly toxic Moonflower, or Angel's Trumpet, as it is called here in Babylon, it was used on Crete by the high priests, with careful precision as to dosage, to sedate victims before the removal of their living hearts in homage to their particular god. Ironically, it is the very substance that Mochlos would have used on Rah the day he was to sacrifice him on Mouth Ida.

Now, with the surgeon's assistant, Kalak, as his helper,

Mochlos can only hope that the antidote they prepare will break the hold of the coma on the boy and bring him back to the land of the living. But the key ingredient, Ma Huang, secured in his days as a High Priest in Knossos from a Chinese trader, could as easily kill him as cure him.

"It will, if it works at all, cause him a complete inability to differentiate reality from fantasy. His heart will race and kick, and he may become violent. His pupils will expand. This is his body fighting the god who has imprisoned him-"

"Upelluri," offers Kalak, who has been sent to the House of Seven Cisterns in the stead of the surgeon, who suffered an inexplicable heart attack this morning in the palace pit. The news was not surprising to Mochlos, who was familiar enough with that particular heart attack, having had it weighed upon his chest on more than one occasion himself.

"Yes, Upelluri. He will be intolerant of light for several days."

"So he will wake?" asks Kalak, who, though Egyptian himself, has a working knowledge of Greek and is quite able to speak to the priest in his native tongue.

"Pray he will," answers Mochlos, and, hearing a commotion at the door three stories below, he quickly covers his mortar and pestle with a cloth, stashes it in the vestibule behind the drape, and motions for Kalak to follow him.

Downstairs in the great entry, Nipu is blocking his view of the intruder, now being hauled out into the front garden by two strong house slaves.

"What is it, Nipu? Do I see blood there?" asks Mochlos, who has become so accustomed to his association of blood with the assassin that the crimson droplets he spies on the polished stone floor at Nipu's feet sends a bolt of alarm up his spine.

"The man's ear has been sliced off, Sir," answers Nipu, closing the door as the man is dragged out.

Oh, dear gods, thinks Mochlos, shoving past Nipu without ceremony and thrusting open the door. "Bring him here!" he shouts at the house slaves. "Bring him to me this instant!"

In the greeting room, the man is deposited on the polished floor. His hand immediately moves up to cover the stump that was his ear, which is now bleeding profusely as a result of his tussle with the house slaves.

"What is your purpose, coming here, man?" spits Mochlos. "Get him a towel, Nipu, quickly!"

"The biggest rat," pants the man, who is out of breath, "biggest rat... in Babylon... Bab...Babylon, has caught a cat, and he desires that this cat," he stops to gulp air, "This cat, which is the property of the sovereignty of Hattusha ...be kept safely.....and away from prying eyes.....until he comes for it." The man collapses onto his elbows. "I lost it," he continues, "In your garden, Sir, when your men grabbed me."

Confused, Mochlos looks to Nipu, "A cat?" he squints, imagining the man carrying the comatose Rah to his door.

"He was carrying a cub of some sort, Sir, spotted, quite wild," answers Nipu, pursing his lips and drawing his elegant, long-fingered hand up to his breast. "It jumped from his arms when the house guards grabbed him."

"That man, Nipu," begins Mochlos, pinching the bridge of his nose with his thumb and forefinger, for his head is throbbing, "That....'rat'...." He shakes his head. "Never mind. Do these walls," he waves a hand at the exterior walls, "Circumvent the yard? The entire yard?" He looks up hopefully.

"The only entry is the iron gate in front, Sir, which is locked at night, but left opened during daylight hours. It is still open, Sir."

"WELL CLOSE IT!" screams Mochlos at the top of his lungs into the faces of the two big slaves who still stand behind the intruder. They blink at him, look at one another, and trot off to close the iron gate.

"Did anyone see this animal escape out the gates?" Mochlos grabs the intruder by his good ear and pulls him, screaming, to his feet. "You? Imbecile? Did the cat escape?"

"I could not see, Sir!" cries the man. "They were holding me, your men!"

"Gates secured, Sir!" cries one of the two house slaves from the front of the yard.

"Do not let anyone in or out without my knowledge, do you hear? NO one! And find that cat!" screams Mochlos, throwing his arms into the air above his head. A nudge from Nipu causes him to turn to take the towel his man has offered him. Grabbing the intruder by his good ear a second time, he presses it against the man's bloody stump.

"Where is Kalak?" mutters Mochlos miserably. He turns to see that the surgeon's assistant is standing in his shadow.

"I am here, Sir," answers the young apprentice.

"Can you do anything with this wound, Kalak? Stitch it? Sterilize it?"

"It needs to be cauterized, Sir," answers the young man. "I will need a fire, and a good blade."

"No blade!" cries the would-be thief from his knees.

"Well, do it then." Mochlos releases the man's ear and drops the towel in his lap. "Keep pressure on it," he says to the thief, and, turning to Nipu, "Give Kalak whatever he requires to patch this fellow up, Nipu, for he is the property of a very dangerous....and stern... master." The priest runs his palms over his bald scalp, then presses the heels of his hands into his eyes.

"Sir? Are you ill?" asks Nipu.

Mochlos lowers his hands, clearing his throat. "Listen to me, both of you," he takes Nipu and Kalak each by a shoulder, "If the cat this man brought with him is not found, *his* suffering now will seem like the bite of a mosquito in comparison to *ours*. You understand?" Both men nod, giving each other a quizzical look.

"Who owns this man, Sir? Who would slice off his own servant's ear and then send him here to you with the property of the Hatti royals?" asks Nipu finally.

"It is the merchant from Knossos! It is Ameg!" cries the thief. "I am his mule! I must return to him!"

Mochlos gazes at the man briefly, then turns to head for the stairs, intent on completing his antidote for the dreaming tea before the palace guards arrive with the comatose Rah. "I have work to do, Nipu. I must wake the Rah. For the King. The fate of this city rests on my shoulders. All you need do is cauterize that ear, and send this man back to the one who cut it off. And find that cat. Or we will none of us have ears... or eyeballs, or skin on our backs, for that matter."

A trifle, that's what you are, thinks Mochlos later that evening, watching the palace guards carry the body of the Rah through the iron gate and up the red brick path to his front door. The cub has not been found, but the silence in the trees gives the priest hope that it is making a living in the veritable jungle that is his front garden.

Mochlos watches as the house guards close and lock the front gate. When the litter bearers reach his front door he leads them through the greeting room. The evening light plays in Rah's curls, turning them safflower and silver, his ridiculous lashes copper.

A trifle, a notion I had, an itch I had to scratch. That is all. A Minoan hoax, a fraud, a scheme. I wanted to cut your pretty white chest apart and hold your heart in my hands, such was my lust for your beauty in agony, and what has it got me, that lust? Satisfaction? When does lust ever end in satisfaction? You are my seal ring and my noose. That which allows me into the grandest society I can imagine, that which every hour threatens my neck. I would be nothing without you. Not even alive, truly, for the assassin would have left me to scorch, my ashes drawn out into the sea to be spat out by fish. Or had I somehow survived the eruption of Thera, somehow been informed early enough to escape without the help of Ameg, I would be wandering, where? Caanan? What would I be? A poisoner? A druggist? Certainly not a priest. And so here I am, chained to you, chained to your corpse, if that is what you've become. A marriage of terrible inconvenience.

Mochlos wipes his damp palms against his robe, leading the litter bearers toward the long, shallow staircase at the back of the receiving room. He waits at the bottom step as the men carefully lift the body of the boy, which is covered completely by a sheer shroud, and lay him on a stretcher, which two men can easily carry up the stairs. Mochlos leads the men up the steps, lifting the hem of his robe like a woman ascending a temple stair for her nuptials. His expensive, pearl-beaded sandals glitter as they peek out from the robe with each step he takes, giving his long, monkey-like feet an elegance they have never enjoyed before. Ah, he is worth it. He is. Every horror I have had to endure. I would be nothing, I would be ash spit out of the mouth of a carp somewhere in the deepest crevice of the floor of the Great Sea. But you, my marvel, my beauty, have brought me here to Babylon to be a rich man, a highly regarded priest! I need only be resourceful, and circumspect, and clever, which, of course, I am. Surely I can bring you back from the land of dreams, though why my emerald has failed to keep you safe escapes me.

Upstairs in the tower room one man lifts Rah's shrouded body from the stretcher and sets him down carefully on a chaise at Mochlos' direction. The men turn to go.

"Not so fast," snaps the priest, lifting the shroud from Rah's head. "Where is his emerald? Where is the stone I charged to protect him?"

"It was removed to stitch his scalp, Sir," answers Kalak. "I suppose it is in the hands of the Palace Guard."

"That emerald had better be safe," snarls Mochlos, examining Rah's stitched scalp, and then noticing the mended ear. "Hog shit! The pearl as well? Where is the pearl earring? Where is his *pearl?*" Mochlos has turned to grab Kalak by both shoulders. His bony fingers dig into the man's flesh like tiger claws.

"I did not know he had a pearl, Sir!" cries Kalak. "It must have been ripped out of his ear when Hatu-Hadu struck him with his whip!"

The litter carriers have been standing by dumbly, listening to this exchange. Mochlos looks over Kalak's shoulder at them, his eyes burning with fury. "*Find it!*" He throws his hands in the air, clasps his head, pacing. "Amorite imbeciles! They strike the Rah like a dog! One hair, ONE, would have cost you your heads. Now," he turns to scream into Kalak's face, "We will be sliced up like bacon," he pushes Kalak aside and cries at the litter men, "And stitched to a pirate's flag in bloody strips to sail the Great Sea! Do you understand?" The men are backing away from the raving priest with wide eyes. "We are the walking, talking dead," continues Mochlos, clutching his head, eyes closed. "We are less alive than the shit that falls from a chicken's ass!" He shoves Kalak toward the stairs. "Find that pearl, Kalak, for your life depends upon it!"

"Yes, Sir!" Kalak has pushed past the stricken litter men to stumble down the stairs as the priest shouts at his back, "Find that pearl! And bring me that emerald crown!"

CHAPTER 10

Rah is sleep here, with Ono, thinks Rah as the man lays his shrouded body down on the sky blue chaise.

"Ono not here, Rah," answers Ting Ya. "Ono still at palace. Rah has temple here, now, here in Babylon."

Rah sees himself stretched out on the chaise under the death veil. The priest, his priest, shouts at the men who have brought him here. Not so fast! The priest snarls, lifting the sheer cloth from Rah's head. Where is his emerald? Where is his pearl?

"They are like ghost," says Rah to Ting Ya, who stands beside him, at the foot of the chaise, observing his own body, and the priest's anger, as if through a curtain of thick air. "Why like ghost?" He turns to Ting Ya, but the little priestess has no face, only a glowing where her face should be.

"They are the dead," answers the little figure beside him, shaking her veiled head. "Everyone here, slave to the body! No discipline. Bad place. Chaos. No one here can deny their body. Always yes, never no. Cannot fast, cannot wait. No discipline."

Rah looks down at his sleeping form. "Rah must dance for King, Ting Ya. Dance to save city from plague."

"Jin yu," answers the diminutive spirit, "Plague already here, in heart of people," she thumps her chest with a fist, making a hollow sound. "People always hungry, until they learn to fast. Rah must sleep, and the people will learn this. Learn to deny body, purify soul. Body is like a lion, always hungry. Always want more. More it has, more it want. Now

133

priest of Rah, he teach this city how to fast. How to deny the body. Plague in this city is appetite of people. Priest of Rah, he tame this lion. Then plague is no more."

Rush has returned to the palace in the guise of Ameg the Merchant.

He arrives in time to intrude upon the installation of yet another foreign guest in the wing across the courtyard from the King's chambers on the third floor.

"Sir, you will find your wife and son in the large suite at the end of the hall," says the flustered Host of Foreign Dignitaries, seeing the obese fop swishing down the hall toward him in his outrageous yellow robes. The Host of Foreign Dignitaries, who has been juggling his duties as Host of Foreign Dignitaries with his secondary occupation as Tutor to the Princess in Royal Decorum since his forced migration to Babylon from Larsa two moons ago, is developing a profound headache. Is it my fault, thinks the Host of Foreign Dignitaries, that my excellent organizing and greeting skills should make me the best choice of Host of Foreign Dignitaries, when I am in fact, being the son of the son of the governor of Larsa, and having been raised amongst impeccably well-mannered and highly educated nobility, though I was but a bastard, far more important to the Babylonian throne as Tutor to the Princess in Royal Decorum? Can the Steward of Employment not find someone else, perhaps not quite as organized or diplomatic in nature to coordinate, install and placate this constant stream of foreign visitors while I focus on the princess' courtly etiquette?

"Just there, Sir, the door on the left," he points over Ameg's shoulder, but the corpulent merchant merely belches behind his ring bedecked-hand and offers the Host a facile smile.

"I had assumed this wing would be ours alone, but I see we will be sharing our quarters?" The dandy makes no effort to disguise his less than manly interest in the tall, striking visitor who stands in the doorway of a small but beautifully appointed chamber.

The stranger makes a crisp bow from the waist at Ameg.

Ah, these military types, thinks the Host of Foreign Dignitaries. Always making military bows at everyone. Utterly inappropriate under the circumstances. Isn't it obvious that the man he offers such respect is nothing more than a graceless, overfed magpie with less experience in the area of warfare than the palace pastry chef?

"Good afternoon, Sir," says the foreigner, over his head, to the merchant.

"And to you, you handsome thing," answers the merchant, his dark eyes shining with obvious, homosexual delight, as he extends a limp, if enormous, palm. "I trust your journey was pleasant?"

"Hardly, Sir," answers the grey-eyed stranger, taking his hand briefly. "I came straight from the coast, returned there first to take stock of my superior's homestead, before I made my way alone, on horseback, to Babylon. I understand the Minoan Rah is here, in the city, Sir."

"Indeed he is, soldier," answers the merchant, stuffing his hands into the folds of his robe and rocking back on his heels. "Indeed he is. And how does your master's home fair? Unruffled by the terrible sea winds that have followed the great eruption, I hope? I myself have only recently come from the coast, and I understand that the weather is unseasonable and peculiar there, making travel by ship especially dangerous."

"The sky is black, Sir," answers the grey-eyed foreigner, "And the winds are strong. But my superior's home is secure, his wife, though she grieves the death of her guest from Crete, is well, and his sons are her comfort."

"Her guest is dead, you say? By what means?" asks Ameg, his dark eyes sharpening on the stranger's with such intensity that the man coughs and takes a small half-step backward.

"She fasted, my Lord," answers Nikolaos of Thrace, losing interest in the ruse. "She fasted for the safe return ... of her son, and his return never came."

A palpable stillness has thickened the air in the hall and the Host of Foreign Dignitaries, always alert to the nuances of emotion in the conversations of others, clears his throat and waves the merchant toward the suite of rooms at the far end of the passage.

"Come, Sir," he says, attempting to draw the big man away, though inexplicably hesitant to touch him or guide him in any way other than with his voice and gesture. There is more to this merchant than meets the eye, he hears himself thinking. "Let me take you to your wife and son."

"When you see your master's wife again, soldier, you will tell her that Ameg the Merchant is sorry for her loss," says Ameg to the newcomer, turning to follow the Host of Foreign Dignitaries to his own suite of rooms. "Truly, truly sorry."

Nikolaos is three days out of Amega. He has spent the past month traveling, first, in the company of the Amegan army, through the foothills of Urgup to Hattusha, then, with only a handful of men, back to Amega in pursuit of the Rah. Having missed Rush by mere hours, he set off for Babylon alone, now in the garb of a Cyrian Palace Guard Captain. His plan is to enter the city as he would have had he never met Rush the Assassin, a loyal subject searching for his lost queen, whom he last saw a day before the fall of Cyrus, when she charged him to follow and to guard the Rah with his life.

A dab of mud and chicken grease is all he needs to hide the Tears of the Bull, but to be sure, he ties a triangle of blue cloth about his head and over his left eye and cheek. If asked, he will say he lost that organ in battle with one of his own soldiers, who intended to flee the city and his queen to pillage the countryside when the quakes came.

On the evening of his arrival, as the palace sleeps, Rush untangles himself from the surprisingly firm grasp of the sleeping Tiamat and slips silently off their bed. This arrangement is not his choice, but is thrust upon him by the Host of Foreign Dignitaries. The suite of three rooms he and his 'family' are assigned has only two beds, one large and obviously marital, and a small, raised pallet in a separate room, meant for a child. Incapable of sleeping clothed, Rush slipped under the feather quilt naked but for his crescent blade and ankle holsters, lay down on his back, as was his habit, and considered the weaknesses of Babylon. There were many, and on this pleasant journey, he had found sleep.

When he awakes three hours later, refreshed but dismayed

by a dream in which he held Samsu-titana's detached and still talking head in his hands, he finds himself quite entwined in the girl's grip, and it is not without considerable effort that he manages to disengage from her without her waking, for she continues, even in sleep, to grasp his side, his arm, his neck, even his thigh, each time he disengages.

Free at last, Rush sits at the end of the bed and pulls on his assassin's leggings.

"M-m-m," murmurs Tiamat, the fingers of her left hand crab walking across the bed in search of his heat.

Rush tosses the feather quilt over her roughly and frowns. Had there not been another bed for the boy, even I could not have escaped these two, he thinks, moving noiselessly past Makkan's door and out into the hall.

Oil lamps illuminate the passage, which is wide enough to bring an ox cart through. The footsteps of a guard patrolling the west hall echo in the otherwise still, damp air. A light rain patters on the roof. Rush waits for the footsteps to recede north, then steals down the corridor to Nikolaos' door. The door is ajar.

"Come in, Master," says the captain in a hush tone. Rush pushes open the door, to see Nikolaos standing, fully dressed, by the courtyard window. "I would have come to you, but did not wish to disturb you," he looks down, "and your new wife."

"Pictured me in congress with a woman for a change, Captain?" Rush smiles, crossing the room to stand beside him. It is a shark's smile, thinks Nikolaos, the last thing you see before it pulls you down into the sea by the leg.

"I- I have not-," he stumbles. Suddenly he is engulfed in the man's embrace. All the air in his lungs is pressed out of him in one monstrous squeeze. Nikolaos grits his teeth, fighting the wild urge to struggle.

"Ah, you are a fine Lieutenant, Niko," says the assassin, his hot breath scalding the younger man's ear. "You do me proud. Poisoned their horses! Hah! Using that pit viper priest like a weapon!" He releases Nikolaos, spins him to face the window, and just as quickly stuns him with a congratulatory thump on the back and a sideways hug as he tucks him under one arm. "There, you see it? Where the light still lingers?" he points across the black courtyard. "There is the princess' chambers. Ephtheta, she is named. Our prize, Niko. Her head," he holds his empty palm under Nikolaos' nose, "Here, and this city is mine without a fight. Done." He gives Nikolaos one more slap across the back, nearly pitching the man through the open porthole.

"You intend to behead the King's daughter?" blurts Nikolaos, squinting up at him. "Here, while we sleep under his roof? Does this befit the Master of Amega?" No sooner has he said it than his face blanches white. "Forgive me, Sir," he swallows the words, head lowered. "I have no right to question-"

"Not and keep your handsome head, Nikolaos of Thrace," hisses Rush, still smiling, but now like a wolf, his black eyes burning into the captains as he grips his shoulder tighter. "Remember whose you are, and by what means you have remained in the land of the living."

"I do, Sir, every day, I remind myself why I... why all of us, are still alive," answers Nikolaos. "But I thought you were a man of war, Rush," Nikolaos, whispers, peering up at the man in the near dark. "Not the kidnapper of children."

"Why so? Did I not kidnap the Rah, and he was younger than this one?" Rush looks out across the courtyard, "One Babylonian girl, or ten thousand of my good men, hmm? You tell me, my cautious Captain, whose blood you would prefer to spill."

For a moment, Nikolaos says nothing. Finally, he asks, "*Will* you kidnap her, Sir?"

"Not I, Nikolaos, not I. I have had enough contact with that minx already. Now you are here, you will do it for me."

"I, Sir? Would such a feat not require a man who can move through the dark like a nightmare? A man well versed in the act of disguise?"

"Not a problem. I have been busy, Captain, whilst you wandered hither and thither across eastern Anatolia like a goat in the rain. I have relieved a certain tanner of his skin, and had a suit made of his hide. I have it here with me. You will collect it tomorrow night on this very hour from my wife. You will put it on, face and all, and then you will visit the princess where she sleeps. She is a sickly thing and will give you no trouble. The shock of your costume will relieve her of her breath, at any rate, for she is an asthmatic. Advise her to silence lest she become my next garment. And spirit her to the House of Seven Cisterns in the Kullab district. Tell the priest to keep her healthy and make her comfortable."

"But you said–"

"Her head, yes. All in good time, Niko. Your best bet with a snake is to cut off the head, yes? All the more, the female, lest she should spawn. But a dead princess is worth nothing. I cannot bargain with her corpse. Therefore keep her breathing, for now."

Rush gives Nikolaos one final slap on the back, jolting his teeth. "Do me proud, Nik, and there could be a promotion in this for you," he grins before slipping through the open window and disappearing.

"Where in Hades are you going now?" Nikolaos asks the dark, "A promotion. To what? To what I am? You drag me up and down this chain of command as if you were grating a radish." He lifts his palms to his head to press his temples. "Gods, I have a headache."

In the night courtyard, Ephtheta sits on a stone bench under a date tree. The soft rain has moved off to the north, leaving in its wake a dry breeze that smells slightly of tar and ash. Beside her, Yesh sits, weaving tiny, delicate designs into her basket work with skilled fingers.

"What is it that comes to us from the south like smoke from a dampened fire?" murmurs the princess, as if to herself. "My illness is worse than ever. I choke on this air, which is thick, and gritty in my susceptible lungs. Why must Pazuzu bring me this suffocating tide?"

"The winds are born of the heat of the Egyptian deserts, my sweet. Your Pazuzu rides them across the Great Sea, where they pick up water to bring Babylon rains for her crops." Yesh stops her work to press her wrist against the girl's forehead, looking for fever. "Perhaps something dark has latched on to the god's chariot."

"Perhaps Pazuzu brings us the Cretan air, Yesh, to

suffocate a princess first, and then her city." The girl smiles wanly. "Or is the Cretan disaster already here?"

"You have no fever, Theta, but your lungs are weak, and you say yourself that you can taste the winds of the underworld in the air tonight. Why do you insist on sitting out here in the damp? You court your *own* disaster." Yesh stands up to offer the princess her arm. "Come inside now. Surely you will breathe better indoors."

"No, Yesh," Ephtheta shakes her head. "I cannot stand to be inside tonight. My mind prowls like a hungry beast. Let me be. You are dismissed for the evening."

Reluctantly, Yesh takes up her weaving basket and, curtsying, bids the princess goodnight. When she is gone, Ephtheta bows her head and covers her eyes with her palms, soothing them with her own heat. Where are you tonight, enemy of my father, sweet breath of life, she thinks. Have you vanished like the wolf you are back into the forest night? Or do you prowl my city? A man. A man with warm lips to kiss with, iron limbs to hold with, strong lungs to save me. You are a murdering phantom, and yet I will your return. Will you take my father's life tonight? Or are you here only to steal back your Grain God, to spirit him away from us before he can heal our starving soil. Will you return with a horde of Hatti warriors to sack our city now that Babylon is as vulnerable to you now as I was last night?

A rustle in the date leaves brings her head up out of her hands.

She is on her feet, craning her neck to peek through the veil of fruit into the dark. The closest lamp is twenty feet away, across the paving stones, its light barely illuminating her bench. It is only a monkey, thinks the princess, and yet she whispers, "Demon!" as her fingers pull her veil across her face to cover the mouth he took mere hours before, the mouth that still feels his heat pressing down on it.

"It is you. I feel it. I feel it in my womb, I swear I do! Rush." She lets this last word slip through her teeth like a tongue.

But the date tree is silent.

And Ephtheta's heart turns to ice.

"Come to me, Wolf!" says Ephtheta, as loudly as her shallow breath will allow. "Show your enemy's daughter you are not a coward!"

The soft purr of a nightjar cuts the stillness over her head. But the date tree gives no answer.

In the House of Seven Cisterns, Rah sleeps. He has been moved to a pallet beneath an eastern window of the tower room. His bed is made of lambskin, stuffed with the softest hay. The wolf skin he slept beneath at the House of the Moon is his blanket, and covers his lower body. Mochlos watches him from a beech wood bench beside the pallet. The priest is dressed in his night robe, a simple, unbleached Tanitic linen: "woven moonlight", as the Egyptian's call it. It is the purest garment he has, appropriate for the magick he is about to perform.

Mochlos has not been alone with the body of the Rah until now. All day he was forced to entertain a seemingly unending host of visitors from the palace, nobles mostly. All were there to pay their respects, to bring gifts of copper, gold and silver, precious oils from Egypt, incense, exotic fabrics, and mouth-watering delicacies that Mochlos could barely keep himself from taking right out of their hands to sample as they presented them. But these gifts were all to be recorded by a palace scribe, so that just consideration could be given to those who contributed to the swift recovery of the Grain God. And these gifts came at a price. All but one of the callers wished to see the sleeping god-slave with their own eyes, and so Mochlos was forced to take them, individually or later, when he was exhausted from climbing the four staircases to the tower, in groups, to the foot of Rah's bed. Without exception, each caller stood dumbstruck at the end of the god slave's mattress, blinking and open-mouthed, gawking at the boy's ethereal beauty until finally, and only with a harsh cough from the priest, they were jarred back to their senses, and not a little embarrassed, they stepped back from the boy's pallet, in unison prostrating themselves before him.

"Well, my little albatross," murmurs Mochlos from his bench, "It is time we get started."

The priest rises, crossing the tower room to the blue and gold drape that hides the recess wherein he keeps his magical effects. He finds the crushed Ma Huang stems which he left in his mortar earlier that day when the commotion at the front door called him from his work. He taps them into a cup, then tucks a loaf of flax bread under his arm and pushes aside the drape. He walks to his altar, which has been moved to the center of the room and faces the curving south wall upon which Enlil impales Ninlil with his enormous phallus. He sets the loaf on a Minoan plate. He pours a bit of wine from a jug on the altar into the cup of poison, swirling the mixture together, thoughtfully. When he is satisfied he dips his pinky into the brew and tastes.

My pharmacy will be my salvation, he thinks, lifting the cup to his lips to take a small sip.

When his tongue goes numb, he sets down the cup and raises his arms above his head, hands extended.

"Mighty Rah, god of grain, of all harvest, abundance, fertility, and plenty, hear the prayers of your city, this city of Babylon. Your people see that you have abandoned them, and bring you gifts as acts of contrition. They see that their soil has become tired and bitter, and can no longer support their crops. They see that they have angered you and they are repentant. The mighty lay on their bellies, begging forgiveness for their disloyalty and disobedience. They see now that their Marduk is a god of lies and death. He demanded that they immolate their own children, insulting your life giving generosity. Be merciful, Mighty Rah. Come back to your people through this servant, this, your slave and host. Come back to reside in this body, and I promise you that this city will serve you, above all other gods."

Now Mochlos lowers his hands. He picks up the cup, and, pulling the flax loaf in half, he tears a moist ball from the center and presses it into a coin-sized disk with the tips of his fingers. He drops the disk into the cup of poisoned wine and allows it to soak.

"Incarnate, god of plenty, into this boy once more, and I will give you Babylon on its knees."

Mochlos slides the disk of soaked bread from the cup

onto his palm, kneels beside Rah, and drops the medallion into his half-opened mouth.

And waits.

Rah watches his priest slip the lozenge of poisoned bread in his open mouth from his vantage point at the foot of his mattress. He can feel the lozenge melting on his wounded tongue, though he watches his body from a distance. He can hear his heart begin to bang against his ribs, like a spooked horse kicking at its stall door.

"Priest is bring Rah back, Ting Ya," he hears himself say as he floats toward the body on the bed. But the little priestess is no longer at his side. He is alone with his priest.

And his heart is racing, racing like the heart of a horse that has been galloped through the spires of the Table in the dark, ridden near to death, and having thrown its rider, flees riderless now before the headless ghost soldiers of Syria.

And he is flailing his arms and legs, the howl of a stricken beast emanating from his mouth. His body is soaked with sweat. He sweeps the wolf skin from his lower body with one spastic arc of his arm, his head jerking back at the sight of the priest kneeling at his bedside. He tries to speak, but words are grunts, his disobedient tongue jumping like a worm in his mouth. Tremor runs through his maverick limbs so violently that he rolls from the mattress. His thighs Charlie-horse and his brain screams with pain, but from his mouth comes only an ugly cawing.

"Praise you, Rah!" sings the priest, clapping his hands over his mouth in relief and joy, tears springing to his eyes. "I *do* believe, I do, I do. Forgive my disbelief!" Jumping to his feet, he yanks at the bell rope beside Rah's pallet for Kalak.

"M-m-m-m-m-a-a-a-a-A-A-A-A-A-G-H!" cries Rah, limbs flailing as he crab walks backward into a wall.

"Easy, boy, easy now," says Mochlos, moving gingerly toward him, his palms out. "It is the Ma Huang. You mustn't fight it. I cannot lose you to a heart attack now that I have put you back together again!" he clasps his hands before him, then brings them to his lips in supplication. "Oh I do, I will believe!" he whispers into his fingertips as Kalak rushes in from the north stairs.

"Great powers of heaven!" cries the surgeon's assistant, when he sees Rah flailing beneath the mural of Enlil's engorged penis entering Ninlil. "You have awakened him, Holiness!"

"Go to him, Kalak. He trusts you. Soothe him, before he dies of fright!" hisses Mochlos, who presses his hands to his chest and chews on his lip, thinking hard.

"He trusts the Captain's valet more, Sir. You should send for Aamat," says Kalak, who has dropped to his knees and is now inching toward Rah as if he were approaching a frightened animal.

"No. NO! We cannot let them know he has returned! Not yet! If we do, they will take him back to the palace. He is mine, Kalak. I made him. He is mine. He has no other master." Mochlos is moving forward, slowly, toward the gibbering boy. He stands beside Kalak, staring at the strangely beautiful fear in the face of the Grain God. How is it so, thinks the high priest, how can fear be so lovely? Is it in the face? This particular face? These particularly arched brows now flattened in feline panic? This particularly succulent mouth, now open, shining with spittle, panting? These unimaginably jade eyes, wide with dread? Mochlos can barely keep himself from reaching for the boy, or for imagining himself now, whip raised, the *reason* for the fear. But as soon as he does so, his head is underwater. His neck, squeezed between the thumb and palm of the assassin, is pressed against the smooth edge of his drowning pool in the House of the Moon, his lungs collapsing.

Mochlos gulps the air, brings his hand to his throat involuntarily. Kalak turns to him, his brow pinched. "Sir?"

"Go on, Kalak, soothe him. Or perhaps... yes! A woman! A woman will soothe him better than any man. Go and find Awiti, quickly! Bring her here to me." The boy will know what sex she is. He has a nose for it. Even in this state, thinks Mochlos.

A moment later Kalak has returned with Awiti. The girl is dressed in a yellow silk robe, her head covered by a veil. She walks on bare feet across the room to stand beside Mochlos while Kalak remains at the head of the stair.

"Go to him, Awiti," says Mochlos, taking the girl by the arm. "I have brought him this far. I am his father, his creator, yes, but I see now that a father can do only so much. It will take a woman to complete his rebirth." Mochlos turns to Awiti. "Take off the veil."

Awiti looks to the high priest, unsure. She has been required to wear the veil, a sheer halo of matching silk, since her head was shaved at the inn and the priest proclaimed her Babylon's first hermaphrodite. "Yes, Sir," she concedes, seeing the determination in his face now. She pushes the veil back, revealing a perfectly balanced skull; a flawless, ebony face; her pillowy, peach-colored lips parted.

"Ah, there's my lovely," smiles Mochlos, pressing her forward.

Rah's panic seems to have lifted with the girls' entrance into his temple. He is still breathing heavily, his fine chest rising and falling as he flattens himself against the muraled wall. But his focus is now on the girl. His brows have softened, a look of confused wonder on his face. He scans the girl's features, his grunts becoming rhythmical, chimp like.

"Tell him you are Siriona," hisses the priest into Awiti's ear as she begins to lower herself onto her hands and knees to approach Rah.

"He is so beautiful," she responds, as if she has not heard him. "He is like a lion, as pale as the sun..." she kneels back on her haunches, placing her hands on her knees. Rah follows her movement. The contrast of her ebony fingers on the yellow silk has captivated him. He watches her palms come to rest against her knees, cupping them. His eyes lift to her face. His grunts accelerate, soften. Now they are little huffs, still deep, but gentler. Curious.

Awiti lifts one hand, palm up. Her palm is a pale pink, in perfect harmony with her ebony skin. "Come, Rah. Come home to us now," she says simply, smiling at the boy.

Rah croaks. His brows bunch, frustrated. He lifts his own hand, which is stiff and unyielding. His fingers spasm. He tries to speak again. It is a bark.

"He is trying to say it! Yes, Rah, it is your Siriona!" cries Mochlos, clapping his hands together.

The percussion of the clap flattens Rah against the wall. He crushes his ears with his hands.

Mochlos spits through his teeth in a whisper, "Damn me. Where is my brain? This house must be silent!" He turns to Kalak, still standing at the top of the stairs, as if it were he who clapped. He motions him forward impatiently. Kalak slips across the tiled floor, careful not to make a sound.

"He cannot endure noise, Kalak," Mochlos hisses at the surgeon's apprentice. "You must go and tell the household immediately. I will not tolerate so much as the rattle of a pan in the kitchen! There must be absolute silence!" He spreads his fingers under Kalak's nose. Then he looks back over his shoulder at the cowering Rah. Awiti has slipped several feet closer to the boy, who is whimpering, regarding her with his hands still pressed against his ears, his eyes big as the emerald that no longer sparkles between them. "Silence here in the Temple of Rah," Mochlos murmurs, gripping Kalak's shoulder. Observing the boy's naked forehead, his eyes widen, struck by an idea. "Yes! This entire city must submit to my dictate, if they want their barren fields to bear harvest again. There must be silence throughout the entire city! Go! Send a messenger to the palace immediately! The Priest of the Rah has determined that the entire city must fast, must pray, and must observe complete silence!"

As Kalak races down the stairs with his message, Mochlos turns to see that Awiti has edged even closer to Rah. Still on her haunches, she is stroking his shoulder with long fingers, cooing as if to a babe. Rah no longer presses himself against the wall, but sits cross-legged on the floor, his hands on his knees. Mochlos smiles. Yes, he thinks. There you are, my beauty, there you are, soothed by the softer sex, easy as baiting a kitten with a string. You will not leave your Siriona, now you have found her again. And while you play with your concubine, this city will fall on its knees in obedience to your priest.

Mochlos has retired to his own kingly chamber and is pacing back and forth between the columns of his terrace when a loud knock on his door disturbs his scheming. Did I not tell them to observe compete silence? He shakes his bald head with indignity and crosses the veranda, arranging his face in an appropriate scowl as he reaches for the bolt.

"What is it, Nepu?" he asks the tall African, softening his features when he sees it is the senior house slave. "Have you found the cat?"

"No, Sir. But we have the emerald headpiece," the man turns to wave a palace guard forward. This man is quite imposing. He is easily as tall as Nepu, but twice the man in girth. He wears the red tunic and elaborate breastplate of the Palace Guard of Babylon. His leather helmet is in his hands. His waist is belted, and along its jeweled breadth is an array of weaponry: two daggers of different length, a short sword at his right side, a battle-axe on his left. I would be on my knees carrying all of that metal, thinks the priest, his eyes lifting to meet the cold gaze of the soldier.

"Your Holiness," barks the man, clipping his boots together and making a swift, abbreviated bow at the priest. Mochlos flinches backward as the man chops himself in half at the waist, sure that head would brain him like a mace if he did not.

"I am Petuk, Captain of the Palace Guard," says the brute as he straightens himself. "I have brought you the Rah's emerald headdress." He shoves his leather helmet at the priest, and Mochlos flinches a second time.

"Indeed," murmurs Mochlos, considering the possibility of head lice as he takes the offering.

"This is a dangerous city, Holiness," continues Petuk, watching the priest as he gingerly opens the helmet, which is folded into an elongated triangle. "Even I cannot traverse it safely, not without a contingent of soldiers. And your message suggested too great an urgency to assemble one."

"So you hid it in a hat," Mochlos looks up into the man's fierce grey eyes. Some grey is flecking his beard and brows as well, but for the most part the man's facial hair is still chestnut. "Very clever, Captain. Yes, my message was urgent, for it is the removal of this magical emerald band from the boy's forehead that allowed the god to escape from his body in the first place. And the god will surely not return to him without its guiding light." Mochlos' fingers have reached the charmed mail band in the point of the helmet. A smile draws back his lips. He lifts it out, holding it in the light. Prisms of color shoot across the ceiling of his chamber, dashing among the rushing chariots carved into the plaster. "You see, Captain, it is a powerful stone."

"I see, Holiness. It was my own man who took it from him, at his request, so that the surgeon could stitch his head. It seems that the removal of the stone from the little god's head has cost us dearly. That very night, The Hatti Wolf visited the palace, killing a number of guards, leaving his mark, and taking with him the leopard cub that he himself sent the king as a gift."

"Did he, now," says Mochlos, pocketing the emerald band with one hand and stroking his new beard with the other. He turns quickly from the soldier so as to hide his own surprise. "An odd message, no? What kind of leopard was it, Captain? For your King will find his answer there. As I have already informed the palace, I have had considerable dealings with this man, and I have made it my business to understand him. To get him right the first time, you might say, for there is no second. You see the mark on my face, proof of this? I may well be the only man alive, not directly under his service who lives to tell the tale of this mark's creation."

"I see the mark, Holiness," answers Petuk softly.

"And was there anything special about the animal?"

"It was the Anatolian leopard," answers the soldier.

"Anatolian? And what is the custom of the sovereignty in the region? Do they generally allow the great beasts of their kingdom to be exported?"

"They do not. They are strictly the property of the royals," responds Petuk.

Mochlos turns back to the Captain, his lids at half-mast. "There you have it, then," he says.

Petuk's brows bunch over his piercing gaze. "Sir?"

"The message, Captain, is in the gift. Don't you see? The leopard is the property of the Hatti. The Hatti royals, to be specific. Have you not yet heard? That a division of your own Amorite army attempted to kidnap the young Hittite king, Mursilis? The plot was fouled, of course. The Hattushan king lives and sits upon his throne as we speak. Though I believe you will find proof of my story, despite what your generals return home saying, by the fact that the Hattushan king's seal ring is in this very city! The plot was actually quite excellent, and may have succeeded, if it were not for the fact that you are dealing with the devil himself. It is only by the interference of the one who sent this leopard to Babylon that the king of the Hittites remains on his throne."

Mochlos looks up at Petuk, wagging a finger. "The Wolf is telling Babylon that he intends to repay the offense! Like for like! An eye for an eye!" The priest balls his fists together. "Hammurabi's law! YOUR law!" he cries, his fists rising over his head. "He is playing with you! He *wants* you to know! He wants you to fear his next move!" Mochlos turns to strut toward his balcony, then spins suddenly back toward Petuk, his white house robe flaring about his ankles. "He walks in and out of your palace like a ghost, unseen, laying out as many men as he chooses," the priest gesticulates, his arm arcing and slashing as he paces back to stand before the soldier, "Slipping in and out right under your nose!" Mochlos reaches up to tap Petuk's nose for emphasis. "Mark my word, man." He shakes one extended index finger over his head. "He intends to return! He intends to return and kidnap a royal!"

"The princess!" blurts Petuk, his eyes wide with horror.

"The princess," nods Mochlos, smiling. "The King's favorite. And now, with the boy asleep, and the crops failing-"

"How could you know this?" Petuk's eyes narrow.

"How could I not, man? Am I an idiot? Do I not have servants, and do servants never gossip unwittingly within earshot of a clever master? Your crops are failing. Your soil is tired and overused. And the King expects a miracle of me. First, to return the Cretan god, Rah, to the body of the slave he has escaped, by the folly of the palaces own surgeon I might add, and then to obtain the monumental favor from that god of restoring the land! A strange land! Not his own Crete, but Babylon! A city that has worshiped every insignificant, hostile, nay, *homicidal* god known to man! And so here I am, ensconced in this temple like a monk, with a comatose slave-god, courtesy of a handful of palace idiots, expected to patch up this sinking

149

ship, to avert this catastrophe, to repair the irreparable."
Mochlos takes a moment to catch his breath. He wipes his
moistened brow with the bit of linen he keeps in a pocket of
his robe for just such a moment. Now is his chance to put to
the King the entirety of his importance to this city. He must
choose his words carefully, he must not amble into reckless
speech which could get him staked, but he must wander near
enough to let the King know that he is confident enough to do
so. Confidence! That is the key! This is a confidence game if
ever there was one.

Petuk is regarding the priest silently. He has not moved
from his parade halt in the priest's chamber doorway. His jaw
is set, and in his fierce grey eyes the priest can read a gathering
tempest. This might, to any other High Priest, council
moderation, but Mochlos is in the middle of his dissertation,
and poise now is key. He must allow his righteous indignation
full rein. He storms on.

"A man does not build a pyramid without first
determining whether the earth below can support its weight,
Captain, nor does a general confront an enemy army until he
has sent out spies to gauge its strength. And a high priest, a
good priest, does not undertake a miracle for a King without
first understanding what opposes it, both in the world of the
gods, and here on earth." Mochlos fondles the emerald band
in his pocket as he turns to give the Captain his back. Cut me
in half now, if you dare, he thinks. You see how self-assured I
am that you will not? A man's back can be an awesome show
of strength, if used properly. But to Petuk he adds in a near
whisper, forcing the man to come out of his stance to hear
him, "The fates have predesigned this to prove my power as a
magician here in Babylon." He turns, now confidentially, to
sidle up to Petuk, hands clasped together as in prayer. "This
city has been rampant with wickedness for too long, Captain,
and the hand of the mightiest of all gods is clenched against it!
We must appease him! The King must order a fast! A fast
from sin, a fast from the worship of Marduk, who demands
that men immolate their own babes! This is a terrible insult to
the god of abundance and plenty, the god of fertility! And so
he withdraws, flees from the god-slave I made for his worship

on Crete, a god-slave who brought abundance to every city he entered. This emerald will hold him, once I have restored him to the body of the boy, but unless Babylon falls to its knees in worship, I will never succeed in seducing him back into the body! The fields must be rested. No wine, no wheat or barley or any grain nor fruit must be harvested! And no more can the priests of Marduk demand the offspring of their flock to be fried like eggs in the arms of the scorching statues of their dark god!"

CHAPTER 11

Horus sits on the corner of his bed, feeding Mushezibit chunks of dried lamb from a covered bowl he keeps on his dresser.

The cheetah's large, thickly lashed eyes watch Horus's right hand as he lifts each piece from the bowl. The cheetah is well trained, and subtle hand signals, unrecognized by a mesmerized audience, inform her. A lifted index finger: sit. Fingers collected and up, wrist over: down on your belly and roll. Finger to painted lips: a feline to human kiss, nose to nose.

Horus sighs as Mush licks his face eagerly, then snuffles his hand for a treat.

"Not so fast, Mushmush, try again," he says, lifting his index finger to return her to a sit. He taps his lip. This time she gives him one quick punch with her nose. He drops a treat. "Good girl!"

Horus runs one long-fingered hand down the cheetahs wither as she licks up the chunk of dried meat, flops her great paws down in front of her, and chews. "Oh, I miss him, Mush. I do." He rises, tapping on his elevated sandals to the bureau to study his own pale reflection in his hand mirror. Losing track of his thoughts for a moment he props the mirror against the wall, presses his palms to his temple and smoothes his corkscrew mop back into a pony's tail. He checks his profile, notices a blemish on his cheek, feels about the top of his bureau for his pot of face paint and dabs the spot with a bit of flesh color, lifts his chin to examine his image, and sighs again, heavily, slapping the bronze mirror down, defeated.

"It's not the same without him. I feel fat." Horus has moved to Rah's mattress to lift the crumpled linen that the guards left in a heap when they rushed in to take him to the priest. He brings the linen to his nose and sniffs. Hyssop. Cherry. Without thinking he turns, unfurls the linen sheet, letting it drift and settle onto his own mattress like an angel's wing.

The movement brings Mush up into a lazy sit. She watches the sheet settle, then finds an imaginary quarry under a wrinkle and pounces, great paws coming together like silent cymbals. Horus pats her head.

"Gone, Mush," continues Horus, who, as saddened as he is by his loss, is nevertheless stimulated by the drama of it. "Our Rah," he clasps his hands to his breast, "Spirited away by the Guard," he makes a sweeping gesture toward the doorway, "To be kept like a princess in a temple spire high above our heads," Horus turns to his elongated casement window, leaning to see if the top of the House of Seven Cisterns can be seen from it. "If only we could find some reason for them to need us..."

His musings are interrupted by Rhinna, who suddenly appears in his doorway, her falcon head tucked under one arm.

"Eliabus wants your act between the Dance of the King's Falcons and the Chorus of Marduk," she announces, pouting. "I think it's ridiculous, but nobody asks me my opinion." She stops to peer keenly at the magician. "What's that on your face?"

Horus turns from the window to the wall mirror.

"You can't go on stage like that," chirps Rhinna, padding cautiously into the room, one eye on the cat. She points to the blemish on Horus' left cheek, the stiff blades of her waxed papyrus wings lifting lightly in the breeze from the window.

"I thought I'd covered it," mumbles Horus, exasperated when he sees that the blotch has defied the makeup and reappeared.

"Looks like you'd had a visit from the Amegan," chuckles

153

Rhinna. "Well, better get yourself put together. Eliabus is doing a run through this morning. You're up next after us. And when I left we were half way through." She turns to scamper out the door, remembers the cheetah, and slows to a walk.

When she's gone, Horus returns to his bureau, rifles through a few pots, finds what he's looking for, and pats a dab of face paint on the spot.

Suddenly he freezes. He snatches up a make-up rag, dabs the tip of his tongue, wipes at the mark. It's true. The boil is surfacing just under his left eye. A bit of clever cutting with a boiled and sharpened fish bone, the kind used for tattooing, would not only relieve the tiny pimple, but mimic the Tears of the Bull.

Horus locks eyes with his own reflection. Hazel eyes, tip-tilted with the new line Rah showed him, regard him. What was it the Assassin said? A woman's heart is fiercer?

But do I really have the courage to steal the trademark of the Wolf? Just to trick my way into service of the House of the Rah?

Horus pulls open a drawer to fine the fish bone tattoo knife his father used to mark the royals of Egypt. His father had been an excellent artist of living flesh. He had taught his only son how to boil the tiny implement before dipping it into the various inks he used to create his perfect lines, lines that were permanent, lines elongating the almond eyes of powerful faces, lines which, if even slightly askew, would cost him his hands. Eliabus will be furious with him when he fails to appear for his practice, but that is not what frightens him. It is that one, slightly sad, onyx eye of the Amegan, regarding him now from somewhere in his brain.

"Lucky for you he set your bone before he dropped dead of fright," says the Stable Master's assistant, tacking up the King's Turkoman in the main aisle as Hatu-Hadu watches. Hatu-Hadu's right arm is bound and splinted, and hangs from his shoulder like a slaughtered lamb hangs from a butcher's hook. His assistant is the only man Hatu-Hadu has confessed the truth of his injury to, and he would not have done even this, except that, having heard Hatu-Hadu's cries of agony shortly after the assassin's visit, Buhuru-Hatu had come to see if a horse had somehow escaped his stall and trampled him.

His shattered elbow, the pain of which came upon him like a second Wolf after the first had gone, caused Hatu-Hadu to bellow like a lost cow, and had awakened his brother, who had been sleeping in the grain room at the far end of the aisle for the past month in an effort to discourage thieves in a city which was starving.

The fact that his assistant is also his bastard brother, and ties him to silence, is a small relief. The man has been needling him for striking the Grain God since the incident, and the assassin's nocturnal visit has only enhanced his jibes.

"You think I don't know that?" spits Hatu-Hadu, referring as much to his 'luck' as to the fact that the surgeon's death was surely the result of a visit from the Beast of Amega. "All the same, I am a horseman with one frozen arm, am I not? The joint is locked forever. It is only by grace of a high birth that I am allowed to remain in my position."

"You are a fine enough horseman to ride with one arm," answers Buhuru-Hatu, shrugging. "And I am a fine enough horseman to train any horse that needs two."

"You'd like that, wouldn't you," mutters Hatu-Hadu miserably, always and forever aware that his bastard brother is by far the better horseman, though he is, in Hatu-Hadu's opinion, far too generous with the animals, coddling their moods like a mother, and far too unwilling to show them just who wields the whip when needs be. "The Turkoman is the descendant of gods, brother," Buhuru-Hatu would often remind him, and "You cannot dominate a Turkoman like you might a plow horse. Break his spirit and you will be riding a golden ass, an animal with no courage, into battle."

And when was the last time the Palace Guard of Babylon rode into battle? We are peacocks, thinks, Hatu-Hadu. No one rides a Turkoman into battle, unless the King himself goes to war. It is the Babylonian army's job to keep Babylon's enemies at bay, not the Palace Guard.

"They say he had a pearl in that ear," says Buhuru-Hatu, tightening Samsu-titana's girth, while stroking the animal's neck with his free hand. "There, now, no nipping. Have I ever pinched you?" he says gruffly to the horse, which has turned to him with pinned ears. Not too tight! say the ears. I warn you!

"A pearl?" repeats Hatu-Hadu. "What sort of pearl?" A cold chill has rushed up his back to his shaved hairline, and at the same time a nervous quiver in his bowels causes his sphincter to clench involuntarily.

"A pearl worth a fortune," responds his brother and assistant, who slips three fingers under Samsu's girth to assure that it is not too tight nor loose. "A pearl given him by the Amegan Wolf." He looks over his shoulder at Hatu-Hadu, a ghost of a smile on his lips.

"What are you saying? That my whip dislodged it? That it is lost somewhere in the dust and shit?" He looks about wildly, as if he would find it now with fear as easily as he displaced it in anger.

"Unless a clever and observant man has already found it," answers Buhuru-Hatu, reaching for Samsu's bridle, which is hanging on a peg on his stall door. His face now turned away from his brother, Buhuru-Hatu hides the lingering look of satisfaction on his brow. Too long has he been his brother's lackey, all resulting from an accident of birth. Do you think I love you? he asks the Stable Master silently. I have had to listen to your ignorant authority long enough. Now we will see who is the better man. Now we will see who deserves to be the Master of the Stable of the Palace of Babylon. But to his brother, who is already on his knees, feeling along the base of Samsu's stall for the lost pearl, he only sighs, "I fear you can only trust yourself now, to find it, Brother, for any other man who does will only pocket it. I am sure that the man who returns it to its rightful owner will be well rewarded."

"Your father has sent for you, My Lady," says Mefali to the princess. She is standing in her garden, feeding berries to a brightly colored parrot perched on her arm. All morning she has been considering the whereabouts of the Amegan. How is it that he comes and goes in the palace so easily? Is he truly a wraith? A spirit-man who can walk through walls at will? Or is he flesh and blood, heat and temper, mass and strength.

A monkey chatters in the palm above her head. On the couch behind her, her black Egyptian sight hound lies like a sleek-coated skin, paws outstretched and hanging over the seat, taut belly moving evenly in the pattern of sleeping breaths. The morning sun reflects in the dreaming pool, a thousand sparkling stars, blue-green, like the Cretan Grain God's eyes.

"Can it not wait, Mefali?" Ephtheta puts one slender hand to her breast, causing her veil to billow lightly in the still air. "I am not feeling my best this morning."

Mefali purses his lips. "I'm afraid not, Princess," he responds, genuinely disquieted by her confession, for even at her worst he has never heard her complain of her illness. Far from it, since her babyhood, she has steadfastly refused to recognize her limitations. "I am sure he will not detain you long," he adds, hoping to mollify her.

"He wishes to tell me that the Amegan Wolf intends to kidnap me," she says, turning her back on the old guard. "That a special detail of guards will be watching my every move. That I can no longer move about freely, that I can no longer leave the city, nor even the palace until the threat is past. But the threat will not pass, Mefali. The wolf will eat."

"How can you know this, Princess?" asks Mefali, stunned.

"Servants talk, Mefali," answers the princess calmly, turning to him as she gently passes the parrot to a eunuch. As the young man moves off with the bird, she adds, "And the wise listen."

"I cannot tell your father you have heard this from a servant, unless you wish that servant to be staked."

"Of course not. For then how else would I come by such information in the future? The palace protects me from all useful intelligence." Ephtheta offers Mefali a weak smile. "Come, then. Let us pretend, you and I, that we have not had this conversation, and allow my father the illusion that he insists upon."

In the evening, Rush returns to the Palace. He has been on his feet, or in the saddle, for two days. During that time, he has rendezvoused with Aleksandus and Agrippa at the Lake of Fire, on the border of the two kingdoms of the Hatti and the

Amorites, where the skulls of a thousand of his enemies' heads lay under the ever moving sands. He has given orders for an attack in twenty one days; a chariot attack from the southeast, where the gates of Babylon are most easily overwhelmed and unprotected, and a water attack from the south end of the river itself, which bisects the metropolis, a perfect entry for boatmen to inject hordes of the wolves of Amega directly into the city at the service doors of the palace. Twenty one days: three weeks. Not a moon. Not half. But enough time for a town now ordered to live on the grain and produce imported from its southern neighbors to wither. In a week, Agrippa, Commander of the First Division, will have cut off the trade route though Syria from the south. In two, he will have launch hundreds of boatloads of Amegan soldiers into the Euphrates twenty miles south of the Samas Gate. And in three, while the palace fights desperately to control the attack from the river, which has effectively cut the city in twain, Aleksandus will attack from the Uras and Zababa gates, taking the districts of Suanna, Eridu and Te-Eki, the unsuspected, and furthest quadrant of the beleaguered Babylon.

She is mine, thinks Rush, dismounting the Black in the courtyard of the Eridu stable and handing the animal's rein to a stable boy, who leads the steaming warhorse into the barn. But I will put her on her knees first.

Rush has kept his suite in the hotel in the Suanna district for his own purposes. Dressed as an Amorite soldier, he enters through the front room, where a cluster of well-dressed men recline at a low table, eating a late supper. Rush pays them no mind, finding his way past the kitchen to the back stairs leading to the upper rooms. On his way a young slave carrying a basket of fresh bread trots past him, trailing the aroma of the yeasty loaves. Hunger overtakes the assassin like a fever.

"Boy," Rush slams a palm against the wall in front of the lad, "bring a braised goose and a jug of good wine up to the suite of rooms above." He takes a loaf of barley bread from the basket and rips a chunk from the heel with his teeth. "And a tub of fresh butter." He pokes the basket with the loaf in his hand. "This man can wait for one who serves the King."

"Yes, Sir!" the boy sets the basket down on the stair and

backs away, then turns and flees toward the kitchen. Rush palms a second loaf from the basket, shoves it into the sack he carries over his shoulder, and continues up the steps to his rooms, ripping chunks of barley bread from the first loaf with his incisors and consuming them as he goes. Thrusting the door of his suite open with one shoulder he hears a soprano yelp on the other side. The aperture swings wide and Rush is confronted with the sight of a young woman hopping on one foot and holding the other in her hands, howling.

"Hush, girl," barks Rush, tossing his sack on the floor and moving to the washbasin. "You'd think you'd broken it. What were you doing anyway? Has no one taught you a servant never stands behind a door?" Pulling off his tunic, he slaps cold water on his face, then grabs a linen from the side of the basin. As he turns to face the girl, he begins lathering his chest with a chunk of goat milk soap.

The girl has released her injured foot at the sight of his naked torso. She stands quietly, mouth opened, watching his hand move in circles over his chest.

Rush lowers his lids at her, lathering his arms, his neck, his belly. "Have you never seen a man bathe before?" He turns his back to her, rinses the linen in the basin, wipes the suds from his upper body. "Where are you taken from, hm? Open your mouth girl. Let me hear your dialect."

"I am Hatti, Sir," says the girl carefully. She has not finished her words before the assassin has swung round to face her, surprise lighting his obsidian eyes, the only clue of emotion in a death-mask face.

"A Hatti girl?" he whispers, wiping his face with the cloth. "Here?" He slaps the cloth on to the rim of the basin. "Serving the Amorite dog?"

"A spoil of war, Sir," answers the girl softly, peering at him.

Slowly, she allows her eyes to drop to the black star of hair over his heart a second time. "Master," she whispers, pointing feebly to the star. "You are also Hatti!" she drops to her knees, slaps her palm on the floor making a diamond of her thumbs and forefingers and resting her forehead upon it. "You are the Assassin!" she weeps into her hands.

Rush moves quickly to shut the open door, then take the girl by one wrist and pull her to her feet. "Hush, child," he says gruffly as she throws herself into his arm, weeping against his chest. Reluctantly, he allows her to cling to him.

"I am saved," weeps the girl, who has turned her lips to the star and now kisses it reverently.

"Indeed you are, but for a little while yet, you must pretend for me that you are not," says Rush, gently pushing her from him by her shoulders. "Has anyone, any one of these Amorite pigs defiled you?"

"It is there custom, Master," answers the girl, haltingly. "I was taken in the battle of Nesa. It is now the fifth year of my slave life. For one year I was made to endure the soldiers' use. Then I was sold by the army to the proprietor of this inn for the price of a battle axe."

"And does he also use you?"

"As he pleases, Master," answers the girl.

"Five years," breathes Rush, "And for one, defiled by dogs. But now you become the servant of Ameg The Merchant here in Babylon. You will take this," he hands her his smallest dagger, from the harness at his right ankle, "And you will put it the innkeeper's eye when next he mounts you. Then you will find his wife and marry their deaths on this blade. If you can do this, you will walk out of this place a free woman. Go then directly to the palace and announce yourself to the Master of the Palace Stable. And before the next moon, you will see your homeland."

The girl falls to her knees a second time, weeping, to kiss the assassin's feet, which are still booted.

"Can you prove yourself a Hatti woman, and accomplish what I tell you?" he asks her as he unbinds the waist tie of his leggings.

The girl rises and turns her back to him before he begins to remove them. "I can," she answers, an unexpected fierceness tingeing her child-voice.

"Do it then, and you will return to Nesa a rich woman, on my word."

"I will, Master. Or die trying."

"Yes," says Rush, "You are a Hatti woman." And turning

to the basin he begins washing his lower body. "And are you also a Hatti female in your fondness for jewelry, daughter?"

Still turned respectfully from his nakedness, the girl nods to herself, smiling. "I am, Sir."

"Then I suspect you could find a pearl in a manure pile, if I know the women of my country," says Rush, soaping his belly.

"I suppose I could, Sir, if I had a mind to," she answers calmly.

"Then that is what I will expect you to do when you reach the palace. Ameg's servant girl will scour the stable of the King for the Pearl earring of the Rah. You will have no difficulty obtaining access to any corner of that place, for the man who struck the Rah with a reed, and tore the pearl from his ear, will make himself your footstool. That man is easy to distinguish," Rush continues, rinsing his washcloth in the basin and then removing the soap from his body with it, "For he is no longer in charge of the arm he struck with. Indeed it will hang by his side, quite useless, for all of his days. He cannot even wipe his posterior with it, let alone pick up a whip. Nevertheless, his mouth functions, and with that mouth he will, with a few words from you, Hatti girl, order every groom in the stable on his knees, searching for that pearl. Now how do you suppose this is so?"

"Shall I mention you, Sir?" whispers the girl, unable to keep from peeking over her shoulder to look upon the broad, powerful back, the hard, clean line of the waist, the tucked and athletic buttocks of the Wolf of the Hatti. "And if so, by what title?"

Rush, hearing her voice has turned to him, shakes his head with grim amusement. "Hatti girls," he murmurs to himself, then reaches for his tunic. "Just tell him you are the property of the puppeteer," he looks at his own image in the mirror above the basin, "That should suffice."

When she is gone, Rush pulls an Amorite tunic over his head. He waits in silence at the window, staring out toward the House of Seven Cisterns, whose pale blue tower can just be seen over the north walls of the palace. He imagines the Rah, still, lifeless, perhaps shrouded in a silk so fine as to be transparent, lying on a narrow bed. Lamps burn on the frescoed walls, reflecting red and orange over the perfect planes of his face. Leonine lashes sweep his cheekbones. His boy's beard is growing, and beneath the shroud, golden bristles shade his jaw, his chin. He will never have a proper beard. Muttonchops will be the best he'll manage, if he even manages to reach his third decade of life.

Seventeen. Seventeen summers, you are. What will I do with you? Am I cursed with this longing so long as you live? Will manhood make you somehow unappetizing? I am not one to love my own kind. But are you male, because you reside within the body of a male? Or are you something else altogether. I have heard the Hebrews speak of angels, creatures made by their beloved "one, true God," to adore him, before He made mankind. Is this what Josepha sees in you? A Hebrew angel? Neither male, nor female, taking on shape in the world of men to walk among us, to change us, to turn our hearts to God? She told a story once, of two of these, so beautiful that when they entered the city of Sodom the men there would have raped them, had a Hebrew man, recognizing what they were, not hid them in his home. And how did the story end? Those men destroyed the city, did they not? But took the good Hebrew and his family with them to safety.

You have destroyed Crete, my angel. Perhaps it was not I who rescued you, but you, me. And my family. Will you now destroy Babylon, this wicked city, as well? So be it. I have no use for it. I will take it, then let it fall. But you, you will come with me. You will walk again along the Bridge Road, while the bells of all four Houses clang announcing your return. I will install you in the Palace of Knossos, and I will be your King, and you will dance for me, and be mine alone. You will not escape me, nor return to your God, however powerful he may be.

When his dinner arrives, Rush eats hurriedly, devouring the goose in its entirety, and washing it down with an amphora of excellent wine. I will go to see him, thinks the assassin, wiping the grease from his lips with a linen, then setting the serving tray down on the bed, pulling off the contemptible Amorite tunic, and slipping into the muslin rags of Rush The

Assassin. I will visit him in his stillness, and perhaps I will bring him back, as I did in Cyrus, simply by the force of my love onto the body he inhabits. Little angel of god, why did I not see it? How is it I was blinded? Was it by pride? I am a proud man. What I do, I do better than any who have been nor will be. But I could not take your head. And so I hated you, or perhaps you caused me to hate myself, having failed in my work. But if you are an angel, inhabiting the body of a man, how could I help but love you? It was no fault of my own. For who can kill a divine creature? This wound, you have inflicted, it is only love of the divine. It is nothing to fear. It is nothing to despise. It does not work against my pride. I am still The Assassin.

Rush leaves his rooms by way of the window, and the ubiquitous trellis of vines clinging to the northeast wall of every house in the Mediterranean world. In the alley, he pulls his hood over his head, then moves from deepest shadow to deepest shadow, on silent feet, up the Eridu Road, along the base of the palace walls, toward Kadingirra and the Ishtar temple. Under the nose of the Lower Fortress of Babylon, the enemy of the Amorite people moves freely, blacker than black in a moonless night, to the new House of the Moon, where his own beloved nemesis sleeps.

"You were marked, and lived?" says Petuk, blinking with incredulity at the perfect Tear of the Bull beneath Horus' left eye. A moment ago, when Eliabus informed him of the magician's tale, the brooding guard had snatched the man's jaw, fairly pulling his head off his shoulders in Horus' opinion, to examine the mark. Now he shoves Horus' chin from him with a loud harrumph. "This is impossible," he grumbles. "You must have been dreaming, and opened a boil in your sleep, that is all. If you wear the mark and live, you are his property. And what would the Wolf of the Damned do with a foppish magician like you?"

"Train a cat?" The magician responds feebly, denying himself the luxury of rubbing his wrenched neck. He has always had a ferocious crush on Petuk, with his falcon-sharp features and his positively gorgeous salt-and-pepper beard, but the man is a bull. Such strength, thinks Horus. I could never endure it. Still, a sweet chill has lifted the damnable wooly red hair along his forearms. Oh, I must shave my arms before I leave. I just must.

"Train a-? Ba-h-h-hah-hah!" Petuk's stern face has shattered in a burst of laughter. It is not a pleasant sound. This is how you sound when you laugh? thinks the magician. Dear gods, I'll labor to keep you sober from here on.

Just as quickly, the Captain of the Guard straightens, as if in surprise, turns his back to Horus and Eliabus, and coughs. "You mean the little Grain God….."

"Well, he is cat enough, Sir, but no. That one is beyond training. Wild as a civet. I only mean, that is my specialty. He did not tell me what I was to be, in his employ. Only that I was to report to the House of Seven Cisterns by the end of the week, or else the Palace would enjoy another visit from him."

Oh, I cannot believe I just said that, thinks Horus, feeling queasy suddenly with his own boldness. Kishar save me, I must watch my tongue before I lose it.

But Petuk is suddenly all business. "Well, then, Magician, he may have you. Pack and be gone by nightfall. I have a job to do, and so I will do it. I will not visit that hell upon the house of the great Samsu-titana by denying the lord of the underworld a silly stage magus. Did you not here me, man? GO! Get out of my sight!"

"Yes, Sir," says the magician, dipping to one knee feebly before he scurries off to pack his things. And now what? What do I tell the House of Seven Cisterns? Well, only the truth, really. He *did* tell me to watch over the Rah like a mother hen, didn't he? Am I to take responsibility for a boil shaping itself into the mark of the … well then, I shall tell them the Palace has sent me, with orders to wait on the Rah…oh by now they must know of the assassin's nocturnal visit. Servants talk, Kishar be praised. And who is to question it? Who has the nerve? Not that nasty priest, certainly, he with his 'hermaphrodite' temple concubine. If the gods made hermaphrodites, I would be the first! Why she is nothing more than a pretty bit of Africa come from some rich man's slave quarters, bought for half the worth of my Mushezibit. He bought her on the way into the city, or I'm a princess! And I shall expose him just as fast as he does me, and shall tell him so, too! We've all got our secrets. I'm not above telling him so.

But as he packs, Horus is thinking of Rah's long lashes, fanning his cheekbones as he sleeps, or snarls, or spits or bows....bows like a puddle of silk off the finest roller, his honey-gold ringlets brushing his tawny shoulders, lakes of curls on the floor...and he thinks of the little Grain God's poor split tongue, so pink and wet, and his cupid's bow mouth and apricot lips... and his tip-tilted almond eyes, blue-green eyes like the sea, and Horus knows that if ever a hermaphrodite lived in Babylon, if ever such a creature passed through this city, this sinful and decadent place, she would surely be ravished, for how could she survive? "Someone must protect him from this city," thinks Horus aloud, as he stuffs the last of his tunics into his sack and turns to take Mush's leash. "Someone must," he sighs, throwing the sack over his shoulder and tapping out of his cell for the last time on his platform sandals.

CHAPTER 12

Nikolaos of Thrace is sitting on the end of his bed, staring at the edge of his short Grecian sword. Today is the day, he thinks. Today I must kidnap the princess. What was it he said? Something about her head. I used to enjoy taking heads. But that head, that one I am not so fond of the idea of taking. Better to leave it attached, to leave the veil of a princess undisturbed. This is a bitter business. It is not in my nature to raise a sword, nor a hand, to a royal. I am far more at comfort serving the monarch than severing her.

Nikolaos rises and moves to his narrow window. From across the courtyard, he can see the lamplight in the princess' bedchamber. If I stand here, I will see her walk across the room. Has no one addressed this issue? To allow a guest to peek at the intimate movements of a royal from across a courtyard, simply because some fool Host of Foreign Dignitaries has chosen a hall directly opposite the royal bed suites for his guests? Does he not understand that this is a strategic disaster?

Nikolaos turns, a grim determination molding his brow to a hard line. On the floor beside his bed is the tanner's skin. The thing is hideous, and the Captain cannot imagine the level of fear that must have propelled the seamstress who made it. She will have seen him in his entirety, thinks Nikolaos. There is a seamstress, somewhere in the seediest corner of this city, who lives a nightmare, having worked upon the thing. She will have had to tan it, too, for he will hardly have done that himself. He will have thrown the whole wet and bloody mess at her, arriving like doom at her door, and barked his orders. And the only thing more hideous than the skin will have been that eye, that exposed eye, looking at her through that muslin mask and the simple phrase he will have used, something symmetrical no doubt, to yoke her to it. "Do it, or be it," he will have said. Something to that nature.

Nikolaos picks an edge of the skin up with the toe of his boot, his lips curling in disgust at the feel of it through the thick leather. I cannot bear this. How can I? What have you made me into, you devil. Would that I had never followed you here. But it was not you I followed. It was Rah.

Be a man, says another voice in his head, a deep voice, deeper even than his own. Wear a dress or wear the skin.

But is this being a man? Can I not accomplish this thing without wearing the skin of another? A flicker of light across the courtyard takes Nikolaos' attention away from the grizzly skin momentarily. He turns to peer again out the window, and as he does so, he sees that someone is crossing the gardens below with a lamp. Intrigued, he blows out the two lit lamps on his own wall, then returns to the aperture. The light is moving along the path, under a canopy of fruit trees, toward the south wing. It approaches the Dreaming Pool in the middle of the courtyard, then stops. Whoever is holding it is resting on a stone bench beside the pool. But the figure is cloaked in darkness. It has no distinguishing features.

"Perhaps?" Nikolaos speaks the word aloud. He licks his lower lip, steps away from the window, and suddenly, with a burst of decisive energy, kicks the skin under a dresser and rushes out of the room, tossing his sword on his bed as he passes it.

Below, the girl from Nesa has settled on a bench beside the Dreaming Pool of Babylon to rest. She has been searching all day for the pearl earring of the Rah. The stable was all but torn apart. Hay bales tossed hither and yon, the grain room sacked, the grain itself poured out, bag after burlap bag, and run through with anxious fingers. Each stall was stripped, horse shit was pulled apart with pitch forks, then fingers, buckets emptied, aisles inspected on hand and knee. But the elusive pearl could not be found. Now the girl from Nesa, determining that the thing *was* found and stolen by some individual visiting the palace, is inspecting every room, every drawer, every pocket of every bit of clothing, to find the thing and expose the culprit. I will have it, and I will return it to my Lord. On my knees I will return it, or die trying.

The girl from Nesa had no difficulty dispatching the innkeeper and his wife. Infused with the exhilaration of her salvation and the release of not only her spirit, but her Hatti fury, she lured the innkeeper to the laundry room after serving the couple their dinner, lay back on a pile of linen (a pile she had lain over the assassin's blade moments earlier) and arched her back, a black dog in heat. The innkeeper responded, only too glad that tonight the girl would not have to be caught and subdued, for he had had a tiring day. She is finally learning to love her master, he thought, pulling his tunic up and kneeling between her legs. "Let me," said the girl, her left hand dipping into his loincloth for his organ and opening her legs to allow him to creep closer on his knees. The miserable thing was hard, as usual, and bent slightly to the right. She smoothed her hand over it, biting her tongue so as not to vomit, and pulled back the skin along the shaft.

"Oh-h-h-h," moaned the innkeeper, unaccustomed to such enthusiasm, from slave nor wife. He closed his eyes, and as he did, her right hand darted under the linen beneath her arched back like a viper, found the hilt of the assassin's dagger (oh, smooth as silk, you are, organ of my King, metal of my Master) and just as quickly plunged the blade into his left eye socket, releasing a spurt of blood that quickly soaked her sheath as he pitched forward on top of her, groping at the wound.

But the wound was deep, the blade razor sharp, and the man bled out in minutes. The hardest part of the thing was getting out from under him, for he was fat as a pregnant sow and twice the girth. The girl from Nesa pushed and wiggled, shoved and kicked, and finally tore herself free by cutting the shoulders of her dress and slipping out like a kitten being born from the blood soaked mess. "Just as well," she said, kicking the brute in the same eye as she rose to find a lamp, then rifle through the laundry until she found a black cloak suitable for movement in the dark. She wiped the assassin's blade on a corner of the cloak, then put the weapon in her teeth as she swiped the house key from the innkeeper's apron pocket and slipped out into the hall and up the stairs. At the landing she waited, flat against the weeping stone wall, as a boy rushed up the steps from the kitchen pantry with a basket of pears and apricots. Unbelievably, he paid her no mind, though he nearly struck her with his extended elbow as he flew past. I am invisible, thought the girl from Nesa. I am under the protection of his power, his blade protects me. And she slipped up the stairs well behind the boy, making a left to his right at the top, and drifting like a bat down the hall to the master's quarters.

The wooden key slipped into the lock noiselessly. Thanks be to Taru, the innkeeper was modern in his thinking, and had installed an Egyptian pin tumbler lock into the door of his own chambers. There would be no bar on the other side, requiring someone from within to throw it.

The girl from Nesa moved on bare, if bloody, feet, into the room. The innkeeper's wife was snorting like a boar in her sleep, and the bed was easy enough to find in the dark. The girl from Nesa put one hand over the woman's nose and mouth as she lifted the assassin's weapon. She turned the dagger blade sideways, thinking of the innocent chickens she had been forced to pluck and debone in her years here as a slave. Then with all of her strength she plunged the point downward, deep into the woman's chest, severing her aorta.

Blood rushed out of the woman's mouth, ear, eyes, pumping upward from her split breast over the fingers of the girl from Nesa. "Pah, heathen bitch," muttered the girl, pulling up the woman's white bed skirt to wipe off her hands before taking the assassin's knife to the wash basin to cleanse it. When she had finished she kissed the blade like a lover, pulled open her cloak, pricked a hole in the lining, and slid the shaft in to the hilt. "There now, you may join your husband in the underworld. I have spared you the terrible fate of widowhood."

The palace bell tower had struck the fourth hour of night by the time the girl from Nesa had made her way out of the Suanna District, past the Marduk temple, and west along the Road to the stable entrance at the south west corner of the palace. Unable to find an open shop in which to find proper clothing at this hour, she determined to nevertheless introduce herself to the hapless Stable Master in her current garb, which, she found, she enjoyed enormously. It completely concealed her from the eyes of the world, and yet she experienced utter freedom of movement in her nakedness beneath. Whose had it been? Perhaps a traveler had mistakenly left it behind in his room. No matter, it was hers now, a disguise that happily imitated the assassin's wraps.

"Identify yourself," barks Nikolaos of Thrace, jarring the girl from Nesa out of her revere.

"I am the property of the Wolf of the Hatti," returns the girl coolly, rising to her feet. "And I am here to do his bidding, that is, to find the pearl earring that has been stolen from him."

"The Wolf?" Nikolaos chokes. "You? You think the great Antares of Amega needs a girl to find what he has lost?"

"I know only what my Master tells me to know. And what I know is that a certain stable man struck the Rah, dislodging a rare jewel from his ear, and that the earring is lost somewhere in this palace or else taken by the first thief who spied it lying in debris. And I know that I will be the richest girl in Nesa if I find it and return it to him. For it was he who put it in the Rah's ear in the first place."

"I see," muses Nikolaos, whose handsome face looks as if he has bitten a tart apple. "So you are Hatti born, and by some happy twist of fate, discovered by your hero here in Babylon, and now, released as you are from whatever slavery you have been subject to, you are his minion. Well then, girl from Nesa, we are of like employment. I, too, work for the Master of Amega, the one they call the Hatti Wolf, but I am afraid my task is far more compromising than that of finding an earring, no matter how lost that earring may be."

The girl from Nesa has pushed back her hood to better examine the face of the one who calls himself a servant of the

Wolf.

"You are his also? But yes, there is his mark." She points to the Tear of the Bull beneath the Captain's left eye. "It suits you," she murmurs, her eyes wandering over Nikolaos' features. "I have no such mark, but I can prove my service to him nevertheless." With that her hand snatches out the little dagger from within her cloak, holding it up for Nikolaos to inspect in the lamplight. "Do you recognize it?"

"I do," responds the Captain, squinting at the blade. "It is his ankle weapon. He carries its mate still on his person. But why would he give it to you? Were you sent to murder, here at the palace?" For a moment, Nikolaos is hopeful. Perhaps Rush has had second thoughts, and decided it would be better to send a woman to kidnap the princess. After all, she could so much more easily breach the royal bedroom, as a serving girl, a laundress, a chambermaid.

"My murdering is done," responds the girl casually. "I have only now to find the pearl. And find it I shall, or die trying. But you," she pushes a lock of hair behind one ear. "Who are you here, at the palace? Besides the property of the Wolf?"

"The palace knows nothing of my loyalty to the Assassin," answers Nikolaos, "Here, I am what I was before I met him. Captain of the Palace Guard of Cyrus, lost city of the Minoans. A soldier looking for his lost queen."

"Captain of the Palace Guard of Cyrus," repeats the girl from Nesa, "Lost city of the Minoans. How sad, Captain, to find yourself now in the position of undermining the royalty of Babylon."

"Indeed," sighs Nikolaos, looking down at his hands.

"Perhaps we can work together," says the girl, watching the man's face. "After all, we are servants of the same Master."

"Finding the pearl is easy enough," says Nikolaos, settling himself on the bench beside her. "I could have if for you by daylight."

"You are either a fool, or a braggart," says the girl, tossing her head at him. This causes her hood to fall to her shoulders, revealing her face.

"You are indeed a Hatti woman," says Nikolaos, looking

her over. "Pin straight, jet hair, decisive, manly features, wide lips, a square nose," he allows his eyes to travel down to her midriff, which exposed itself when she sat down and the cloak fell open at her lap. "Shapely."

"Yes, Sir," the girl responds, pulling the cloak around her. "I am a good example of my race. I am also clever, dangerous, and fond of luxury." When she receives no reply, she continues, "And how would you go about finding it?"

"Not so fast, little murderess," says the Captain. "Tell me first whom you have dispatched with my Master's dagger. Then I will tell you how to find the pearl."

"Easy enough," the girl sighs, pulling her hood back over her head and standing. "My master and mistress, that is, the innkeeper and his wife. Took me not a half hour, once I was given the courage." She lifts the dagger, turning it in the lamplight. "To think it sat upon his ankle," she muses, then kisses the weapon a second time.

"Day and night," says Nikolaos, "For as long as I have known him."

"I have told you what you asked. Now tell me how to find the pearl by sunrise."

"By letting me complete your assignment, while you complete mine," says Nikolaos.

"And what is yours?"

"I am to kidnap the princess."

"Kidna-?" the girl is incredulous. "This is what he ordered? But how can you? How can anyone? She is a prisoner in this palace. Never leaves it, except under heavy guard."

"A woman would be far more suited to the task, don't you think?" continues the Captain. "She could enter and leave without notice, a laundress, a chamber maid, an entertainer. She would only have to know how to use a blade. And of course, she would have to be clever ... and dangerous."

"And fond of luxury," smiles the girl from Nesa, thinking now of the princess' chambers, of the heaps of jewelry there must be, and finery, and shoes!

"Such a girl would have her pick of the princess' things, too, and who would be the wiser? Merchants must come and go daily, carrying bags and pushing carts of merchandise for her to choose from. Leaving her chamber with a bundle, under the guise of a merchant, that would be relatively easy. But how does one smuggle a body out of the palace? A woman cannot carry a body. No, a man would be needed, a man-" she turns to peer up into the princess' window, which is dark now. The girl from Nesa gnaws her thumb, thinking aloud. "A carpet cleaner, perhaps? Yes! A rug has been stained by a sloppy serving girl bringing Her Majesty her breakfast. The plum jam has turned the peacock's throat purple. Ah, my Lady, forgive me! I was only purchased for the palace yesterday. I was serving an innkeeper, pouring drunken soldiers jugs of wine, and today I find myself at the palace, before the princess of Babylon! Let me have it removed to be cleaned."

Nikolaos allows himself a chuckle. "A good start, but I think a girl like this would have her hands cut off at the elbows before the palace let her spill another pot of jam on the princess' carpet."

"Shit, then," the girl turns to glare at him, her dark eyes hot with hatred. Her voice has dropped an octave. "I'll find some animal's shit. The woman loves her beasts. A monkey! Look there, on the corner of your favorite Egyptian rug, My Lady! I'm afraid one of your pets has had an accident! Let me have it removed to the laundry-"

"Right. Monkey shit on the carpet. And then? When and how is the princess subdued? Shall you pull the assassin's dagger from your robe, hypnotizing her while I bound into the room to wrap her in the soiled rug?" Nikolaos, slaps his hands on his knees and rises.

"Not at all," snaps the girl. "I will subdue her myself. I need only be alone with her for an instant. She is dainty of limb and frail of spirit, more ill than well most of her life. Then I will wrap her in the carpet. All you need manage is to disguise yourself as a carpet cleaner. And summon the strength to carry her," she adds, somehow managing to look down her long, Hittite nose at him, though he stands a good hand over her.

"And you think a carpet cleaner will be allowed to walk

out of the palace without his burden being inspected? No, we will have to find a place to hide her here, within the palace."

"So find one." The girl from Nesa pulls her hood over her head, takes up her lamp, and begins to move into the shadow of a fig tree. "Get out of the sight of prying eyes, you fool," she hisses at him, "Or we shall be caught before we've begun. Now tell me, ill-chosen kidnapper, how you intend to find the pearl earring."

Nikolaos, unaccustomed to being called a fool, has his hand on his empty belt before he has reached the sound of her voice through the leaves. "I should take your head," he spits, grabbing her cloaked arm and spinning her to face him.

"That would leave you yet with only one," snarls the girl. "Touch me again and I will give you something to remember me by."

"If you are a good example of a Hittite woman," thinks Nikolaos aloud, "It is no wonder the assassin was born a Hittite."

"Thank you," smiles the girl from Nesa, pleased.

"I need only find the man with a secret, most likely in the stable itself, and I have found the pearl," says Nikolaos. "I was a captain of many men. If I know anything, it is how to read them."

"Well, Captain," says the girl from Nesa, "You will have to bring me the earring first. I have no intention of risking my life until I have it in my hands."

"Neither will it be in your hands until the princess is in mine," answers Nikolaos.

"But you will prove to me you have it, at least?" the girl peers up at him with distaste. "Or do you think Hatti women are like the Greek girls you no doubt have been lying to all of your handsome life, eh? Willing to lie down for you on a promise?"

"You will know I have it," answers Nikolaos, tiredly.

"Excellent, and when I do, you will keep your pretty eyes open, for I will send you a sign that I have her also." And with that, the girl from Nesa disappears into the dark garden leaves, leaving nothing but the chattering of a monkey behind for the Captain to contemplate.

Rush enters the House of Seven Cisterns at midnight. Considering the goons at the front gate his own employees, being underlings of his servant, the High Priest, he slips over the wall along the east side of the estate, a deliberate vanity, since the wall is just across the Ishtar road from the Southern Fortress. Atop the buttresses of that massive structure, Amorite guards pace the parapets, oil lamps lighting their way in the moonless night, while that which they seek tops the high garden wall of the Temple of the Rah mere yards from the circles of their lamplight, then makes his way through the vegetation to climb the staircase at the back of the house to the High Priest's terrace.

"Ugh!" the wind escapes the High Priest's lungs like a fart, for he has dined on pigeon in garlic sauce that evening, and the assassin claps his hand over the man's mouth in self-defense.

"You stink, man, what do you eat, you pompous glutton, to make you stink so?" mutters the assassin, thinking better of his decision to interrupt the priest's sleep with his terrifying presence before he visits the Rah.

"I am a man of excellent gastronomic discretion," snarls Mochlos, making a weak attempt to wrestle out from under the assassin's bulk. "And the cook here is a genius with sauces. You might try his inky cap mushroom in wine, or perhaps his puffer fish, or his immature bullfrog soup..."

But the assassin ignores Mochlos' poisonous suggestions, and merely gives him a light pat on one cheek with the back of a hand as he rises.

"How is our little god, priest? Have you brought him back from the land of dreams for me?" The hooded beast looks up, his exposed eye scanning the carved, ivory tile ceiling as if he might see through the floor of the priest's apartment with the ferocity of his desire.

"As a matter of fact," pipes the priest, straightening his night gown and throwing back his covers to expose two, hairless stick legs, "I have."

Instantly the black wraith is on him. "What is this?" he rumbles, nose to nose with the priest, his massive hand encompassing the better part of the man's neck.

"Wouldn't a bit of good humor be more appropriate, given the circumstances?" squeaks Mochlos through his bruised windpipe.

"How," the assassin's lashes sweep the priest's brow as his eye darts over the man's face. "How did you accomplish this, priest?"

Mochlos takes a determined breath, staring that single eye down. "I am a high priest, am I not? I have ordered this city to fast, in supplication to the god. Two birds, one stone. If they must fast, the land may rest. If they fast, they are too weak to further insult the Rah with their sins. Goodbye gluttony, sexual perversion, the immolation of their babes." Mochlos shrugs. "All that is left is sloth, and sloth can harm no one."

Rush is peering at the high priest with the intensity of a pit viper. At last he blinks, and Mochlos twitches his brow, casually. When the iron grip on his throat is released, he says simply, "Well, I suppose you shall have to see him."

"Indeed," growls Rush, lifting himself off the priest for the second time.

"Well he isn't alone. There is a girl with him."

"Isn't there always?" answers Rush, moving toward the doorway.

"Well, for heaven's sake, man," hisses Mochlos, shoving himself off his mattress and straightening his gown. "Must you scare her to her death? Mightn't I…. prepare them first…for your entrance?"

"Pah, when did Rush The Assassin ever announce his coming," scoffs the enormous darkness in the doorway, but as if thinking better of his dispassion, the beast stops, rests one paw on the doorframe, and turns back to the priest. "He is weakened by his state, no doubt?"

"Of course he is weak! He has the mind of an animal. He grunts and growls, snarls and swats. It is only the girl who has kept him half human since he woke, and the sight of you, *you* of all people, is likely to send his spirit straight back from whence it came forever. And the girl's too, I would imagine. You are a bull in the pottery, Sir, and I wonder no one has ever told you," says the priest, planting his fists on his hips.

At this, the monster drops its head, and in the lamplight the priest is sure he sees that one exposed eye smiling.

"Indeed someone has, priest. And it is time I take our little cat home for her to pet and coddle. She has only recently lost a dear companion, and she must be ill at heart."

"You speak of your wife," nods Mochlos, inching forward. "And of the Asian woman, the grave keeper."

"Ting Ya," affirms Rush, raising his eye.

"I am ... truly sorry then," says the priest, after a tense silence. "She was a ... remarkable creature."

"I would not have him know," says Rush, his baritone cracking.

"No, of course not. Only we cannot protect one who walks with the gods from what he can see."

"You amaze me, priest," says the hood, wagging cynically. "Sometimes I actually consider the possibility that you might believe your own deceptions."

"Sometimes I do," answers Mochlos softly.

"And the cub?" Rush lifts his head suddenly. "What has become of the Anatolian leopard?"

"Still up a tree somewhere in my gardens," responds Mochlos casually, one hand waving toward his terrace door. "Where can it go? The walls are taller than two men standing one atop the other, and the guards have been keeping the gate closed day and night."

"Those idiots? I could walk a bull past them," scoffs Rush.

Indeed you have, thinks the priest, for you stand in my bedroom while they snooze at the gate, lucky to be breathing from their noses and not out of the stump that was once their neck. But he says nothing. Instead, he perfunctorily nods toward his visiting room. "Perhaps you would make yourself comfortable in my absence. I will not be a moment."

But the assassin snatches his arm with a grip that could break a neck.

"Do not condescend to me, priest," says the wrapped head leaning down to breathe cinnamon scented breath into his face. "I told you once, no one announces Rush The Assassin."

CHAPTER 13

Rah is sleeping in the arms of his concubine. He dreams of a triumvirate of brilliant white horses, pulling a gilded chariot. He wears the blue and gold robes of the Cretan Sun God, and he is no longer a boy, but a man, the colt, Hali, no longer a dappled, leggy, two year old, but a silver-white stallion. Hali leads the triple horse chariot from the center, flanked on either side by mother and sister, and Rah races along a flat plain, flanked by seven other charioteers. He is in the lead when the colt's mother, running along on the right, snaps her pastern and continues running on the shattered bone four more strides before she collapses at the finish line.

Rah awakens to the sound of his own screams.

Awiti has drawn up on one elbow beside him. She peers through the dark at his face, pinching and shaking his shoulder.

"Rah! Rah! It is a dream, it is only a dream," she coos into the silvery curls at his ear. "Only a dream, sweet Rah. Come back to me."

"Gah," says Rah, raising his fists to his eyes, then pulling himself up to lean against the wall behind the bed, fold himself over onto his own drawn up knees and expel a great, human sob.

"Sweet Rah, you cry for ghosts," soothes Awiti, petting the yellow-gold curls.

"Hali no race," says Rah, gasping, pounding one fist on the mattress. "Hali no race."

"Oh!" Awiti hops from the bed. She is on her feet, pulling a linen sheet from the mattress to wrap around her naked form. "Oh, Rah! You speak! You are speaking! I must go and tell the priest, Rah!" She dashes toward the stair, tripping on the ends of her makeshift robe.

Stumbles into a black breathing wall on her way down the stairs.

She is lifted by her throat, slammed into the stairwell wall.

"Leave us," says the monstrosity. And Awiti, having dropped the sheet in fright, lurches down the staircase naked, her shapely, and unquestionably female buttocks claiming Rush's attention momentarily before he pulls off his hood, tucks it in his weapons belt, and finds his way to the bed of the still yowling Rah.

"What dreams torment you, my little cat, eh?" laughs Rush, and sighing with relief at the sight of the Grain God he bends to tousling the blond mop.

Rah looks up at him with a tear stained face, scowling.

"Is Wolf," he says. "Wolf again. Pah. Wolf he kill cat. Always kill. Always chase, like death."

Rush takes the boy's chin, shakes it. "Yes, bad wolf. Now what is it that frightens you? Or must I enter your dreams myself and wreak havoc against these shadows?"

"Hali," Rah begins, searching the assassin's face for understanding, "Was race. Hali, Hali mare, also one more. Three. Hali mare, she break leg again. I dream twice now. Hali no race, Wolf! You promise Rah, Hali no race!" Rah takes the assassin's shoulder, squeezes the iron deltoid.

Rush settles himself on the bed beside the boy, stretches out his long legs. He draws his hands up to rest his head in them against the wall at his back, covering the rape of Ninlil. "Ah, Rah, sometimes a dream is only a dream," he says. He crosses his ankles. "And who would dare race your Halix in my absence?" he asks, his baritone a fatherly rumble.

"Maybe Grippa son, no?" answers Rah, wiping tears from his lashes.

"Pah, hardly, Rah. Your horses are safe." Rush leans forward to pull his remaining ankle dagger from its holster, then absently begins trimming his cuticles.

"Where other one is?" asks Rah, pointing to the dagger, then to Rush's ankle. "Wolf is lose?" His face brightens. He looks into Rush's eyes, delighted. "Ta-hah! Wolf is lose his dagger! Someone take?"

The assassin's eyes narrow. "One day you will go too far, boy," he says, pointing the tip of the blade at Rah's lips. "It is no wonder you lost half your tongue. Don't make me take the other half."

The boy's grin collapses. "Rah bite tongue," he returns, sullen. "Nobody take. Rah no speak, many year. Only speak again in Illyria. Only after Rah has horse to train. Begin to speak to horse. Later, to men."

Rush stares dumbly at the boy. The blade he holds to those apricot lips wavers, the hand drops limply onto the bed. Rah is glowering up at him under his silvery, fox-tail brows, waiting.

"When did you bite your tongue off, boy?" whispers Rush, hoarse. "Do you remember?"

"Yah, Rah remember. Rah is this big," the boy flattens one hand and chops the air at his own navel. "No speak until this big," he lifts the hand. Now it is under his chin.

"What..." Rush begins, then takes a deep breath, picks up the dagger, slips it back into its holster. "What else do you remember, Rah? Do you remember when you became....when you were taken to be a slave?"

But the boy only shrugs, looks down at his hands. "Maybe remember. Maybe only dream." He looks up. The blue-green eyes glimmer in the dark. "Maybe dream is only dream."

Rush peers at the perfect face in the lamp light. "You use my own words against me. But you remember. Tell me, Rah. Tell your Wolf. Perhaps he will go a-hunting one day, eh? A-hunting for the one who took you. I owe him much, after all, do I not? I would have never found you, had he left you where you were. I would have never..." but the assassin's voice drifts.

"How you find?" scoffs Rah, lifting his chin. "Even Wolf can no find piece of hay in stack of hay. All alike," he spits, nodding his head, strangely, toward the north wall of his temple. On it, the sky god, Enlil, stands on a mountain and blows his golden breath down onto a lush plain of waving barley.

At first Rush is confused by the image, which is lit by a small oil lamp embedded in the wall below Enlil's feet. Then an idea enters his head and he sits up, swinging his feet to the floor. "Do you think there is a man alive I cannot find, Rah?" he murmurs.

"Maybe dead already," answers Rah. "Rah be seventeen summer now. This man, he be old. More old even Wolf." He shakes his head. "Hard life, kill, kill. Live to kill. One day, be kill."

"One day you will tell me, Rah. One day you will remember, and I will go a-hunting," he nods at the mural, at the plain of waving barley. "Far north."

In the morning, Nikolaos visits the palace stable. The first man he sees is Buhuru-Hatu, who is whistling a little peasant tune his mother used to whistle to the chickens to make them settle and lay. Buhuru-Hatu is graining the horses, and he is in a capricious mood. Today is a very special day, for Buhuru-Hatu has been keeping a secret, a secret he has sewn carefully into the hem of his tunic, and today he intends to smuggle his secret out of the palace and reap his reward. Once the horses are grained (he would never leave the horses hungry, and if he did, they would most assuredly kick their stall walls and cry out in outrage until Hatu-Hadu came running to see what the racket was all about) he will leave on his mission to secure his fortune and kiss his brother's overbearing ego 'good-bye'! He will slip out the southwest gate and head directly to the House of the Seven Cisterns, where he will present to the Priest of the Rah of Knossos the missing earring. This, surely, will result in an enormous reward, and he will be free of his brother Hatu-Hadu forever.

Buhuru-Hatu is all but finished, having just deposited a double portion of sweetened barley and oats into Petuk's feed trough through a slat in his stall door when he notices a tall man of exceptional bearing striding toward him from the arena entrance. The man wears a short blue cape, an odd leather helmet, and a broad, highly-jeweled weapon's belt. A short, fat blade hangs from his waist, slapping his thigh rhythmically as he walks. Buhuru-Hatu blinks. The man appears to be striding quite confidently, indeed angrily, toward him. Buhuru-Hatu drops the grain scoop on top of a bag of oats and stands up, swallowing a bit of bile that has risen in his throat.

"You there!" says the man in the cape. "Show me the place where the Stable Master struck the Rah of Knossos!"

Just like that, and Buhuru-Hatu, born and raised a man of lesser class, jumps like a rabbit to attention at the authority of the man. Though by whose authority he speaks, is anyone's guess. He is not a soldier of Babylon, nor a palace guard, and yet by the very fright of his voice, which cuts through Buhuru-Hatu's morning like an executioner's axe cuts through a neck, he is able to bring the stable master's assistant to his knees before his cart. Dear gods of the underworld do not let this man take my head before I have time to speak! thinks Buhuru-Hatu, shaking like a foal just dropped from its mother's womb and attempting its first steps.

"Get on your feet, man, and if your tongue fails you, point! Show me precisely where it happened!" says the caped man.

Buhuru-Hatu stumbles to his feet, then trots past the man to Samsu-titana's stall. "Here, sir!" he burbles, eyes fixed on his own feet, he points to the stall of the king's Turkoman, his wrist quivering like a virgin on her wedding day. "Just here! But the entire aisle has been searched, sir! Every stall torn apart! There is no earring here, sir!"

Buhuru-Hatu's knees begin to tap out a crooked tune as the shadow of the cape swims like a shark toward him on the cobblestone floor.

"Who asked you for an earring, grain man? And why do you tremble so? You bring suspicion on yourself with your fear even as you blurt your secret."

The man's voice is a whisper, a puff of air against his shaven pate. Buhuru-Hatu drops to his knees a second time, this time to beg for mercy.

"Of course," the man in the cape continues. "The one who grains the horses would have found it, and kept it, hoping it would buy him a new, and better life."

Buhuru-Hatu lifts his hands to take hold of the caped
man's tunic in supplication. But before he can utter a word, he
is struck in the head with a fist like a rock. He rears back on
his haunches, his hands slapping the ground.

"How dare you touch your better? I would take your head
now, if I were in my own country."

The point of a wide, flat sword slices the air above
Buhuru-Hatu's head. He cries out. The point finds his larynx
and rests there.

"Give it to me," says Nikolaos, "Give me the earring."

Buhuru-Hatu rends the hem of his tunic, shakes the pearl
into his palm, offers it up to Nikolaos with head bowed.

"This now is *our* secret," says Nikolaos, slipping the
earring into a pocket within his weapon belt without giving it
more than a glance. "Your master has spied us, you see? Over
there? That shadow by the door of- No! Do not turn to look.
Let him believe he has seen something he cannot prove. Do
you know I have saved your guts being spilt today, grain man?
For if the Assassin had found the ring in your possession, he
would have opened you like a sack of grain just for touching
the thing. There would be your reward, to watch your own
entrails leak from your slit belly in loops. And lucky you would
be, that the man had no tree nearby to hang you from before
he slit you. Else you would be feeding the birds for hours."

Buhuru-Hatu is weeping into his hands, muttering
apologies for his mother having whelped a fool. He barely
notices when the tall man shoves him onto his side and strides
toward the Stable Master's apartment.

Hatu-Hadu has been watching from his doorway. He has
no reason to believe he has been seen. The door is opened
only the width of his hand, and he is completely hidden,
standing as he is against the wall of his room. He is unaware
that the torchlight behind him has created an elongated shadow
of his silhouette on the stone floor of the aisle.

He draws back into the apartment as the tall, elegantly
dressed stranger strides across the distance of six stalls toward
his room. What is this? thinks Hatu-Hadu. Who is this man
that he charges about in my stable like he owns the place,

questioning my man, putting him on his knees with a blade to his throat? And yet Hatu-Hadu has no inclination to step out into the aisle and confront him. Indeed, the very force and determination of the man's approach melts his bowels. Hatu-Hadu grips his useless arm with his good hand and flattens his back against the wall. He cannot be coming here for me. What have I to do with this, this, whatever has transpired between himself and my brother? Perhaps Buhuru has over-grained his horse. Yes, that must be it. The soldier came in on a fine Egyptian animal and the animal is pacing, pawing, turning in circles in its stall. The man is justifiably angry. Do you not know how to grain a hot-blooded Egyptian? You will founder him. I will have lost a horse and for what? Because Babylon is the city of the Turkoman? Is it my fault that your animals are so proud and brave? Is it my fault that Babylon will not sell a Turkoman, and so I am forced to accept second best? This animal of mine is as fragile as a reed on the Nile. And you have poisoned it with your rich concoction of sweet grains. Why, I could eat that myself and live on it for a month it is so rich. Yes, yes. This is what has transpired. I will make amends to the foreigner, who is certainly here from some far off land--look at him. I have never seen such a uniform. Nor such a countenance, such bearing...

Hatu-Hadu's thoughts are interrupted by the crashing of his cell door against the wall upon which it is hinged. He jumps, still clutching his useless arm, then steps forward to fall on his knees. He is immediately met with a boot to the chest, and falls backward, both arms akimbo over his head.

"You imbecile. You think you can spy on a man with your back to a lantern? You are the piece of shit that struck the Rah! There is the signature of the man who took your whip arm, right there on your cheek. How did he manage to keep himself from opening your head with a blade I do not know, except that you must be of greater value to him alive than dead. Therefore I will leave you alive. Tell me what you have seen and heard."

Nikolaos kicks the man in his kidneys for good measure, settles his fists on his hips, waits.

"I heard nothing, Lord!" cries Hatu-Hadu from the

packed dirt floor. "I saw you speaking with my brother there, saw him fall to his knees, I wondered what had upset a guest of the palace, and what I might do to correct the situation, that is all!"

"You saw him lead me to that stall there," Nikolaos nods at Samsu-titana's stall. "And you wondered, was he showing me where the Rah's earring was lost? And now you snivel like a dog denying it. You have lost the use of one of your arms already because of your overbearing conceit, yet your conceit continues, for you refuse yet to tell the truth, considering yourself a better liar than I a judge of liars!" Nikolaos sets the point of his sword against the stable master's sternum. "I should thrust you through, but I am bound by a greater man, and that man chooses that you should live. But I tell you this, if you speak a word of what you have seen to anyone, anyone at all, I will come back and take your eyes."

"I am already blind, I swear to you, good Master. I saw nothing, I see nothing. You were never here at all!"

"Good," nods Nikolaos, replacing his sword in his belt and pulling the stable master to his feet. "Now saddle my animal. I must return what I have found to its owner."

"Gladly, Sir," says Hatu-Hadu, bowing low, then, as Nikolaos turns his back on him, waving frantically at his brother. "Saddle this man's horse at once, Buhuru!"

And as his brother rushes off to find the Cyrian's oddly familiar saddle (where has he seen one of these before?) Hatu-Hadu collapses back against the wall of his cell, heaving and holding his kidneys with his good hand. "Mother of Marduk, ever since that boy appeared my life has gone to the underworld. Curse him! May he never wake! May he wander in the land of Upelluri for all eternity!"

It is early evening when Horus arrives at the front gate of the House of Seven Cisterns. The two house guards look him over, arms crossed over their massive chests, and burst out laughing.

"Did the master call for a eunuch?" says the taller of the two, wiping tears from his eyes.

"We've got one upstairs in the tower, do we need

another?" cries the second, slapping his thighs and doubling over with mirth.

"What is that on your head, girl?" asks the taller, reaching for Horus' strange plate-on-a-cone shaped hat, but the magician steps quickly out of his grasp, holding the sides of his cap to his ears for fear that his unruly red curls will spring from it, making him even more ridiculous than he is.

"I am a magician, Sir, from the palace, and a friend of the Rah," squeaks Horus, trying with all of his stage experience to accomplish a look of distain. In fact, he is terrified of these burly apes, and has visions of himself being hauled kicking and crying into the tropical gardens before him and being abused unmercifully. "Why, I shared a room with him and-" Horus is startled from his discourse by an unmistakable sound in the olive tree just above the tall guard's head. His head rocks back, and he loses his hold on his hat. "Shhhhhh!" hisses Horus, his finger to his lips. He glares at the two men, who, at the sight of his hair, have collapsed in guffaws.

"Is the face paint not enough?" cries the one, gasping for breath. "Must he have hair the color of a baboon's ass?"

"What is all this?" a noble voice snaps the two goons to attention, and Horus is still pointing into the tree when the man, running down the red brick path from the house, stops in front of them.

Horus turns to see a tall, slender house slave wearing a gold-trimmed green gown, his long, braided beard reaching the gold sash at his waist, his head and brows shaved.

"There is a wild cat in that walnut tree there!" hisses Horus. "Has someone lost a cat?"

Hearing this, the guards step back, hoping to melt into the brickwork of the garden wall.

"A cat? You saw it?" Nipu steps closer, follows Horus finger with his eyes and peers up into the tree. "Oh my! Yes! There it is! Well we must catch it somehow, and quickly. The Master is desperate to find it." Nipu looks over at the goons beside the wall, who lower their heads. "But we have no one with any skill with wild things," he adds bitterly.

"I am that person, Sir," says Horus. "I am sent from the palace. An animal trainer, and magician. An entertainer. I shared a room with the Rah at the palace, for he is a wild thing himself, you see." Horus looks back into the tree, purses his lips, makes a string of soft, kissing sounds. "Ah, you see? She is used to human affection. Someone has raised her by hand. She knows this sound." Horus lowers his bag carefully to the ground, then approaches the trunk of the walnut, turns his back to it, and leans against it. "You must back away, Sir, and these two also. Perhaps they can move off down the wall and out of sight for just a moment."

Nipu gives the two guards a stern look, and the men do as Horus asks.

Horus fishes for something in the pocket of his tunic. Then he lifts his hand, opening his palm to offer the cub a few bits of dried herring. There is a rustle in the leaves. Silence. Another. And suddenly, the cub is visible sliding awkwardly and head first down the trunk. Horus gives it his shoulder for purchase and lifts the treats to its muzzle. The cub licks up the offering hungrily.

"There we are, little one. I have more. Here you go. All of Mushy's fish-fish. Ah, look here. A collar." And Horus is kneeling with the cub in one arm and fishing in his sack with the other. He soon pulls out a red leash and fashions a harness around the kitten's chest. "He will slip a collar," says Horus, rising with the cub secure in his arms.

"You are marvelous with wild things," muses Nipu, motioning a lesser house servant, who has been standing in attendance behind him, to pick up Horus' bag. "Do you think you can get it inside the house?" He raises a hand toward the front doors of the ziggurat.

"It seems to me that he must be quite accustomed to the inside of houses," answers Horus, walking along side Nipu as the guards surreptitiously return to their posts at the gate. "He was quite confident to climb on my shoulder, and to take treats from my hand. This animal is tamed, Sir, though I cannot imagine who might have owned it. It is certainly an Anatolian leopard, and must have been smuggled into the city by a very brave poacher indeed."

"That is quite possible," is all that Nipu returns, swinging open the great, golden doors of the House of Seven Cisterns.

"Oh!" exclaims Horus, looking about as he enters. "Oh, this is enchanting!" He gasps as he sets the cub down on the polished green and white stone parquet. As if accustomed to a harness, the animal requires only a gentle tug to keep it at the magician's side.

A rush of footsteps down the staircase at the far end of the room brings Nipu to attention. He steps quickly to the side, gesturing to Horus and the cub as Mochlos, his white robe billowing about him, hurries toward them.

"A visitor from the palace, Sir, has recovered the lost kitten," says Nipu, bowing ceremoniously at his master.

"Indeed!" sings the high priest, his hands pressed together anxiously. "Indeed he has, Nipu! How auspicious! And who is he? Who may I thank for turning our fears to joy?" Mochlos reaches for the magician with both hands, then, seeing the newly cut scar on his left cheek in the house torch light, withdraws them and steps back. "Welcome, welcome!" he babbles, one eye on the cat, the other, on the magician.

"I am Horus The Magus, Master, and I was the Rah's companion at the palace before he came to you here," answers Horus, giving the leash a tug as the kitten paws Mochlos' toes.

"Are you, are you indeed. That is a peculiar scar, there," swallows Mochlos, "for an entertainer…"

Horus, remembering his ploy, touches the scab. "I, that is, do you," he fumbles, calling upon his training on the stage, "Do you recognize it?"

"I would be quite the fool to fail to recognize the scar I must live with myself," answers the priest, setting the tip of his index finger on his own matching Tear.

Horus turns to take his hat from the servant that has fetched it, and followed him inside. He takes a moment to stuff his corkscrew hair back under it, adjusts it, raises his eyes to the high priests. "May we speak in private, Master?" he stage whispers behind a hand.

"Yes, yes, of course," says Mochlos, waving Nipu and the others out of the room. "Come, sit," he motions Horus toward a couch. "Bring something raw for the beast, Nipu," he calls after his servant. The tall slave turns, bows, disappears into the back of the house. Mochlos settles himself on the couch and pats the seat beside him.

"Well, Horus the Magician," he smiles his tigerish smile, "How is it that you come to wear the Tears of the Bull and live? It can only be that you are in his service, but by what means? Were you discovered by him when he went calling on the Rah at the palace one night? Or are you a hired spy from Amega, here in Babylon, and a longtime vassal of the beast. Ah, but your Tears are fresh, and so it must be the former."

"I am most certainly in his service, Sir, for he told me himself to watch over the Rah as if he were my own cub," answers Horus, lifting the leopard into his lap as Nipu returns with a plate of scraps from the kitchen. He takes the offering, sets it before the kitten on his knees. "I would have come in either case," he continues, eyes on the cub as it gobbles the tidbits of raw meat. "I ... I wish to serve the Rah, Sir, in whatever capacity I can. I became quite attached to him at the palace–"

"Yes," nods Mochlos, "I'm sure you did. But," he points to the weeping wound on the magician's cheek, "Not enough to pretend to have been marked by the assassin, I hope, for that would make you either a fool or a mad man, using the beast's mark without his consent."

Horus takes an even breath, sets the plate, and the cub, down on the tile at his feet. "Yes," he nods, "And such a foolish ....or else mad.... man would hardly come to the house of the High Priest of the Rah, knowing full well that he, too, wears the mark of the assassin, and must certainly know a fake from the genuine article!" He gives a half-hearted chuckle, turns to the priest, presents his cheek.

"Mmmmm," says Mochlos, peering at the replica of his own, hard won Tear. "How true. And even if that priest could not determine its authenticity," he motions for Nipu, who has returned from the kitchen with a plate of confections, to leave the sweets on a low table, "The assassin himself, who, by the way, was here only last evening, would surely sniff it out." He takes a small, round cake of honey-dipped mashed pistachios and nibbles on it. "Mmm. Delicious. You must try one," he offers the plate to Horus.

CHAPTER 14

Princess Ephtheta is dreaming.

In the hour before dawn, she is awakened by a dream, a dream of the Wolf of Amega, and of two younger wolves, twins, the likeness of their father, all except for their eyes, which are not pitch, but pale amber, like her own.

"You will be our mother," says the one.

"We hunt in pairs," says the other.

"The wolf has many sons," says a third voice, a voice made of silver and wind, a voice which touches her shoulder like a hand and then skates up the side of her neck and into her hairline, and it is the fingers of the Wolf, iron fingers, fingers that could crush her head like a pomegranate but do not, are gentle, even tender; and then the mouth, rich, red, succulent, bristles brushing her lips and cheek, her nose, and the warm breath, entering her, filling her with life, ensuring her of a tomorrow.

Ephtheta awakens, brushes the tingle of whiskers from her mouth, the tickling breath from her shoulder, and moans with pleasure. I shall have his children, she thinks, I need no witch or dream shaman to tell me the meaning of this dream. The Wolf of Amega is to be my lover. He will fill me with life. Twins!

Ephtheta stretches for the bell cord. A new handmaid appears, an odd girl with sharp, strong features, eyes that, even cast down, seem somehow dangerous. Madam, the carpet is stained, she says. But who are you? Where is Yesh? I am new here at the palace, she says. Yesh has heard news of her brother's death and she is in mourning today. Yesh had a brother? No, she would have told me. But it is too late, the pillow is over her face, the handmaid's weight pinning her to her bed. She cannot expand her ribs beneath it. Her weak lungs panic, she flails and claws but the girl has the strength of a man. She feels her spirit lift from her body. White light, safety.

Ephtheta's body relaxes. The girl pries open her mouth and dribbles the tincture of poppy under her tongue. And when Ephtheta dreams again, she dreams not of a wolf, but of a fox, with dangerous downcast eyes and a strong, sharp jaw.

Nikolaos returns to the palace shortly after dawn. He has spent the night at the House of Seven Cisterns, which has becoming something of a circus. The assassin, dressed as he came in his black muslin nightmare, wanders about the house and gardens freely in daylight, alone or else with the Rah. He is barefoot, bareheaded, and being so incongruous is such a setting, every bit the monstrosity in light that he is in darkness. He has no fear of discovery. The walls are over sixteen feet, and the guards and servants are like moths clinging to the walls, silent and motionless unless disturbed, their faces molded into clay masks of terror. The priest, somewhat sullen in general but cordial toward the Captain nevertheless, has attempted to maintain the composure and decorum of his household, but it is hard to guide sheep through a ravine when there is a wolf perched on the cliff side. Adding to the spectacle a comic flair is the palace magician, Horus, who lost his hat in the flower garden when the Wolf of Amega, seeing his false Tears, held him over a balcony by his feet. The man is now forced to go about his chores, these being the care of a young leopard and the entertainment and management of the Rah, with his orangey curls springing in all directions from his head. This would be comedy enough, but the man wears a woman's peach-colored shift, platform sandals, and makeup befitting a princess of Egypt. His counterpart, Awiti the

Hermaphrodite, is bald and veiled, dressed in a yellow silk robe befitting a priest. He is nevertheless the epitome of femininity, with his voluptuous hips and lovely round bottom, his enormous, almond eyes and full, sepia lips. They make a most ridiculous pair, these servants of the Rah, each seeming to attempt to steal the other's true sex, neither quite comfortable with his own.

The house is a fortress of secrets, and the priest deals with all contact from the outside himself. The Rah has recovered from the dreaming tea, appears to have recovered as well from his animal state, and although physically weakened from his ordeal, is in high spirits. He speaks of returning to the palace to dance for the King, and the assassin listens with the kindness of a father, nodding and biting his lip. Out of earshot of the Rah he growls through his teeth at the priest for putting these ideas in the boy's head in the first place, for how is he to allow such a thing? The Rah, *his* Rah, performing for the King of Babylon, his bitter enemy? To Nikolaos alone he has confided his rendezvous with Aleksandus and Agrippa, his orders for an attack in twenty one days from that rendezvous: a chariot attack, led by Agrippa, launched from the southeast where the gates of Babylon are most easily overwhelmed, and a water attack made from the river by Aleksandus.

"Hah, you see the genius, Niko?" boasts the Wolf, engulfing the Captain in a single arm hug as he rips at a pomegranate with his incisors. "They will have only the Palace Guard to overcome while the Babylonian Army twiddles its thumbs in the Northern Fortress, watching for Mursilis to attack from the northwest. Twenty one days: three weeks. Not a moon. Not half. But enough time for a city now ordered by my priest to live on the grain and produce imported from its southern neighbors to wither. In a week, Agrippa will have cut off the trade route into Babylon though Syria. In two, he will have launch hundreds of boatloads of my men into the Euphrates, twenty miles south of the Samas Gate. And in three, while the palace guard is busy dying at the blades of my wolves, Aleksandus will attack from the Uras and Zababa gates, taking the districts of Suanna, Eridu and Te-Eki. And with the palace and the eastern quadrant of the city in our hands," the Wolf give Nikolaos' a hearty slap on the shoulder, knocking half the wind from his lungs, "Which is to say, the King, the princess, and the noble families our hostages, Babylon," he crushes the pomegranate in his fingers, red juice sluicing down his forearm, "Is defeated."

"But the princess," stammers Nikolaos, "Am I not to kidnap her? To avoid all this bloodshed?"

"That is a personal matter," answers Rush, releasing the captain and biting into the defeated pomegranate. Red juice runs into his beard and a servant is instantly at his elbow with a clean linen. Rush grabs it, neatly wipes his chin.

"Because of the attempt on Mursilis," says Nikolaos, nodding. "This kidnapping, it has nothing to do with sparing Amegan lives in battle. It is a conceit. It is your retribution for Mursilis. You want the King to feel your strength, your absolute dominion of his territories. Even to the extent that you would take his most precious possession."

"You forget his maggots gave up Mursilis for my Rah?" answers Rush evenly, his eyes suddenly cold, hollow.

Nikolaos swallows, only just realizing the depths of the pool he has just wandered into. He opens his mouth, but has no words to speak.

"Captain," whispers Rush, who in an instant has taken Nikolaos by the throat and pinned him against a wall. His lips brush Nikolaos' cheek as he speaks. "Will you never learn not to question me? Must I explain myself to you, Niko? Like a wife? And if you say yes, you may nag me like a wife, might I not be due some husbandly pleasure from you?"

"She will be kidnapped, Master," answers Nikolaos through closed teeth. "And delivered to you. Forgive me my insolence."

"Forgiven," nods Rush grabbing the Captain's head in both hands and forcing a terrible, toothy kiss onto his lips. "Now go and finish the task you have been given. By tonight the girl is to be here at the House of Seven Cisterns, and no one the wiser."

By noon, Nikolaos is back at the Palace, a reasonable facsimile of a Syrian rug salesman's robe stuffed in his saddlebag, along with a merchant's cap and enough twine to wrap a rug the height of a princess. He has found a bit of papyrus paper stuffed under his door with a crude stick figure in charcoal drawn on it. The figure is prone and sleeping. Assuming this is the girl from Nesa's message to him that the princess is in her possession, and quieted, he dons his costume and makes his way to the north wing. The palace is oddly quiet today, no doubt as a result of the High Priest Of The Rah's orders for penance and fasting throughout the city.

He has no difficulty reaching the princess' rooms, but finds the door bolted. He taps out the syllables of his name, Nik-o-la-os, and waits. Presently the girl from Nesa, dressed as a chamber maid, opens the door.

"She is subdued. Use that rug, there. I have stained the corner with monkey shit, in case you are stopped," she hisses.

"Lovely, a princess of Babylon, wrapped in a shit-stained rug," mutters Nikolaos.

"The hand-maid, Yesh, is drugged and sleeping in her own chamber in the inner room there." The girl from Nesa points toward an alcove and a hall. "The princess lies in her own bed," she cocks her head toward a beaded curtain door on the opposite wall. "Quickly!" she waves Nikolaos toward it. "I am leaving you to your task. And where is my proof that you have found the earring?"

Nikolaos turns, hands the girl a bit of cloth, folded and basted lightly into a little envelope. The girl from Nesa pulls the stitching out quickly with her teeth. The cloth falls open in her palm. In it is a curl of golden hair.

"Proof enough?" asks the Captain dully.

The girl looks up at him, nods, folds the cloth over the curl and slips it into a pocket. Then she is at the door, peering down the outer hall. She tosses a sly look over her shoulder at Nikolaos, and disappears.

The Captain steels himself for what he is to find in the princess' bedchamber. He pushes aside the beaded curtain, thinks better of it, and crosses the visiting room to the hall and the handmaid's quarters. He passes a vaulted door on his left, opens it, finds a bath chamber, an enormous bathing pool in the center, ringed with statuary and plants. The noon sun beams in through lattice windows facing north, and a triplet of small fountains stir the water. Nikolaos backs out of the doorway, continues down the hall, where he finds an archway on his right. The room is heavy with the scent of proteas and orchids, flowers of the southern Nile. Lying on a simple raffia mat is a tall, slender African woman. She seems to be sleeping peacefully, but on closer inspection, Nikolaos notices foam on her lips. Beside her in a rattan cage a small, narrow-faced blond monkey chatters at him angrily, even jumping onto the bars of the cage as he moves closer to the drugged Yesh to lift her wrist and feel for her pulse. The beat is barely perceptible.

"What on earth has she given you," murmurs Nikolaos, pulling a coarse hemp cover sheet over her from the base of the mat. Beside the monkey's cage, on a small table, is a blue iron cup. Nikolaos reaches for it as the monkey screams, indignant. He picks it up, sniffs the contents, dips a pinky in the amber liquid and tastes; sets it down where he found it.

Then, intrigued, he lifts the cup to the monkey.

The animal jumps onto the bars of its cage, snatches the cup, tilts it expertly against the rattan bars and licks at the perfumed brown liquid. As suddenly as it took the cup, it flings it down, screaming, wobbles to a corner of its domain and curls in a corner, quieted.

Nikolaos strides swiftly out of the room and down the hall to the princess' bedchamber. He pushes aside the beaded curtain and is struck dumb by the sight of the drooling and convulsing body of the princess, her bed gown drenched with sweat and clinging to her body like a second, transparent skin. A large black housecat lies beside her on a cream silk pillow. It gives the Captain a malevolent look, hisses, then flies off the mattress and past him, tinkling the beaded curtain as it disappears into the antechamber. Nikolaos wastes no time lifting the moaning and delirious princess off her bed and carrying her into the visiting room. He lays her on the unsoiled end of the rug, which is red and gold damask, and rolls her unceremoniously into a silk cocoon. The braided gold tassels bounce cheerfully as he lifts the six foot cylinder over his left shoulder, where it bends in a neat V, the princess bending at the hip within. Nikolaos gives his burden a shrug to adjust it and then, pulling his short Grecian sword from his belt and kissing the ruby hilt for good luck, he slips out into the empty hall toward Ameg's rooms.

He is in the east wing when he hears the voice of the Host of Foreign Dignitaries echoing down the far hall. He will recognize me, thinks the Captain, making an abrupt about-face toward the northeast stairwell. It is a servant's stair, and Nikolaos meets no resistance as he pads quickly down to the ground level, which, to his amazement, offers an exterior exit into town.

"Precisely the exit a rug salesman would take," whispers the Captain to himself, hoisting the cocooned princess more comfortably over his trapezius. "You are as light as the Rah," he murmurs into the carpet, disquieted by the comparison, "And will no doubt cause me as much trouble."

Workmen are rebuilding a broken garden wall running along the western flank of the palace. Their activity, together with the dust they raise in their work, makes good cover for Nikolaos' departure. His long strides take him swiftly into the crowded street and he is soon striding purposefully through the Eridu Market toward the House of Seven Cisterns like any other man with a task to accomplish.

"There is a man here with a rug," says the gate guard to the doorman at the House of Seven Cisterns. It is Nipu's turn to watch the Rah, keeping him from the exterior wall, which he alone could easily scale. The assassin is away, having disappeared in the night on some private business. Horus is enjoying a bath, and Awiti has spent the morning repairing Mochlos' best sleeping gown, which was torn last night when the leopard wandered into his chamber and made a game of catching his kicking feet as he dreamed.

"A rug? But the master has not ordered-" begins the doorman. But when he looks up into the fierce grey eyes of the rug salesman he finds himself stepping back, making a short bow. "I was not informed-" he begins, but is cut off by a voice behind him.

"Is Fox!" cries the Rah, shoving the doorman out of his way and throwing his arms about the Captain and his burden.

Nikolaos responds by enveloping the boy in his free arm as he gentles the cocooned princess to the floor.

"Easy, Rah, easy," says Nikolaos, but he holds the boy to his heart a long moment before he releases him. "I must see the priest at once, Rah. And the Wolf, if he is here."

"Wolf gone. Go hunt, maybe," quips Rah, looking suddenly down at the wriggling roll at the Captain's feet. "Rug be move. What you bring Rah, Fox? Nice girl, maybe?" Rah gives the rug a nudge with one toe.

Behind Rah, Nipu rushes across the tile floor toward his charge. When he sees the moving rug, he draws Rah back by an arm. The voice of the priest at the stair landing draws both Rah and Nikolaos to attention.

"Lieutenant General Nikolaos!" Mochlos limps lightly toward them. "What in heaven have you-? What ... my goddess...what misery have you brought to me now?" He looks down at the convulsing rug with chagrin.

"The Princess of Babylon, priest. Poisoned with opium tea, and barely breathing. Do not question me. It is the will of the Assassin that she be kidnapped. Now see to it that she lives, or you will be held responsible."

"*I*? What have *I* to do with this?" Mochlos chokes. "What fool gave an asthmatic princess opium tea?" He is on his knees, waving Nipu to join him in unraveling the rug. Princess Ephtheta moans and arches in her soaked bed dress. "She will surely die," moans the priest. "Get me a blanket, quickly, you fool!" he shouts over his shoulder to a house slave. "You are sure it was opium?" he looks up at Nikolaos.

"It is one drug I am familiar with. I was in charge of the Palace Guard of Cyrus, you remember. It was a favorite pastime of the less...qualified ...of my men. Of course, when I found the source of their somnambulance, they suffered the consequences."

"Of course," Mochlos frowns, returning his attention to the princess. The house servant has returned with an arm full of blankets. Mochlos grabs the pile and begins covering Ephtheta.

"She be like Rah, now, maybe," says Rah. "See Ting Ya, too."

"She is barely breathing." Mochlos slips his fingers under the blankets to find a pulse at the princess' throat. "I cannot trace her life's blood beating. Carry her to my chambers, Nipu. Tell Awiti to bring me the small trunk, the one with the triple phases of the moon painted on the lid. It is in the alcove behind the drape in the tower room."

Nipu lifts the princess; starts for the stairs.

"Who did this, Captain? At least you can tell me that? Must I always be forced to work in the dark?" Mochlos gives Nikolaos an exasperated look.

"A girl from Nesa," answers Nikolaos, "A Hittite woman. Apparently in service to an innkeeper here in Babylon, and lucky enough to be assigned the Assassin's rooms. He gave her....an assignment. To find the pearl earring at the palace. I gave her my assignment, expecting that her sex would gain her access to the princess I could not possibly gain, and in turn I found and returned the pearl."

"I see," says Mochlos, stroking his salt and pepper beard. "And where is the woman now? Still at the palace?"

"Do you need her?" snaps the Captain, who has had enough of Mochlos and his whining, "You are a high priest, well versed in the practice of poison. You must know of an antidote. Use it."

"Yes, yes, of course. But the girl, the Hittite girl, she knows too much, you see. She now knows the whereabouts of the missing princess, Captain. She holds your life in the palm of her hands." Mochlos watches Nikolaos guardedly.

"She is in the Assassin's service, priest," responds the Captain, but his voice wavers. "She would not dare-"

"No?" answers Mochlos smugly, "Any woman brazen enough to do this, surely has the audacity also to give up her secret, for a price. Imagine," Mochlos folds his arms over his vestments, casts a glance toward the stair, "What the King would give for such information."

"Perhaps, but nothing would save her from the Assassin, should she expose me," answers Nikolaos.

"I would not return to the Palace, if I were in your sandals, Captain," says Mochlos. "In any case, I think it best you remain here at the House of Seven Cisterns as a precaution, lest, finding the princess, and their guest, Captain Nikolaos, were missing at the same time, they wrestle the truth from your limbs in a very," he pauses for effect, "Unpleasant way."

Turning to limp across the green and white parquet toward the stairs, Mochlos hesitates a moment, looks over his shoulder at the Captain, and nods at a house slave.

"Show the Captain to an empty guest room on the second floor, Farah, if we have one. And tell Nipu to move my things out of the Royal suite and up into the Tower." The slave bows and leaves. Mochlos turns to face Nikolaos.

"You know that the city awaits the Rah's return to the palace. And that I have been ordered to reawaken him, so that the god I worship within him, the Minoan god of fertility, blesses the vineyards and plantations of Babylon with renewed life. So that they might flourish as they did before this foolish people farmed them to death. But do you know what will happen to me if he is not returned? Or if his return does not bring health back to this sick earth? Unlike Crete, my friend, here in Babylon, when a High Priest's prayer, and a city's penance, fails to accomplish what he promises it will, that priest is put in a golden pot, to be boiled slowly, so slowly that his poached flesh might fall from his still living bones over the course of many, many hours. Have you seen it? The steps leading up to that massive vessel in the center of the Palace Public Courtyard? That is not a decoration, Cyrus. I have been doing my homework, here in the city. They mean to put me in it, if, given sufficient time in the King's mind, I have not returned a dancing Rah, and a prosperous harvest. That is how they deal with frauds here in Babylon."

Nikolaos blinks at the priest, horrified. "The Assassin-" he begins, but Mochlos waves him silent.

"That monster has my replacement, your *wife*, Captain, safe in Amega. What does he care what happens to me? Will a wolf, once he has taken all the meat off it, fight for a bare bone?"

Mochlos flashes Nikolaos one more, dark look, then turns and begins again toward the stairs.

"Priest!" barks the Captain, and for a moment his voice is as deep as the assassins.

"What is it, Captain Nikolaos?" answers Mochlos, turning tiredly to face him once more.

"They will have to boil me with you," smiles the Captain, and to his relief, the First High Priest of the Rah gives him a courteous nod, and smiles back.

"What a stew we will make," he quips. Then, lifting the triple-moon pendant that hangs from his neck like a toasting cup, he kisses it, and disappears up the stairs.

General Agrippa stands beside a fire at the banks of the Euphrates, drinking a tea made of nettles and cinnamon. As the morning fog lifts, he stares northwest toward Babylon, contemplating his next assignment.

Agrippa's forces are crowded along the banks of the Euphrates, blocking trade from Uruk and Eridu and the Great Gulf. The spoils of this task are massive, and Agrippa has ordered a division of men to begin transporting much of the plunder back to Amega. A portion of grain, fruits, livestock and beer, as well as weaponry, have been appropriated for the troops, and Agrippa himself enjoyed a delicious roast lamb the previous evening as a result.

But his next assignment will be far less pleasant. In two weeks, the boats that have been commandeered will be refitted and manned by Amegan wolves to sail into the heart of Babylon and breech the palace walls from the river. Rappelling lines and hooks will allow commandos to grapple over the wall and take down the guards on the roof before they can summon for help. After that, it will be a matter of the bulk of his forces storming the walls from the river, using the same ropes, as well as ladders and each other's backs, while the commandos saturate the palace and sabotage a counter attack.

Agrippa sips his tea and turns to the southwest, toward Amega, where a bank of strange red-grey clouds are gathering over the plains. At first it appears as if a storm must be brewing off the Great Sea, but as the General lowers his cup, staring, he sees the morning go dark, darker than any storm, as if a great veil had been drawn over the world, as if the curtain were closing on life itself. A wall of red darkness, hurtling across the plain, galloping like an army of charioteers, like the dust that might billow about the feet of a thousand, thousand men: an impossible truth that could not be blinked or rubbed away from the eyes, charging toward him as an army charges, a tide of furious clouds consuming everything in its path.

The city sleeps. The tinkle of a donkey cart bell, the rustle of a beaded curtain in a doorway, the crow of a cock, nothing more. The first to see are the guards patrolling the western wall. They shout the alarm, and the rams horns blow. The palace awakens, and there is panic, because the city is starving, and there is no strength for war.

Then the world goes dark, the army that rushes over the wall is an army made of dust and ash, of elegance and plenty, of laughter and music and art and grace, of what is left of Crete. A red-grey ghost, a blanket of souls, a choking darkness.

One city will be buried. One city will be reborn.

CHAPTER 15

There is no blood, no army of wolves breaching the walls, no river choked with enemy hordes, only the red-grey dust covering the city like a blood-dimmed tide. A profound silence, a sooty, airless sleep has overcome the City of Light. For three days, darkness. And on the fourth, his daughter taken, his kingdom choked in ash, King Samsu-titana declares defeat. Aleksandus' troops march into Babylon through the Marduk Gate, unopposed, even as Agrippa's boatmen row into Tumar, dock, unchallenged in the channels under the palace, and take control of it.

The city is soon accustomed to the sight of Amegan warriors in the streets, in the markets, in the brothels. They are even welcomed, for with them comes the fruits of their piracy on the Great River. The cargo boats the Amegans have pirated, laden with grain and oil, figs and olives, sheep and cattle, from Egypt and Elam, Susa and Ashani are unloaded and the goods distributed throughout the city. King Samsu-titana is imprisoned in his own dungeon, while the generals of Amega await the return of their master.

In the House of Seven Cisterns, the princess has awakened. No longer imprisoned in her father's palace, nor by his fears, she watches from the third floor terrace of her new home as Aleksandus' Wolves march up the Kadingirra Road into the Lower Fortress. Beside her, Awiti stands, veiled and silent, a soft yellow ghost. The two have become friends in the days that have followed the princess' recovery from the opium tea. Like Yesh, Awiti, though a slave, possesses the quiet dignity and noble bearing of a queen. Like Yesh, stories of her homeland at the root of the Nile flow like the waters themselves. It is not long before the princess uncovers the hoax of the Nubian's sex.

"As if anyone could believe you were less than entirely female," she laughs, after catching Awiti in the bath one evening.

"But you mustn't tell, Princess, I beg you," responds a giggling Awiti. "The priest, he saved my life! He did! I owe him everything. If he wishes for me to pretend to be half-male, then I will do it. I will do it until all of the women in Babylon are half in love with me!"

"Does the assassin know?" wonders Ephtheta now, standing against the balustrade of the north terrace, for she has thought of little else than that cinnamon kiss since she has awakened, and in her mind now, every circumstance relates to it.

"He surely does," answers Awiti, her eyes flashing at the memory. "He came upon us, that is, the Rah and I-"

"I see," says the princess. "How extraordinary," and she sets the palms of her hands flat against the polished stone. Leaning over, she watches as a tall man wearing an unusual, short blue cape, dismounts a fine palace horse, hands the reins to a soldier, and strides purposefully toward the Lower Fortress gate. "Was he here while I slept, Awiti?" she wonders softly, "Did he visit me?"

"He has not been here for a fortnight, Princess," Awiti responds, following the princess' eyes. "That is the Cyrian, Captain Nikolaos," she points as the man in the cape disappears through the gates. "He has been here, at the House of Seven Cisterns. He is in great favor with the assassin. And with the Rah."

Ephtheta turns sharply. "In great favor with the assassin? Who is this man?"

"They say he was a captain in the land of the Sea People. On the lost island kingdom of Crete. He swore his queen an oath that he would protect the Rah, and when the assassin rescued the god slave and his high priest, Captain Nikolaos came with them." She gives Ephtheta a shrug. "He is the assassin's now. As we all are."

I, thinks Ephtheta, have been in the Wolf of Amega's possession since the night he kissed me. But he thinks of me only as his enemy's daughter. What will he do with me, I wonder? Could my love despise me so, for being the whelp of his foe that he would throw me in my own father's dungeon? Or worse? But she can imagine no such thing. And swooning with desire, she places her wrist to her cheek, turns to lean against the balustrade.

"Are you well, Princess? May I bring you something to drink? A cool cloth? You look as if you might faint." Awiti opens her arms, as if she would break the princess' fall. Can I touch a royal now? she wonders fleetingly. My world is turned inside out and upside down. I no longer know my own place in it.

"It is nothing, Awiti," answers Ephtheta, smiling weakly. "Only when I think of him..." she trails off, frowning.

"Oh, me too," nods Awiti, remembering the great black terror that interrupted her lovemaking with the Rah, and how it boomed at her, shaking the candlesticks, and tore the sheet from her back as she ran past him down the stairs. "He is a fright, and no less so in daylight."

Strange, thinks the princess then. I have not seen my love in daylight. Nor do I wish to! Let him come to me again in my dreams, in cover of darkness, and press his lips against mine, and fill me with more than breath alone. Oh, what a beautiful monster you are, enemy of my father. So fitting, that you should be called The Wolf. For even now, I can still feel the bristle of your muzzle on my cheek!

"I am weaker than I think today, Awiti," smiles Ephtheta then, taking the concubine's arm. "Help me back to my bed, please."

In the two weeks' time it has taken for Babylon to fall to hunger and ash, Rush has returned to Hattusha with the King's seal ring.

It was easy enough to find.

"He is a noble in the Court of Ishtar. But he will certainly have sold it himself by now," sighed Mochlos, his head in his hands. "What use is it to him? He will have sold it to a trader, perhaps even to a Hittite agent, who would have been expecting a reward for its return. He," Mochlos lifted his head, looked miserably into the assassin's black eyes. "He gave me a fortune for it."

"Describe him, priest, if you cannot give me his name. A scent is all I need to track a man, and I am in no mood to remain here, in this house of flaming fops."

"A typical Amorite with some money in his pocket," shrugged Mochlos. "Decked in jewels, purple robes, long-braided beard, bald and oiled. He had a-" Mochlos waved a hand.

"He had a what?" Rush looked up from his nail trimming. He had been lying on the priest's bed. The leopard cub beside him, had caught its own tail and licked at it elegantly. Rush dropped a hand and ruffled its head. The assassin wore his muslin leggings. His holster straps crisscrossing his broad, pale chest, hiding the star of curling black fur over his heart.

"He had an odd…well, odd to me at least…accent. As if he had been raised in another district. I couldn't place it. Not Egyptian, nor Greek… nor Hittite of course. Perhaps Illyrian…or perhaps some southern town. Eridu, Nippur…and I recall he wore an unusual scent."

"Come priest," said Rush, fiddling with the cub's left ear as he turned to lean on his hip. For a moment Mochlos imagined he reached for one of his blades. He started, then, confused, pointed at the assassin's left ankle.

"What has happened to your dagger?" he lifted his fingers to his lips.

"Gone a hunting without me. But Papa will come collect it soon enough. Now let us get back to the business of the King's seal ring. I go to Hattusha to assemble the Rah's retinue. The leopard and the ring come with me. Or else your head, priest, if you cannot tell me where to find this man."

"Well of course our business was done in secret! How could I ask him a name? I simply made sufficient inquiries to discover who might have the means, and the desire, to purchase such an item. I sent the girl with a message to the Ishtar Temple guard that, if such a man existed, he might make a transaction that evening in a local opium den. I met him there. No names were exchanged, I wore my hood up. And that is that."

"That is not that. You mention a scent." Rush sat up, set the leopard cub at his feet. The animal batted at the straps of his leather boots.

"Yes, very unusual. Exotic. Not a flowery scent. More of a musky herb. Not at all sweet. Cumin? Perhaps cumin. Yes. I would bet on it." Mochlos waved a finger in the air.

"Build?" posed Rush.

"Build? Oh, well…quite rotund, actually. Not a man concerned with his health, I can tell you that. He did imbibe in the opium as if he were quite accustomed to it. And quite fat. Not especially tall, as these Amorites seem to be. Again, as if he were born elsewhere."

"Eye color?"

"Well, I suppose … yes, brown! Not the typical blue-eyed Amorite."

"A wealth of information, priest. Though he believes he has maintained his secret identity, he will be as easy to find as a weasel in a hen house."

Two nights later the Ishtar noble was relieved of the Seal Ring of the King of the Hatti. He had not yet sold the thing, for his normal trade route down the Great River had been closed by none other than the Wolf of the Hatti himself. He had in fact been wearing the elaborate golden band since he had purchased it, and was already grieving his error, to spend such a sum on a bauble that could not be sold in his own city so long as the shadow of the wolf loomed over it. Then, one early morning, when a light rain fell so that the ash laden streets had become strange, white, molten things, pools of red-grey mud collecting here and there with sinister intent, he met the very beast himself. Leaving his homey warren of rooms along the western flank of the Ishtar edifice, Dan d'Dmaha, was headed to the noble's bath, a grand open air structure at the rear of the ziggurat, when he noticed a large, heavily decorated man in a fine yellow robe and a merchant's cap approaching under the colonnade. The man carried a rolled bathing mat and a second set of sandals, a real dandy, thought Dan d'Dmaha, who huffed to himself while arranging his face in a suitable greeting, for the two would pass under the portico in a moment and, though he did not recognize the man, he could only assume he was some palace popinjay, come to the Ishtar to pray his fat backside be spared another day of fasting.

"Good day, Sir," bowed Dan d'Dmaha courteously as the man minced, toes first, up to him. "How fairs the King?" It was a common enough expression, when one greets a member of the palace staff, but the stranger made no effort to respond in kind. No "the greatness of the king is the blood of his people," no "may he live a thousand years and may you prosper by his rule," just a strange glint in those unusually dark eyes, so unlike the demeanor of the man. Prevailing, even fierce.

"Give it me," said the smiling mouth, and for a moment Dan d'Dmaha could only stare, stare at the generous, well-formed lips under the brush of black moustache, the sides of which were long and braided, the ends held with golden bands which trotted against the trimmed beard like a pair of fine ponies as the man spoke.

"Give you what, Sir?" answered Dan d'Dmaha politely. Perhaps the man was asking for a certain greeting? A blessing? Unusual accent, in any case. And such strange, dangerous eyes…

And Dan d'Dmaha was no longer standing. Somehow, he was on his belly, his front teeth chipped on the rough paving stones under the colonnade. And an elephant's foot was crushing the air from his lungs through the center of his back.

"My gods, man, what is your will?" gasped Dan d'Dmaha, realizing now that this was a robbery. This beast was not what he seemed. A clever thief, probably some damned Hittite exiled from his own country for just such behavior, had dressed himself up like a wealthy merchant, no doubt in stolen clothing and jewels, and on this most unfortunate of all unfortunate mornings, Dan d'Dmaha has made his acquaintance. Well, he may take my very teeth. But he will not take what I have paid a fortune for. Dan d'Dmaha slipped the seal ring of Mursilis off his left hand, which was, opportunely, trapped under his own body at the moment. He palmed it, then shoved it in a crack between two paving stones.

"The ring or the finger," grunted the elephant into the back of Dan d'Dmaha's head. And he was rolled expertly onto his right hip, his left wrist instantly twisted up and behind him, straining the ligaments in his shoulder to unprecedented limits. Marduk protect me! Thought Dan d'Dmaha. It was the ring he wanted! He must have followed me here for this very purpose! Curse that priest! Why did I ever-

But the thought was never finished. His head was twisted back, his temple smashed into the paved walkway. And he was lifted, peacefully, from his nightmare to rest among the lost souls between worlds until a temple sentry man, patrolling the portico, found him and brought him to with a pail of bath water.

"Gone!" cried Dan d'Dmaha, as, coming to his senses, he groveled and groped about on the paving stone looking for the seal ring of Mursilis the Hatti. "My fortune wasted! Gone!"

"You should be happy, man," answered the sentry man. "For whatever you've lost, you did not lose your purse." And the man handed him a silken moneybag, the size of his fist, and bursting with coin.

"What?" Dan d'Dmaha snatched the pouch. He pulled at the opening, revealing a king's ransom of Babylonian marked gold. "My gods be praised!" he sang, stumbling to his feet. "The heavens blessed!"

"What did you lose, Sir?" asked the sentry, looking about for the missing item. "Perhaps when you fell-"

"No, no!" answered Dan d'Dmaha, "It was nothing. Nothing at all. Here it is, right here," and he lifted the purse up for the man to see, then brought it to his lips and kissed it. "I had tripped, you see," he pushed at a raised stone with the toe of his sandal. "And struck my head." He rubbed his temple, where a bump the size of a Bantam egg is rising. "All is well," said Dan d'Dmaha, nodding and smiling to himself. "All is well," he repeated, turning from the sentry man to find his way back to his rooms on the western tier of the temple.

Now, with the King's seal ring on his own hand, Rush the

Assassin gallops over the plains of Urgup toward the valley of Goreme and the city of Hattusha on the black Amorite warhorse. A cold rain falls, turning the crusted earth to mud. The weather is inside out, thinks Rush. The volcano has turned the world on its side and summer is winter.

But the rain is clearly needed, and evidence of drought lies all about him. The carcasses of roe deer, dead of thirst, the low and muddy rivers, the rock beds that were, a month earlier, gaily burbling, all indicate that Anatolia has suffered from the strange turn of the world since the eruption. And what of Crete? thinks the assassin. What is left of her? But I will know. In a year's time, this thing will pass, just as all things pass. And I will be the first to return, lay hold of her, reclaim her. She will be rebuilt, though her people are scattered across the shores of the Great Sea, two queens I will return to her, and one god.

It is evening when the assassin enters the city, a dark wraith in a Hattushian soldier's cloak, the hood pulled over his head and hiding his face, astride a soaked black beast in Amorite tack.

"Who are you? And what is your business" barks the guard, a single man wrapped in a Hattushian cloak himself, booted and helmeted, but approaching without sword drawn.

That is enough to jangle the assassin's ever-present contempt for apathy. He is dismounted and pressing a blade to the man's throat before the guard can utter another word.

"I should cut you down myself," rumbles the Assassin, "You are not fit to breed. On whose orders is this gate guarded by one man? And that man answers the door like a lady having a bath." Rush spits in the man's face, shoves him aside, turns to confront the seven sentries who have rushed down the inner stairs of the gate wall to defend their post.

"Slackers!" bellows Rush. "An army could have marched through this wall before you flatulent goats came to arms!"

"Who are you, Sir?" answers a man from behind the group. He pushes past his men, one hand raising a gleaming and decorated sword, the other grasping the hilt of his battle ax.

"Better you answer me," snarls Rush. "Who *you* are, Captain, that I may demote you myself. What in Tartarus has become of this city since I left her? I should have put a guard of Amegan Wolves at these gates and left you ladies to bathe in the palace pools."

By now the Captain of the South Gate Guard understands who he is speaking to. He drops to his knees, his men, in turn, dropping to theirs about him.

"Master!" is all that the Captain can press from his lips.

"You call a man master who has not identified himself?" booms Rush, and one great fist smashes the man in the head, putting him out on the ground. "Draw your swords, you imbeciles, get on your feet! Defend your city from one who could take it by himself!"

The men are on their feet instantly. They back against the gates of the tunnel through the great wall, swords drawn. They peer through the drenching darkness at the monster, knowing full well who it is, terrified to disobey, terrified to obey.

"Now demand my identity like men worthy of my mark!" bellows the brute. The cloak flies back, exposing two powerful naked arms, hands like bear claws, and the crescent blades of the Assassin glittering in the torchlight along the tunnel walls.

One man steps forward, his sword held before him, trembling. "Show your seal, Sir," he demands, his voice cracking, "That we may escort you in."

"You need further proof of who I am than these, pup?" says a now smiling voice under the drape of the hood.

The man's swallow is audible, even in the lashing rain. "There is only one in all Hattusha who can carry the crescent blades of the Assassin without losing his head to a better pair," he murmurs miserably, quite sure he is about to lose his own.

"Wise answer," says the wraith. The hand that takes his shoulder still grasps the falcate razor, which is now pressed against the man's neck. The man flinches involuntarily, recovers, drops back to his knees. His companions follow suit.

"You are now Captain of the South Gate. This fool," he kicks the former Captain with the toe of Iamhad's boot, "could not captain a bath house. He is sufficient proof of nepotism in my city to make me think a little house cleaning must be done before I go. Let the city of Hattusha know that there will be no nepotism here. Get to your feet, fool."

The former captain, still dazed by the blow to his forehead, rises unsteadily to his feet. In the morning he will find the proof he should have asked for on his forehead: the indentation of two seal rings, one that of the King of Hattusha, the other that of the Wolf of The Hatti.

It rains for four days over Hattusha. During that time, the Assassin has paid a visit to the King, returning his seal ring to his finger as he sleeps. Eight guards at the South gate can confirm that the Wolf of the Hatti, greatest among men, entered the city, demoting the Captain and promoting his Lieutenant (no one dares question the man, who still bears two ring-sized bruises on his forehead, one of which, though blurred, configures eerily with that of the lost seal ring of Mursilis). His face hidden within the hood of a Hattushian cloak, his crescent blades unmistakable, the Wolf of the Hatti disappeared through the tunnel in the wall and into the city, leaving the guards at their post with renewed enthusiasm for their vocation. By morning, an exquisite black warhorse was found munching hay in a stall in the palace stables. Amorite saddle, bridle, pad and war boots lie in a heap beside the stall. There is no mistaking whose horse this is. The animal wears the scabbed over Tears of the Bull on his left cheek.

But no one else has been favored with the Assassin's appearance, at least, no one who dares come forward.

The walls of the palace flash white in the pale light of a three quarter moon as a rush of clouds chases the storm. The lashing rain has moved north, over the mountains to froth the Black Sea. Rush the Assassin moves through the city, a beggar here, a tax collector there, a pigeon merchant, an opium addict. For four days and three nights he has spied upon the city of Hattusha, a man in the street, a commoner. And he knows he has chosen well, for the streets speak. They speak of a King who is fair and good, generous and noble, calm and decent, a King who has the heart of a young leopard, brave without conceit, wiser than his years. Hattusha will prosper, and with the training the assassin's own soldiers have supplied them, the armies of the King will hold and defend the Hittite

Empire, greatest of all of History's warrior nations, and its borders will expand west and south.

Was it his hand that saved Hattusha? Or was it the coming of the Rah, as in Knossos, where crops and waters teamed with life during his presence there; as in Cyrus, where drought was quenched; as in even Amega, where great warriors became greater still by his gift of the three man chariot.

Was it the dagger? Or was it the dance?

Rush stands on the balcony of the King's chambers. Tossing in his sleep, Mursilis, awakened briefly by the chill and damp, glimpses the silhouette of a great beast wrapped in muslin rags, inhumanly tall, inhumanly silent, burst like black lightening against the racing clouds. His young heart jolts, as much in fascination as in fear.

"Rush!" he whispers into the darkness, but a breeze has tossed the silken curtains across the figure, blocking his view for only the space of a breath. And the figure is gone, though forever imbedded in his mind to the day of his own death.

For the assassin has already leapt to the roof above, crossed the parapet to the next balcony, and descended on a wolf's soft feet to the stone floor. Then, making his way noiselessly through the incense and pillows, the silks and satins, the entwined arms and legs of thirty two concubines, male and female, he heads for the light beneath the beaded curtain of Numira's private chamber, unimpeded by the ten burly eunuchs that guard the harem doors from the interior hall.

CHAPTER 16

"Numira," the low growl in her ear is a tickle, the delicious curling rough of his beard pricking her lobe; the warm, cinnamon breath is wet. Instinctively she turns her head toward the luxurious baritone voice.

"M-m-m-m," murmurs Numira, nuzzling in her half sleep against the ropey neck beneath the muslin hood. One long-fingered hand has found the bottom of the ragged tunic and slipped beneath it to stroke the exquisite symmetry of bunched muscle and heavy, male bone. Before he has had time to snatch her wrist and pin it to the bed beside her, Numira's fingers are licking at his taught nipples like tongues.

Still dozing, spinning in the erotic dream, Numira's mouth yearns forth to find his.

"Wake, woman, I am not here to service you," chuckles the assassin.

"Oh, OH!" Numira's eyes fly open, and though she can see nothing, her thoughts quickly congeal into logic. It does not dim her passion, but confirms it. "Terror of my enemies!" Numira submits her pinned wrist, pulls back her other arm against her pillow, as if the intruder were pinning that one also. "Take me, beloved of my people!" she breathes. "Oh... oh, Rush, take your servant!"

"Woman," answers Rush, pulling off his hood and wrestling himself out of the surprisingly strong grip of her legs, which have slipped around his waist with remarkable dexterity and skill. "You are half tigress. It is no wonder that what Hattusilis loved, his pup cannot yet handle." Chuckling, he withdraws from the bed. "Hatti women," he murmurs, shaking his head.

"How may I serve you, Guardian of the Hatti?" whispers the still swooning Numira as she slips off the bed and on to her knees at his feet.

"You are a woman capable of keeping secrets, Numira. You have kept some of them for decades, even from your King and lover, Hattusilis. Now you may serve me also by keeping my presence here in the royal harem secret, though you have a multitude of mouths to stop from telling it. I have come for the entourage of the Rah. Face painter, seamstress, dance master, troupe, all these I saved from the volcano for him, then sent them north from Amega to serve him here in the palace. But," Rush shakes his head again, "The Rah is no longer here, is he? He has fled with his priest. He has chosen Babylon. And so I have taken Babylon."

Numira stares, open-mouthed, into the blackness above her. "Taken Babylon?" she utters the words dumbly.

"It is in the hands of my armies," responds Rush, "while I have business here. And so for the time being," he continues, taking her by one arm and lifting her to her feet so that he might speak softly into her ear in the dark, "I will make my headquarters here, in your chamber." He brushes his lips against her throat. "I trust you will not deny me your bed?"

"Oh my Lord and Master, it would be my greatest honor to serve-" begins Numira, falling instantly to her knees a second time.

"Excellent," responds the Wolf. "Leave me now, I have been awake for days. Find yourself a pillow then, out in that mass of mischief," he nods toward the harem.

Stunned momentarily, Numira hesitates, before coming to her senses and putting her forehead to the floor.

"I am your grateful servant," she sighs, rising to her feet, then bowing several more times on her way out, though the room is pitch. Then she slips as quietly as she can through the beads to find a comfortable couch to lie on in the outer room.

In the morning, Rush awakens to find himself surrounded by a flock of harem concubines, male and female. The assembly, to his astonishment, has gathered about his bed without waking him. They stare down at his form in awe, for he is naked but for his leather holsters and blades: painted eyes, tipped with mirth, peaking over delicate, shell-blue fans. Most are dark-haired and brown-eyed, but two or three are exotics, one grey-eyed boy who rivals Tiko for Asian beauty, and a willowy African lad, his flawless skin as black as the finest Egyptian ebony.

Rush lifts himself onto his elbows. At his movement, the congregation of beauties sways back in a single wave, like a field of lilies in a breeze.

Presently he realizes what has captivated his audience. He reaches for a coverlet and tosses it over his sex, which does little to improve the situation. He has created a tent.

Several of the girls giggle.

"Where is your Mistress?" grumbles Rush, slipping off the bed and tucking the coverlet about his waist.

"She is off to see the King, Sir," answers one of the boys, a tall lad with a warm brown complexion, full lips and jade eyes.

"And how would you know, boy?" mutters Rush, attempting to find his way to the sack of clothing he dropped on the floor the night before. "You are her offspring, are you not? Could she do no better for you than conscript you to the royal harem?"

"I am her grandson, Sir," answers the youth in a lilting, girlish voice. "And it was I who begged her that she find me a place in the King's harem. I am a good concubine, Sir. It is my greatest hope to serve our new King one day."

"Yes, well," responds Rush, finding his sack in a corner and tossing a sardonic look over his shoulder at the boy, "Pity for you, then, that the King I have chosen for Hattusha is not interested in his harem as a whole," he rises, a Hattushian guard's leather chest protector and skirt in his hands, "and I trust, in your, no doubt extraordinary, abilities, in particular."

The boy can only frown in disappointment and bow at that.

"Now get out, all of you," barks the assassin suddenly, and the group jumps in unison, but makes no move to leave.

"We have been instructed to serve you, Sir," says one girl finally. She is slight, no more than a child, her eyes as green as Numira's.

The other's nod and murmur in agreement.

"I have no need of you," says Rush, his eyes wandering down the girl's sexless body. "Nor does any man in Hattusha who cares to live to see tomorrow," he adds, tying the soldier's skirt about his hips.

"It looks as if you do," titters a tall lad in pearl earrings and a sea-blue shift. His hair is long and pulled back atop his head, a woman's comb holding it there. His eyes drop to admire the assassin's swollen skirt.

Rush gives the lad a deadly look, then turns his attention back to the child. He puts himself on one knee and lays his hands on the girl's shoulders. The others hush as he tips her chin up to admire her perfect features.

"You are Numira's progeny also," he says gently. "I see it in your eyes. And those eyes will make a king swoon one day. But you are yet a child. Your mother has put you in the mouth of the lion."

"I am orphaned, Sir," answers the girl. "My mother died the day I was born."

"You miss my meaning," responds the assassin, his frown deepening. Edgily he looks about him. "Is she the youngest?"

"Oh, no Sir!" answers the boy in the pearl earrings. "There are younger still, if you wish."

"Has anyone abused these children?" Rush growls, rising to his feet, but the room is a circle of blank stares. "Has anyone laid hand one these younger ones? Has anyone touched them, to train them for this act? Do not force me to fill my sack with your silent tongues."

"They are the King's property, Master," answers the boy with the lilting voice at last. "King Mursilis has never visited the harem, and King Hattusilis …. was fondest of women, Sir. And in his dotage, loved Numira alone."

"No one wants a trained child," blurts a plump girl whose pillowy breasts, rising like pastries above her braided bodice, distract Rush momentarily.

"This ends today," says Rush, reaching for his weapon's

belt, which he spots lying on a bedside table behind a wisp of a girl. She looks up into his face ingenuously as he snatches it.

"There will be no child less than sixteen summers in this harem. In any harem, nor in any brothel in all of Hattusha. Nay, in all of Hatti!" Rush turns to shoulder his way through his unmoving crowd of admirers. At the doorway, he turns to face them, his face darkened with rage.

"And that is a bit of gossip you may let fly upon my leave: that the Wolf of Amega will personally hang and gut the next man or woman who touches a child for pleasure," he pulls the beaded curtain aside. Outside in the seraglio, he is accosted by several dozen more concubines.

"Give me room to breathe! You are a pack of ninnies, all of you!" he barks.

"Yes, Master!" a chorus of voices responds gaily, and the garden of bodies sways to make a path for the assassin.

By the evening of his third day in Hattusha, Rush is more than ready to quit his Hattushian headquarters. He has moved about the citadel unrecognized by any but his own men, left in place in Hattusha under the command of an elite force to guard and counsel the new king after the defeat of the Amorite army. He has arranged for the passage of the Rah's coterie by donkey cart, under guard, through the land of the Hatti and into Babylon. His men in Hattusha have maintained his anonymity, and the harem has done the same. But he has yet to spend a night in the seraglio without fighting off a handful of kittenish maidens, eager to cuddle against the legendary and well-equipped warmth of the Wolf of the Hatti and perhaps, if the gods be willing, bear him a son for their trouble.

On the fourth morning, before the cock crows, Rush slips from a small mountain of lovely young bodies, male and female, sleeping peacefully beside him on Numera's bed. He changes into the black muslin garb of the assassin, leaves a gift of exquisite Minoan pearls on the Harem Mistress' pillow, and departs through the same aperture he entered by four nights earlier. He scales the wall of the palace, stopping briefly to visit the King, slip the seal ring onto his finger, and tuck a very different gift under his sheets beside him. He kisses the boy's head, as he might his own sons', then makes his way to the palace stables to tack up the Black.

The guards at the gate offer him no resistance, but only fall to their knees, in unison, to bump their chests with their fists in salute before he gallops off into the morning toward Babylon. And in the morning, King Mursilis will find the lost seal ring of Hattusilis on his hand, and a Hatti leopard cub curled contentedly against his belly.

In Nesa, his dagger finds him.

Nesuetu has returned to her own city, on the banks of the Singing River. With the dagger of the Wolf as her proof, her once lowly status has elevated her to such a social level that within a week of her arrival she has received no less than five marriage proposals, two of these coming from older gentlemen with royal blood, the other three from sinfully rich merchants, one in spice, one in tin, one in woven goods.

But Nesuetu has refused them all, for it is the man whose dagger she holds that she intends to have.

In a city the size of Hattusha it is not impossible to hide a monster under the cloak of a Hatti soldier, the tunic of a sandal merchant, the robes of a priest. In a city such as Nesa, a city built on river trade, inhabited by soldiers and merchants for hundreds of years, it is less easy to keep such an identity secret. For Nesa was once Assyrian, and still conceals many a mercenary Assyrian spy, lurking within its nest of cobbled streets, beneath the smoldering volcano, the Nipple of the Goddess. From these spies, kings of both nations have collected their intelligence, and they have lived comfortably off the earnings of their trade for generations.

In his own country, the Wolf is not concerned with such spies, and he makes little effort to conceal himself, except to keep his face obscure. Indeed, he is unconcerned when, resting at the banks of the Singing River one evening after two days travel, he becomes aware of one, passing on his way to Larsa, who takes note of the Black, tethered and grazing not a dozen yards from where the assassin lies. And when the man, having realized what he has discovered, backs away from his finding like a terrified woman who has just inadvertently kicked a hive of sleeping bees, Rush makes no move to prevent him from taking off at a run back toward Nesa with the news, fully aware that Karum Kanes, the merchant colony, will be buzzing with reports of the Wolf's presence by morning.

"You are the woman! The girl who owns the dagger of the Wolf!" the silk merchant steps back from his tables of exotic fabrics, a hand on his breast, as if he might capture the air that has escaped him at the wonder that confronts him. His words instantly draw a crowd, and Nesuetu is soon surrounded by a crush of curious bystanders.

"Indeed I am," answers Nesuetu, smiling the proud, even-toothed smile that only a Hatti woman could by her association with the Amegan Assassin. "And live to tell, without his mark upon my cheek." She unfastens her batula and turns in a slow circle, allowing the crowd to examine her face.

"How is it possible?" shouts a man in back. "No one can identify the Assassin and lives to tell, save those who are in his service!"

"Indeed, fool," responds Nesuetu. "And so you have it. I am the property of the Great Wolf of the Hatti, the Lord of Amega, Delight of our People, and safeguard of the line of the Tudhaliya Kings!"

The crowd murmurs in assent at the girl's use of the full customary address of their champion.

"But I heard only this morning, as I was beginning my day here in the Karum Kanes, that the Great One, riding an Amegan warhorse, was seen resting at the edge of the Singing River, most likely traveling east to the country of his enemies!" The shopkeeper lifts his jewel-bedecked hand to point with distain over the heads of the crowd toward the Lake of Fire and Babylon. The crowd's murmur becomes a rabble of voices as their excitement heightens.

"Is he here?"

"Perhaps he comes to Nesa today!"

"I have heard it said that the King was kidnapped, and that the mighty Amegan army crushed the Amorite hordes like grapes in the fields of Urgup!" shouts one tall man with a blue-grey beard and hair like a lion's mane.

"I have heard that the Wolf sits astride an Amegan ghost-horse, an animal killed in battle and returned from the land of the dead to serve him! The beast cannot be seen beneath him as he rides, and the assassin seems to fly through the air unaided at the speed of a gallop!"

"I have heard that Babylon has fallen!" cries another, which sends the crowd, now fifty strong, into a frenzy.

"Enough!" Shouts Nesuetu in a shrill Hatti-woman countertenor that threatens to break the pottery in the next stall. She raises her fists over her head, a feminine parody of the Amegan battle signal. The crowd hushes.

"You!" she points to the man with the blue-grey beard over the crowd. "You will take me to him! Get him a horse!" she shouts at the crowd, and two men charge off toward the soldier's quarter.

"Not I!" Cries the blue beard. "I will not look upon the face of the Wolf!"

"Nay, you will not," answers Nesuetu, "For you are a coward and do not deserve to see it. I will go myself, for I was given the dagger for a purpose, and that purpose is accomplished. Now I must return it to its master."

Over the city of Babylon and the over-farmed fields surrounding her, the blanket of ash, the dust of the Minoan kingdom, the souls of Crete, settles like a cape. Following the ash cloud, a soft rain pelts the earth, nourishing the soil with the songs of Knossos and Cyrus, of Gornia and Malia. And the earth accepts the food that is the ash-body of the lost empire and the crops green and grow, thrive and prosper. In the months to come, the priest of the Rah of Knossos, so nearly boiled like a pudding in a golden vessel in a public courtyard, will be lauded and eulogized, and his riches will exceed those of the King, though not those of the Wolf who owns him.

But first, the Rah must dance, for so his priest foretold, and even now, under the crescent flag of Amega, Babylon demands it. And so while Aros the dresser and Pyrus the face painter, Dimius the dance master and Tuma the bath master, make their way west across the foothills of Urgup, the Valley of

Goreme and the Table of the Gods to join him, Rah prepares his dance.

It will be the story of his beginning, his slavery, his rise to stardom in Knossos, his capture by the assassin, his death sleep through the explosion of Thera, his arrival in Amega and his creation of the three man war chariot. It will include his terror on the Table of the Gods, his second capture, his ride to Hattusha on Dashuri. Finally, it will depict his kidnapping by the Amorite bandits, his lone journey into Babylon, and his meeting the Princess on the Royal Road. But Rah has two demands for his performance. It must be performed in the People's Theatre, and it must be performed for the imprisoned King.

Behind the theatre the Lower Fortress crouches, overrun with Amegan soldiers now, at the head of which the mysterious Greek stranger in the short blue cape issues orders. Beside the theatre, its reflection shimmering in the Sacred Pools of the Ninmah Temple, is the House of the Moon, where Ephtheta remains a captive.

And as the Princess Ephtheta watches from the balcony of the House of The Moon, the People's Theatre comes alive with activity. Droves of scene painters, prop makers, costume designers and seamstresses move up and down the two staircases, east and west, leading up to the third tier, while actors and dancers, costume designers and hair weavers, face painters, singers and musicians come and go along the paved ramp that rises to the great golden doorways of the second level, their dress and their chatter as colorful as the rainbow walls of the ziggurat.

And while Ephtheta watches from her balcony the goings-on outside, Rah rehearses the Story of The Rah, dazzling those privy to his practice with his speed and grace, his strength and his ethereal beauty, upon the stage within.

"There is no use denying it," says Rush to the Black, as if the beast's stamp and blow were a reply to its master's unspoken thoughts. "I am sick with it, this lust of the heart, this lust to please him. Only a god deserves a hunger such as

221

this. He has made me weak, as a woman for her babe. All for a slave boy, for a boy from the north with the sea in his eyes."

The assassin grunts, lifting the heavy Amorite saddle up onto the animal's back. "Ey, Ey!" Rush raises a warning finger as the warhorse turns to nip his shoulder when he bends to tighten the girth. "When will you learn, eh?" He taps one flared black nostril. "I am the master. Not the other way around."

So deep in thought is he, as he prepares his departure, that he fails to hear the soft trample of hooves trotting up the Singing River Road. But the Black hears and lifts its head sharply, flicking its ears forward, warning.

"That will be my dagger, and the harridan who thinks that because she has held it, she will hold its owner next." He turns in time to watch a dun cart horse jogging up the river road toward him. Upon the beast, wearing the same dress he last saw her in, is the girl from Nesa, her black hair loose and flying about her, in harsh contrast to the pony's blonde mane, which is just as long, wavy and matted.

Fifty feet from where he stands the girl slips from the back of the animal. She drops its rein and steps away from it, her eyes fastened on Rush, who cuts a handsome figure in his Amegan General's cloak and helmet. Elaborate, gold hammered-metal cylinders enclose his forearms from wrist to elbow, and a thick, tall collar of similarly hammered gold encircles and protects his neck. Over his chest his breastplate glitters in the early morning sun with rare and exquisite jewels: rubies from Kush, and Egyptian emeralds, sapphires and even turquoise, mined in the South Sinai. Nesuetu stands, transfixed at the vision of her lord in daylight.

"My King," she breathes, falling to her knees and then collapsing onto her outstretched arms on the dust road.

"Rise, girl," growls Rush, "And take that pony's rein up before she steps on it and cuts her tongue."

The girl rises slowly to her feet, her eyes down, the assassin's ankle blade proffered in her extended palms.

"Give it here," says the assassin, and the girl, taking only a moment to catch the ponies rein and tuck it into her belt, approaches in the same manner, eyes down, the blade laid out upon her palms, gleaming.

"You have polished it, I see," muses Rush, taking the weapon and lifting the point to bisect the early light of the sun.

"Master, I have served you, and I would only ask that I be marked as such; that I be used henceforth as such, for I have proven my loyalty. I have laid low the enemies of your people with your own blade, I have kidnapped the princess of Babylon at your behest. My life is now yours."

"Ah, yes, the matter of the princess," says Rush, with a curious turn of the lip suggesting a smile. "You disobeyed my order, did you not? Switched assignments with my Lieutenant, thereby rendering you both responsible for neither? What general would trust such a soldier, or do you suppose you can command men better than I, woman?"

"My Lord! I did what I had to do, to assure the success of both tasks!" responds Nesuetu.

"And this is why women do not fight," Rush shakes his head. "War would no longer be war between enemies, but a war of words between male and female, both assured by their own genitalia that they are right. You would argue with your Master, argue until I bed you to prove who is the stronger. No, woman, I know your kind. Put yourself out of my sight before this dagger returns to you, less comfortably than it first came." Rush looks over her head at the pony, who has calmly followed his new mistress without dispute. "That pony is a better soldier than you, girl. I will take him with me. I know of a lad who would make a pet of him."

"But, Sir!" cries Nesuetu. "I come six miles on his back!"

"And you shall go six more on your feet," smiles Rush, stepping toward her to take the rein. "Here," he slips his fingers into a leather pouch tied discretely to his weapons belt. "Perhaps you can bribe a cart man to let you ride with him. You will need money, now that you no longer hold the weapon of the assassin."

Nesuetu takes the offering. She cannot keep herself from pulling it open to look inside.

"Oh," sighs Nesuetu, wilting again to her knees. "It is a Kings fortune." For there are rubies and other precious stones glittering amongst the gold coin.

"Not quite, but it will buy me my freedom, I suspect."

"Freedom, Sir? But who is more free than the Wolf of the Hatti?"

"Free from you, girl," answers Rush, jumping into the Black's saddle. "Free from you," he grunts, swiping the pony's rein from her hand and tapping the Black into a trot toward Babylon, the pony trailing obediently behind.

CHAPTER 17

In Babylon the former palace dancers, now known as the Dancers of the Rah, are joined by the newly arrived Troupe of the House of The Moon. Dimius and his assistant, Akbar, are quickly installed in Eliabus' place as the Masters of Arts of the City of Babylon, but Eliabus is not unhappy. He is assigned the daunting task of remaining Rah's own, personal choreographer and assistant. Proud beyond measure of his new title, Eliabus is determined to design a dance for the god-slave that will set Babylon on fire. No move, no expression, molded into the flesh and bone of the little acrobat will be too shocking, too frightening, too erotic to employ. Against Dimius' objections, Eliabus soon creates a ballet of such provocative magnitude that even Aros, who can deny Rah nothing, is pacing in the skene, wringing his hands with worry.

"This will not sit well with the Wolf," he hisses into Pyrus' ear each time he passes him, for many are coming and going down the long hall in which they stand waiting to be called to dress and paint the Grain God for his second act. Dancers and costume makers rush back and forth, some trailing extraordinary creations the likes of which the pair has never seen: horse heads made of peacock feathers and doves made of…well, of doves, stuffed and mounted on thin metal wands of various heights which actors, dressed head to foot in black, will hoist and wave when Rah performs his Dove Dance.

"It's none of our concern, Aros," answers Pyrus, who leans

against the hall wall, now and again lifting his tray of face paints over his head to avoid a collision with a costume scurrying down the hall. "It is what it is. Remember, we are in Babylon now, and Babylon, though in the jaws of the Wolf, is nevertheless, Babylon."

"That is easy enough for you to say," continues Aros, pressing his palms to his cheeks. "You have not seen what I have seen. You were not there the night he entered Rah's chamber, the night he came to .... discipline the priest, and stood like a great, lovesick demon over the boy's pallet. You did not see what I saw in that monster's eyes..."

"That is ancient history, Aros. If anyone is going to pay for the lewdness of this dance, it is Eliabus, the pompous bastard. And he will well deserve it."

"Gentlemen, you are needed!" cries a skene runner, a boy whose sole purpose is to call the dressers and painters waiting in the wings to their tasks in time to prepare their actor for the next scene. Pyrus nods at Aros to clear his way, and the pair trot off to climb the stair to the Rah's temple above the People's Theatre.

Rah is pacing in his golden prism when they arrive. Two attendants, both sweating profusely and looking belabored, sigh with relief at their arrival.

"He will not dress without you present, Master Aros, though I tell him these are the very garments you sewed for him with your own hands! Look here! He bit me, bit me on the hand when I tried to pull the dove wings over his head!"

The man extends his palm to Aros, who ignores it and snatches the silken costume from his hands. "It does not fit over his head, Reyhab, and well he knows it. Look here, the straps fits under the shoulder plates, here, then under the arm, like this, and then back around and lace up under the wings in the back, like so."

"What is it, Sunlight?" says Pyrus, who has put down his tray of paints to examine the attendant's hand. "Why do you mistreat your servants like this? Were you not a slave yourself, once?"

"Rah is no like so many attendant," snarls Rah, who is nevertheless allowing Aros to secure his wings. The dresser pulls the laces tight, causing Rah to catch his breath in mid-snarl.

"Don't be unkind, Rah," says Aros behind him, still holding the laces firm. "Beauty without grace is nothing."

"Why Rah is have so many servant now, eh?" Rah continues, adjusting the straps of his wings under his armpits and pulling the laces out of Aros fingers. "This one, he want to be everywhere Rah is. Even Rah take shit, he want to be here. Pah!" He spits at the man's feet, but his furious brow only serves to add a breathtaking new beauty to his face. The man shrinks away, head bowed.

"I only didn't want to lose him. I didn't think he could find his way back from the latrine, you see-" he blathers.

"No!" snaps Rah, pointing a finger in the man's face. "He want to see Rah! See if this god is maybe big like horse, or maybe have two, three, maybe make like gold-" he gesticulates at his skirt with great emphasis.

"Enough, Rah!" shouts Pyrus. "Aros and I will attend you, we will speak to Eliabus about it. But you mustn't treat your servants this way. You are offensive."

"Bah," barks Rah into Pyrus face. And pouting, he pulls a stool away from a vanity and plops down on it, the tips of his wings bending against the floor.

"This wings is stupid. Why Eliabus make Rah wear like this? Can no move like this. Big, stiff wings. Like dead bird. This no wing for dance. Aros, where wings you make Rah, eh? You get. Rah wear." Rah tilts his face up to Pyrus, crosses his arms over his chest, closes his eyes.

Aros and Pyrus exchange a look. Pyrus nods for the two extraneous attendants to leave, picks up his tray of paints, and begins to rediscover Rah's face.

When Rush arrives in Babylon the city is a bustling and joyful place. Trotting through the Royal Gate and up the Enlil Road he is surrounded by celebration, and even here in the poorer, western district, good will and cheer. The Enlil Road is jammed with carts loaded with fresh vegetables, bags overflowing with barley, farro, spelt and amaranth, chickpeas, lentils and garlic, baskets of figs, grapes and pomegranate, dried fish, live goose, duck and quail. Women dress in their brightest attire, decorating their veils with flower wreaths. Rush, having revealed himself to his own men at the Royal Gate, pulls his Hattushian hood down over his features and heads east toward the bridge and the palace.

At the east end of the Kumar Bridge, Rush dismounts the Black and hands both animals to an Amegan stableman, who drops to his knees, head bowed, and bumps his heart with both fists at the sight of his master.

"Get me a fresh mount," Rush barks. "And a decent Amegan meal, something half-cooked or still breathing." Four soldiers rush toward him to kneel at his feet as the man trots off with the horses. Rush pulls off the Hattushian cloak that had covered his general's uniform. He throws it down onto one of the men's heads. The man quickly wraps it in a roll and rises to his feet, awaiting orders. "Get me a fresh one, and some fresh clothing. I stink from days of riding in mud and dust."

"Sir!" cries the youth, a bit too sharply, and trots off.

"I will occupy the King's chambers tonight. And tomorrow I will behead my enemy in the common."

"Yes, Lord," answers a man dressed in a captain's uniform. "But the King," he lowers his eyes as if he were to blame for the situation. "The King has been taken to the House of the Moon."

"On whose orders was he released from his prison?" snarls Rush, grabbing the man by the collar of his cloak and drawing him in.

"On Captain Nikolaos', Sir," answers the man, his face reddening.

"Niki?" Rush squints, releases the man. "Ah, I see. For the boy. Because he demanded it. Because he 'must dance for the king'," his words trail off. "So now he orchestrates my Babylon. A slave child. A babbling, tongue-less boy who owes me his head."

"Sir?" the man swallows, adjusting his collar.

"Never mind. It is the will of the gods, of *his* god, that I must serve he who is my servant, though I hold the world in my palm." Rush shoves the man out of his way, shaking his head. "Whether I am in hell or in heaven I am never sure, not since I lay eyes upon that golden head."

And grumbling to himself, he turns to take the reins of a fresh horse from the stableman, drop his sack into the arms of the captain, and trot off down the Kumar road toward the Kullab District and the House of the Moon.

Inside, Mochlos is nervously entertaining the former King of Babylon, Samsu-titana, and his daughter, the Princess Ephtheta in the jade-green and pearl-white visiting hall. The former king is trussed up in most of a bolt of gilded silk, a man-sized babe, swaddled from cheek to toes. The situation would be comical, except that for Mochlos, it is also appallingly profane. Here he sits, at the pinnacle of his career, in a home several times the size of his villa in Knossos, surrounded by every luxury, making every attempt to make pleasant small talk with the King of Babylon and his princess daughter, all the while maneuvering what conversation he can stimulate around the painfully silly sight of Samsu-titana, the great and powerful, swaddled and prone, with no more free will than a stuffed apricot.

When did my life become a farce? A parody of my own dreams of riches and fame? considers the High Priest of the Moon, the thought of stuffed apricots drawing his attention back to the piles of delicious fruits and sweetmeats on the low table before him. But how can I partake? While the King of Babylon drools onto his swaddling. Poor man cannot have eaten in days, whisked as he was from his own dungeon, like a sack of barley, tossed into the back of a cart, and deposited here on my couch. Do not put that filthy creature on my lovely upholstery, I hissed into the ear of the man who carried him. But to no avail, for Captain Nikolaos had given the order, insisting that the king was to be 'entertained here in the House of the Rah until the Rah was ready to perform, at which time he was to be made present in the People's Theatre.' Well kiss a jackass and call me an uncle, I said, put a robe on him then! For he is running with lice and sores. He is a contagion! And so they ordered my Nepu to bring a robe, but Nepu, seeing that they were about to dump the hobbled and gagged King on my chaise regardless, snatched up the bolt of fine silk I'd ordered for my own Performance Day costume, and wrapped the poor man, head to toe.

And so here we sit, or lie, in the case of the King, awaiting what? It will be days before the performance. Can I untruss him? Do I offer him a bath and proper garments? Will the assassin make a soup of my head if I treat him with any kindness or honor at all? And where is Captain Nikolaos now that he has saddled me with this mortification. Why put this preposterous situation on *my* shoulders? I am too refined for this buffoonery.

"Can my father not at least be allowed a bath, Sir? What chance has he of escaping? His city is swarming with the hounds of hell," pleads Ephtheta, who is seated beside her father on the chaise, his head in her lap, patting his bristly pate.

"I would not mumble such things if I were you, Princess," snaps Mochlos, and immediately slaps a palm over his mouth, for should the wrong ears hear him call the girl princess still, he will surely spend his final days decorating a stake in the palace square.

"Call me by my given name, Holiness," responds Ephtheta gently. "I am no longer a princess, and I would not have your good manners be your downfall."

"Very well then," answers the priest, drawing his palm across his breast and offering a discrete nod in apology, "Ephtheta. But my child, you must not touch your father, for he is…well, he is…"

"Unclean? Then I will be also, for we are one flesh, are we not?"

"You are, child," answers Mochlos, brushing the crumbs of a date bar off his lap.

"And if we are one flesh," continues the princess, "and I am bathed, then should my father not be bathed also?"

"My dear, it is not I who-" begins the priest, reddening at the thought of defying a royal, no matter how defeated a royal.

"Dear Mochlos, you have been kind to me, more than kind. You are a noble man. But it is the assassin whom you fear, and the assassin is not here. Can you not allow my father the dignity of a bath, under guard, so that he might be presentable to the Rah when the time comes for him to witness the holy dance?"

At this Mochlos draws himself up, blinks, licks the date syrup from his lips. "I see your point, Your Majes-, yes, I see your point, Ephtheta. It could be dangerous to anger the Rah by providing him anything but a clean and well-oiled King in full regalia, as dangerous as upsetting the assassin himself. Very well," Mochlos rises to his feet. Reluctantly, he pushes the tray of pastries away and claps his hands, calling the five Amegan guards that have been assigned to the House of the Moon by Captain Nikolaos.

"You will allow my man to bathe him and send for proper royal attire. I take responsibility for this decision, but if he escapes from you, Captain Nikolaos will deal with you himself." The men lift the prone king from the couch as Mochlos summons Nepu to take charge of the operation. "He won't get far in this city at any rate, the place is overrun with Amegan wolves," he murmurs to himself, returning to his settee.

"Holiness," Ephtheta folds her hands over her heart and offers Mochlos a dainty nod, "I am in your debt for this."

The priest blinks, for once at a loss for words. "It is nothing, my dear," he stammers, wondering if he ought not drop to his knees himself. Instead, he mimics her gesture of gratitude. "I should have thought of it myself, only the whole scene…these Amegan barbarians hauling the great Samsu-titana himself into his own visiting room, trussed up like a roast, naked but for a stained loincloth…forgive me, child but my nerves are frayed. Shall we share an amphora of the last of my Minoan wine? Yes, yes, let's do, before that hulking monstrosity returns to pull my eyeballs out of my head for showing your father some common decency. A thing I would venture to say he knows nothing about."

But Ephtheta only lowers her eyes and smiles behind her batula. Any mention of the assassin brings the same reaction from the princess, Mochlos has noticed, and she has yet to join him in his invectives regarding the beast.

"Rah be here. Die," Rah is pointing to the parquet tiles at

the foot of the King's Theatre Pavilion, a structure of stone built on concentric circular steps in the center of the People's Theatre. Eliabus is nonplussed, for it was his decision to entertain Rah's ideas about performing the most sensual dance of his career directly in front of the King's pavilion. But to install the former king in the pavilion is suicide. How can he allow the deposed King to sit where by rights, only the assassin himself, should be sitting? Only a headless goat would do of such a thing, given the fact that the assassin would certainly either hear of it, or witness it himself. Suddenly, the great joy of being Rah's personal choreographer loses its color. Eliabus automatically touches his throat, stroking his neatly pointed beard as if bidding it farewell.

Yet how can he say no to the Rah? If the god who inhabits him demands the audience of Samsu-titana, and is denied, will not all of Babylon be punished for the transgression?

The solution strikes him like a flame igniting a torch. A trussed and gagged king Samsu-titana will be deposited in the choir pit, fittingly kneeling on a black hassock, his neck wrapped in a red cloth, his final act as a 'king' being his own beheading before the audience of the Rah following the last act of the play. But the Rah will not see this for the king will enter the theatre in a shrouded palanquin. And the Rah will have been hustled back to his temple, while this monstrous deed is performed by the Amegan Captain Nikolaos.

Eliabus points to the choir pit. He clears his throat, takes Rah by the shoulder and turns him around to face the stage.

"No, Rah, the King will be there, close to the stage, the better to see your performance."

"King here," responds Rah, pushing Eliabus around in turn and pointing to the Pavilion again. "Rah die here," he points to the tile at his feet. "Priest, he is have table," he draws his hands out, describing the altar upon which he must die, "cut out heart of Rah, lift, this way," he raises the invisible heart up to heaven, in full view of the audience. "See, real heart, maybe cow heart. Real blood. He hide heart under altar, here, little space no one can see. He push knife," Rah plunges the priest's knife down with such force and promise that Eliabus jumps, though there is nothing but air in Rah's clenched hands, nothing but air where his altar must be. "Into Rah, but no real knife. Make from papyrus, something soft, look like sharp. No really kill Rah. But Rah is die. Here. So King can see." Rah turns casually to Eliabus, his pantomime complete. "Then lamp go out, all over, no light to see. So Rah can be gone. When lamp is light again, Babylon is have great joy. Big sun, lot of flower, lot of animal on stage. Many sack of grain. People dance."

"Very well," sighs Eliabus, exhausted by the constant demands of the little performer. "But you understand, the King must wear his ceremonial costume to the performance. He will be wearing his battle garments, you see? This is what the people expect when our leader appears in public."

"This no problem," responds Rah, waving the thought away, a distraction. He turns to leap onto the stage, using only the tips of his fingers to scale the edge, which is the height of a horse's back. He stands over Eliabus' head, naked but for a white loincloth which has been expertly twisted around his golden belt, and his golden bracelets, collar and circlet.

You are a jewel made flesh, thinks Eliabus, but he shakes his head at the boy, turns his back on him and crosses his arms. "You understand that the King wears a helmet, Rah? You understand that you will not see his face?"

"What kind hell-met?" Rah hops off the stage to land at his side, so lightly that it is only the slight breeze his jump creates that alerts Eliabus to his proximity. Now Rah is looking up at him, eyes wide with interest. "Crown like Rah? Can see face," he assures Eliabus, pointing to his own.

"Not like this, Rah," answers Eliabus, tapping Rah's emerald. "A battle crown. A golden circlet, yes, but a thick leather mask attached, to protect the royal countenance from injury in battle. You will not see his face."

Rah shrugs. "No problem. But Rah is die here," he points to the spot he were he has determined his finale must occur.

"Yes, yes, you may die there," responds Eliabus, sighing. "Now let us get on with rehearsal, shall we?"

"Ya, rehearse. Is good. Many time. Make perfect," nods Rah, leaping back up onto the stage where his priest awaits, enormous prop dagger in hand, blood bucket at his feet.

"You kill Rah there, front of King," Rah orders the man, who shoots Eliabus a furious, wide eyed look, then picks up his bucket and heads for the choir pit stairs.

Rush returns to the House of the Moon at daybreak. The house is still sleeping, none harder than the guards at the gate, who were napping when he found them, and now sleep the sleep of the dead. His fresh mount has been left loose in the front garden, and Rush has scaled the priest's balcony to awaken him with his usual greeting.

But the slender bundle of silken sheets on the King's summer bed are not shaped like a Minoan monk, nor do they smell of the temple incense (myrrh, poppy, hibiscus) that is Mochlos. This little bundle smells of woman, and for a moment, Rush is confounded. Has the priest become a man at last and taken a woman to his bed? But no. The lump of silk moves, a single body. It turns to face him, two slender arms stretch up, fists clenched, a soft feminine moan, and the top half of the face of the princess exposes itself above the bedclothes.

It is the first time that the assassin has seen the girl in daylight. He blinks, approaches, squints, gives the sheet covering her cheek and jaw a tug to expose her face. Blinks again.

She could be the Grain God's sister.

A perfect nose to fit the aristocratic face, narrow nostrils and a pointed tip, small but elegant; cat-like jaw, sharp mandibles clearly defined under the petal-like earlobes. And though her hair is the color of wildflower Meade, her lashes are as long and thick, her hairline shaped in an identical peak.

Youth, thinks Rush, it is only their youth, yet the similarity draws him. What are you, girl? Daughter of my enemy. Shall I rape you? Is it not fitting? Yet he cannot bring himself to contemplate the thought. That sweet, honey-colored mouth drawn down in pain and fear, her whimpering. Even her whimpering. It would ...

It would....

"Tah," gruffs Rush, turning back to the balcony. "This is a child," he rumbles aloud to himself, disgusted, "Be it mine

234

enemies spawn, yet a child. I will not do this."

"Not a child, my Lord," the soft, entreating voice of the princess tickles his ear. He turns, and she is raised on one elbow, her hair streaming down over her pillow. Her eyes, those tip-tilted eyes, the Grain God's eyes, only amber, regard him. The brow pleads.

"I am not a child, my love, I am of age to be married." She is looking up at him from the bed, indeed a child, and yet composed and determined as any monarch. Rush clenches his jaw. The world is a perverted place, he thinks to himself, when the monster of the Aegean can be spoken to thus, by kittens.

"You are how many summers, girl?" grunts Rush, planting his fists on his hips.

"This will be my seventeenth, and already last summer my father had begun his search for a proper husband for the future Queen of Babylon." The girl has risen from the bed to stand naked before him. "Well?" she gives the assassin a confident smile, then lifts her hand to touch his hood. Rush stands his ground, but his eyes have narrowed to slits. Even so, they take quick inventory of her body. "You are a worldly man, Wolf of Amega. Do you see before you a girl? Or a woman?"

I would be hard pressed to rape this creature before *she* seduced *me,* thinks Rush, shaking his head, then snatching the slender wrist. In the time it takes a snake to strike he has turned her around and pinned her to his chest.

"I can take your breath as easily as I gave it to you, woman," he snarls against her ear.

But the Hittite rumble only causes her to giggle. She twists, and nips his mouth. "Take my lungs, my love, for they are weak, and you have already taken my heart."

Rush is losing ground against his own will. This is my enemy's daughter. Would I make his seed a Queen, though I have defeated him? But his breath is quickening at her throat, and as she sighs sweetly in response, his flesh betrays him.

"I don't want to hurt you," he groans, and hears himself saying these exact words to Rah so long ago, there on the dirt track to Ting Ya's door, and he remembers Rah, soaked and struggling in the mud, those little nips and yowls.

"Then take me, Wolf," responds the princess, twisting in his arms and somehow managing to pull the general's leather helmet from his head, one-handed. "My father searched Babylon in vain. I will have no other but you."

"If you would be so disposed, Your Greatness," squeaks Eliabus the following morning in the kings' visiting room, "The performance will require you to wear the garments of an Amorite of great bearing."

Eliabus is on his face, his lips brushing the stone floor as he makes his entreaty to the devil himself. He has never seen such a monster, and at the same time, could not identify the man if he had to do so. The beast is dressed head to toe in black muslin rags. He is a great, shredded wraith, shoulders like a Minoan bull, arms like an ape, face hidden in a sudarium with one hole ripped out over the right eye. The eye that burns through it is terrible.

"And so now I must wear the garment of my enemy? To witness the god's dance? How have you managed to orchestrate this insult? I will wear your head as a hat before I watch the Rah dressed as my enemy!" the thing booms above his head.

"Your Greatness! I could not imagine such a thing! It is the little Grain God who wishes to dance before the King of Babylon! If we do not allow it, will we not anger the god who inhabits him? Is it not the god who demands it? And how can we put the deposed King in the Pavilion? Would that not be an even greater insult to you? But we cannot allow the little god to see the king-who-was, trussed and readied for beheading, in the choir pit. He must believe that whoever occupies the pavilion is the King, for he insists that his finale be played at the foot of the pavilion for the King. And your Greatness," Eliabus dares to lift his head to talk to the booted feet of the Assassin, "You are, of course, and always have been, King of all you survey."

"Pity you Amorites didn't acknowledge that before I lay your armies in the dust of Urgup," answers the assassin, reaching down to pull Eliabus to his feet by his beard. Then, his one unveiled eye regarding the choreographer, he gives the beard a tug, pulling out a chunk of it in the doing. "I will wear the garb of the mercenary, Samal-Etatani, for I have used it to infiltrate your city on more than one occasion. But the battle helmet of the deposed King I will not don, and so you had better make me a mask befitting a murderer, for that is what I am. His crown I will wear," Rush releases Eliabus, kicking him aside, "His battle helmet I will not." He waves to a guard.

"Blindfold him," he orders. And when the man has done so, Rush removes his hood, tucks it into his weapons belt, and addresses the choreographer. "See to it that the little god is not apprised of the fate of the King once he's left the stage. And see to it that the former princess is equally unaware of the fate of her father. I am done with Babylon, and the House of the Moon is to be packed and ready to return to Amega by the new moon. I will leave Captain Nikolaos in charge here."

When the choreographer is gone, Rush turns to the guard that still stands at attention beside the doorway.

"You are Petuk, are you not? You, and the girl, Ephtheta, found my little cat," says Rush, studying the man. He has a fine build, robust and tall. "You remind me of another," muses the assassin, taking a step toward the Amorite. The man drops to his knees, his head bowed, one fist over his heart. "You are a good man," continues Rush, tilting his head and stroking his own beard. "A smart man, a man who knows when to be silent, when to be still, when to speak."

"Master," responds Petuk, punching his chest with his fist.

"Exactly. While others scurry about, looking to find favor with me with their fawning, you remain silent, yet at my side. Always at my side, here in the palace, at least, ever since my return. You are the son of the old advisor, Mefali, are you not?"

"I am, Lord," answers Petuk, raising his eyes. "He is in prison here," he adds carefully.

"For what purpose?" asks the Assassin, motioning Petuk to stand. The man is very nearly his own height.

"He is to be beheaded with the deposed King," answers Petuk, "As is the custom," he adds, knowing full well that the Assassin ordered it himself.

"If he is as good a man as you, Petuk, the one who ordered this is wasting assets. Remove him from the prison, and send him to the daughter of my enemy, for I understand that she is fond of him, and I..." the Assassin trails off, gruffly nods toward the door. "Go!"

"I have no power here, Master, to give such orders," Petuk replies.

"My word is power enough, amongst my men. But if you say that you would wear my mark, then you must also be ready to die in battle for me," Rush counters. "Or on a whim."

"My King," answers Petuk, "You have spared my father's life, and of she who was my princess. I owe you two lives."

"You will indeed bear my mark," nods Rush, "But you will first prove your loyalty. Go and do as I have ordered. The Tear will find you when you earn it."

CHAPTER 18

The ziggurat sleeps. The players dream. And while the moon is rising, the sun is setting in the injured brain of the Grain God of Knossos. In twilight sleep, Rah rises from his perfect human form and travels. His spirit sees the ghosts of earlier gods who dwelled here, men and women chosen for one extraordinary feature or another: a woman with no pupils standing at the window; and infant with two heads lying in a gilded crib. He sees his own form, golden curls spilling over a silken pillow, one graceful arm slung over his head, palm up as if in defense of a blow, golden diadem, bracelets and nipple rings catching the flickering lamplight and casting it around the prism-shaped room like the northern lights he watched as an infant twin.

Rah rises. He rises above the haunted temple of the ziggurat, he marvels at the moon-drenched white-gold exterior of the shrine, the twinkling pools surrounding its base, the sheer size of the theatre. He thinks, "King", and he is in the House of the Moon again, not in his own tower chamber but in the priest's suite, where Samsu-titana has been installed in the room that was the hermaphrodite's. The King is sleeping on his back, his head and beard clean shaven, his aura a dirty yellow. He is a man near death, and inside his bones rage a disease that eats his marrow like a wild dog.

Rah can feel the heat of the disease, radiating off the man's body. "He will die soon," he hears the soft voice in his head.

"Either way, he will die soon."

"This is King?" Rah hears his own spirit voice. He can no longer remember his early language. Even his spirit must press itself now through the glue of a foreign tongue. "No look like King. Look like old man, wait to die."

"The limp was the monster, eating his bone. The monster entered through the injury." The voice is sweet, not man, not woman, not child, but lovely beyond imagining.

Why must he know this? But Rah knows. He knows that the King will be beheaded in the choir pit, that the assassin will wear the battle gear of an Amorite to please him, and watch from the King's pavilion. And he knows that this is how it must be, how it always must have been. For the King is no more a king. The Wolf is King.

"Close this secret in your heart, and take this heart to the mountain, and give it back to me."

And now Rah knows another thing. He knows where he belongs, where he has always belonged, why he was born, and captured and why he danced and why he could not speak, could not be understood, his voice always muffled by a clotted tongue, a strange language.

"It is for you I made the mountain, it is for you I made the priest."

Backstage, a river of dancers waits for the choir to call them forth. The King has been dressed for death: a red scarf to catch his blood, a brown tunic to cover his shame. He will be forced to kneel through the entire performance, watching from the stocks he is fastened to, inside a box upon which the choir master will conduct his chorus, separating the high voices from the low.

Rush leans forward on the railing of the pavilion, the floor of which is a man's head above the stage. A walkway from the stage, the width of a cart, will allow the Rah, his bearers and his priest to the foot of the pavilion, where the death scene of Mount Ida will be enacted. The walkway passes through the center of the choir pit, directly in front of the choir master and the deposed and soon to be headless King Samsu-titana. But for now, only Rush, Eliabus, the choir master himself (who would in any case have been disturbed by the grunting and moaning under his feet), and the man who will behead the monarch knows of the plan.

The people's theatre is filled with the aristocracy of the former Babylon, the Babylon before the ash cloud, before the dancing god, before the Wolf. There will be no sabotage, no undermining of his power here, and when he is gone, the eyes who have witnessed this horror will remember, and will remain his subjects, though he will leave only the skeleton of an army to maintain his hold for five more years.

He has what he wants from Babylon. Its surrender. And his Rah.

Rush wears the battle garments of Samal-Etatani, the mercenary whose identity he stole before first entering the city. Covering his features, the Assassin's hood screens his identity. Pinning it to his forehead, the King's crown winks blood red rubies in the torchlight.

But at his waist, the Amorite tunic is drawn tight against his body by his own weapons belt, and the straps of his crescent blade holsters crisscross his chest and back over the tunic, so that the entire horror of who he is revealed to all.

Only the daggers at his ankles, concealed by Iamhad's boots, and one other item, also confiscated from an enemy, remain hidden.

His is a wardrobe of victims. He is the Assassin King of Babylon.

On the stage, a village of hay. Women pantomime the washing of clothes in a lake, a bolt of blue silk waved by two boys dressed in black. Three children dance and chase each other, giggling, around a straw hut center stage. A woman, a horse-tail of yellow hair braided and trailing to her feet, steps from the hut with two bundles of swaddling in her arms, identical. Twin babes.

The chorus follows her voice up a scale, and for a moment Rush wonders if Nikolaos somehow transported Cara here for this scene. Hers is the only other voice as true that he has ever heard. The voice wavers at an impossibly high place, then takes him where he would not go again.

He fights, but the fight is in his heart, the only battle he could never win.

It is the lullaby....

And Rush is no longer wearing the monstrous costume he has chosen for Rah's performance, but the robes of a Minoan Priest of the Dead, and he is striding down Mount Ida toward Knossos after ridding himself of his burdens of human flesh.

He releases the ponies to graze and moves down the mountain. He will come back for the animals later, and the priests will be sure they have been grained and watered and groomed when he does. He knows many ways down the mountain, many ways back to the Bridge Road, but he is helpless not to take the path that Rah will take today if he visits Ting Ya. An hour's walk down the path he sees the boy coming toward him and his muscles twitch, his mouth involuntarily filling with saliva, as it did when, during his years in the army, he spied a small herd of antelope after having been fighting without supplies for days. He came this way for this very reason, on the chance to pass the boy, to have proximity to him without frightening him. He pulls his cowl over his head. He pins it with one hand at the throat as he closes the distance between himself and the boy, who walks alone, head down, kicking stones with sandaled feet.

Rah is walking along the path, eyes up, scanning to the very tops of the trees for life in the leaves, his face open and pleasant, those maddening dimples bracketing his pearly incisors, his blonde mop of curls brushing his gold silk shoulders. He sings softly, mumbling a little melody, a foreign lullaby Rush thinks he recognizes. The babyish tune, carried on the boy's dusky voice, seems to hum through the soft summer air and alight on Rush's belly like fingers reaching to tickle his loins....

The lullaby. This is Rah telling his story! This is the mother! There are the twins! This is how my little cat began...

Rush is jarred back to the present as a scream peals up into the night sky above the theatre. Estonians! The stage is a war, a war against the innocent! Against women and children. Against the boy's mother.

Rush's hands are on the railing of his pavilion balcony.

Except for the gentle hand of the princess beside him, he would have leapt over, down to the stage, and had his way with a half dozen fops in battle gear. He would have sliced through them like a knife through silk, and would have burned down with the fire of his fury the only evidence left of Rah's beginnings, just as the Estonian marauder now lights the hut, which is carefully walled, he notices, with a brick base, so that the fire will not consume the entire stage.

"It is his mother!" gasps the princess beside him, her hands coming up to cover her veiled lips. Rush turns briefly to look down upon her. She could be his sister, the thought jolts through his mind again. The princess wears a head veil, the silk a shimmering yellow, bound across her forehead with golden embroidery. It covers her dark honey hair, while a second veil covers her face below the cat-like eyes, the bottom falls like snow across her breast as she breathes.

Her eyes are wet with tears.

There is a cry from the stage. It is the woman in the horse-tail braid. Her babes have been taken from her, dropped like stones, and the brute is on her.

Though it is a dance, it is clear that he is raping her.

How could he know this? thinks Rush. He was a babe. But there are many things that he has known that he should not have known, comes the answer, a softer voice inside his head than his own. Many things.

Now the lamps have been dampened. The choir is wailing, the fram drum, cymbals, clappers and rattles are jarring, deafening, but the Wolf's acute hearing can make out the backdrop and props being cleared away, and his keen eyes can distinguish the outline of movement. It does nothing to quench his desire to slaughter the actor who played the part of the Estonian who raped Rah's mother.

In his imagination he is hacking the man to bits small enough to feed to a housecat when the lamps relight.

The cacophony of the orchestra has dimmed. A reed pipe lifts a trill of notes into the theatre, soft, sweet. A boy and a girl of equal height, dressed in rags, their hair white-blonde and disheveled, hanging down their backs (more horse-tail?). Their faces are carefully painted. Blue tears run down their cheeks

243

like rain. On their ankles, shackles leading broken chains; on the chains, tiny bells ring each time they take a step.

The single reed pipe becomes two. The two pipes entwine their notes, up and down, sweetness and sorrow. The children, too, embrace, release, circle each other like those notes. Beauty and sadness, entwined, embracing. Releasing, the same, yet separate.

Rush blinks. His eyes sting. The smoke from the lamps. Angrily he rubs them through the hole in the assassin's mask. Fools, he thinks, and then he understands. Of course, it is on purpose, that smoke. He looks down and about him at the audience on the benches horseshoed around his pavilion in concentric half circles. People are raising their hands to their faces, just as he has done. A mass of people, weeping.

He has made his audience part of the play, thinks the Assassin. Just as he has always done.

The reed pipes drift, musical clouds, higher, leaving room for other instruments to fill the void beneath them: the lyre and shofar, the drum, like a heartbeat, like the heartbeat of two children dancing. A crowd of people, men in fine cloaks and others in battle dress, well-dressed women, have begun to gather around the twins. They throw coins at the children's feet, and the boy darts away from the girl to scoop them up. He spins and jumps, handsprings, end over end, circling the girl, disguising his motive, but all the while the calves bladder tied to his waist is growing, until he can no longer jump, or so it seems, from the weight of it. He draws himself up, takes his sister's hand, and the two bow, in unison, to their audience.

It is the Grain God's bow. Rah's bow. Rush squeezes his eyelids tight. This smoke, this infernal smoke. That bow. That bow that defeated me.

The torches are extinguished a second time. A brief respite. Then one halo of light draws his eyes to the far left. The girl child lies on a bale of straw. The boy kneels on one knee beside her, a wooden bowl in his hands. He puts the bowl to her lips, but the girl is motionless. He puts the bowl down beside him, rises to his feet, turns to the audience, his face ashen, his hands raised to clasp his head, elbows out. Another familiar gesture, expertly copied by this child actor.

He looks to heaven, wails like a wild thing, a cub torn from its mother. He turns, falls upon the breast of the girl-child, shaking the stiff corpse. The halo of light fades. The audience gasps.

The bale has been lit! A second fire ignites the theatre, shadows leaping across the faces in the first rows. The audience watches as the girl child's pyre consumes her. Rush looks about. The women in the audience are weeping openly. The men have set their faces like flint. Stage hands in black pull a damp skin over the pyre and douse the flames. And as they do so, the theatre is once again pitched into darkness.

More movement on the stage. An enormous prop is being pulled in on a low cart by several men. When the torches are relit, a great ship dominates the theatre. The trolley beneath it cannot be seen behind the billowing blue silk waves. There is a man on the prow, a merchant. His face is kind, his hair and beard white. Some hidden source of a breeze is blowing them back over his shoulder, and he holds the railing hard, as if he fights that breeze for purchase, as if he travels across a vast and angry ocean, as if the furious wind has not seen land for many days and runs wild, a horse without a rider, over the waves, unhindered.

Behind the man, a shock of white-gold hair, the trim, exquisitely graceful body of the Grain God rides the wind and the waves easily. He wears a deerskin vest and linen breeches. The golden collar is gone, or hidden by the standing collar of the vest. The emerald crown is also gone, and the golden anklets hidden in leg wraps. Aros' work, thinks the assassin, nodding and smiling wryly under his hideous double hood. Good man, Aros. He had no crown, no gold, that slave boy. Only beauty and talent.

Enough to make him a god.

Everything about the boy that will become Rah indicates that he is fighting to stand in the pummeling forces of nature, and for a moment even Rush allows himself to believe that the boat must surely be tossing, jolting him. The breeze, lifting the hallo of curls, completes the illusion.

Even the boy's brows seem to fight the wind.

Another halo of light illuminates a figure at the far right of the stage. Rush's attention is drawn to a tall man in a white robe, exquisitely embroidered in gold. The man stands with his back to the audience, his arms extended out on either side of his body and lifted, palms up, as if in supplication to the arriving ship. Rush's heart kicks in his chest. He peers at the figure, and for a moment is convinced that the choreographer, Eliabus, has somehow convinced the High Priest to play his own part. Five enormous heads of golden wheat spread from a single stalk, from shoulder to shoulder across the back of his robe. It is Mochlos' Minoan robe, certainly. But the man is not Mochlos. The tigerish features are not present. This man is a bit too filled out, and lacks the peculiar, too-straight posture of the priest. His shoulders are broader, and as the lamp light passes through the robe lifted at his sides, Rush can see that his arms are more muscular, and not the slack limbs of a man who has never worked except to lift a chalice or a whip.

The boy has leapt from the ship. He turns to lift a hand to the captain-merchant, who mirrors his gesture while the ship is pulled back on its trolley off stage. Now the boy is seized by two men in golden loincloths. Their skin is as black as the wings of crows, men from The Land Of Punt. They drag the struggling boy before the priest, who makes a clawing gesture with one hand. Bare him! it says. The men step between the boy and the audience, and the vest and breeches are tossed aside. When they step away, the boy is naked, but for a loincloth and his golden collar, the Minoan ring of gold about his waist, his bracelets and anklets. He backs away from the priest, and where the ship disappeared into the dark, a troupe of dancers step forward. A jolt of recognition strikes Rush like a lightning bolt. Tiko! When did they have time to import him? But no, he peers at the boy. The Asian features are exaggerated. They have been painted on to the actor's face. Rush scans the remaining dancers. He sees familiar faces and relaxes. Of course. Rah would not have forgotten Tiko. But the others, he himself sent them here from Hattusha for this purpose.

Rah fades back, a breath of pale motion, into the body of the troupe. The choir has hushed. The heartbeat of a single fram drum, which Rush only now notices has been palpitating beneath the other instruments from the beginning, remains. The orchestra is silent but for that single reed pipe and the organic beat of the drum. The dancers begin to move out in an irregular circle, leaves blown erratically in a lop-sided wind. They dip and wave, they spin about one another. Chaotic. Confused.

Suddenly Rah reappears, crouched in the center of the dancing feet that spin about him. Rush notices that his curls have grown out since Aros cut them into a spiky mane in Amega. Rah lifts his head. His face is now a maze of yellow and green stripes, bursting outward from his eyes, which have been outlined with a deeper blue-green that streaks back and up into his hairline. It is the face that Queen Media's ladies gave him for his dance in Cyrus, the paint that would smudge into a soft green blur that would remain on his cheeks for days after the Queen and her ladies had their way with him. But right now the paint is sharp, the blue-green line below his blue-green eyes intensifies them, sharpens his feline cheekbones, lifts his cat-like brow. Motionless, he is already exquisite.

Rah rises. He begins to join the dancer's concentric circles of disordered merriment. He moves through them, flows through them, spins one girl, squares off with one boy. Despite the seeming randomness of his movements, he is organizing them. They are becoming something new and cohesive now as the boy stalks and spins and weaves through them.

"He *is* dance!" Rush hears Ephtheta draw in a breath, delighted. "He plays dance itself! Do you see it?" she is pointing, an excited child, at the stage. The corners of her eyes confess an unchecked smile under the veil, and that hidden smile competes for Rush's attention with the beauty on the stage.

Rush too smiles, under his mask. But he is confused for a moment by the face paint. Why the tiger? Ah, yes, that was the boy's first dance, was it not?

It was the story of a boy created from the forbidden love between the Moon Goddess and a tiger. The boy, half god, half tiger, so beautiful, with stripes made of moonlight and eyes the color of the sea, that he was hunted down, ravished and stripped of his pelt by the people of Knossos. And when the Goddess learned that her son had been defiled by the people, she called forth the wrath of the Aegean, which rose up and drowned the city in a great tidal wave.

In Knossos, the audience threw saffron flowers and yellow lilies at Rah's feet and roared with delight when the King stood up and stepped down from his place on the dais to honor the House of Mochlos with his acceptance of the boy as the new Grain God.

It is not the Cyrian performance that the boy is returning to. It is the performance that made him a god.

A whip cracks. On the right side of the stage the priest, Mochlos, stands between the two slaves from Punt. He points his whip at Rah, and the men stride across the stage to pounce on the boy, tearing him from the center of the dance. As they do so the dancers flee like sheep whose shepherd has been struck. The men drag the struggling boy before the priest. One lifts a long rope of chains up for the audience to see, then the two men take the boy by his wrists, lift him, seem to fasten him to the air. When the men step away, the boy's back faces the audience, his wrists are raised above his head so that he appears to be hanging from his bracelets against a wall. But there is no wall. The boy keens like a trapped fox, pulling against the invisible, even tearing at his own arms with his teeth.

The audience gasps. Blood trickles from the bites he has made in his forearms.

The priest lifts the reed whip. The audience gasps again. A dramatic pause, then the High Priest brings the whip down on the boy's golden back, splitting it, again and again, so that rivulets of crimson run down his torso, his thighs.

The boy writhes. He cries out like a wildcat, he struggles violently against his invisible shackles. Is this real? Rush thinks, squeezing his stinging eyes shut against the smoke-spiced air. His broad palms lay flat against the pavilion half-wall, ready to take his weight and propel him over the side, into the audience, and onto the stage.

"My King," says Ephtheta, who has risen to stand at his

side. She touches his arm, "He plays out his past. See, there is nothing holding him. It is an act, that is all."

But I saw those thighs, thinks Rush, breathing like a bull. Split and raw, so raw that his grace was lost for many days. Act or no, I will not watch this monstrosity. And when I am through here, I will skin that priest and eat his belly raw while he watches.

Now the stage is dark. The halo of lamp light has jumped to the opposite side of the theatre. And Rush grunts and steps back in shock as the audience screams.

For there he stands, a black muslin horror wrapped like a mummy from head to foot, huge, grim, revolting.

A woman in the second row faints into her escort's arms. Her slave scoops her up, rushes her out of the theatre. Her escort turns to nod at the man and wave him off, as if to say, yes, take her home, but I will stay.

The beast has disappeared into the dark. The halo that he stood in remains, empty. Another halo returns where the boy was flogged. Center stage, the beast appears in a third ring of light. He stands over a pallet upon which the boy lies. He bends, gracefully bizarre, as the choir pit comes softly awake with lute and reed pipe, a love song. The beast lifts his head; beacons to the audience, come look! He gestures, a sweep of his fingers over the boy's sleeping form, he balls his fists, lifts his gaze to the stars above the theatre. Howls.

A wolf, baying at the night sky.

At first the sound is mournful, but soon it wavers, becomes a growl. The wraith-wolf lifts the sleeping Rah in his arms and disappears into the darkness with him.

So you have changed our story, muses Rush, stepping back from the balcony of his pavilion. The theatre torches are relit as the audience murmurs, awakening from the hypnotic spell the play has cast. Silly little cat, Rush nods to himself and sits down beside Ephtheta, who has returned to her place on the Queen's chair. He chuckles with relief.

You have managed to tell your story without telling mine, and that is good, little cat, else I should have to chastise you.

Hawkers are milling through the crowded bleachers below, selling snacks: roasted hazelnuts, stuffed dates, fried dough, even hot meat pies and kibbeh. Wine sellers are also taking advantage of the intermission. They carry their wine in amphora strapped to their backs, and poor the beverage into the cups the audience brought with them. Rush watches as a half dozen slaves clear and sweep the stage, which is no doubt covered in a fine ash. Two fires already, and we are only just finished with the second act. There is much to tell, but how much of it will be true? How much of it, the Rah's twisted perception of the truth? How much of it pure fantasy, pure drama, dreamed up in that fluff he calls a head.

Beside him, Ephtheta sits, her palms resting face up in her lap. Her fingers are decked with jewels, for he has had her entire wardrobe moved to the House of the Moon, along with his own bag of villainy. Nikolaos has been ensconced in the Palace for the time being, and will remain there until Rush needs him elsewhere. Then Babylon can fall to the Assyrians for all he cares. She is a harlot, taken, used, tossed aside for the next man.

Rush allows his hidden eyes to visit the cleavage at the princess' breast. How exquisitely sweet youth is, he thinks. And how did such beauty spring from my enemies loins? It is almost a pity that I must cut off your father's head to keep you.

But then his mind turns, blind hands seeking something lost. A treasured light. How much sweeter is your wisdom, my heart, my lamp. And he is aware that his longing for Josepha's welcoming kisses, her possessive caress, her blind love for him is calling him home once again. Josepha, wife and mother.

Still, he cannot help but admire the creature beside him, the perfect union of what he cannot have, and what he can. She has given herself to me, though she knows full well what I must now do to her father, the dethroned King. It must be, or else I may as well give Babylon back right now. No conqueror can hold a city while the former king lives.

But she will not witness it. This I will not have.

Without thinking he lifts her veiled chin with a finger. She turns her head obediently, flicks her amber eyes at him. She takes his hand in both of hers, kisses his knuckles.

Knuckles that have broken heads.

"You will be taken back to the House of the Moon after the final act," he hears himself growl under the double mask. "I will not have you witness-"

"I understand, my Lord," responds Ephtheta. "I have understood since the day you gave me breath," she adds. "That when you took his city, and I knew that you must, you would take my father's life. It is the way of things."

Rush shakes his head gruffly. "You Amorite women," he moans. "You are a ferocious breed. Like lionesses, you are," he looks back at the stage, for the theatre has gone dark again. In the dim, starlit shadows he can see a pale head full of curls. "You will make a mighty queen, girl, if I can keep the breath in your body."

"My sickness dims in your presence, my Lord," Ephtheta smiles up into the black eyehole. "I am at peace with you beside me, for what is there to fear when the Terror of the Aegean himself is my own master? Even my illness fears you."

She slips her hand onto his thigh as the stage torches light. Rush flinches, looks down at the slender, jewel-bedecked fingers, settles. Despite their frailty and youth, there is no question that those fingers are possessive of that thigh. What heart you have, he thinks. Truly the blood of queens runs in those veins. He shakes his head and grunts, returning his attention to the stage. In the center is another ship, this one Minoan, the single great eye that is the emblem of Nanaea flying from the mast above a central sanctuary. The black devil that plays himself stands astern. Beside him, in a short blue cape, Nikolaos (and Rush must chuckle to himself for even Babylon the Whore could not find an actor to properly represent the striking Captain); a fat monk, a woman in a white robe, a white chicken and a white goat in her arms, (Lydia and Ephram!) and four priests, one wearing a wig of extraordinary thick black hair, the three others bald, each in robes embroidered with the emblems of their houses: Earth, Sky, Moon, Sun. The water bearers charge about the stage creating great, billowing waves. The torch handlers, dressed in brown and saffron hooded robes, have drawn together at the back of the stage, becoming a mountain erupting with fire and lava.

The audience is in awe, and Ephtheta has taken her hand

from his thigh to point at the flames.

"My gods," her soft voice is trembling, "It is the volcano! Look how they have created the eruption that destroyed the Minoan kingdom!"

Now the burlap shade that covers the canopy of the ship is rolled up to expose the Rah on a bed of straw.

And beside him, reaching over a railing to nuzzle his hay-colored curls, a silver-white Turkoman, no doubt pilfered from the King's own stables. Hali.

The ship rolls off, the volcano disperses, becoming a row of guards along the back wall of the stage, and where the ship disappeared, the Wolf and the others, Rah on a hammock carried between two soldiers, stride into the Fortress of Amega. Stage left a woman sits on a simple bench, chickens at her feet, a dove flapping on one arm. Josepha.

And another mule-kick to his chest. For there, beside her, sits the diminutive Ting Ya, wearing a thin white veil that covers her entire head and face and disappears into the folds of her robe, one long grey braid draped over her left shoulder, the tail of it sweeping the floor at her tiny feet.

Ah, Pyrus, thinks Rush. And you, Aros. More face paint, more excellent costume making. Not Ting Ya. Only an actress. And probably a child, at that, playing the part of the deceased tender of the cemetery of the ancients.

An hour later, after which, to Rush's relief, Rah has told the story of Sophina, his own struggle with the ghost soldiers of the Table, and his flight from the assassin on horseback into Hattusha, but has completely left out the building and testing of the three man chariot, a second intermission brings the venders back to mill about amongst the people. A slave from the palace has entered the King's Pavilion from the stairs at the rear to offer the Assassin and the Princess an array of dainties from a golden tray. Another brings a small golden amphora with the King's insignia hammered into the bowl. Rush grabs the amphora before the slave has had a chance to fill the two golden cups on the tray. One-handed he takes a long draught through a slice in his hood that would have otherwise remained hidden, for it is nothing more than the lack of a seam between two horizontal strips of muslin. Then he thinks better of himself, looks down at the princess, whose eyes are smiling with a mixture of embarrassment and mischief at his faux pas, and pours some of the excellent wine into one glass. Nothing else on the tray interests him. Ephtheta, however, out of courtesy, and perhaps sympathy for the slaves who once served her father and must now serve a Hittite assassin, takes a few grapes from a bowl and nods politely at the men.

"Thank you, Wadum," nods the princess.

The man smiles at her appreciatively, then drops his gaze to the floor and bows. Before he has time to turn and head for the stairs, Rush has snatched the tray from him and handed it down to Petuk, who stands on the steps leading up to the front of the pavilion.

"It pays to stay close, eh, cub?" his eye is smiling sharply at the man, who is guarding the assassin's pavilion without being ordered to do so.

Petuk takes the tray gratefully. He has not eaten since morning. Rush has taken the wine bearer's skirt with his other hand as the man turns to go.

"Bring me a raw rabbit," he growls, "and don't bother to gut it."

The man's eyes grow wide. He nods, trips, and rushes down the stairs. Rush turns to Ephtheta. "You don't mind watching a wolf eat a rabbit, do you, girl?"

Ephtheta blinks away the shock in her eyes. "So long as you don't eat it while it still lives, Lord."

"And if I did, little Ephtheta? What then?" Rush has taken her veiled chin in his hand. "Are you wolf enough yourself to run with this wolf?"

"I am, Lord," answers the princess, meeting his eye. "I certainly am."

"I believe you are, little enemy," nods Rush. "At least there will be peace in your city for a time. For no one will dare enter what I have taken," he looks down at the princess, "Even after I have released it."

CHAPTER 19

While the dance plays on in the People's Theatre, a girl with one breast and a boy with no father pack all that they have purchased in the merchant's quarter for their passage to Amega. They will be leaving ahead of the Assassin and his 'guest', the princess, Ephtheta.

But far south of Babylon, on the coast of Canaan, the former Queen of Knossos and the former Queen of Cyrus know nothing of the celebration of the Assassin's taking of Babylon. Nor do they know that the god-slave, Rah, did not perished in the apocalypse. Their own houses are relocated to the Minoan settlements of Sidon and Arwad. Nanaea will never know, and will remain in Sidon to her last days, her pregnancy, the gift of Ameg, having provided her with the daughter she prayed for, a strong-willed tigress with the heart of a warrior, who will leave home at the age of eighteen summers and follow a Hittite army into Syria, killing dozens of men before her sex is discovered and she is married to her own general, finally settling along the Euphrates River herself during a Hittite reign of Babylon now obscured in history.

As for Media, who settled her household further north, in Arwad, mourning has returned her to her former madness. She sleeps all day, then, dressed in the queenly gown she left Crete in, now little more than glittering rags, she wanders the streets through the depths of the night until Fillius and Bacus, or one of the few remaining loyal men from the Cyrian Palace Guard, find her and return her to her husband. The household of the Queen is no more than a skeleton, the ribs of a once-lovely temple surrounding the heart of a city: Fillius and Bacus, Ikarus and Cyrus, Media and four old guards, and two ladies in waiting, their four oxen long since eaten, the few valuables long since pawned. The former occupants of the palace of Cyrus live together in a small, two story house in the merchant's district on the eastern coast of the island city. There Cyrus plays senet or twenty-squares with old Ben-Jahar, who is seventy if he is seven, while Ikarus cheats Phoenician soldiers at dice for wine. Only Fillius and Bacus are able to make enough money for the household bread, as both have found work in the garrison, Fillius mending high-rank military garments and Bacus stewarding for the admiral himself. It is enough to keep a roof over the household and an occasional chicken in the pot. But it is no life for a king, and while Cyrus watches old Ben-Jahar toss the knuckle bones he considers the fate of his city, and the fate of the Assassin and the boy-god, Rah.

Here in Arwad, all of the house of Cyrus, but the King himself, have long since forgotten the Assassin. Media is mad, and the others are busy with the business of survival in a new settlement.

But the Assassin has not forgotten them. And as the monkey bones clatter along the packed mud floor of the inner room of the little house, spelling out the king's future, the polished hooves of a Babylonian Turkoman clatter down the cobbled street outside, and the tall, broad-shouldered man who sits astride, calls out, "House of Cyrus! House of Cyrus! Who knows the whereabouts of the Philistine King? A dog's weight in silver for the whereabouts of the Philistine, Cyrus, and his Queen!"

The Turkoman's palomino coat is polished like a king's chalice. It blinds passersby and peddlers, shimmering in the noonday sun. People take cover under awnings as if the beast were a glittering knife, cutting the pedestrian traffic in two. The animal snorts, dances sideways, nearly knocking over a stooped old woman pushing a cart of fresh fruits along the lane, hawking her goods. The rider is foreign, dressed like a palace guard in bright red cloak and tight leather helmet. He speaks in Greek, but his accent is coastal Hittite. One man steps forward from a door to hail him. The man is a potter. His hands are white with clay.

"That house," he points to the king's front door, across the street and two doors down from his own. "There is a madwoman lives there, claims she is a queen. Walks the streets at night, calling for her 'kitten'." And hopeful for the promised prize, he wipes his hands on his apron and follows the Turkoman to the king's door.

"Watch him for me and I'll pay you for your trouble, potter. If this be the man I look for, you'll be rich before the sun passes that tower there." And dismounting, the foreigner slaps the potter on the back, a blow that causes him to step into the horse and wrap his arms about the glittering neck, warning him as well that if this is *not* the man he searches for, there will no doubt be consequences also.

Inside the little house Cyrus is startled by the sound of his name called out in the street. He looks across at Ben-Jahar, his mouth gaping open. The two stare at each other, and Ben-Jahar's hand is frozen in the air between them, still clutching the last three knuckle-bones to be tossed, bones that will spell the future, just as the first and second three spelled the past and present.

"Luxury and greatness," said the first toss. "Love and wine."

"Poverty and sorrow," said the second. "Madness and water."

"Shall I toss them, Highness?" asks Ben-Jahar. But Cyrus is already on his feet. He has lost almost three stone since his arrival here on the island city of Arwad. Though nothing has changed his love of comfort and a good meal, his circumstances have carved a new king. This one is no taller than the earlier, but he looks so, for he is straight and trim, his shoulders and chest no longer caved from carrying an epicurean's belly. Forced to live on little more than fish and cabbage and the fruit that hangs on the trees in his own yard, he has become a younger version of himself. And, too, his daily walk to the opposite side of the island to gaze out across the Great Sea toward his own incinerated kingdom has toned his muscles and strengthened his lungs.

So Cyrus is already at the door when the foreigner knocks, three great raps, like a gong for the dead, or like a call to prayer.

Cyrus opens the door to a man of considerable height and girth. The man wears elegant clothing for a traveler. His salt and pepper beard is long and braided. His eyes are like flint. Cold, piercing. He makes a quick assessment of the king.

"Lost some flesh, yes?" he squints, pushes at the king's hard belly. "Wonder you're alive at all, you plush bastard," he says, snorting. He shoves the king aside with one stroke of his arm. The startled king blinks. Even here, where he is nothing, even here in Arwad, he has never been treated with such disrespect.

"I am he who was once a king," he blathers, knowing full well where this man has come from, who this man is sent by. "I am Cyrus, whom you seek!"

"And I am Peleshet," answers the foreigner, "It is your queen I seek, man. The one who loved the Rah."

But I too loved the Rah! Cyrus nearly blurts out, then thinks better of his words and motions, suddenly a king again, to Ben-Jahar. Go on, man, bring her down! Ben-Jahar is on his feet and up the stairs before Peleshet can grab the old man's wrist and stop him.

"Do not attempt to hide her from me, Cyrus," he turns to the King, his deep-set eyes stabbing Cyrus, like a pin through a butterfly. "It is the Assassin who sent me to find her. Woe to him who lengthens his search."

"I know who it is who sent you, Peleshet," nods the King, undaunted. "For I can see his mark upon your cheek. She is mad again, you can tell him. She sleeps all day and wanders the streets at night calling for the boy, her 'pretty kitten', her 'pet', her 'dove.' See for yourself." He raises his eyes to the top of the stairs, where a pair of small and gracefully arched feet, crusted with soot from the streets and talon-nailed, appear beside the worn leather sandals of Ben-Jahar.

"My love," coos the King, stepping forward to watch her descend. "We have a visitor. A visitor from Knossos." He turns and winks at Peleshet, making a small, waving gesture with his fingers behind his back.

"Knossos!" The little feet take flight down the staircase, leaving those of Ben-Jahar on the upper landing. "Is it my little dove? Is it my sweet kitten?"

The thing that has descended the stairs is half woman, half witch. The black hair is knotted and wild. The face is a hysterical painting made by a madman, kohl eye liner dripping down gaunt, too- rosy cheeks, lips talc-white, cracked and bleeding at the corners.

But the king opens his arms to embrace her as if she is a beauty. She stops, square- footed, on the bottom step. Still, she must look up into Peleshet's unimpressed face.

"Where is my kitten? Where is my little dove?" cries the queen, her voice cracking like her lips, bleeding at the corners. She lifts her fists, cutting her palms with her ragged nails. She rushes at the warrior, raises her arms to beat at his chest.

Peleshet has her wrists in one hand before she can land a blow. Without ceremony, he lifts her by them, a dirty goat for slaughter. He turns and puts one shoulder into her midriff, adjusts her weight against his trapezius, and she is helpless, hanging head down, legs kicking at the air behind him, her tiny waist trapped between his trunk-like neck and his deltoid.

"Is this necessary?" the King raises his hands unsteadily, thinks better of it, puts them at his side. "She is not well. She is delicate."

"She is not going to get better here, wandering the streets until some scoundrel makes her a curiosity in a whorehouse." Peleshet is done with the King. He puts him out of his way with the palm of his free hand, turns, ducks out the doorway with the writhing Queen of Cyrus on his back.

"But she will fall if you carry her thus, on horseback!" cries the King, "Let me come with you! Let me-"

"Let you what?" fires back Peleshet over his open shoulder. He has already grabbed the reins of the Turkoman from the potter, lifted himself and his burden into the saddle, and swung the gleaming animal around. "Lie to her? Your lies have this to recommend them," he pops his deltoid, giving the Queen a little bounce in the air. "I will show her the truth, and we will see who is greater, he who possesses her, or he who possesses Babylon."

And tossing a money bag at the potter, he kicks the Turkoman into a trot and heads up the street toward the wharf.

Watching them disappear behind a hay wagon, King Cyrus presses his palms to his temples, lets out a terrible groan, and falls to his knees. Fillius and Bacus are running up the street towards him, having just seen the Queen being carried off on a foreigner's shoulder, still kicking at the air.

"My King," cries Bacus, dropping to his knees to shout into the King's moans. "What has happened? Who has taken our Queen?"

"It is-" but Cyrus' words are choked by his sobs. "I did not lie, Bacus, but for her. Only for her..."

Ben-Jahar has appeared at the doorway, holding a damp towel which he applies to the King's forehead. "There now, it is all for the best," he mutters, looking over Cyrus head at the two stewards with a warning glare. "Don't you see? If the assassin sent this man for our Queen, it can only be because the Rah lives! What other use has he for her, Sir?"

At this Cyrus quiets. He collects himself, rises to his feet, bringing Bacus up with him. "Yes, yes of course!" he nods, the color in his face returning. "He is... he is..." he makes a gathering gesture with his hands, looks down the street as if he might still catch the golden tail of the Turkoman disappearing around a corner.

"He is gathering us, My Lord," Ben-Jahar finishes his thought. "And for what purpose? Except to restore us."

"To restore us," murmurs the king. And he is half right, though he does not hear the Turkoman's hooves galloping north now, Peleshet having crossed the bay on a black market barge, to bring the prize that is tearing at his chest with her teeth, to his master.

"Your Greatness!" shouts Wadum into Rush's left ear, and though he is not startled, Rush rewards the man's impudence with an elbow to his solar plexus, and a bruised rib.

Rush ignores the man's muffled "ughff" and takes the tray upon which a skinned and lightly roasted rabbit, paws and tail removed, head intact, lies in a bloody sauce. He takes the carcass in one hand, pulls his mask up to his nose, and tears a mouthful of muscle from the flank.

"Mmm, not raw," he lifts an embroidered napkin from the

man's forearm to dab his beard, "But very nice. My compliments," he swats the man in the cheek with the back of his free hand. "More wine. Go."

On stage, the Rah has been making rather realistic love to two concubines in the kidnapped Hattushan King's bed. The seats are less crowded than they were during the first and second acts, nevertheless. Some of the ladies in the audience have retired to the front hall, their chaperones having sent them away when the scene became too risqué even for Babylonian gentry. They are gathered now in a clutch, like hens, their fans beating a bit too frantically, as they gossip with a mixture of delight and scandal, that the scene is quite offensive. In truth, without their husbands' insistence they might have never left the theatre. The boy is simply too beautiful to take one's eyes off, even (and especially) when he strips and falls into the arms of the beauties on the enormous bed, his delightfully athletic rump pumping with dramatic vigor. None have ever seen a manhood as bright and erect as the soft pink head of a calla lily, nor framed in honey-gold curls. Some of them are swooning into their sister's arms. When did it get so hot? It is the fires. Too many fires in the theatre tonight.

But the former princess remains beside the new Master of Babylon, her eyes peeking over a shell fan, her free hand no longer lying possessively on the assassin's thigh but curled in her own lap, soft and passive. She has stayed of her own accord, though had she risen to leave her monstrous escort would not have allowed her to do so. He now lays one great paw on *her* thigh, and the weight of the thing is unhinging her. The heat of it sears, and she imagines the delicate pale skin beneath her yellow silk robe turning pink with it. The fingers clench now and then as well, all but encircling her leg just above the knee. She is sure she is bruised there, where his thumb and ring finger press into her thigh each time the Rah roles over in the bed of the king to mount again the alternate girl. He has had them both several times at this point and quite clearly is nowhere near sexual exhaustion. Eliabus is pacing between the choir pit and the stage, hissing at the trio on the bed, and titers of laughter are starting up here and there amongst the more adventurous ladies, who have remained beside their chaperones in the front seats.

Apparently Rah has lost himself in the scene. And once again, his play is an empty chariot pulled pell-mell across a field of boulders by a hot colt.

"Did he think *he* could tame him?" mumbles Rush, not a little drunk. "Keep that head of fluff from drifting off his shoulders and into the clouds? Pah," he spits a bit of grizzle from his rabbit into his palm and opens it to Wadum. The man whips another embroidered towel from his belt and removes the offensive bit from the enormous palm as if he were picking a crocodile's teeth.

Finally Rah, giggling, rolls off his most recent concubine and onto one hip toward the audience. He plants his chin in his hand and closes his eyes, dreamily. His face is a soft green blur. He begins to purr.

The audience is tickled. There is a corresponding giggle erupting from the bleachers, and the front row has begun to clap in appreciation. Rah's sweetness is mesmerizing, the scene, a delightful success. A pleasant romp, risqué and rude, a declaration of the little Grain God's capricious and whimsical nature. Eliabus has brought his hands up together at his breast, grateful that his greatest achievement did not turn into a humiliating fiasco as a result of his poor judgment.

But a drunken Rush only chuckles, a rumble like a faraway thunder. His little cat never lost track with his performance, no of course he didn't, not even in the act of copulation.

He has been dancing all along. That delicious little rump danced in time with the fram drum, even as he pumped his maidens.

Rush slaps Wadum on his bare belly with his knuckles. "More wine," he belches rudely. The tanner's dried skin is itching his cheek beneath his assassin's hood. Casually, he pulls off the muslin assassin's mask to reveal Sin-Turami's face.

The slave faints.

Ephtheta turns to see what has thumped onto the pavilion floor beside Rush, and is greeted by the face of the tanner who took Tiamat's breast, stretched in a wretched grimace over her lover's handsome features.

261

Ephtheta swoons. Rush catches her in one hand as she a slides off her chair.

The other slave has dropped his tray and run, his sandals skating and slipping across the polished cypress floor as he dives for the stairs.

But in the same instant three Amorite bandits have dropped onto the stage from ropes strung above, as if they have crawled down from the ceiling of the king's chamber. Rah jumps off the bed as his maidens scream in terror. A forth figure descends from the ceiling: Mochlos. The tallest intruder, a broad shouldered monster with a patch over one eye and a jagged yellow scar across one cheek, huge and rank with wild hair, tosses a spitting, scratching Rah over his shoulder. One of the girls has made it half way across the stage when Ess cuts her scream with a dagger, hurled from twenty paces away with such a force as to lodge in her abdomen to the hilt. The second girl is off the bed and cowering in a corner whimpering when Aych, more boar than man, sets her reeling, and by the time she has struck the ground Aych has opened her throat with his own dagger.

"Put a knife in him and take his jewels!" cries Zee.

"He is worth more than a great hall full of jewels," snaps Mochlos. "I have told you what he is worth, and to whom he is worth it. And do not mar him! We could be discovered at any moment. I know not where or from whence the Wolf is coming, but I know that he is coming."

"He has forgotten the king," slurs Rush behind Sin-Turami's face. "Now how am I to come upon the king if there is no king?" He taps Ephtheta's cool cheek as she slumps in her chair. "Come girl, watch this nonsense with me." But Ephtheta remains limp. "What has gotten into everyone?" Rush lifts his free hand to scratch at his chin, confused momentarily by the strange, stiff skin of the tanner's throat where his beard should be.

"Master, you are wearing another man's face," says Petuk calmly from the third step of the pavilion. He has turned half way around upon hearing the thump of the slave's body hit the wooden floor, so that his boots point toward the assassin on the stage while his eyes watch the one in the King's theatre seat. "The princess has fainted as a result, and the slave, well, you see." He raises his open hand, gesturing at the slave, who is now on his elbows, coming to.

"Ah, yes, the tanner," smiles Rush under the very man's lips. "He was cutting open a girl I rather fancied when I came upon him," he hiccups. "Took one breast, but the other was still in splendid shape. So I skinned him."

Petuk, one eyebrow raised, nods appreciatively as the Assassin on the stage lets out a baritone howl of dismay that sends two ladies up the isle for the front hall.

"What am I bellowing at?" frowns Rush, squinting at his counterpart through the smoky theatre. There is more smoldering in the theatre than on stage now, as some of the spectators have lit up hookahs and are smoking opium. Rush gets to his feet, allowing the princess to slip from her chair in a silken heap onto the polished cedar. "Idiot. I never bellow," grunts the assassin, planting his paws on the pavilion railing and heaving himself over.

He lands on the step above Petuk's, soundless, even drunk. Petuk steps aside, drops to one knee, thumps his heart with one fist.

The assassin on the stage has stopped bellowing in mid-bellow. He is staring out into the audience, at the man he pretends to be. He pulls his hood off, trips over a prop. His face is ash.

And now there are two assassins on the stage. For Rush has leapt over the choir pit in two great strides, and is circling his alter-ego like a jackal. The counterfeit assassin is looking to Eliabus for direction, but Eliabus is gone. He is a flash of aquamarine and peach foppery flying up the isle to the back of the theater and the exit. The choir has gone silent. Only the sound of the fram drum, knocked over as the man holding it leaps to his feet to flee the pit, breaks the silence, the jingles sewn into the sides adding a disconsonant lightheartedness to the scene.

"What am I bellowing about?" snarls the Wolf of The Hatti behind his human mask. But the phony assassin can only lift his hands, imploring mercy.

"I didn't write the play, Sir!" he squeaks, falling to his knees.

"Let's do this right, shall we?" hisses Rush, pulling a dagger from one ankle holster, flipping it, snatching the handle in mid-air, all in the space of a breath.

"Beg pardon, Master, it is only a play!" answers the fraudulent Rush, his voice now a trembling tenor.

But Rush has lost interest in his alter-ego. He turns to the choir master, pointing his dagger at the raised platform upon which he stands. "Get off that, I am done with playing."

The choir master scurries off the box.

"Time for Babylon to see whose teeth it is in," roars Rush, leaping into the choir pit. With one blow, he smashes the former king's prison into splinters. A woman in the audience shrieks. Samsu-titana kneels amidst the debris, bound and gagged, a red scarf wrapped around his neck to catch his blood.

But Rush has turned him into a blood spouting stump before the king can find his sad, assassin's eyes in the hollows of Sin-Turami's face skin.

Women in the front row are stumbling to their feet, pulling free of their husband's hands, pressing handkerchiefs over their mouths as if to hold back their vomit.

"There is what is left of the man who tried to take Hattusha! See what becomes of those who challenge the Terror of the Aegean!" he bellows, his baritone causing ladies to clap their hands over their ears as they scurry and shove, pell-mell, up the aisles and out through the theatre entrance doors.

The theatre is a mass of confusion now, the choir having stampeded down the stairs of their platform and darted through a secret door under the stage to safety. The orchestra pit is nothing more than a tumble of instruments, thrown hastily to the floor and shattered by their master's feet as the musicians do the same. But not everyone is dodging for safety. At least half of the audience remains in their seats, riveted by the turn of the play. For surely this is part of the performance! It is not the first time a criminal was beheaded in the theatre, and in the eyes of this new and formidable king, his predecessor *is* a criminal. Men in the first row of benches are standing now. They clap their hands, at first hesitantly, then with vigor. The blood-soaked Wolf of the Hatti is standing over the spouting neck of Samsu-titana, whose body remains upright as a result of its bondage. The former king's head has rolled under a chair in the choir pit. The flautist that had been occupying that chair, too paralyzed with fear to bolt with the others under the stage, lifts her feet just as the king's cranium flops in a lopsided roll beneath them to rest on its nose under her bottom. This alone gives her the courage to explode from her seat like a pheasant from the brush and dive through the open door beneath the stage.

"Wine!" booms Rush, only now determining that he has left his amphora above, in the pavilion, beside the fainted princess. "And bring me the daughter!" he adds, his powerful lungs shaking the still air like a quake beneath the theatre.

Two slaves rush down the stairs of the pavilion, one with the amphora of wine, the other with a wineskin the size of a small pig strapped to his back. Petuk, his features controlled, turns to take the steps up to the pavilion with two strong strides. He bends to lift the princess gently from the floor, his eyes unable to refrain from stroking her slim white neck, nor stealing a glimpse of the sweet crease of flesh between her breasts just above the neckline of her dress. Then he grits his teeth, lifts his hungry eyes, turns to his new king, and determinedly stamps down the steps to the bridge over the choir pit.

Now he stands above the assassin, the princess limp in his arms.

Rush, ignoring the amphora offered by the first slave that has reached him, has sliced the pack off the second's back with two strokes of his gutting knife, which until then had been glittering amongst the array of weapons across his hips. He lifts the wineskin, takes a draught to challenge that of a hot horse, and hands the skin back to the man.

"Give her here, man," he burps, "Or would you have her for yourself?" The dagger-sharp black eyes hooded by the tanner's brows burn with wicked knowledge.

Petuk swallows hard, but maintains that gaze. He jumps into the choir pit with the slim body of the princess held easily against his chest, lands on his feet, lifts her toward the assassin, drops to one knee.

"She is yours, my King," says Petuk.

"She is indeed," roars Rush. "Bring her back to the House of the Moon, and have the priest wake her with one of his potions. Then ready her, for I am taking this frail spoil of war with me to Crete," Rush gives the stage a once-over, as if the Grain God might have suddenly returned to plead with him for the princess, as he did for the leopardess on the road to the Valley of the Gods.

Petuk is on his feet and striding up the center aisle toward the lobby. The torch lights have all been doused, having been dropped in the quenching pails when the light bearers fled the theatre. The theatre is dark, the play ended. With no orchestra, the silence signals a finale, and with only the stars above illuminating the exits, those remaining in the theatre make their way out, satisfied that this was all part of the production. They murmur amongst themselves, those with breath left in their lungs to murmur. Exquisite, masterful, a true work of genius! Eliabus' name will be remembered for generations as the finest playwright in Babylonian history.

Rush has pulled off his revolting head-covering. He tosses it into one of the quenching pails on his way back up the stairs to the King's pavilion, where he retrieves his hood, and pulls the familiar muslin over his head. Now where is that little cat of mine? Have they kept him off-stage, far from the action, as I ordered? Is Pyrus still fussing with his makeup for the next scene? The scene only Pyrus and Aros knew would never come? Of course he is. And even now, Niki bursts into the little god's dressing temple to proclaim that the stage is on fire, a coal from the hut scene having smoldered throughout the second act, finally igniting the straw beside the pyre, which was foolishly placed nearby while the stage hands were moving props in the dark. And now the place is ablaze and the people have run, screaming from the aisles. But no matter, for the King has seen you dance, and the play was nearly over, at any rate, and your remaining scenes only brief glimpses of you, lying on an altar in your tower, and then, and who can say why you insisted on such an ending when it is not to be? your evisceration by the priest in the last act, at my feet. Yes, yes, that was your favorite scene. Well, there will be a sequel, no? It is all the fashion these days, sequel after sequel, the same tripe regurgitated over and over again ad nauseam.

Rush plunges through the doorway under the stage, losing even the starlight to guide him. But his quick eyes yet see, like the nocturnal predator he is, and he slips through the channel of beams holding up the stage, brushing aside the guide ropes, meant to lead members of the choir and orchestra back and forth from the pit to the skene during intermissions to relieve themselves, for they, too, would have no light to guide them. And finding the opening at the far side, he climbs a narrow channel of steps into chaos. The drama behind the stage is far more intense than it was on it. Men and women still in costume, some with masks under an arm, trailing peacock feathered headdresses, some in nothing but body paint and flesh-toned loin clothes, are fleeing before him up the stairs on either end of the wide corridor, which is stocked with the various backdrops and props used during the first three acts of the play. Rush reaches out one monstrous claw and takes a dancer by his arm. The green and yellow paint on his bicep is still wet and the boy very nearly slips from his grasp before Rush lifts him by his throat with his free hand and presses him against the cool stone outer wall.

"Take me up to the tower, pretty," snarls Rush, his hot, cinnamon breath burning the boy's cheek.

"Ma-ma-master, no one knows the w-w-"

"*You* do," smiles Rush under the hood, "For this is Pyrus' paint," Rush slips his grip lewdly up and down the boy's arm, "And no other. You are the stand-in tiger boy, and only Pyrus can paint you. His studio is in the tower, with the Rah, is it not? Now would you rather be flogged by that candy-licking Eliabus, or licked and chewed up slowly by the likes of me, mm?"

Rush releases the boy's throat and the lad, trembling, nods to a blue and gold striped curtain on the far side of the corridor. "Behind that curtain is a stair that leads up to the tower from the inside. There is another entrance off the fifth tier, but it must be reached from the exterior stairs."

"Take me," Rush pushes the boy ahead of him toward the

striped curtain.

"But Master! I am only a dancer-"

"And I am only the man who portrayed me. Remember it. There will be less blood to slip on when we come back down this way if I am taken for my own forgery on the way up."

Half way up the stairs a wail interrupts the sound of their feet brushing the stone steps.

"That is he," says the assassin, more to himself than to his escort. "Someone has told him that the king is dead. Damn them! I would have kept it to myself. Now there will be hell to pay, and time wasted."

The clatter of platformed sandals above causes Rush to melt into the shadows behind the counterfeit cat-boy. Horus appears suddenly on the third landing, a lit torch in his hand, his strange hat teetering to the right as he turns to make his way down the second story stairs.

"Oh, Arammu, he has gone wild! He has bitten the dress maker! He has leapt up onto the sky ledge, he will fall to his death! I must find that man, the one in the blue cape, the one the Amegans call Captain. He can calm him!" and he has fled down the stairs, one hand holding his hat upright, the other extending the torch out in front of him in the dark, and even so, failing to light the corner in which Rush has pressed his bulk.

"Aptly named," says Rush, giving the stand-in a light whack on the buttocks to get him moving again. "Now is he calling you *his* love? Or are you named 'love'? Not much chance for survival on the battlefield with *that* name, I'll guess, not even for an Amorite dog."

"Horus calls us all Arammu, Lord," responds the boy, now taking two stairs at a time to keep out of the way of the assassin's hands. "All the male dancers, anyway." He has reached a golden door at the top of the fifth level. "This is it," he winces, cringing back against a wall in order to allow the assassin's volume onto the fifth landing, which is minute.

"Mmm, but is he not up on the sky ledge?" Rush settles one enormous palm against the cypress door, as if taking its pulse. "He will leap to his death at the sight of me, just to spite me, for killing that insect, Samsu. No, I cannot take that chance. You will have to find us another way, out onto the upper parapet, beneath his fall. There *is* an upper parapet, is there not?"

"Yes, Lord, but the only way out there is down again to the fourth level, through the priests' quarters, and out a western window."

"Priests? In the theatre of the people? For what purpose, priests. Pah, to pick and choose from among the most delicious flesh, no doubt. City of sins, I will burn you to the ground," Rush grumbles. Then, leaning down to squint into the cat-boy's eyes, he smiles behind his mask. "Yes, introduce me to these 'holy men' of the arts. It won't take a moment, and then I shall catch my little cat on the temple ledge."

The boy nods, gulping, then squeezes himself under the assassin's extended arm to lead him back down to the fourth level, the Level of the Theatre Priests.

"There, Lord," he points to a red door with a strange character carved into the face of it. "That will take you into the Priests' quarters. Every chamber has an exit onto the parapet, you've only to choose which."

"Ah, there you are, Marduk," Rush snarls, tracing the character with a finger. And without another breath taken he has drawn back his fist and smashed it into the symbol, cracking the thin wood into two halves dead center. "Dark god of the Amorite dog, coward who demands the burnt flesh of the children of his own people, face me on the battlefield, and not in the hearts of fools, and I would tear you limb from limb. But as it is, all I can do is tear those hearts from the fools who have sworn allegiance to you."

The unhinged half of the door has fallen backward into the priests' lair. Rush crashes through the opening he has made. Before the tiger boy has followed him through, shadowing the monster now more out of sheer curiosity than pluck, a Priest of Marduk hangs from the assassin's fist by the hood of his crimson robe.

"Tell me, priest, what has Marduk to do with the theater?" Rush is breathing through his muslin into the priest's flaccid face.

"I-we-" he stutters, swiftly losing air as his windpipe closes with the weight of his own gluttony pressing against his collar, for his gown is a seamless woven wool.

"Have you touched my Rah?" Rush slams the man's back against a wall, a dagger appearing in his free hand as if by magic, then disappearing beneath the priest's robe, the flat of it pressed coolly against his scrotum. "Have any of you murderers touched him? Even to smooth a curl on that moonlit head?"

"None!" squeaks the Priest of Marduk, his hands clawing at the collar of his cloak, once such a joy, being of one piece, richly died with the madder plant tinctured in urine, and greatly prized, now a thing he wishes he might slither out of and never put on again.

"Ah-hah, but you had plans, you priests, no? Marduk feasts on innocence, and that one is more innocent than any babe. Your ilk would defile him, you are set in your ways. Let me relieve you of your lust while I am here to do it." And with one thumb against the dagger blade so that only the tip is functional, Rush has severed the man's testicles with a single surgically neat slice.

The man screams, faints. Rush drops him in a heap. "Such a simple solution, really. Make note, Arammu, a new law in Babylon. All priests of Marduk must be castrated." Rush has been scanning the layout of the priest's quarters as he speaks, and now strides toward a curtained archway to his left. "Here, I think," he muses, while his new secretary, dizzy from what he has just witnessed, launches his legs after him.

"That should thin this flock of fools," Rush mumbles to himself, drawing back the curtain with the same bloodied dagger to find a triumvirate of priests enjoying a midnight meal. At the sight of the towering black hell that has entered their refectory, the men shove themselves away from their table, toppling over their stools to flee in all directions. But Rush pays them no heed. He has leapt onto the table and launched himself through the window above, the boy Arammu behind him.

"Rah! You will not escape me!" bellows the beast, who stands on the narrow parapet below the sky ledge of the theatre tower. When Arammu reaches the ledge he looks up to see the

Grain God, painted now in preparation for his final act, a human rainbow, walking along the ledge, as easily as if he were strolling on the Kadingirra Road. Lengths of curling silk attached to his golden Minoan collar, bracelets and belt, extending the colors painted in stripes on his body, billow in the cool evening breeze. Rah sees the Assassin and his own double at the same time. He lifts his lip, snarls at Rush, showing a starlit row of perfect teeth, except for the exceptionally long incisors. Then he makes a half turn to Arammu, causing Rush to launch himself onto his knees, arms extended to catch the boy's fall. But Rah ignores him, lifts his arms above his head, and then sending himself into a graceful spin back and away along the ledge on his hands, his costume exploding outward in all directions like an aurora.

"I will climb that wall with my teeth and eat you whole!" screams Rush, his fingers crawling over the slick Iberian marble, mined in the Anasol peninsula and paid for with a thousand child slaves. But he can find not a single flaw in the surface of the temple tower wall, not a solitary chink upon which to hang a nail for purchase.

"Wolf is kill King!" barks Rah from the ledge, which is a good twenty meters over the assassin's head. And with a violence that Rush has never seen erupt on that handsome brow, Rah tears the emerald circlet from his hair and flings it down, though a warm breeze, heavy with the coming evening showers, gentles its fall so that it only wafts on the current, skating along the marble on the last half of its descent, and like a golden dove, settles softly in the assassin's outreached palm.

Rush cannot help but cringe at the sight of a dozen golden curls, some blooded, insinuated in the minute mail that makes up the jeweled headband.

"Rah," he sighs, shaking his head and blinking back up at the Grain God of Knossos. Tiny beads of moisture have begun to collect on the surface of the marble, making it even slicker. Without realizing what he is doing, he brings the crown to his muzzle and inhales. Cherry blossom, hyssop, myrrh.

No. Not like this.

"Rah, it is done in every conquered city," he shouts upward, up the unhearing marble of the temple, up into the unhearing heavens. "The king must die. Or the city will never accept its conqueror. I am your king, Rah. And the new King of Babylon. And you have danced for me," he swallows the fire in his throat. "Come down, boy, I cannot lose you thus," he says, so softly that only he and the rain can hear him now.

"Kill, kill, kill!" shouts Rah, moving back and forth along the ledge as if he had the floor of a stage upon which to balance. But in fact, the ledge is only half the width of the heel of his foot. "Always you kill. Can you *make*, Wolf? CAN YOU MAKE WHAT YOU KILL? No, even chicken you no can make. Only what is make *you*, can make chicken to *feed* you, feed your army. Kill cat, kill king. Always kill. No more for Rah. Now Rah take what you love, Wolf, and kill. You see. You see."

And he is gone, vanished off the ledge.

And as quickly as he has vanished, the assassin has pushed Arammu aside and disappeared back through the window into the priest's rectory. By the time the imitation Rah climbs onto the sill, he is gone.

CHAPTER 20

Peleshet has covered the distance from the coast of the Great Sea to Aleppo in a day. By twilight, he is riding into town, along the back streets, to find lodging with an innkeeper along the canal whose owner is in the assassin's pocket. Peleshet has had enough of the scratching, biting bitch on his back. An hour into his journey he was forced to dismount his animal, as much to water the beast at a well as to bind the former Queen of Cyrus with a few strips of red cloth he has had to cut from his own cloak. He has bound her mouth as well, and for good measure has given her a mildly concussive hit to the temple, effectively silencing her for the remainder of the trip.

At the inn, Peleshet pays up front, a bag of gold that could silence the entire city, let alone one innkeeper who is already convinced that his best action, when dealing with anything of or related to the Terror of the Aegean, is to hand over his keys, order a shipping amphora of the best wine he can find and half a roasted pig for his Amegan guests, and lock himself in his own room until daybreak. Now Peleshet climbs the back stairs of the inn to the third floor, whose occupants have been hastily relocated to the first level. The Queen is awake but dazed, no longer squirming. Her knotted hair hangs down his back like a horsetail, still black, despite her forty years, beneath the red road dust that powders it.

"Mmph," she says behind the partly chewed gag as he kicks

open the door of the room they will share and tosses her on the bedding.

"Mmph yourself," responds Peleshet, striding to a window to throw open the shutters. And leaning out of the aperture to regard the alley below, he adds with confidence, "You may jump, but you won't get far on two broken ankles. A nice sheer drop and cobblestone below."

"Mmph," says the Queen again, this time into the bed linen, for she has squirmed her way onto her face and is inadvertently smothering herself in an attempt to sit up.

Peleshet, striding past the bed to the door, gives her ankle bonds one quick jerk, effectively turning her onto her back. Then he secures the bolt, an exceptionally heavy length of olive wood that she in all likelihood could not lift on her best day. "Try pulling that off the door without waking me," he says, gentling it into its iron tracks.

He turns, satisfied, hands on his weapon laden hips, to see that she has righted herself, and now sits on the edge of the bed, though her wrists are still neatly bound behind her.

The two regard one another evenly, the Queen, looking less mad than surprised, the warrior, merely studying his options in this new battle.

Finally Peleshet breaks the stand-off by marching up to her and tearing the red gag from her mouth.

"Go ahead and scream if you like, it's nothing they haven't heard around here when the Wolves of Amega are in town. You won't get any help, not from this lot of misfits and thieves. This whole town is not worth one Amegan archer with a broken bow."

The Queen, breathing more easily now without her gag, gazes up at the soldier towering over her. Despite her wretched condition, her wild and knotted black hair, her blackened eyes, kohl-streaked cheeks, and cracked, bone-white and bleeding lips, she is more kidnapped queen than deranged mad-woman. It is as if the harsh treatment, or perhaps the act of riding on the broad and indifferent shoulder of a handsome warrior, has brought her back to herself. I am not a prisoner, say her eyes, but a monarch in a difficult situation. It is not my first, and shall not be my last. She takes one serene breath, lifting her breast with regal patience for her circumstances, and manages to look down her nose at the man in uniform who stands above her. She is not bound and sitting on a filthy straw bed running with lice. She is perched on a golden throne in her own country, a city surrounded by saffron meadows and bleating sheep and undulating fields of grain; she is in a hall filled with Minoan aristocracy, gaiety, ladies with hair curled into ringlets and flowing down their backs from golden headbands, dressed in many-tiered, belted skirts, blue, red and gold, skimming the floor, their bodices cut to their bellies and cupping their exposed breasts: men trim and brown, wearing their own colorful knee-length skirts, golden anklets and hair as long and curled as their women's.

Peleshet is a giant in comparison to them, a foreigner from the mainland. His crimson cloak, his leather boots, his plain sheeted muslin tunic, his gruff manner, all suggest that he is Hittite. She must handle him carefully, for they are a volatile race. How she came to be in his possession, when the last thing she remembers is stepping off a Cretan pier in the dark onto a pitching ship, she cannot recall. But it hardly matters. She must use her queenly bearing to secure appropriate handling by this man, who is after all a soldier, a man who has an understanding of who his betters are, regardless of race.

"Sir, we have been traveling for some time," pronounces the bedraggled queen. "I am filthy, and I am tired. I require a bathing pool, access to a latrine, and a handmaid. These bonds are unnecessary, as it is clear to me that I am in your care now and that you, a gentleman of some position within your master's service, are assigned to my safe passage wherever it is that you are taking me. Therefore, I now give you my word as Queen that I intend to make no attempt to escape you, for you are my lone guardian, clearly a well-chosen one, and my safety depends upon you."

Peleshet can only wrinkle his brow at this unexpected oration. He frowns, considers her words, slips a short filleting knife from his belt and cuts her ankle bonds.

The queen gives him a barely perceptible nod. "Thank you," she says sweetly, and then stands to turn around and offer him her wrists.

"I will escort you myself to the latrine. There is a bath of sorts on the ground floor, more of a drinking pool for the innkeeper's beasts, but it will have to do. You will bathe in your clothing while I watch, madam. Then we will have a meal and rest, for I intend to be on the road at dawn."

"Excellent," smiles the queen, "You are a good man, and your master will reward you, if he has a bone of grace in his body." And even in her present condition her smile sends a shiver of pride through Peleshet's belly.

Media has lifted the fingers of her right hand in such a gesture that Peleshet offers her his arm without thinking.

"Take me then to the bathing pool, my handsome guardian," says the Queen of Cyrus, looking up at her escort with a glimmer of girlish coquetry on her sooty face. "And tell me your name, dear, that I may recommend it to your master," she says, giving his enormous bicep a squeeze as he throws the bolt with his free hand to ushers her through the door.

Rah has leapt from the tower sky ledge, not back into the tower room as the assassin believes, but into a rain chute that runs down the northern face of the pyramid. The chute collects the rain from a cistern atop the tower, then sends it down into the Theatre pools below. The channel is visible in only one direction, north, where, directly below, Captain Nikolaos, is just leaving the Theatre and marching up the torch lit road to the Northern Fortress.

The trough is just wide enough to accept Rah's narrow hips, and the light rain that has begun to fall has slickened the surface, making the shaft a perfect slide for his paint-greased body. He shoots down the channel head first, hands extended, so that his entry into the pool below makes no more noise than that of a seal slipping off the arctic ice into the ocean.

Instinctively, Rah remains underwater a full minute. When he is satisfied that his escape has not been noticed by the Fortress Guard, he presses his body against the moss along the pool wall and peeks over the stones. He sees Nikolaos broad, blue-caped back receding up the Kadingirra Road toward the fortress gates, watches the guards bow to their captain, and in that blink of time when their eyes are lowered, lifts himself up and over the stone wall and slips into a hedge of white lilies planted six deep along the entire circumference of the pool.

When the Captain has disappeared into the fortress, the Grain God of Knossos follows the pool wall east, on the opposite side of the Theatre and out of sight of the House of the Moon and the Fortress. Here the city declines into a district of modest three story homes, neatly pressed together amongst gardens of olive and apricot trees, date palms and lemons. The wall around the theatre is broken by a bridge over a pristine canal lined with stone benches and plantings. Tonight the iron gates are open, offering the people of the Kulab access to the theatre during the performance of the Rah. But all have fled back to their homes after the beheading of their king. And the gates are unattended.

Rah pads softly down the path to the canal. Despite his elaborate costume, he is little more than a drenched housecat, his curls pasted to his head and streaked with blood where he tore off his crown, the strips of silk attached to his wrists and ankles twisted around his torso, or dragging and hitching along the paving stones. His body paint is melting in the rain. He is a colorful blur with kohl rimmed, iridescent eyes.

Miserable, chilled, his scalp pounding in a ring of pain where his circlet of gold once nested in his hair, the little Grain God hops onto the ledge of the bridge wall, and dives into the canal.

To be continued................

ABOUT THE AUTHOR

Susan Shepherd is a retired law enforcement officer who has spent most of her career interviewing criminals and writing reports for the Court. She lives on the North Fork of Long Island, New York with her husband, three horses and four cats.